Also by Liselle Sambury

Blood Like Magic

BLOOD LIKE FATE

A BLOOD LIKE MAGIC NOVEL

LISELLE SAMBURY

Margaret K. McElderry Books

NEW YORK · LONDON · TORONTO · SYDNEY · NEW DELHI

MARGARET K. McELDERRY BOOKS

An imprint of Simon & Schuster Children's Publishing Division

1230 Avenue of the Americas, New York, New York 10020

Text © 2022 by Liselle Sambury

Jacket illustration © 2022 by Thea Harvey

Jacket design by Rebecca Syracuse © 2022 by Simon & Schuster, Inc.

MARGARET K. McELDERRY BOOKS is a trademark of Simon & Schuster, Inc.

For information about special discounts for bulk purchases, please contact Simon & Schuster Special Sales at 1-866-506-1949 or business@simonandschuster.com.

The Simon & Schuster Speakers Bureau can bring authors to your live event. For more information or to book an event, contact the Simon & Schuster Speakers Bureau at 1-866-248-3049 or visit our website at www.simonspeakers.com.

Interior designed by Hilary Zarycky

The text for this book was set in Athelas.

Manufactured in the United States of America

First Edition

2 4 6 8 10 9 7 5 3 1

Library of Congress Cataloging-in-Publication Data

Names: Sambury, Liselle, author.

Title: Blood like fate / Liselle Sambury.

Description: First edition. | New York : Margaret K. McElderry Books, [2022] | Series: Blood like magic ; 2 | Summary: While struggling with her new role as Matriarch, Voya has a vision of a terrifying, deadly future, and with a newfound sense of purpose, she vows to do whatever it takes to bring her shattered community together and prevent the destruction of them all.

Identifiers: LCCN 2021043769 (print) | LCCN 2021043770 (ebook)

ISBN 9781534465312 (hardcover) | ISBN 9781534465336 (ebook)

Subjects: CYAC: Witches—Fiction. | Magic—Fiction. | Genetics—Fiction. | Blacks—Canada—Fiction. | Toronto (Ont.)—Fiction. | Science fiction. | BISAC: YOUNG ADULT FICTION / Fantasy / Contemporary | YOUNG ADULT FICTION / Family / Multigenerational | LCGFT: Novels. | Science fiction.

Classification: LCC PZ7.1.S2545 Bj 2022 (print) | LCC PZ7.1.S2545 (ebook) | DDC [Fic]—dc23

LC record available at https://lccn.loc.gov/2021043769

LC ebook record available at https://lccn.loc.gov/2021043770

AUTHOR'S NOTE

While this book is a work of fiction, it does deal with topics and discussions that affect people in real life. As such, I wanted to include content warnings for those who may need them.

Content Warnings: Gun violence, reference to police violence, discussion of eating disorders, blood/gore/violence, death, discussion of substance abuse/addiction, mentions of child neglect, sickness/infection

CHAPTER ONE

The cloying scent of vapor smoke in the lounge is as suffocating and sweet as the memories of my grandma. The last time I came to Chinatown to sell products to Rowen Huang, Granny was with me.

She was alive, and I was a very different girl.

Now I sit on one of the plush red loveseats waiting for the Huang Matriarch to grace us with her presence. The velvet of the fabric invites you to sink into it, but I keep my back straight and lean forward. Lounging into the furniture just makes me look smaller, even more like a little kid than I already do. I fight not to grit my teeth. I'm so hacking tired of being reminded that I'm a "child."

Beside me, Keisha has no problem snuggling into the crimson cushions. She's pulled her knees up to her chest, bulky coat pooling around her neck, scrolling through her phone while I search the room for Rowen.

Around us, the Huang family members stare. When I was here with Granny, they stared too, but not at *me*. I wasn't important then. I wasn't a Matriarch and definitely wasn't the youngest one crowned in our family for centuries. And I absolutely wasn't the girl with two gifts, something rare even outside of our family, in the Black witch community as a whole.

People look at me now.

And no matter what I do, they find me wanting.

I've avoided doing this drop-off for Rowen since Granny died specifically to not have to deal with this—letting Keisha, Alex, or Mom handle the in-person deliveries of the special serum and products that Rowen prizes. Except last time, she insisted that I show my face, claiming that she missed me. I'm sure she barely knew my name before this.

But Rowen loves a juicy piece of gossip, and these days, I'm the juiciest there is.

My fingers twitch on my lap. Every time I hear a whisper, I can't help but think they're talking about me. Me and the family.

No way that little girl can fill her granny's shoes.

Why did they pick her?

How the mighty have fallen.

"She knows we don't have all day, right?" Keisha whines, snapping me out of my thoughts. Today, my cousin is wearing a honey-brown sew-in wig that seems as long as my body is tall.

I swallow. "I'm sure she does."

Rowen never made Granny wait. If I were her, I would have already left. But we're not in that sort of position anymore. Six months ago, when my family decided to do an impure ritual to help me avoid completing the task to become a witch and save my little sister Eden's life in the process, they ruined our purity.

Purity.

Now I know that those labels don't matter. All they do is divide our community even more than it already is. Magic is nothing more or less than blood and intent. Mama Jova taught me that.

But these days, even she doesn't show her face.

And everyone except me is happy to cling to their divisions.

Pure witches like the Huangs treat us with a level of disdain they never did before. In the wake of Granny's death, we've lost our placements in stores owned by pure witches, and I've stumbled through trying to maintain the relationships we do have with the awkward grace of a drone piloted by a toddler.

People talk back to me in a way they wouldn't have dared with Granny. They argue about prices or threaten to pull our stock for better deals. Or they act like Rowen, making us wait because she knows we're desperate.

No one gives a shit that Granny chose me. That Mama Jova chose me. That I did the best I could to protect our family from Justin Tremblay's attempt to control us in his quest for immortality. It's like everything I accomplished six months ago means nothing now. Like I'm the exact same girl who stayed in that blood bath for hours, dreading her Calling.

But I'm not.

Keisha taps her long fingernails on her phone and steupses under her breath. "I just want to get this over with."

"I know," I say, peering at the back room door where I know Rowen is probably sitting and waiting us out. "She'll come soon, I'm sure."

"Like, 'I can see the future' sure, or just 'I hope I'm right' sure?"

I scowl.

When I passed my Calling all those months ago, I was given two gifts—the past and the future. The power to see both the past of a person and the future I created when my actions pushed them from whatever path they had been on before to a new one.

It was only after the Pass that I realized how difficult that is to figure out. How exactly am I supposed to know for sure whether I've changed someone's "path"?

"I doubt I've done anything to change the path of Rowen's life, so I can't see whatever future results from it," I say. "And even if I could, I wouldn't use it to see if she's coming soon or not."

"Boring."

Keisha is and has always been frustrating. But even as irritating as she can be sometimes, she's been there for me. She comes on beauty supply runs or helps coordinate them with our other cousin, Alex. When I'm alone in my room, contemplating how I can make everyone believe that I'll be a decent Matriarch, she'll pop in with a snack and force me to watch a feed show with her.

She's there every time Keis would usually be. Keis, my favorite cousin. My first love. My best friend, who I sentenced to never leave our family home to save the future of a boy who now hates me.

My restless fingers grip the soft fabric of my coat. I'm not the same girl I used to be, struggling with every single choice. I can't be. As a Matriarch, I need to be resolute in every decision I make, like Granny was.

But losing Keis is a choice I don't know if I got right.

Rowen bursts out of the back room, thick hips swaying in a form-fitting gown with a slit up the side that looks like it's made of molten gold. Matching clips are stuck in her chin-length hair to tug it back from her face. Her skin looks flawless, as usual. Granny had a backup stash of the special tonic she made specifically for Rowen, and we've been running through the supply ever since.

"If it isn't my favorite little Matriarch," she coos as she sweeps in front of Keisha and me. "I hope to get an invite to your showcase."

I bite my lip to stop a sneer from coming out and slap my cousin's knee to make her sit properly, which she does with a scowl, her fluffy boots slamming onto the intricate rug underneath us.

"No showcase for me," I say. Like elaborate debutant balls, showcases are rare events in the witch community when those with particularly interesting gifts gather people to show it off. It was more useful back in the day when families wanted to demonstrate how powerful they were. I can't imagine doing something that draws that much attention to myself now or ever. And definitely not just so everyone can gossip about my gifts more than they already do.

"Too bad." Rowen frowns at Keisha. "Who is this? The cousin who always has her nose in a tablet? Ava always said you two were thick as thieves. My uncle was sad to hear you weren't available for his internship."

I twitch at her mention of Granny's name and hate myself for it. I jerk even more when I realize she's talking about Keis. "No." I don't offer any more. I can't. I don't want to talk about it.

"I'm Keisha," my cousin jumps in for me.

The Huang Matriarch makes a little "ah" noise in the back of her throat, latching onto the discord with a gentle joy. I expect her to pry deeper, but even she seems to know not to go that far. Not when Granny's been ashes for less than a year.

Her funeral wasn't even that long ago. I remember standing inside the dining room, the grief hanging like smoke in the air, choking us all into silence. Our family and the Davises were the only ones there. We did invite Granny's old family, the brothers and sisters who left when she decided to be pure. Some had pledged to new Matriarchs or had kept the Thomas name and lived without a Matriarch, our magic separate despite our shared name. Most witches never choose the latter because it means living without protection, and it's a guarantee that your magic will get weaker. But I guess some would rather be Thomases than anything else.

I invited them all anyway.

But none came.

Keisha hefts the tote bag of beauty products onto the low coffee table between us. "Your products for this month."

With a single, long manicured nail, Rowen presses the edges of the bag away and peers with a casual disinterest at the wares. That's not what she really cares about.

"And your vial," I say, grabbing it from the thick inside pocket of my jacket. It's a simple glass bottle, maybe two inches long, with a rubber stopper and filled with blush-colored liquid. I reach out to pass it to her, and it shakes the slightest bit between my fingers.

Rowen's eyes narrow.

Hack me.

I swallow with a gulp audible enough to make me fight a cringe.

Keisha's side-eye is so obvious that I don't have to look at her to know she's doing it.

The Huang Matriarch plucks the vial from my fingers and examines it.

I clear my throat in the same signature "pay me" sound that Granny used to use.

Rowen ignores it.

"We need to get going," Keisha says, dragging the words out and making a show of zipping her jacket back up.

"Do you mind if I pay after?" Rowen says to me.

My jaw drops. "What?"

"I think, given the circumstances, it would be best if I sampled the product to be sure it stacks up to the usual quality."

"But . . . we've been delivering to you for the past six months since . . ." I can't say it aloud, can't admit that she's gone. Can't make it real. "You haven't had a problem."

"There have been some titters about quality dropping." She presses a hand to her chest. "Not from me, of course."

"From who?" Keisha asks.

Rowen smiles indulgently at her. "I don't like to gossip."

My blood heats under my skin. Rivers of it poised at any time to become sharp whips. This time, I can't hold myself back from gritting my teeth. Keisha inhales sharply beside me, though she tries to smother it.

Rowen continues, "They said they got a delivery yesterday and it didn't seem quite up to snuff. I'm just the messenger, so don't be upset with me." She waves a hand and stares into my eyes. "I think it would be appropriate, considering my loyalty to you, to let me try things out. And next month, if everything is good, I'll pay double. No problem, right?"

Every bit of me wants to say no. Granny would have said no. She wouldn't have ever let Rowen play her like this or even deal with the disrespect of the offer. But even as defiance kisses my lips, something in me twists away from it.

"That's fine. We'll be back next month for double." The words don't even feel like my own. They slide out, expanding and spreading from my tongue like soft butter in a pan.

"Wonderful," Rowen preens, clapping her hands. "See you next month."

Keisha doesn't even say bye, just stomps out of the lounge, her fluffy boots clomping. I say a hurried goodbye to Rowen before chasing after my cousin.

The exit opens up into a Chinese food market with rows of fresh produce misted by water and aisles of colorful imported snacks. The woman at the counter stares us down, and I force out a smile for her that she doesn't return.

We leave the store and break out into the frigid cold. February in Toronto is chilling winds and chalky salted sidewalks. Mounds of grime-stained snow and slush. People walking with their hands dug into the pockets of thick down-padded coats and hats pulled low on their heads.

Chinatown is as busy as ever, even in negative degree weather. Bright holos flash, loudly advertising each store, and the block is a crescendo of car horns, streetcars screeching on the tracks, and bicycle bells from the brave (or not smart) few who cycle no matter how much snow is on the ground.

Keisha's coat has a hood as fluffy and pink as her boots, though without the salt stains. I tug my hood, sans any fluff, up over my head. We have to shuffle to the very edge of the sidewalk, nearly into the road, to stay out of the way of the people walking along Spadina Avenue.

"Are your circuits fried?!" Keisha snaps at me. "We just gave her product for free."

"She knows." I press my hands against my eyes. "She must."

"How would she know?"

I think of my shaking fingers as I handed Rowen the vial of serum that I made myself without Granny's help. The problem is that I lack whatever she used to make it special. It's a dud. But we've run out of Granny's stock. It's a miracle that we made it this long in the first place. We needed to do something. I made the choice to sell our homemade batches instead of saying we had run out. The latter would have bought time, but we need money now.

We ran one of the new batches out to a James, and they've already noticed the difference and passed on the gossip. Of course, things couldn't have worked out for once.

"Also," Keisha says. "You definitely yanked on my magic."

I cringe. "Sorry." One of the powers that comes along with being the Matriarch is the ability to pull magic from other members of the family, and it's not as easy to control as I thought it would be. Just another one of my many problems right now. Like how we need that money from Rowen. "I didn't even mean to agree to her not paying. It just came out." I'd wanted to fight more, but then for some reason I didn't.

"Hack me," Keisha breathes.

"What?"

"She used her gift on you."

"No," I shake my head. "She wouldn't do that."

Rowen's gift of a honeyed tongue can compel people to listen to her. To take notice of her words. It's a more direct version of Rena Carter's gift of suggestion. But a Matriarch using her gift against another Matriarch? That's the sort of thing that would make wars break out between families back in the day. No one even tries that mess now.

Rowen wouldn't do that. She's been one of our clients for years, and only a few months ago she was helping me get Keis an internship opportunity with her family.

"She wouldn't do that," I repeat aloud, shaking my head, trying to go back through my thoughts and see if I remember a press of magic. It's hard. That's the whole point of being a strong witch. People aren't supposed to realize when you've manipulated them.

"Um, yes she would, because no one hacking respects us!" Keisha throws her hands up. "Everyone is playing power politics now that Granny is gone. Do you know that Emerald told me one of the Baileys is looking into making beauty products now?"

Great, if Emerald is saying that, it means her dad, Johan, must know about it too. More witnesses to our downfall. Since I pissed him off last year by interfering with one of his family's rituals, things have been awkward. I still fulfill my internship at his restaurant, but we've lost the vibe we used to have. The Thomases and the Davises used to feel like one big family. Now, it's like we're distant cousins or something. At least on my end.

Keisha continues, "The Baileys aren't pure, so Rowen won't buy from them. She's only buying from us because she always has, and we're at least *trying* to be pure. But it's not about that! It's about the disrespect!"

"Magic isn't about being pure or impure, it's—"

"Yes, yes, blood and intent. I get it. But, like, everyone else cares about that sort of thing."

I've tried to get the family to understand why we shouldn't

be bothering with the pure/impure thing, but it hasn't stuck with them, either. "What else did Emerald say?" At least I can have a guess at how far we've fallen in the Davises' eyes.

Keisha shrugs. "Nothing much, just our usual chats. Focus! Rowen Huang used her gift against you."

"We don't know that."

"We need to retaliate! This is hacking war, Vo!"

I let out a breath. "Let's go home."

"We're going to let her get away with it?"

"I'm done."

Keisha grumbles but follows me to the streetcar. We hop on one of the many red and white trains going to the Spadina subway station and ride in silence. I watch the bright holos over shops pass by, and all the places Granny used to point out as old froyo shops. Once, I asked her if she thought about Grandad much. I was thirteen, and it had been six years since he passed. I remembered something offhanded about him when she happened to be nearby. She said she thought about him every day.

I couldn't understand it. How you could think of someone who was gone every single day?

But ever since she died, not a day has passed without her being in my thoughts.

Six years from now, maybe it'll still be the same.

I don't want to believe that Rowen used her gift against me, but Keisha is right. No one respects us, not anymore.

We don't have Granny.

All we have is me.

And if there's anyone in my family people are willing to disrespect, it's their youngest and apparently most disappointing Matriarch.

CHAPTER TWO

We're supposed to go home. Keisha thinks so, anyway. She's happily tugged the collar of her coat up and is tapping away at her phone. Meanwhile, I'm the one paying attention to the stop names as they ring out and eyeballing the salted streets as we pass. The Spadina streetcar drags its way north to the station of the same name, and we should make our way west along the extended subway line to Long Branch Station.

I lean over, trying to sneak a peek at what my cousin is doing, but she has her privacy settings on. "Organizing dates?" I ask. It feels like it's been forever since she's been out with a girl. "Have you been on any good ones lately?" Last year, she put a name to how she always felt: demiromantic. She even included it on her dating profile. She was excited about it. I was excited *for* her.

Keisha shrugs and looks up from her phone. "I'm helping mom organize client orders." She shakes her head. "Doesn't even understand how her own system is programmed. It's tragic."

I notice that she sidesteps my date question.

She must notice too because she shrugs again. "I don't really have time to date right now. It's fine." She flips her hair and grins, but it feels like it's only for my benefit. "Girls will always be around for me."

I try to smile back but can't make my lips do it.

This wasn't how it was before. Now everything is different because of me and my choices.

Everything is worse.

"I'm fine, Vo," she repeats, and I nod because I know she wants me to be okay. And pretending is all I can give her right now.

Arriving at Harbord Street. Harbord Street.

I push the stop request button, and Keisha raises a delicate eyebrow at me. "Why are we getting off here?"

"I wanted to make a quick stop."

"It's cold."

"We'll be inside."

"Inside where?"

"Inside!" The streetcar slows to a halt, and the doors slide open. I hop onto the platform with Keisha dragging her fluffy-booted feet behind me.

In front of us are huge glass and concrete buildings, one with UNIVERSITY OF TORONTO etched onto it. Students walk quickly between the buildings, desperate to not be outside more than necessary. They have trees lining the street and adding a natural flair to the imposing buildings dusted delicately with white snow.

I have the AI on my phone do an AR map to help direct us where we need to go. We follow the projected yellow footsteps through the campus. The tall buildings and their modern insides seem to scream money and are filled with sponsor kids with wealthy benefactors and kids who are just plain rich.

Going to university used to be something you went into debt over, but now the cost is too high. Drowning yourself in loans just to not get an internship in the end is a sad existence, and most people are smart enough to go the intern route first. If they want you to learn more, the company will pay for you to go to university.

Last year, I thought Keis would be one of those kids. She was on track to be. She was *supposed* to be. But I made a choice. I chose to let Luc keep his future because I didn't know that he could ever come back from losing it. I punished Keis for being the strong one, and now she's happy to punish me right back.

I never realized how long she could hate me.

And I didn't picture losing them both in the end.

But here we are.

More casualties of my decisions.

"You're tugging at me," Keisha whines, though her eyebrows are drawn in concern.

I force a breath out and try to calm down. "Sorry."

The AI dings with a joyful tune in front of the Trinity College building. It's huge, made up of gray and beige bricks, tall and old elegant windows, and a large, dramatic arched entryway. It's like a beautiful castle, only open to commoners like us for occasions like this.

"Oh, hack me, are you for real?" Keisha groans. Clearly, she's spotted the sign.

I hike my shoulders up to my ears. "I saw it on my feed. Looked interesting."

"You are so full of shit."

The digital banner tacked on temporarily for this event is the only thing out of place on the ancient architecture. It declares that they're hosting the Thirty-First Annual Innovations in Tech Conference. It scrolls through the different speakers and guests, and emblazoned larger than life is a boy with stormy blue-gray eyes and matching hair.

LUC RODRIGUEZ, CEO OF NUGENE, KEYNOTE SPEAKER.

Keisha shakes her head at me. "We're *not* going in there."

"I already paid for tickets."

"Wow. Are you malfunctioning?"

I let out a deep breath, my heart beating faster in my chest

t the blown-up photo of the boy I fell in love with. "Can
⸻ just go inside?"

"We're gonna watch him do a whole-ass speech?"

"No," I scowl. "Those tickets were too expensive. I got public
floor access. You can walk around and look at the different booths
and stuff. That's it. No panel or speaker access." Part of me felt
guilty pulling the money from the family account, but another
part of me rationalized that it was only twenty dollars for the two
tickets, and as Matriarch I'm supposed to have control of it anyway.

I don't. Not really. It's the same grocery account I've always
been able to access, and Mom still gives me my allowance every
week like nothing has changed.

I'm not a Matriarch. I'm a child with a fancy title.

Never mind that I'm busting my ass trying to save our business. Never mind that I have to learn to be a Matriarch by myself.
Never mind that I'm grieving like everyone else. Never mind that
part of the reason we ended up in this situation is because the
adults refused to believe in me, and now they're fine with doing
that all over again.

I push down the feelings. I need to be calm. I can't keep tugging on everyone's magic.

Staring up at the holo of Luc just makes it worse.

Luc isn't like me. He's flourishing. He's blocked me from his
personal channels, but I can still see him on public ones—which,
and I know this is sad, I have an alert for. It seems like every tech or
science feed is filled with photos of his face. They're talking about
how he cares about social issues the company didn't touch before
his tenure. How he's reviving the seemingly dead NuSap program
now set to launch in a little over three weeks. In six months, he's
become the face of the new generation of genetic and technology
advancement.

People trust and respect him.

"Let's go," I say, and blaze the trail into the building. Someone checks our tickets at the door before letting us inside.

Beyond the front door, the space is a concentrated explosion of colors, sounds, and movement. The ceilings are sky high with arched wooden beams fixed to them. It feels more like it should be home to a museum than a conference. There are what seems like hundreds of people weaving in and out of the many rooms, each of them packed with booths with flashing holos and loud music thrown on top of it all to add to the chaos.

My chest aches as I think about the first time I walked into the Collective with Luc. The awe at the bright and inviting booths. We weren't exactly on stellar terms then, but we were a lot better than we are now.

Part of me thought that after everything, I could carve Luc out of my heart. Slice him away like peeling the fat off a chicken. Except the fat is one of the best parts, and doing without has left me with something dry and disappointing.

I check the time in the corner of my eye, projected into my vision by the hijacker chip implanted behind my ear.

10:15 a.m.

Perfect.

I stride through the crowds—side-stepping other attendees and calls to check out the latest tech or whatever innovation they're presenting.

"Um," Keisha says. "Are we going to actually look at anything or are we just rushing . . . ah, hack me, *really*, Vo?"

I guess that she's caught sight of the giant NuGene sign on the room that we're heading toward.

She grabs my arm. "There's no way this goes well for you."

"I just want to take a look."

"You want to torture yourself."

I tug out of her hold. "I'm a big girl. I can handle it." I continue into the room, and Keisha lets out a steups behind me.

The NuGene display is predictably grand. Life-sized holos project a multicultural mix of people across the walls. There are free giveaways of tech that's definitely not cheap and feed celebrities wearing what looks like luxury athletic gear with the NuGene logo directing people to the different displays.

"Hack me!" Keisha gasps. "Orange Orange is here!"

I can't even bring myself to ask her who that is. My eyes are scanning the room, past the huge crowds of people, past the cornflower-blue NuSap units walking around and interacting with people, right to the biggest crowd in the middle of the room.

And there he is.

Surrounded by a massive group of people, Luc stands in a sleek black suit with his blue-gray hair carefully coiffed exactly the way Justin used to wear his. His eyes are crimson with the spinning lenses his mentor favored.

I walk closer like I'm being drawn by a force bigger than me.

He looks different. Just a little bit. Maybe I'm the only one obsessive enough to notice. Now that he's in front of me, it's more obvious. His jaw is a tad sharper, more on the right side than the left. The lack of symmetry makes his face that much more charming.

Once I'm at the edge of the crowd, I can actually hear what he's saying.

Even his voice has gone through a slight change. Deeper. Like it's coming from further inside his chest. And the way he carries himself too, held straight instead of slouched.

He gestures to the NuSap unit beside him. "We're so excited about the new features of the unit as well as the return of some of the original features. The units will still be able to detect the presence of other units, very necessary if you have multiples.

We've also worked diligently with governments to amend the restrictions on AI control, of course with added safety precautions. We've . . ."

I lose track of what it is that he's saying as I stare.

He doesn't just look different.

He *feels* different.

Charismatic is not a word I ever thought I would use to describe Luc, but it's what fits. The way he waves his hands around just so, this new, perfect, all-teeth smile, and even the casualness with which he throws in the odd joke that makes the crowd burst into laughter.

He stops talking and an assistant opens the floor for questions. His head turns as he looks at the crowd, and it takes only seconds for his gaze to land on me.

I inhale sharply. I don't mean to. It just happens.

And I'm trapped in those swirling bionics, wishing that I could see the familiar stormy eyes underneath.

I feel like I should say something but don't know what.

How are you? This is a cool setup.

I'm sorry.

I saw you on the news. That's pretty impressive.

I miss you.

Abruptly, Luc jerks his eyes away from mine and pulls his lips into that picture-perfect bright grin. Nothing like the lip-biting smile that I'm used to.

It's like being slapped with the cold chill of the blast freezer at Roti Roti. I wrap my arms around myself so I won't shiver.

He hates me.

Of course he does.

Why did I forget that suddenly?

A hand lands on my shoulder and steers me away from Luc. I let her. "Let's go see the other stuff," Keisha mumbles.

I rub away the tears at the corners of my eyes and try not to choke when I mutter back, "Okay."

My cousin struts into the different rooms, tugging me along with her and pointing out anything that looks remotely interesting. The bright sights and sounds wash over me, and I can't make myself concentrate on any of them. I keep picturing Luc's swirling bionics turning away from me. Shutting me out. Shutting me down.

We go to a booth that's drawing people in with a giveaway for a NuGene procedure, which Keisha is desperate to sign up for.

"Gene hacks!" the man at the booth shouts. "That's the future. We're not going to need the machines anymore, just a little injection filled with some specially programmed nanites and BAM, manipulation delivered. NuGene already has the tech! I heard that from a very reputable source."

The guy has barely finished his sentence before some others start arguing with him about feasibility, and his response is to go off on a conspiracy theory involving monkey urine. It's enough for me to doubt how legit the giveaway really is and how "reputable" his source might be.

Keisha wrinkles her nose and, maybe having the same thought, decides not to enter. "Let's move on." She starts to push me toward another display when she stops. "Woah, that dude is hardcore staring at you."

I blink and follow her gaze.

It lands on a Black boy with curls that fan out around his face and drop into his eyes. Those curls might be nicer than mine. His skin is lighter than ours and has a sort of dewy, fresh-faced look to it. Like he takes good care of himself.

And he *is* staring at me. It's intense and singular, like nothing else exists between us. It's hacking creepy.

Keisha nudges me hard in the side, and I grunt. "He's totally into you," she sings.

I cringe. "Keisha, please—"

"You can't keep pining over Luc. For one, it's sad."

Okay, ouch.

"Two, his sponsor dad basically murdered Granny *and* Auntie Elaine."

"Luc tried to help us."

"Yeah, but like, *he* thinks you killed Justin, so . . . Honestly, you'll benefit from moving on to bigger and better things with shinier hair and skin." Before I can protest or ask how I could have time for dating if she doesn't, she drags me toward the boy and the booth.

He snaps out of his intense gaze, and for a moment I swear his eyes narrow at me. But he turns away from us and suddenly becomes interested in organizing the papers on the table.

"He doesn't seem excited to see us," I mutter to Keisha.

She scoffs. "He's shy. He was basically licking you with his eyes a second ago."

"Gross."

"Hush."

We stop in front of the boy's booth, which declares itself HELP-ING HANDS: CHARITABLE GENETIC MANIPULATION and has a logo of a DNA helix split into two, with the ends made into little hands reaching for each other. I've never heard of it, but it's the sort of thing that it seems like I should know about. NuGene will occasionally dole out a free service for someone with a previously incurable genetic disease that makes the news. Someone who usually doesn't look the way those in my community do.

Otherwise, the government will cover any genetic therapy for procedures needed, but it also means being on a waiting list, sometimes for years. People whose mutations could cause immediate death are always prioritized, while ones that cause daily pain or suffering but aren't life-threatening are pushed down the list. NuGene owns the government contracts for genetic therapies, meaning they have to fit those clients in alongside their paying ones, which leads to even longer wait times.

And there obviously isn't anything in place for genetic mutations in the witch community that cause weaker gifts or no gifts at all. If there were, Auntie Elaine wouldn't have had to go out of her way to try to fix it herself. She wouldn't have needed to get Justin Tremblay involved and spin our family down a path that's still stretching out today. Not that those are the same as a life-threatening genetic disease, but still.

The closer we get, the more the boy's lip curls like he's tasted something foul. I half expect him to abandon the booth to avoid us, but he doesn't.

"Keisha . . . I really don't think he wants to talk to us . . ."

My cousin hushes me again, clearly on a mission.

Just as we're about to reach him, a guy from the crowd rushes toward him. "Eli! Man, I haven't seen you in forever. I heard your mom was getting sparked as shit looking for you."

Eli, apparently, shifts in place. "Oh . . . no, it's fine, I just, like . . . needed space from her for a bit. You know how it is?" The last bit weirdly comes out as a question when I'm sure it's supposed to be a statement.

The new guy notices us, and his eyes get wide. "Oh, damn, you got a celebrity over here."

All of us throw confused looks at him.

Celebrity?

"Voya Thomas, right? I'm Henson Bailey." He leans forward and grasps my limp hand between both of his, shaking vigorously. Then he goes back to Eli and gives him a nudge. "This is my boy Eli."

Finally, the celebrity comment sinks in.

Me. *I'm* the celebrity.

I look closer at Eli and see that he and Henson have the same skin tone. Baileys. That's probably why he was staring at me. Not because he was "licking me with his eyes," but because he recognized me. Maybe from his family saying how shitty our product is. The narrowed eyes and intense gaze might have been him trying to figure out if it was actually me.

"Right," I say to say something. "Nice to meet you."

Henson beams. "For sure. Oh man, wait here, yeah? I gotta go find my sister, she would love to meet you. She has the shittiest gift." He cranes his neck around the mass of people. "Hack me, okay, I'm gonna grab her. Don't leave, okay?" Henson rushes off into the crowd without another word.

I do not plan to be here when he gets back. I move to turn away, but Keisha yanks me back, flashing a big smile at Eli. "You're a Bailey?"

He refuses to meet our eyes and instead looks down at the papers on the table. "Yeah." Instead of the casual tone he used with his cousin, what comes out of his mouth is terse and short.

"How old are you?"

"Seventeen."

Keisha tilts her head. "I don't remember seeing you in Johan's school."

"My mom taught me at home."

My cousin eyes him up and down, and he squirms under the scrutiny.

"So, what is all of this?" I ask, gesturing to the booth. I would rather leave, but clearly Keisha won't.

He clears his throat but still doesn't look up. "We're Helping Hands. We gather applications from people who need genetic manipulation treatments but may not have access to government health care or have been on a waiting list for a while. Our group partners with talented geneticists who perform the therapies on a volunteer basis, and we're lucky to get donations that help with equipment costs."

"Where's your volunteer sign-up?" Keisha asks, looking around the table for a tablet. "Voya would *love* to volunteer, wouldn't you, Voya?"

I scowl at her.

How is this girl not seeing how uncomfortable he is talking with us? Has she really been out of the dating game that long?

Eli shakes his head. "We're not recruiting right now."

Keisha raises an eyebrow and points at the sign above him that says, WE'RE ALWAYS LOOKING FOR VOLUNTEERS!

Now this is just getting embarrassing.

Hack me. This guy saw me in a crowd, stared because he thought he recognized me but obviously did not expect to talk to me, and now wishes we were gone.

I would love to make that happen for both of us.

I tug Keisha away. "Let's go." I point into the crowd where Henson is making his way through, dragging a girl behind him. "I would like to avoid that, thank you."

"Um!" Eli suddenly blurts out.

I turn back to look at him. He freezes, staring at me while I stare back, finally making eye contact. "Yeah?"

"Why are you here? At the conference, I mean."

My face heats, and I'm glad blushes don't show through my skin. "Thought it would be interesting."

"Right . . . Well, enjoy it," he mumbles.

"Thanks."

We make our way back outside into the frigid winter air. I take one last look at Luc on the holo sign in front of the building. That same sparked smile. The one I don't recognize.

Maybe the lip-biting one was never real. Like whatever was between us. And this new smile is the better version. The version of Luc with a thriving future. The one I always knew he deserved.

I just hadn't gotten around to understanding the reality that I wouldn't be in it.

And I hadn't figured out that *my* future wouldn't look anything like that.

"Forget that Eli guy," Keisha says. "There's plenty more out there for you."

I fight not to roll my eyes. She's really out here acting like I was thinking of him as a prospect. "Sure," I reply, like I care about any guys other than the CEO who rejected me. Again.

"Home?" she asks, hands tucked into her coat.

"You can," I say with a sigh. "I have to go to work."

Asking Johan to watch their murder rite last year was one of my worst choices, and one of the ones with more lasting effects. My days are eaten up with mornings or afternoons in a kitchen working. I think Johan enjoys lording it over a real Matriarch.

I turn away from the screen with Luc's face on it.

My choices have the power to change futures.

I just never thought they would make mine worse.

CHAPTER THREE

I'm two hours early for my shift. Which means I'll be working two hours for free because there's no way Johan will let me go home early—not that going home earlier is what I want either. I walk in through the main entrance to Roti Roti, where the spiced scent of curry lingers in the air and calypso music blasts through the speakers. A holo flares to life in the entryway to welcome me with a thick Trinidadian accent. It's a woman decked out in Caribana gear, giant feathered headpiece and all. She's wearing the same costume that the Davises used last year—sparkling blue and silver with ash-colored makeup. Staring at her reminds me of gunshots in the air and speaking the words to Mama Jova that sentenced my cousin to life inside our ancestral home.

I close my eyes for a moment and try to pull myself together, but I'm yanked out of my thoughts by muffled yelling.

It's not coming from the dining area of the restaurant with its booths covered in smooth red vinyl. The kitchen is visible only through a small rectangular pass that connects to the space where the cashiers are in the dining area. The cashier space is filled with hanging Caribbean snacks like kurma, sweet and spicy tamarind balls, red mango, and more. Not to mention the pop fridge is stocked with Busta and Chubby sodas of all varieties, the latter recently brought back to life by a new company specializing in retro drinks. And of course, the always necessary peanut punch and Peardrax.

Emerald winces from where she stands in front of the register and taps something on her phone that makes the calypso music go even louder but successfully drowns out the arguing.

Some of the witches in line look over at me. One is definitely a James, and I'm pretty sure we're cousins, but the woman gets real interested in staring at the menu when I look her way.

Being a Thomas used to mean that people *wanted* to look your way. To be associated with and noticed by you. Part of that was us and another was our connections—the Thomases and the Davises sticking together.

But I completely sparked our relationship with them when I messed up that ritual. Johan assumed that I was trying to sabotage the family, and it's clear that things will never be the same between us. Even though I've told him that wasn't what I was doing. There's a distance that I don't know will ever get shorter.

I wave at Emerald with her hair tied up in a bright island-print head wrap. She gives me a nod back, but she's clearly distracted by whatever the shouting is about.

Making my way through the small door off to the side of the cashier area, I start down the hallway to enter the kitchen. The source of the noise immediately becomes clear.

At the end of the hall is Johan's office, and Topaz, his oldest son, is standing outside of it with his arms crossed. The door slams in his face, and he reels back with a snarl.

"He'll come around," Aqua says to her younger brother, walking out of the kitchen to my right.

Topaz shakes his head and rushes past us both into the kitchen, slamming around the pots and pans in the sink.

I raise an eyebrow at Aqua.

She sighs. "Dad doesn't like his new boyfriend."

"Dad," Topaz hisses from over at the sink, "is an ignorant asshole."

Aqua flinches, and her eyes dart to the door. But Johan doesn't suddenly pop around the corner.

I've never, ever heard any of the Davis kids so much as raise their voice to their dad before. They're perfectly obedient. Our family looks like a bunch of barely behaved zoo animals in comparison. Mom or Auntie will ground us and then forget about it a couple of hours later when they want to go out shopping together. I'm not about to call any of them *assholes*, but I've gotten away with some sass.

Aqua goes over to her brother and lays her hand gently on his shoulder. "Why don't you walk around the block for a bit? Do some breathing and maybe call Mason?"

His fingers shake against a curry-stained pot lid for a moment before he lets out a long exhale. "Yeah, okay." Topaz abandons the dishes, shrugs off his apron, and grabs his jacket from the little cubby in the corner.

After he leaves, Emerald sticks her head through the pass. "I don't know how you have the patience for him," she says to her sister.

"He's upset, that's all."

"Yeah, yeah. I have an order coming in." She nods to me. "Are you ready?"

"Just give me a minute." I rush over to the cubby and shove my jacket inside. Off a hook on the wall, I grab a black apron and find a clean black head wrap for my hair. Johan says they look a lot better than hairnets and that the non-Black customers like them because they make us look extra ethnic. We regularly hear compliments on them. The front of house staff like Emerald have cuter multicolored ones with different patterns that Alex made a long time ago. Back of house like me get plain black since it's easier to hide food stains.

It seems like it's only going to be me, Emerald, Aqua, and Topaz on this shift. I'm glad that the Davis kids treat me the same. It would be a lot harder to work here if they didn't. They have rotating shifts; even thirteen-year-old Peridot helps out. Which I guess makes sense. If he's old enough to cut into the body of a man, he may as well be old enough to help in a restaurant.

I push the image out of my head as I join Aqua. Her honey-brown curls peek out of the top of her head wrap, done in a twist-out style. Her face looks the most like her dad's. Almost a carbon copy, but in girl form: the same deep brown, glistening skin, prominent cheekbones, and dark eyes. She's nineteen, the same age as Alex, and the oldest Davis kid. Sometimes I wonder what it would have been like growing up, just Aqua and Johan, at least for the two years before Topaz came along.

Johan doesn't treat her special for it. He's the only parent I know who does actually seem to treat his children equally. If anything, Aqua gets less attention as the quietest of them.

We usually have our shifts together, with me coming in halfway through the day while she's been there the entire day. Johan wanted to force me to do the same, but we never made any terms around how many hours I would work in our deal, and the government minimum for interns is ten hours a week. If he put me on a full shift, I would only need to come in for one day. Instead he has me stretched out to three days a week for two to four hours each, which isn't bad.

These days I kind of appreciate it.

"I'm guessing Topaz's new guy isn't a witch?" I ask, checking the fridge to see our stock of baked goods. It's winter, and Caribbean people are not looking to have weddings right now, so there haven't been cake orders for me to fulfill besides the odd birthday or anniversary celebration. Mostly I've been helping with the day-to-day cooking as well as making black cake and sweet bread to cut up and sell as individual slices. We've even expanded to home-made bottles of sorrel.

Aqua lets out a sigh and pulls a ticket down from the metal holder. "How did you guess?"

"Johan didn't have a problem with the other two guys, and they were both witches. Plus, the whole 'ignorant' comment."

"I don't think any of us thought it would be a big deal. It's not like Topaz has told him about magic either. But . . . I think Dad is having a hard time right now."

"Why?" I blurt out before I can stop it. "Because . . . of Caribana, or . . . ?"

We don't usually talk about this. If anything, it's felt like Aqua purposely maneuvers around those topics of conversation for my sake. We don't discuss my family's failing business, or Granny, or my gifts, or me being Matriarch, and we *definitely* don't talk about everything that went down between me and Johan last year.

Aqua reads the ticket: "Small curried goat, boneless, wrapped in paratha, no spice. One pholourie on the side, extra tamarind sauce." She points to the fryer basket in front of her. "I can drop the pholourie when you're ready."

"Thanks, you can drop it now."

She does so, silent for a moment. Then, "I don't know what it is with Dad," she says finally, glancing over at me. "It's just hard. Things are changing, you know? They have been for a while. But I don't know. He's been doing everything since Grandma went on her vacation, and I don't think even he expected it would be this long. It's a lot of pressure."

"Yeah." If this is about the pressure of leading a family, I definitely know about that. "Where did she go again?"

Aqua opens her mouth, then pauses and frowns. "I . . . I honestly can't remember. Is that weird? I guess it's been so long. But she and Uncle Kane been traveling all around, so who knows where they are now. They send the odd message to say they're okay, but that's it. Grandma has never liked video chats."

"Fair enough. But why would Johan get on Topaz about it?" I pull a paratha roti out of the warming drawer, the fluffy off-white layers thick between my fingers. Slapping it down onto the prep table, I scoop up the boneless goat and potato curry, taking care of how much liquid I include to avoid giving the customer something soggy. Finally, I wrap the roti up until it hugs the filling snuggly and drop it into a container.

Aqua lifts the fryer basket and shakes out the pholourie before grabbing two small containers of tamarind sauce. "Topaz is really serious about this guy, you know? They've already been together for a year. Secret. I guess Topaz knew better than any of us that Dad wouldn't be on board."

"It's shocking that you thought he *would* be," Emerald says, leaning over the pass.

Behind her, the line has dissolved, all their orders taken, and now they're waiting around in the booths for their food. I try to work faster, grabbing the packed pholourie from Aqua, combining it with the rest of the order, and slipping it through the pass next to Emerald's head.

Aqua shrugs. "He didn't seem like he would mind."

"Dad doesn't like anything that he can't control," her sister says. "Witches he can. Some random non-magic guy, he can't." She paused. "Unless he decides to use magic on him."

"He wouldn't," Aqua says with a frown.

Emerald raises her eyebrows. "Wouldn't he?" She grabs the order and turns away from us.

The eldest Davis stands there for a moment, looking out through the pass. Then she turns back to me with a strained smile. "I guess I'm the optimistic one."

"I guess," I parrot, not sure what else to say.

Working here has shown me that the Davises aren't as airtight of a family as I always thought they were. It's not like my situation is better—in fact, it's absolutely worse—but it does make me feel not as bad about it. Not even the strongest families are perfect.

We continue doing the orders, one after another. It's a Monday night, though, so there aren't many to begin with. Eventually, Topaz comes back and after that the shift passes quickly, hours floating by filling orders, cleaning, and chatting with Aqua about things so random that I forget what they were minutes later. My phone is set to Do Not Disturb so that I can't get any messages while I work. I told everyone that was Johan's rule for me in the kitchen. In truth, he doesn't care. After all, since I've started working here, the feed ratings have shot up, praising the sudden increase in the quality of the food.

It's just easier for me to avoid my family that way.

Aqua lets out a long sigh as the last customer leaves, and I laugh. "That bad, eh?"

"Cooking is not really my thing. I get bored." She tugs off her head wrap and shakes out her hair.

As far as I know, she's never sought an internship anywhere. But I guess I've never asked. "Where else would you work, if not here?"

"I wouldn't. This is where I belong." There's something about the look on her face that makes me think that isn't true.

"Or you could get an internship at a company doing something you actually like," Topaz says from over by the sink as he dries the last dish. "You used to want to work in data science."

My eyebrows go way up. Working in a kitchen is a far cry from doing complicated computer science and statistics.

Aqua scrubs at her face. "I wasn't very good."

"According to who?"

Silence cuts through the air, sharp in its suddenness.

From the look on Topaz's face, it's clear enough who said so.

"I wasn't good *enough*," Aqua corrects, looking down at the ground. "Not with all the competition, and it made things stressful." She looks up at me and grins. "I admire you and Alex, Keisha, and Keis. You're doing amazing things, you know? You have your passions. I'm not really like that." She hikes her shoulders up. "I work here and help take care of the family. If I wasn't doing that, I don't really know what else I would do, you know?"

Her brother steupses but doesn't say anything more.

I want to tell her that she shouldn't admire me. That I have no idea what I'm doing. But I don't.

The more I've spent time with her, the more I've realized how much Aqua supports her siblings. After we finish up in the kitchen and get everything ready for tomorrow's shift, she'll go in the front and help Emerald get that clean, then message the rest of her siblings to make sure they either have a way to get home or are home safe already.

Could she do all that and still chase her dream? Maybe she can't. Maybe that's why she stays here.

She's her own sort of leader in the family, just one so far in Johan's shadow that it's hard to notice her.

We finish in the kitchen, and like I predicted, she heads to the front to help Emerald close up.

I tug my jacket on as my stomach clenches.

Time to go home.

CHAPTER FOUR

I've never really looked at our house. Sure, I go in and out. Sometimes I notice the mail if I'm expecting a package. And some days, I'll look up to see who's out on the second-floor balcony. Usually, it's Keis. It's the closest she can get to being outside now. She always pretends that she hasn't seen me, though.

But the rest of the house, I never just stop and stare at it.

Every part of it was built by someone who was enslaved. They helped push the crisp white pillars into place and nailed together the wooden railings before putting on coat after coat of matching white paint. They made sacrifices in blood to get it here to Toronto. For us. So our family could keep going. And every generation has added something.

Granny's granny spent the time painstakingly retiling the flat roof. Her mother built both our balcony benches from scratch. And Granny . . . well, Granny instructed Auntie Maise with an iron fist to create the pottery pieces that house our plants, put Dad to work on making our porch flower boxes, and got Grandad to do the initial planting that everyone in the family now tends to.

Now those planters are carefully wrapped in burlap or transferred inside for the winter.

Of course, Granny also contributed by leading, the way a Matriarch should.

I stare up at the house with its looming two floors and clench my hands into fists at my sides.

Finally, I enter.

I've barely stepped through the doorway when Mom pokes her head out of the dining room. "Voya?"

"Hack me," I mutter. Part of me thinks that if I sprint up the steps now, I can get away in time. Do my usual sad nighttime routine of scrolling through feeds featuring Luc. But chances are she'll come up and find me anyway. The last thing I want is for someone to witness what I already know is a pathetic way to spend my time. "Yeah?"

"Can you come over here?"

"Okay." I hang my coat on the hook by the door and shuffle into the dining room, where everyone in the family sits, except for Keis, of course. And Keisha, which usually wouldn't be common, except they're eating dinner, so it is. She doesn't like to have her meals with us anymore. Hasn't for the last few months.

The huge dining room table is littered with pizza boxes, because if I'm not home to cook, everyone pretends like they don't know how. Behind it, the huge back windows that look out at Lake Ontario are aglow with the moonlight that streams through.

Eden grins at me with her lips around a vegan slice. I can always tell because the faux cheese never melts quite the same. "We're having pizza."

"I can see that," I say with a smile. Sometimes it feels unreal that my sister is here, alive. That I didn't fail my Calling task, lose our magic, and end up with a dead half-sibling. Except, even if I never did my task, she would still be alive. That was the insurance the adults made sure to get—without telling me, of course—so in the end, all it did was attach us to the house more firmly. Our magic linked to its bones. If it ever fell, we would all lose magic, and Eden would die.

Considering that, we've been a lot more careful about keeping up with house maintenance. Now there are about five new smoke detectors and fire alarms when we originally had precisely two.

But that only protects my sister from the external things that might harm her. Not the things inside her own mind. And seeing a man beheaded and your grandma dying in front of you at six years old is not something you walk away from unscathed.

Priya dabs at her mouth with a napkin while Dad meticulously cuts up slices of pizza for Eden like she's not old enough to handle the full thing. I would probably feel annoyed and smothered, but Eden seems perfectly happy with the extra attention.

Only she doesn't just need attention, she needs professional help. But how could we ever take her to someone without explaining that we fake-killed the NuGene CEO, who we now have trapped in a NuSap unit in our basement? Even in the witch community, no families outside our own know about that.

If we were a proper community, then we could all help each other. Except none of the other families will even entertain the idea of forming a council. I have dozens of ignored messages on my phone to prove it.

Alex pushes an open pizza box toward me, and I sink into a chair. At least I'll be happy and eating when they drop whatever it is they're planning to drop on me.

I pull a greasy slice out of the box, topped with pepperoni, mushrooms, bacon bits, and tomatoes, and shove it in my mouth. It's a little cold, but I'm too lazy to go into the kitchen and warm it up.

Granny used to insist on putting pizza in the oven "to get crispy" the instant it was delivered. We never got to slap the box on the table, open it up, and eat.

My throat goes dry, and I take another bite.

Dad and Priya chew thoughtfully on their slices and try not

to look at me too hard while they fuss over Eden and pretend like they aren't itching to chat with me about whatever is going on.

Uncle Cathius, on the other hand, is ignoring the pizza and peeling a honeycrisp apple. In his typical fashion of being as annoying as possible, he refuses to eat takeout. April-Mae apparently cooked every single meal for her children, and the idea of eating something not homemade is appalling to him. Not that he would ever bother to cook anything himself. Just thinking of it makes me want to roll my eyes.

On his left, Auntie Maise nibbles on a hot wing and stares directly at me. The only family member who I can count on to not beat around the bush. Mom glances between her and me from where she sits.

"So?" I say.

Auntie opens her mouth, but Mom cuts her off. "How was work?"

I shrug. "Fine."

Johan wants me to do all his cooking, and I know my stuff is making him more money, and he won't even acknowledge it. I had my shift with Aqua, which was nice. I think she's my favorite Davis. She's clean and polite and isn't nosy. Oh! And you won't believe this. Rowen stiffed us. Wants to try the product first before she pays us because a Bailey is mouthing off. And Keisha thinks she used her gift on me. But she wouldn't do that, would she? Also, why did we get pizza from 241 when we could get it from Heritage, which yeah, is more expensive, but it's better pizza.

Before, I would have said all of that. Chatting with my family was fun. Something to look forward to. Like having almost a dozen friends that you live with, and yeah, maybe some aren't your besties per se (Uncle), but the rest are great. There were non-stop conversations. I didn't think about half the things that came out of my mouth.

Now it's different.

Now I know that the adults keep secrets. That they'll whisper things behind my back that they would never say to my face.

Before, that used to make me sad, knowing they didn't believe in me. Now it sparks my shit. How much do I have to do to earn their respect? I'm tired of trying and getting nothing back.

If I say that Johan won't acknowledge what I've done for him, I'll remind everyone of how I messed up his ritual, and how much power he has over me as my boss even though I'm a Matriarch and he's not. If I talk about liking Aqua, it'll remind them of the fact that, because of what I did, there's a rift between us and the Davises, even if we're still chummy with his kids. That I've now made Johan our enemy. And if I talk about anything that happened with Rowen, I'm admitting that the business is doing worse than ever and that I let myself get walked all over again.

Mom nods a little, trying to be encouraging. Once again attempting to fill that gap between us where Granny used to be. But it isn't working. We're awkward around each other. Tiptoeing. "Who did you work with?"

"Aqua, Topaz, and Emerald."

"How are they?"

"Fine."

At that, Auntie Maise throws down a chicken wing licked clean of meat. "Enough," she snaps. "Are you depressed?"

I blink. Of all the things I thought they were going to bring up, this wasn't it.

"Depressed?" I parrot back the word like I'm confused about what it means. In one way, I am. What does being depressed mean? Like, do I cry all the time? Not really. I think I cried way more while I was doing my task and Granny was still alive, and no one asked if I was depressed then. Am I sad constantly? Yes. But isn't that grief? Aren't all of us sad?

36

I turn to Alex like my older cousin will have a better explanation. In the last few months, she's let her hair grow out in a little fro that reminds me so much of Granny's that it's hard to look at her sometimes.

Alex shrugs and raises her sparkly eyebrows at our aunt.

I look around the table and fix my eyes on Dad, who stares over at Mom with a rising panic in his eyes. Clearly, this wasn't something he wanted to be involved with, but he must have known it was coming. Otherwise he and Priya wouldn't have been giving me those looks. And yet he obviously hadn't done enough to stop the conversation from happening at all.

It feels like years ago when we sat in his bedroom together talking about Auntie Elaine, the ancestors, and his past. For the first time since I was a kid, I felt close to Dad again. Like we understood each other.

Now I don't know. It's like we're friends who haven't seen each other in a long time and aren't sure how to act. Somewhere between him being preoccupied with helping Eden and me being consumed with trying to help the family, we lost the little bit we had rebuilt.

"Is this an intervention?" I ask, turning to everyone around the table.

The entire family groans except for Eden, who jumps in to ask what an intervention is.

Keisha pops around the corner with her arms crossed and says, "It's a thing where people scroll through your feed and point out the posts that make them worry about you, and Carter Fornberry from eLife comes out of the back and says, 'This is an intervention. Your family cares about you and this is to help you.' And then—"

"Stop," Mom says. "It's not an intervention."

"Everyone's magic is being weird, and they think it's because you're sad," Keisha says, and waves at everyone around the table. "I told them to let me ask, but they wanted to do it 'as a family.'" She scoffs, and I don't blame her.

I shove the rest of the pizza in my mouth and stand, pointing at an empty box. "Did anyone take some down for Keis yet?"

"No," Keisha says. "That's what I was coming to do."

I grab the box, arranging two slices of the meat pizza in it and one of the veggie. She likes to have a mix. "I'll take it."

"Is that the best idea?"

"It's fine."

"*Is* it actually?" Mom snaps. "Is everything *fine*? Because it doesn't seem fine."

"Granny is dead," I mutter, my voice low. "So, no. Everything isn't fine. But I'm not depressed. I'm just . . ." I don't have the words for what I am, and if I did, I wouldn't want to share it with a family who doesn't believe in me. Who didn't think I could do my task last year and who now doesn't think I can be a good Matriarch. I'm trying my best, but nothing seems to matter.

Maybe that makes me depressed, I don't know. But I don't have time to worry about it. I need to pull this family together and protect what Granny made. And I need to make it better somehow, like I told Mama Jova that I was going to. *She* believed that I could do this, so I will.

I pick up the pizza box.

Mom opens her mouth like she wants to say something else, but I'm already racing away, and she doesn't call me back. I know Granny wasn't just special to me. But I can't feel everyone else's pain. They seem to be moving forward without her. And without me too.

The basement door is lodged in our weird side hallway. It's a wall that creates a closed path from the kitchen through to the main floor half bathroom, where it opens up. It's a strange construction, but now I'm glad for it, because it boxes the basement door into its own space that you can't see from the entryway unless you walk right up to the guest bathroom door.

I ferry the pizza box into the basement, trudging down the cold cement stairs in my socks.

When I make it to the bottom, I have that momentary bit of shock at how different it looks now. It used to be an open space with two deep freezers and our laundry machines providing a constant low-level humming, plus a bunch of old junk in boxes we never touched.

Now Keis has cleaned up an old couch she found in Granny's room and actually went through the boxes to find a couple pieces of wood that she fashioned into a desk low enough for her to work from the couch without hunching.

She sits there, swiping through her tablet, her hair in its signature pineapple bun. Justin is on the couch next to her, cornflower-blue skin out of place next to her brown shade. He found some of Grandad's old clothes in the boxes and now wears the same three to four button downs with the same single pair of black pants. At his request, I programmed his body to grow hair for him so he could recreate his signature blond coif hairstyle.

I guess his are the only blue-gray eyes that I'm going to see today. It occurred to me soon after getting Justin set up that Luc had probably gotten his modded eye and hair color to match this original unit. He's enough of a fanboy to do it.

"Look who it is, my jailer come for a visit!" Justin exclaims, launching himself off the couch to make a grand welcoming gesture.

He remains an asshole, even as an android.

Keis mutters, "If you kill people, you go to jail."

That gets a scowl out of the former NuGene CEO.

As a family, we activated the spells to keep him contained in the ancestral home. As long as one of us is inside the house to contribute to its magic, he can't leave. And Keis will never go anywhere, so it's a pretty guaranteed security system. Not to mention some extra NuSap settings to make sure he can't exit the basement anyway. We need it all. Justin may be trapped, but he's still a genius, and Keis can't read his thoughts. Her gift, it seems, only works on humans.

I step forward with slow, unsure steps. "Hey."

"You can leave the box there," Keis says before I can make it any farther into the space.

Awkwardly, I set the box down on the floor.

"And what tales of woe do you bring from the outside world?" Justin asks, leaning against the desk, already recovered from Keis's comment. "Another shitty shift at your shitty job? Some light pining over my dear sponsor son?"

I press my lips together and ignore Justin, staring at my cousin as she works.

Justin's tone twists into something deeper, angrier. "She's not going to talk to you, so you may as well talk to me."

I clench my teeth.

Keis and Justin have developed a sort of truce since he's been here, and both of them spend their time working endlessly on some genetics-based video game. My cousin was forced to graduate earlier than she wanted because it's not like she could continue online classes, and now this has become her entire focus. Keis never seemed to care much about games. She spent all her time studying the real world. But now that she can't go into it, the virtual one is her new escape.

She can't go online, since the magic seems to consider that part of being outside, so instead, one of us downloads games for her and she plays them offline. Or we download offline versions of web pages if she needs them.

In this hacked turn of events in my already hacked life, Justin Tremblay has a closer relationship with my cousin than I do.

A voice in the back of my mind whispers that this is my fault. That I deserve to be treated like this.

"I don't want to talk to you," I snipe at Justin and struggle for something to say to Keis.

The first few times I came down, all I could do was apologize. Say that I was sorry things turned out like this. That if I knew what the family was going to do, I would have done nothing. Not completed my task. Lived without magic and saved both her and Luc's futures at the cost of mine.

But it didn't matter.

All that mattered was what I *had* done.

"Say something or leave," Keis says, not looking up from her tablet. "And if you're not going to talk to Justin, you're out of conversation partners."

In the beginning, she would snap at me, every word filled with spite. Now there's nothing. I'm nothing. And she speaks to me accordingly.

"Is everything all right?" I ask finally.

"Fine," she says, then laughs a little. "Oh my God, am I depressed?"

My cheeks burn.

That's the other thing. Keis has lost any reservations or ideas of protest regarding her gift. Now it's a finely sharpened knife, wielded without care. She tugs memories and thoughts from everyone with the same ease that I cut onions.

And her words sting just as much.

"They're worried," I mumble, suddenly defending the adults.

"My mom is worried about our status and how we're gonna make it with you as Matriarch. Uncle is worried about the same thing and about living up to Granny's legacy. Your dad mostly thinks he *should* be worried but he's not actually. Priya is worried about how this will affect Eden. Really only your mom, Alex, and Keisha are worried about *you*. Can't tell what the ancestors think because I can't read them, but they won't talk to you anyway."

I hate when she does that. Parrots back the thoughts that they won't tell me and at the same time pulls out an insecurity and slaps it in my face. Justin chuckling under his breath doesn't help either.

Hearing about Dad's thoughts is . . . a lot. Maybe he's not worried about me because he thinks I'm fine. Not because he doesn't care. After all, I do keep saying that I'm fine. But I have no way to know. "Thanks," I say. "Because I needed that."

Keis shrugs. "You're the one worried about what people think of you. But you don't actually want to know, do you?"

"I'm doing my best."

"It's not good enough. And you know that."

A sharp inhale spikes up my throat and leaves me gasping. I try and hide it as a cough, but I doubt it's convincing. That voice comes back and whispers that maybe she's right. If I were good enough, Rowen wouldn't disrespect me. The family wouldn't question everything I do.

"Voya!" Keisha shouts from the top of the stairs. "I need your help."

"She doesn't," Keis says. "She thinks you're going to cry or something and wants you to leave. You're so unsure of yourself that every time we go to cast something, we get a false start. It doesn't work at first, and we have to try it again until it does. Your insecurities are leaking into our magic. Not to mention we get random tugs on it whenever you freak out about something." She taps on her tablet. "It definitely wasn't like that with Granny."

"Enjoy your pizza," I say, and walk up the stairs without saying goodbye.

Justin shouts up, "Some of us can't eat! Thanks for being sensitive to that!"

Keisha is practically hopping from foot to foot at the top. "Why do you even bother?"

"Because I like punishment," I mutter. "I'm going to bed."

"It's like seven p.m."

"That's fine."

"If everything is fine, you know that means nothing is actually fine, right?"

I do. I probably know it better than anyone else in this house.

But if things *aren't* fine, then I have to admit that they're bad.

And I'm not ready to say that out loud.

So I go up to bed and lie there on my side, scrolling through all my Luc alerts. There's a bunch of coverage of the conference. I pause on one where I recognize myself. The back of my head, full of curls, and Luc in the process of turning away from me. I take a screenshot and save it.

If I were stronger, I would delete every saved screenshot. I would stop the alerts. I would pretend that I never loved a boy who seemed like he might love me back.

But I'm not.

CHAPTER FIVE

My morning routine consists of a small set of actions. First, I get dressed, brush my teeth, and spritz my curls with water to fluff them back out. Second, I go down into the kitchen and make breakfast: today was bacon, tomatoes, and toast. And last, I come back upstairs to my room with a cup of tea and sit in a circle of candles.

The candles are more mismatched than I wanted. I had to gather them from around the house. Some are vanilla scented and squat, others are tall and not scented at all. One, a standout from the rest, is dark purple and more glitter than wax. It was a donation from Alex's short-lived obsession with candle making.

I arrange them in a perfect set of twelve, one in front, one in back, and one on either side, and then two candles between each of those. Using the barbecue lighter, I sit in the circle and light each one. The first time, I made the mistake of lighting them first and then sitting in the circle, which meant trying to get over and situate myself without letting my hips knock them over and starting a fire in our very fragile home.

When Granny died, she left a box that she instructed Mom and Auntie to give to the next Matriarch—both of whom thought it would be one of them. Instead, Mom left it in my room for me the day after my gift was announced.

Part of me wonders if that's some of the reason for the new distance between Mom and me. A sort of jealousy over not becoming Matriarch the way she always thought she would. I know that Auntie has definitely given me the cold shoulder since. I tried not to be too upset about it. I'm sure they're hurting in their own way. I guess I didn't expect for it to be taken out on me.

Accordingly, there wasn't any loving handoff or introduction to what it meant to be Matriarch.

Just a box and a sticky note that read, *From Granny.*

Inside was another note as short and to the point as Granny loved to be.

This is the password to the section of the almanac meant for Matriarchs. Most of it is for impure witches, so it won't apply to us. Contact the ancestors as soon as you can, they'll help. ORLEANS89—that's the password.

It was so ridiculous that I couldn't help laughing. The laughing turned to crying eventually. I don't like to think about it too much.

Inside the almanac were diary records from Matriarchs past, and a list of rules for being a Thomas Matriarch from Granny's mom that was mostly in regard to who got to be Matriarch next, and when children have to do their first murder rite, and how to conduct yourself as a Thomas, etc.

Irrelevant, like Granny said. The only one that mattered to me was the instructions for calling the ancestors to you for guidance. The ritual included sitting in a circle of candles, drawing the name of your chosen ancestor in blood on your face, and focusing your intention.

I press my thumb to the sharp metal tooth in the back of my mouth—the same one Granny had in hers that I fished out of her ashes. Retro Matriarch style. Most modern ones carry a little pen knife.

I like doing it this way. The way that Granny did it.

Blood blooms on my thumb, and I write Mama Jova's name across my forehead. I've done this so many times that it's second nature now. The first time I had to use a mirror to check my face and made such a mess of it that I was sure that was the reason no one had answered.

Except every single day, I continued to get no answer.

As Keis hadn't been shy about mentioning.

I swallow and close my eyes, focusing my intention on getting Mama Jova to come to me.

Intention focusing happens in three steps.

First, blocking out distractions.

Second, clearing your mind.

And third, choosing an intention and focusing on it singularly.

Magic rises in the air, prickling goose bumps on my skin and making the tight curls at the back of my neck straighten in attention. I take a deep breath in and focus my intention harder on the exhale.

Mama Jova.

I need this to work. I need her to come.

Mama Jova.

Please, please, please work.

Mama Jova.

I grip my hands together, wishing, *begging* for her to come.

The magic keeps rising, getting stronger and stronger, working toward a crescendo . . .

The door to my room bangs open, and I jump, the magic deflating like soufflé taken out too soon.

Keisha stands in the doorway with her hands on her hips wearing a white blonde bob wig and a cream sweater dress with knee-high boots.

"You didn't want to knock?" I ask.

She shrugs. "I did, and you didn't answer."

"Most people would take that as a sign to leave."

"Why do you use the candles? You know they don't actually do anything, right?"

I carefully blow out each of the candles, since I'm clearly not going to get to do what I want to. "They help me focus my intention."

"Do they?"

I don't know, but they were in the ritual, and now that I've been doing it with them for so long it feels strange to not use them. I press my palms against my eyes. "I was trying to contact the ancestors."

"I know. You do it literally every morning."

"What is it?" I snap out finally, tired of going back and forth. I eye her for a moment. "Did you seriously take out a whole sew-in just to put on this wig? Isn't that a lot of work?"

"Uh, I used magic. Is your shit that sparked up?"

Right. Magic. Sometimes I forget about the little things you can do with it. Half the time I find myself methodically putting my hair into twists by hand before I realize I could have done it in a minute with magic. Growing pains of being a new witch, I guess. "What do you want?"

"Mom said that Rowen sent her a message all pissed off about the product."

I blanch. "To your mom? Why would she send the message to her?"

"I dunno, she's an adult."

"I'm the Matriarch!"

Keisha shakes her head. "I told you that she doesn't respect you. You need to do something. We should go over there and show her that we are not to be trifled with."

"By doing what?! You tell her when she's uncomfortable while I say something interesting about Justin's past?"

"Rude."

I stand and shake my head. This is so hacked. I'm so tired of this shit. First whatever happened in her lounge, which I'm now thinking that her using her gift on me wasn't so farfetched. And now skipping over talking to me? I'm not a child! I'm the leader of this family. Or I'm supposed to be, anyway, but I feel like no one else seems to have gotten the message.

"Whatever," I say finally. "Let's go to Rowen's place and clear this up."

Keisha's eyes light up.

"Just to talk!"

"Boo," she whines. "Let's bring Alex."

"Why?"

"For numbers."

I can't with her. I really hacking can't. "Whatever. Go get her."

Keisha lets out a little squeal but pauses before rushing away, pointing at my bloody face. "You may want to wash that off first." Then she leaves to collect our older cousin.

Meanwhile, I look back at the abandoned circle of candles.

Again, no one came.

Even the ancestor who supported me being Matriarch can't be bothered.

We look like the world's shittiest witch gang standing out front of the Chinese market store that houses Rowen's lounge. Me at five feet in my puffy yellow jacket, a color choice that at the time seemed fun and cute but now, in combo with my black hair and matching buttercup-colored knit hat, makes me look like an angry bumblebee. Keisha on my left in her bright pink jacket that's so long it goes to her ankles, where her slush-soaked fluffy pink boots begin. She drew a cat-eye because she said it gave her a strong feline energy and stands with her arms crossed, looking like a bouncer for a kitten café. Alex on my right at least has the height to be more intimidating and wears a dark cape with thigh-high black boots, but she insisted on using a green sparkly eyeshadow she called "witch chic" paired with a similarly bold green lip.

The ancestors are laughing at me. I know they are. I've rolled up to face Rowen Huang with a teenage clique that emphasizes how out of my depth I am. This is going to be something great for Keis to pull from my head and cackle over later.

"What's the game plan?" Keisha says, turning to me.

Alex scoffs. "Well, we're gonna make her pay us, right?"

"We couldn't make her pay us before she got the product, so why would we be able to now that she *does* have it and is mad?" I say with a sigh.

Keisha points a finger at me. "You can't just roll over, Vo. You're a Matriarch! The Thomases are hot shit! You have *two gifts*, for ancestors' sake. Go in there with your back straight and don't let her talk down to you."

Alex nods along to everything Keisha is saying. "Also, she used her gift on you. That's hacked. We can't let her get away with that."

I want to curl into a ball and cease to exist.

I want to not be the one who has to do this.

I want to hear Keis tell me what she thinks I should do.

"You're uncomfortable!" Keisha snaps. "Get out of that mindset. Get angry. Get tough." She bumps her fist against my shoulder, where the impact is absorbed by my jacket.

People walking past the market have started to turn and stare at us suspiciously as they go by. "Let's just go in," I say.

We walk into the store, and the woman at the cash looks at us with raised brows.

"Don't even look at her," Alex mutters under her breath. "Keep going."

I force myself to face forward and walk through the doorway, past the freezers at the back, and into the lounge.

We get about two steps into the door before I freeze in the entryway.

Usually, the lounge is a haze of vapor smoke and jazz. Now it's silent, and the air is clear enough to see Rowen leaning against the bar, alone.

She came by herself to solve her problem like a strong Matriarch, and I've rolled up with my squad like a hacking child.

My cousins look at me expectantly as Rowen stares at us. She's wearing a crimson gown with a fur shawl over her shoulders. It's like walking into a glamorous Hollywood movie every time we meet.

I'm tempted to shrug off my ridiculous coat, but don't.

"I understand that you have an issue with the product?" I say to Rowen.

She smiles and points at her cheek, where I spot a barely discernible red bump.

"Serum should clear that right up," I respond.

"Look, Voya, I've done business with your family for years now. Had your Granny's serum for almost all that time. Specifically developed for me, you know. And never since starting that regimen have I *ever* gotten a pimple."

"First time for everything."

Rowen laughs and leans back. "I don't want to make this into a big thing. I only wanted to honor your grandmother's memory and tell you in person that I won't be purchasing any more of your products."

Honor my grandmother's memory?

"Are you hacking kidding me?" I choke out.

Keisha actually gasps beside me.

"Honor my grandmother's memory? Was it honoring Granny's memory when you stiffed us yesterday? Was it honoring her memory when you used your hacking gift to make me agree? You don't give a shit about my grandmother's memory the same way you don't give a shit about your own family."

Rowen's eyes go dark, and she stops lounging and leans away from the bar to stand up straight. "Excuse me?"

"I know you and the Baileys split so you could kick out your Matriarch because she had a kid without magic. You aren't some magnanimous leader, so stop pretending like you are." I can't stop the words now that I've started. Every little nasty thought I've ever had spilling out. She doesn't want to respect me as a Matriarch, so why should I respect her? Because she's older? Because she's not a *child*?

"Are you threatening me?" Rowen hisses.

"With my words?"

"No. With those."

It takes me a moment to realize that in the midst of chewing out Rowen, I must have bit my lip and now little needle pins of blood are pointing out from them, straight in her direction. I force myself to calm down, and they fall, two drops of blood slipping down my chin. I wipe them away.

My magic feels like a physical thing bouncing underneath my skin. Wild. Sparking and warming my blood. There's too much of it. Too much of everything. Being a witch for the first time. Being a Matriarch. Having two gifts.

Not having Granny.

"Fine," I snap. "Don't buy from us. Here's something for you: We won't sell to you either."

Rowen scoffs.

I twist on my heel, ready to stomp out, when the Huang Matriarch speaks again.

"This is not how your grandmother would have wanted you to run your family."

My mind is flung back to Granny squeezing my hand, our blood mingling together, the sound of Eden crying in the background. Granny's fingers going limp in mine.

How dare she? How dare she try to act like she knows what Granny would have wanted. Like it's easy to step into her place as if she was never there. To become a perfect Matriarch.

How dare Rowen poke at the wound that says I'm disappointing Granny's legacy?

It's one step too far.

My body flares, magic rises hard and fast to the surface, rushing for somewhere to go. I grab at it, but it slips through my fingers, heating the air to a suffocating temperature, searching for some way to lash out and snap back.

"Voya!" Keisha screeches, voice shrill and scared.

My brain feels like it's cooking. Too hot to bear. Too hot to think.

I need to find somewhere for the magic to land. All this excess power that comes with being Matriarch that I can't control. That comes with *feeling* so much all the hacking time. I need to put it someplace. It needs to be big.

Gifts don't use bandwidth. That's the whole point of them. But I can still pour that power into my gift to get rid of it.

My gift that I've only ever used once before.

Months ago, I used it to see into Justin Tremblay's past and give Rena Carter some peace over her daughter's—my friend Lauren's—death. Her murder.

Since then, I haven't even tried to see any other aspect of Justin's past. I didn't want to dig more into someone who had already hurt me and my family so much. I can barely live in the present that I created when I fake murdered him.

But I don't know anyone else who meets the conditions of my gift. He's the only one whose path I changed with my actions enough that he can never get back on his original one. If I want to put the magic into my gift, he's my only choice.

From across the lounge, for the first time since I saw her at the Pass, Mama Jova is standing in the corner. My ancestor who set that impossible task for me. Who gave me my gifts. Who has refused to answer any of my calls since I've become Matriarch.

She mouths the word "forward."

The direction she wants me to go. The one I'm afraid to see.

Of course, that's what she would want.

For a moment, I think of disobeying her.

But I don't.

I open my eyes with a sharp snap. I'm not in Rowen Huang's lounge anymore.

I'm in our backyard, which is buried under thick sheets of white snow. The air should be cold and crisp like every other winter, but it's not. Smoke sweeps into my lungs, ash forcing its way into my throat and sticking there.

I push through the screen of it and almost fall to my knees at the sight that's revealed.

Our house—our centuries-old house—is *burning*. The flames lick at our ancestors' handiwork, what they built through hard labor under the stinging whip of their enslaver. Great black clouds of smoke billow out of broken windows. And it screams. The shrill and piercing sounds of the new fire alarms blare, but it's too late for their warning.

I stumble forward on shaking legs and run around the side of the house to the front. I keep my hand out in front of me, peeling the layers of smoke away like I'm prepping apples for a pie instead of rushing through ash.

As I get around to the front, someone bursts out of the double doors. Cries like nothing I've ever heard before ring in the air.

Louder than the alarms. The thing that comes out from the house is barely a person, only person-shaped, covered in hungry crimson, orange, and yellow flames.

But for one moment, I can see its face.

Her face.

"Auntie Maise?" I cry, the words slipping from my mouth.

Her fire-conjuring gift. But . . . it's never been like this. It's *hurting* her. And it's out of control. She has *never* been this out of control.

"Auntie!" I scream at her, but she can't hear me over her own shrieks.

Until finally, they stop, and she collapses to the ground.

I dart for the doors to get into the house, but the flames are too hot. Even though I know this is a vision, everything feels real. Getting close to the fire singes my skin.

I stare up at the windows but can't see any sign of Mom up in her bedroom. Desperate, I run around to the back of the house, searching for any other signs of my family.

That's when I spot her.

Keis, smashing her head against her window. Again, and again, and again. Her blood splatters across the splintering glass.

"Stop it," I whisper. Then scream, "Stop it!" I try to slam my hands on the lower level windows to distract her, but my fingers go right through.

And Keis doesn't stop. She's lost in hitting her head against the glass.

Finally, the window breaks.

I watch as my cousin flies headfirst out of the second-floor window and lands with a dull thud next to me, her eyes wide open with sharp pieces of glass embedded in her skull and rivers of red running into her hair and down her face.

The magic of the deal I made with Mama Jova should have

immediately transported her back inside. But there's no point to it now. Not if she's dead.

I stumble back with my hands pressed against my mouth, tears springing to my eyes. I run from her body, back toward the front of the house without even looking where I'm going, hands pressed against my eyes.

When I finally manage to whip them away, I spot a boy sprinting down the street. A boy with blue-gray hair and swirling crimson bionic lenses, his dark peacoat flapping in the wind.

"Luc?" I shout, but he doesn't pay attention to me. I realize, finally, that no one can see or hear me, like when I shared that vision of the past. I'm a witness, not a participant.

Why is he here? Does he learn about Justin somehow and come to collect his mentor? Did they do this together? This is Justin's future, after all.

Or . . . maybe not necessarily. Mama Jova only said I would see the future that was created when I changed their present. She never said anything about it being that specific person's future. Luc may not know that Justin is in the basement. Which still leaves the question of why he's here.

Luc rushes right up to the house and stops, staring wide eyed at the destruction. Tears pool in his eyes and slide down his cheeks. "This wasn't supposed to happen," he whispers.

He sinks to his knees in the grass and curls forward into a ball. His shoulders shake, and the sobs that come from him are obvious.

If he and Justin planned this, he's not exactly acting like it. But then what was *supposed* to happen?

Luc's tear-filled eyes glaze over as he stares out at whatever is showing on his bionics. "We need to stop it. V-Voya's family are dead. *Dead*. We need to do something. There's still time."

I freeze. It's a call. Whatever is happening right now, Luc

definitely knows about it, and someone else does too. But it's hard to tell if he knows because he did this or if he just knows what's happening.

Whatever the person on the other end is saying doesn't seem to be what he wants to hear. "This is a hacking massacre! All the witches are dying!"

The glaze of his eyes abruptly cuts off, and I know that whoever he was talking to has hung up.

Luc lets out a low wail so familiar that it makes me clutch at my chest.

It's the sound he made when Justin "died."

Witches. That's what he said. This isn't just about my family. Whatever is happening is happening to the entire community.

I look back at my home, burning.

He has to be wrong. They can't all be dead. They can't.

Leaving Luc where he is, I run around to the back of the house again, remembering that my hand went through it, and rush at the back windows. There's a moment where it feels like I'm walking through a cold wind, but suddenly I'm inside the house in a blazing hot inferno. Smoke floods into my lungs and chokes me, but I stumble forward.

In the kitchen, I find Uncle Vacu lying down on his front. What is he even doing here? My uncle has been estranged from the family for years since he abandoned Alex, his own daughter, in their apartment when she was little because of his addiction to Mod-H. He's magically banned from coming into the house, and yet here he is.

I stumble past him, the clogged air making my eyes tear up, and stop dead. In the hallway to the entryway, Dad and Priya are collapsed on the floor. And Eden, my baby sister, is crying and coughing as she tries to drag her parents out.

"Eden!" I scream.

But she doesn't hear me. Just like everyone else.

"No! Mommy! Daddy!" she cries, her fingers digging into their clothes.

I can't handle it. I kneel down beside her. "You have to go! You have to get out!"

But she won't leave.

And I can't leave her either.

I crawl closer to her, as near as I can get. Breathing is becoming impossible. My eyes start to close even as I fight to keep them open. I try to grab at her, but my fingers go right through. I can't touch her. Eden's eyes begin to slide closed as she slowly collapses onto Priya's and Dad's bodies. If the smoke doesn't get her, the destruction of the house will when the magic in it protecting her dies.

Staring at her face, I try to guess at how old she is. The thing about kids, I've learned, is that in a year, they change a lot. But this Eden? She looks exactly like the one I know now.

I stay next to my sister and gasp for air until there's none left.

The next time I snap my eyes open, I'm staring at the crimson and gold of Rowen's lounge. I'm lying on my back with Keisha, Alex, and the Huang Matriarch herself hovering over me. None of them have blood in their eyes, but I can feel it sticky on my own face. They didn't see the vision. Only I did.

For all her bravado, Rowen actually looks concerned. Her eyebrows knit together as she examines me. "What happened?"

My cousins nod their heads, as eager to know as her, but I can't make my mouth work to explain what I witnessed. That was the future that looms in wait for us because of what I did to Justin.

Because of the choices that I made.

CHAPTER SIX

I stare at the pholourie and plantain in the fryer. The black wrap on my head feels suffocating in a way that it usually doesn't. Today, Topaz and Peridot are in the kitchen with me. I'm assuming the situation with Topaz's dad hasn't gotten any better, because he seems to be in a perpetual bad mood. I've heard more of him banging around dishes than speaking.

I stay in my position, methodically wrapping and packaging rotis and combination plates, and frying side dishes when needed.

I've yet to share the vision I had yesterday with anyone.

After Keisha and Alex picked me up off the floor, Rowen Huang of all people ordered a car to take us back to the house, citing that I couldn't be expected to walk in my condition. She was like a parent sending their naughty child home. I had mouthed off to her and she still helped.

I hunch my shoulders up under my ears and use tongs to stop the pholourie balls from sticking together in the fryer. I wish I was on the early morning shift today. I love that one, because it's just me in the kitchen with Aqua, silently cooking up everything we plan to serve that day. It's easy to get lost in the cuisine and forget about everything else.

Working on a night that isn't very busy to begin with, especially without Aqua, is very different.

I meant to tell everyone about the vision when we got home. After I lay down for an hour recovering, I made my way into the kitchen to dig up some leftovers and snack options. I got macaroni boiling in a pot, getting ready to make fresh macaroni pie, when Mom came into the room and paused.

After making sure I was okay, she launched into a long discussion about the seriousness of the fact that we had lost Rowen as a client. She listed exact numbers. She strongly suggested that I go back and apologize to the Huang Matriarch.

But I wouldn't.

Nothing I could say to Rowen would fix what happened there.

Mom has to know that.

Either way, it didn't seem like an ideal situation to be discussing the fact that I had a vision where the house was burning and our family was dying while Luc cried. That Justin may or may not have been directly involved, but that it was a future caused by what I did to him.

But the conversation would need to happen soon.

I grip my fingers around the tongs.

I won't get caught out again this time. I'm going to show them that I'm a worthy Matriarch. That I'm who Granny and Mama Jova chose. I need to have a plan and a way to solve things. I can't be floundering anymore or give anyone more reasons not to believe in me.

And for that, I need Johan. I need to get together the Black witch council that used to exist. Granny, April-Mae Davis, and Lee Bailey-Huang used to be the most powerful Black witches in the community and formed their own council. It's how they ended up working with Auntie Elaine and Justin. When everything went wrong, when Auntie realized that the NuGene CEO was after immortality more than he was after helping people, she sacrificed her life to take away his memories of us and protect the family.

The result was that the council was dissolved.

Not to mention that Lee was stripped of her title, and the Bailey-Huangs became Bailey and Huang.

But this is exactly what a council should be doing. Bringing together the community and working toward a common goal. The way Luc was talking, this goes beyond our family. It's something that's potentially a threat to *all* witches.

Johan has a lot more clout in the community than I do. If I could get him on my side, we would have a real chance to bring everyone together.

There was snow on the ground in that vision. It stays like that until February, maybe even the beginning of March . . . but not much further. And Eden didn't look older. The future I saw is not far off. I need to move fast.

And so I fry my plantain and pholourie, wrap my rotis, and pack my dinner sets diligently for the three hours of my shift until closing. I clean up my station in record time and slip into the hallway, making my way toward Johan's office, tucked away near the back door.

Once I get close enough, I hear some sort of shouting going on inside. The door bangs open, and a Black man stomps out. His skin is on the lighter side, still brown, but not as dark as mine or my family's. His hair is cut short to his scalp, and he's got a generous amount of facial hair. His lips are pinched, and the skin around his eyes is just as bunched.

"Don't be so immature," Johan snaps at him. He comes forward and tries to put a hand on the man's shoulder.

The guy jerks back and growls at him, "Hack you. We don't need your help. Your family aren't the only ones with strong magic."

"Come back into the office and we can talk about this. *Privately*."

"I'm done talking!" He turns to storm away, and that's when he catches me watching and narrows his eyes. I think he's a Bailey; he has that look about him. Like that Eli guy and his cousin from the conference. Tons of people in their family have this signature sort of square jaw in addition to being generally light-skinned.

Johan lets out a deep sigh and goes back inside his office.

The front door slams as the Bailey leaves, and I slip into the doorway of Johan's space.

When Johan spots me, he groans. "What? I'm not in the mood for this."

"I've had a vision."

"Hack me, you got two gifts and now you wanna be all ominous and shit?"

My face heats, and I slink farther into his office, crossing my arms. "There may be some . . . incoming danger for the witch community. I thought you could help me get the Matriarchs of the major Black witch families to form a council. Like the one your mom, Granny, and Lee used to have."

Johan leans back in his leather armchair. Around him, the space is meticulous: Metal file cabinets carefully labeled with likely alphabetical files inside. His desk completely clear of clutter with only a laptop and photo of his family on top. From the looks of it, this was on one of their many family trips to Trinidad. He and his kids are in their swimsuits on the beach with big grins. I wonder for a moment if he ever gets lonely, running the family by himself. A long time ago, he was with a guy named Seamus for a few years, but it fizzled out. And his mother and brother seem to be taking their sweet time coming back.

You would think that he would want this council too. If not for the company, then to ease some of the pressure on him and his family, who have been supporting the community on their own for so long. Besides, now we actually have a threat to worry about.

I watch Johan as he watches me. Our eyes meeting across the desk.

Finally, he speaks. "My mother joined that council as a favor to your granny and as a means to an end. Once it went sideways, she was more than happy to leave. Why should I, in her name, get involved again now?"

As a favor to Granny? I didn't know that. And a favor for what?

I shake off the distracting thoughts and say, "There may be a danger to the community—"

"According to you."

"What?"

"This is your feeling, based off your 'vision,' right?"

I stumble over my words. "Yes, but . . ."

"And you've had your gifts for, what, a few months? Now you want to run off and have us doing all sorts of things to adapt to it? This was something from the future, right?"

"Yes . . ." I don't know where he's going with this.

"The future changes. It bends and twists. And how do I know that you have enough control of your gift to know what's a future we need to change and what's one that may be different tomorrow?"

"I—"

Slowly, a grin spreads on Johan's face. I don't have anything to say back to that, and he knows it.

"If you want to be out here looking a fool, that's up to you. But don't try and drag me into it. I've learned what comes from helping you. I've got the scars to show it."

I flinch and stare at the ground. I haven't forgotten that moment in his family's basement after I'd begged him to let me watch them do an impure ritual in the vain hope that it would help me learn how to kill. I still have nightmares of the whips of magic that lashed down. Johan took the brunt of it for me.

He's right. Him doing me favors hasn't done him any.

"Fine," I say. "Sorry for bothering you."

I turn to leave, but he calls me back. "Wait a minute now."

Pausing, I turn back his way with raised eyebrows.

"How is the whole Matriarch business going for you?"

I force a smile onto my face. There's no way I'm letting on to Johan that it's going anything but well. "Good."

"Of course," he says, voice pleasant in a way that feels anything but. "I gave my brother a call the other night."

"You call each other?" I blurt out.

"We're brothers. I like to see what he gets up to."

Like to see what he gets up to? Or like to try and pry into our family's business? "Oh, and . . . ?"

"He did a little flinch. I recognized it." He leans toward me. "Did you know, when our mother wanted to punish us, she would tug our magic away. Just for the day."

I feel my smile melting and work to keep it in place.

"And it reminded me of that, for some reason. I called him right before you came in for your last shift. Did anything happen?"

Before my last shift . . . that business with Rowen or even seeing Luc in person for the first time in forever. Hack me. I definitely tugged on everyone's magic with Rowen. I could have done it again with Luc without realizing.

"No," I say. "Nothing that I can think of."

Johan steeples his fingers together. "There's no shame in growing pains as you become a Matriarch. Some people don't have the emotional stability for it."

Why, after months of ignoring me or being snappy, does he suddenly want to help out? How come he wants to go back to being my honorary uncle now? "I'm fine," I say.

His lips press together in a flat line. "Well, then." He waves his hand at the exit. "Close the door on your way out." He picks up his phone and starts scrolling through it without waiting for me to respond.

I do as he says.

I shouldn't be here.

The house in front of me is a modest two-story with a homey bay window, navy blue vinyl siding with crisp white trim, and enough room in their driveway for two cars. Both sit on the asphalt, a tiny eco-friendly one and a huge Suburban that seems giant for the sake of being giant. It's dark out now, the air even colder than usual, and their porch light illuminates their front stoop where I stand.

It only took me a few minutes of AI searching Baileys in the area to find him: Aaron Bailey. The Matriarch of the family is one of his older cousins. He's Mom's age, in his thirties, and apparently has enough money that he and his family could get this house out in Mississauga.

I should have gone home. But I remembered what I overheard from his conversation with Johan. He was looking for help.

The last time I actually helped someone was when I used my gift to show Rena what happened to Lauren, and that was ages ago.

It was also the last time someone other than Keisha or Alex really seemed to respect me as a witch and a Matriarch. As a leader.

Maybe there's something that I can do for Aaron.

The thoughts were enough to have me hopping on a bus to come over here in the cold instead of going straight home.

I take a deep breath and knock on the door.

There's shuffling inside and shouting for someone to "go get that," along with questions of who could be knocking.

The bay window curtain jerks to the side, and little eyes peek out at me. The boy must be eight or nine. He spots me looking back at him and jumps away from the window.

"It's that girl! The Thomas Matriarch!" His shouts reach me from outside.

I hunch my shoulders up.

Hack me, why do witches have to gossip so much?

"What are you talking about?" a voice calls back. There's more shuffling, and a woman appears at the curtain. She's got a silk head wrap covering her hair, and she's darker-skinned than her husband, more my shade.

She blinks at me, and I give a little wave.

Her lips contort into an awkward smile, and she leaves the window, appearing moments later to open the door. "Come on in," she says.

That's the thing about Black witches. Even if they want to be rude, they aren't. I'm one of them, and so I get ushered into the living room with the bay window that everyone was peeking at me through.

"I'm Sara," she says, gesturing to one of two plush cloth-covered couches. "Have a seat. Did you want anything to drink?"

"I'm okay."

"What about orange juice? We have pop too. Coke, Diet Coke, ginger ale."

"Water, thanks," I say, giving in. I don't want any, but I get the feeling she wants something to do to make this less awkward.

The boy sits on the other couch and stares at me while Sara leaves to get the drink.

I put on what I hope is a child-friendly smile. "What's your name?"

"Kevin."

"Cool. I'm Voya."

"Is it true that you had to do a murder rite so you could pass your Calling?"

I choke on my spit.

"Kevin!" Sara shouts from the kitchen. "What did I hear you ask?"

"Nothing!" he yells back.

His mom, seemingly desperate to not have me alone with her son and his questions, comes back into the living room with a glass filled with ice and water.

I take the drink from her. "Thank you."

Sara sits beside her son with a sigh. "So, what brings you out here?"

I open my mouth to answer as a toilet-flushing sound reaches our ears, and Aaron walks out of a door tucked into the corner of the entryway.

He spots me immediately and blinks, bewildered.

It's strange to see him now, normal, when he was so furious at the restaurant after talking to Johan.

"Hello . . . ," he says.

"We have a visitor!" Sara says, her voice with that air of trying to be chipper when she's actually annoyed that I popped in unexpectedly. "This is . . . um, Ms. Thomas."

"Voya is fine." I take a sip of the water to give myself something to do.

Aaron makes his way to the couch and sits with his family, all of them staring at me in my puffy coat. Their hospitality hasn't yet extended to asking me to take it off, meaning they hope I won't stay long.

"What can we do for you?" Aaron asks.

I swallow hard and put the glass down on the coffee table. "I . . . um . . . I noticed that you seemed to be looking for some help from Johan. And I thought, maybe, if that wasn't working out for you, I could see how I might help?"

Sara's eyes cut fast to Aaron, and it takes me that long to realize my mistake in coming here. His lips thin.

She didn't know.

"I'm sorry if you misunderstood," Aaron says, voice forced into politeness. "I was pitching a little business idea to Johan. He wasn't too keen on it. I know you're a bit of a businesswoman yourself, but I don't think you can help with this."

Since when does a business idea have anything to do with a family having strong magic? I mean, it could. But I don't think that's what he was asking Johan about. Especially if he took the time to hide it from his wife.

But this has gone further than I thought it would.

This is what Granny would call "sticking my nose in the shit," which is the last thing I came to do.

"Sorry that I misunderstood," I say, parroting his words back to him. I smile at his family and stand. "Um . . . well, if you ever need any help, you can let me know. We're a community, you know, so it's important to help each other out."

They nod along as I talk, but I can tell they think it's bullshit. Johan's been operating within our community on a give-and-take basis for too long. They probably think I'm looking to get something back from them. The desperate Thomas Matriarch.

"It was nice to meet you." Sara reaches out and shakes my hand.

Kevin sticks his out too, and I shake it very professionally, which seems to please him.

But when I make contact with Aaron's hand, a shock goes up my arm, and I gasp, yanking my hand back.

My heart is pounding in my chest, though the pain of the shock is already gone.

He stands there with his hand still in the air and jaw slack.

"Oh my gosh!" Sara cries, coming over to examine my arm.

I flinch away automatically.

She cringes in response, eyes darting to her husband. "I'm so sorry, he didn't do it on purpose."

Since when do people not mean to use their gifts? There was no blood shed, so that must be what that shock was. Maybe if Aaron was a teenager who had just passed his Calling, I would buy that, but not a full-grown man.

"Why would you do that?" I hiss out, voice breathy.

Aaron stumbles back. "I don't . . . I can't . . . I'm sorry." He rushes out of the room.

His wife reaches out for me again. She grasps my arm with a trembling hand. "I'm so sorry. He's telling the truth. He didn't mean to."

"What's wrong with him?"

"We don't . . . we don't know." Her hand drops away from me, and her gaze follows it.

This. This is what he went to Johan for. The desperation in Sara's face and the way he left so abruptly feel genuine. He really can't control his gift.

My mind snaps back to Auntie Maise in my vision, running on fire, screaming. Her gift acting completely wrong and out of her control.

Snow on the ground.

Eden being the same age.

"How long has he been like this?" I ask her.

Sara swallows. "Not long. It comes and goes. Enough that he forgot that he probably shouldn't touch you. It's been maybe a week since the first time it happened." She crosses her arms. "I can't believe he went to Johan. We don't have anything to give him."

Clearly they didn't, because he had refused to help.

"My offer still stands. I'm willing to do whatever I can to help with this."

Sara gives me a small smile. "If Johan can't help, and our Matriarch can't help, then I'm sorry, but I'm not sure what you can do. You're a lovely girl, but we need . . . more."

More than me.

I stare down at the flooring and nod. "I'm going to try anyway."

I don't wait for Sara to reply before I leave the house.

Like the coward that I am, when I step into the house, I tiptoe carefully up the stairs and hope that no one hears me. It's around nine p.m., which isn't late for my family, but it's usually the time when everyone is holed up in their rooms. That's confirmed when I get to the top of the stairs and see all the doors closed.

I mean to go straight down the hallway to my room but don't.

I turn to the other end of the hall, where Granny's room is. Her wardrobe was too big to fit inside her room alongside the bathroom, so she left it in the hallway. I walk over and run my fingers across the whitewashed wood. It's not an ancient relic or anything. Just particleboard and paint, but it was hers.

Her clothes are still inside too.

I make my way to the door of her bedroom and push it open.

It used to be the biggest room in the house, but Granny insisted on having her own bathroom built in so she wouldn't have to share with the rest of us. It made for a tight squeeze, but she managed. The queen bed has soft sheets and a quilt overtop of it that looks handmade, though likely not by Granny, who would have never had the patience for it.

I sit down on her bed and look at the boxes by her bedside table. I'm not sure what's inside, and I don't feel like prying right now.

This is supposed to be my bedroom now. It's traditional for the new Matriarch to move into the room of the old one when they take the title. But I can't.

How could I empty this room of everything that's Granny and put myself inside instead?

I lay down on the bed and let out a shuddering breath, tears slipping down my face.

I'm hacked.

I've lost Rowen as a customer, and our business will only get worse once she tells everyone how things went down. We're out of Granny's product and have no idea how we're going to make more. Our business is on the brink of collapse.

And now I've had this vision. Johan has already brushed it off as nothing, but the shock that Aaron Bailey gave me wasn't nothing. His wife wasn't that afraid for *nothing*. But she still didn't want my help. How am I supposed to convince everyone in the family to take this vision seriously?

I can't even blame them. What have I done since becoming Matriarch to prove that I can do this? No matter how hard I try, nothing seems to come out right.

My phone pings and pulls up the notification in front of my eyes. I blink hard to open the full thing.

It's a video of Luc presenting somewhere, talking more about the NuSap launch. It's everywhere now. Companies are excited about replacing their subpar drones with them, and now with Luc's new and improved pay plan, the average person has access to them too. Before, no one I knew would ever buy one. But now that you can make small payments, who wouldn't want a robot that can clean your house, cook dinner, and give you an after-work shoulder massage?

I stare at him in his slim-fitted black pants and matching dress shirt. Like a more grown-up version of his usual black jeans and shirt combos. Jasmine and Juras are off to the side of the stage, happily supporting him. I clench my jaw. They had been so cold to Luc when I last met them, but with Justin gone, they flipped a switch and now they're the ones who get to stay in his life. I supported Luc even when I thought I needed to kill him, and I'm the one on the outs.

I should be trying harder to distance myself from him. He has.

A month after everything went down, I found a container on the front step—the one that held the food I gave to Luc so long ago. The one he didn't want to return because then he would lose his excuse for seeing me. Now it's hidden under my bed. Sometimes I take it out and turn it in my hands.

Luc is done with me.

But I'm not done with him.

He knows something about what's to come. Whether he knows it now or will know it, I'm not sure. But I can't shut him out. He's a part of my future.

And if I'm honest, I wasn't doing a good job at keeping him out anyway.

Whatever Luc is saying in the video washes over me. I can't even make myself comprehend it. He fits into his new role so perfectly. And why not? He's been working toward this since he was a little kid, and he's brilliant on top of it.

Never in a million years did I expect that I'd become the Matriarch of our family. No one did. The ancestors are supposed to help me, but they won't come when I ask for help.

I need to form the council to make everyone take my vision seriously, but can't even manage that much.

I wonder if this is how Luc always felt. Like he knew who he should be but couldn't count on anyone else to understand it. But he was wrong. Everyone has embraced him as the leader of NuGene.

How am I supposed to make people accept me? I've tried so many things already. Nothing has worked.

If everyone could see what I could, then it would be different. It's not that easy, though. I can't just jump on a stage like Luc and have their attention.

Or could I?

I jerk up in the bed. There *is* a way that I could make people pay attention to me. A way that I could have a captive audience.

A showcase.

Rowen mentioned it offhandedly, and I brushed it off, not exactly wanting to present myself to a huge audience. But now things are different.

I close the video of Luc and connect to our family almanac, racing through the entries until I find one from 1992. One of my cousins, Sheryl, got a special gift around the same time that our family and the Davises were butting heads over power. They did a showcase where they gathered the witches in the area who were curious to learn more. It backfired a little for them because it turned out her gift of being able to tell when people lie wasn't as theatrical as the gathering required.

But mine would be different.

If I could show people the vision in my head, they would feel it the way that I did. It would make them take it seriously, and it would show them that I have enough power to be taken seriously too.

Enough people are curious about me and my two gifts that they would come.

Assuming that I can pull it off.

And also assuming that I can get the family on board.

I'll have to.

This is the only chance I've got.

CHAPTER SEVEN

I 've managed to gather everyone at the dining room table using two very effective assets: food and Keisha's ability to annoy people into action. Across the huge wooden table are big trays of macaroni pie with its crisp crust, curried chicken swimming in a thick sauce with tender potatoes, and homemade paratha roti buss up shut–style, and an apple crumble is warming in the oven for dessert. I even made a version of curry with potatoes and chickpeas only for Dad and Priya.

My family sits around the table with both eager and suspicious eyes. I haven't been cooking much given everything, and this is the first big homemade meal we've had in at least a few weeks. Cooking used to be my escape, but not at home, not anymore. Now it only feels remotely relaxing far away from here at Roti Roti. And even that's not perfect, because I don't really want to be there.

Either way, the smell of the food is enticing enough that even Keis slunk up from her little den, though she keeps her eyes on her phone, away from me. Justin watched her leave from the doorway of the basement, his arms crossed, unable to go farther than that.

Now at the head of the table, Granny's spot stays open. It's almost worse than if I forced myself to sit in it. Her absence cuts into my skin and leaves the wounds exposed and stinging.

She would have loved this meal.

I can picture her plopping down with a huff and barking, "What are you all looking around for? Eat!" and nudging Uncle Cathius to fix her a plate.

I suck back tears and wave around. "You can eat. I'll talk at the same time."

My family wastes no time, doling out roti and scooping curry and macaroni pie onto their plates.

Keisha, on my left, takes a tiny piece of roti and tears it into little pieces without putting anything into her mouth.

I can't remember the last time I saw her eat. She does. I walked into her room without thinking last week and she was asleep on the bed with a pile of snack wrappers next to her—chips, candy, ice cream, the works.

She woke up and immediately shoved them under her bed, snapping at me for coming in without saying anything. We didn't talk for the next two days, and after she pretended like nothing had happened.

Keisha has always had trouble with food, but it's only gotten worse. She's spending all her free time helping me or her mom. She doesn't have time to date, which used to be her favorite pastime. It's like Keis left this giant hole and her sister is falling through the cracks trying to fill it.

"There's fruit in the fridge too, if you want," I say to her. Usually, that would have her hopping up, glad for the alternative to my more caloric food.

She shrugs. "I'm not hungry. Maybe after your big announcement."

I don't know what to say. How to push back. How to help. So I don't. "I wanted to gather everyone together to let you know about some things."

A small laugh escapes Keis's lips, but she doesn't say anything.

I ignore her. "I had a vision . . . of a future with the house burning down."

"Don't leave out the bit about your ex-boyfriend crying on the front lawn," Keis adds.

"Getting to that," I grind out.

"Wait, what?" Auntie Maise barks, swallowing a piece of macaroni pie. "Tremblay's boy burns down our house? Is that seriously your vision?" She shakes her head, frustrated or disappointed. One of the two.

"He doesn't burn it down. He just, like, knows something about it. Look, I know it sounds strange. But that's the future that's coming for us since 'killing' Justin." I make little air quotes, since we know he isn't really dead. There's a snort from down the hall, and I snap, "Go downstairs before I make you go downstairs."

There's a door-slamming sound and heavy footsteps as Justin makes his way back into the basement. He doesn't like listening to me, but he doesn't like being forcibly controlled either.

Uncle Cathius shakes his head. "Not all predictions are certain. The future is always in flux. The ancestors should be teaching you that. I've told you time and time again that we should sit down together and discuss your duties."

I try not to scowl openly. Uncle has made multiple offers to hand down his wisdom to me, and I've brushed them all off. The last thing I want is to give him a forum to lecture me.

"Oh, so *you're* going to teach her how to be a Matriarch?" Auntie says with a laugh. "Because you're the expert?"

"I spent quite a bit of time shadowing Ava—"

"Shadowing? Why? You were never going to be a Matriarch." She crosses her arms. "None of us were, apparently." The bitterness in her voice is clear and as sharp as her tone.

I force myself to take a deep breath. To try not to take it personally. But how can I when it's so obviously personal?

Keis smiles, making no effort to hide her rising glee. No one in the family except for her and Keisha know that none of the ancestors have talked to me since I became Matriarch. It just seemed like another failure that I wasn't eager to share. And especially not during "coaching" with Uncle.

Maybe it was a mistake having Keis up here. I want to see my cousin, to feel like she's still a part of this family, but she's also a loose cannon. She doesn't care how what she says affects anyone or anything. She should probably be down in the basement with Justin.

I shift in my seat. "There's something strange happening with one of the Baileys. It's in line with what I saw in my vision. I feel very strongly that this is something that's going to happen. And it's going to happen soon."

"Maybe you need to wait a month or so and try for the vision again, see if it changes?" Mom says, leaning against her hand as she sets down her fork. "We really should be focusing on the business. Like making things right with Rowen."

Did she not hear me say that we need to do something soon? "Rowen is one customer."

"She's a big client, Vo. We have no product anymore, and you know that she likes to talk with everyone. I think you need to go down there and apologize to her."

Not this again. "What will that do?"

"Attitude! And it'll go a lot further than ignoring her." Mom's eyes have these crow's feet at the edges that I never noticed before. They deepen as she stares at me, pleading with her gaze.

But I can't let her derail this conversation. "That's not what this meeting is about. It's about the fact that this vision showed that our lives are in danger. I think we need to form a council. I'm going to do a showcase and invite the Matriarchs of the major Black witch families."

Dad's jaw actually drops, and something like hope lights in his eyes. Succeeding in forming a council would mean being a proper community, protecting each other, and sharing enough to find a therapist who Eden could talk to that would be trusted to know what went down with Justin.

He and Priya might be the only ones out of the adults who could believe in me enough.

But as I think it, his eyes turn wary. "A council would be amazing, but . . . you need to be able to show them all your gift. Is that something you can do?" He fumbles over his words as he tries to backtrack. "I'm not trying to question your judgment . . . It's up to you, but . . . is this something you're confident about?"

It isn't.

But there's no way I'm letting them know that. And I didn't want to hear him say it. "I can do it." I *can* do it because I have to.

"Absolutely not," Mom bursts out finally. "This is ridiculous. The last thing we need is a bunch of people up in this house while we're struggling with the business."

Priya leans against her hand. "It might be a good opportunity. My family has always had a lot of success with showcases. It's a positive coming together of the community." The shine in my stepmom's eyes has me sitting straighter. I'm sure that she wants this for Eden too. Last year, Priya asked me to save her daughter, and even though she tried to take it back, I still did it. At least *she* seems to hacking remember that. "A council could really turn things around for us."

I'm opening my mouth to thank Priya for saying so when Mom cuts me off. "Ancestors help me, no."

Dad scowls at Mom, who scowls right back. He didn't express a lot of confidence in the idea, but at least he's loyal to Priya if he won't be to me.

Keis has a huge grin on her face now watching the family go back and forth. She turns to me. "Tell them. You have to tell them now."

"Tell us what?" Auntie Maise asks, narrowing her eyes at her daughter.

"The invites have already been sent," I say, revealing the tidbit that delights Keis. "It's happening."

"What?!" Mom cries. "Sent invites? When?"

Keis grins. "As we've been chatting. The dinner is a distraction."

"And you didn't want to say anything about that?" Auntie snarls.

"It's more fun to watch it unfold."

Mom slouches back in her chair and shakes her head at me. "I cannot believe that you did this. This isn't you. This is . . . impulsive! Rash! It's like you've lost your common sense. I think I actually preferred it when you were more indecisive."

"Well, I'm not anymore," I grind out, and Mom gives me her most scathing look. A look that before would have had me closing my mouth for fear of many months of a lost allowance. But I'm not a kid worried about pocket money. I am the Matriarch of our family. "That girl is gone. I'm here. *Me*. Granny and Mama Jova chose me. And I've already made this decision. We need this council."

We need it to protect the future.

And Eden needs it right now.

Mom seethes at me. She's so mad that she can't even speak. She keeps shaking her head like she can knock the last moment loose from her memory.

"Do you even know what a showcase involves?" Auntie Maise asks.

I attempt to look confident. "Showcasing my gifts."

Uncle Cathius lets out a loud laugh. "It isn't just about you. A showcase puts the entire family under scrutiny."

"Scrutiny that we don't need," Mom spits out. "Did you discuss this with the ancestors? They agree with this?"

I open my mouth to lie and then shut it. I can't. For one, I've never been good at outright lying to my family, and for another it feels like one step too far. The white lie of not mentioning my issue with the ancestors is one thing but saying they agreed to something they didn't is another.

"Voya," she pushes. "Why are you doing this?"

"No one is taking this vision seriously." I try to keep my voice even and measured. "If you could all see it, you would. None of you will listen to me. So maybe after this you will."

"This is childish," Uncle Cathius scoffs. "Which I guess we shouldn't be surprised about, because you're a child."

I am so *hacking* tired of being called that. "I'm your Matriarch."

"They're not mutually exclusive."

I stare down at my clenched fists in my lap for a moment. When I dare to look up, I catch Keis looking back at me, for once without contempt in her expression. It doesn't even have the mirth that it did earlier. It's blank.

She could easily spill the secret of my failure to contact the ancestors, but she doesn't.

Maybe it shouldn't, but it fills me with the tiniest bit of hope.

Keisha sighs. "Okay, we get it, everyone is uncomfortable with the showcase thing. But it's happening. We'll only make Voya and the family look bad if we take it back, so we may as well get ready for it."

"When is it?" Priya asks.

I say, "Saturday night." The entire table groans. It's Thursday now. I know it's not a lot of time. "I told you that this needed to be addressed soon."

"Well," Alex muses, licking her lips after a bite of macaroni pie, "I haven't done any formal wear in a while, so that'll be fun."

"You don't have to make new stuff."

"Um, yes, I do. It's a showcase. The point is to show off. Hence the name."

Mom presses her palms against her eyes and lets out a long, agonized groan.

"I'll look into Granny's things and commune with the ancestors about the products. To see if we can figure out how they were made." I sit myself up straight and look at her. "Does that work?"

She doesn't even notice, hands still covering her face.

Dad blinks at me while wiping Eden's face of excess sauce from the curry. "You haven't already done that?"

I'm saved from answering by a loud banging on the front door. It's as if someone is smashing their fists against the wood. It's frantic and inconsistent.

My baby sister's entire disposition changes. She jerks back in her chair as if her circuits were literally fried and starts shaking.

Priya and Dad move into action, closing in and trying to soothe her.

It breaks my heart.

The banging. There are so many things it could be reminding her of: her and Luc's futile attempts to escape the glass chamber, her own pounding and screaming when Granny fell dead to the ground, the loud thud of Justin's head on the floor . . .

A wealth of bad memories to choose from.

Uncle Cathius is the first to stand, and I scramble up after him along with the rest of the family. We make our way to the front door, and instead of throwing it open, I step over to the front window, not unlike little Kevin Bailey, and flick the curtain aside to peek at whoever is knocking.

"Get sparked," Alex breathes.

As if sensing us looking, the man at the door reels back from it to look at us staring through the window.

Dad comes closer with Eden in his arms, her small hands shaking where they grip his shirt. "Who's that?" she asks, voice quiet and trembling.

"Uncle Vacu," I say.

And I have no idea what he's doing here.

Uncle Vacu paces on our front porch, running his fingers along his short-cropped hair. He's in a pair of dark-wash jeans and a thick mustard sweater. No coat. The shoes on his feet are beat-up sneakers. He's been addicted to Mod-H for most of the time that I've known him, to the point where he even lost his job as a doctor and ended up neglecting Alex so much that Granny took her away from him when she was eight. But still, he's always managed to be calm and collected for the most part. Cleaned up. It was why it took the hospital so long to realize that he had a problem.

"He's high," Uncle Cathius snarls.

Alex shakes her head. "No, he's not. That's the problem."

She would know best. Even though she and the family haven't seen him for at least six years. I only saw him last year because I thought he could tell me something about his late wife, Auntie Elaine.

"Who's Uncle Vacu?" Eden says, her curiosity beating out her earlier fear.

Priya shakes her head and grabs her daughter from Dad's arms, though she sags under my baby sister's weight. "Come on, why don't we go color something upstairs?"

Eden has gotten savvy to when she's being herded away from something interesting. She squints at her mom. "But I wanna know!"

"Eden—"

"He's my dad," Alex says, turning to Eden. "He'll probably be going home soon. Why don't you go color with your mom? If you're a good girl, maybe I'll bring you some glitter."

Eden's eyes go wide. Alex has an unrivaled collection of glitter. A hundred little vials at minimum that my baby sister is very aware of. Either way, it's a lot more enticing to her than staying here. And she's learned that being a "good girl" means listening to adults.

"Okay!" she chimes, wriggling out of her mom's arms and then proceeding to half drag Priya up the stairs like going faster will somehow mean she gets glitter faster too.

I exhale a little, glad that she's okay. That it didn't take much to calm her down and get her back to her normal self this time. There have been days when it's not as easy to snap her out of the fear. Days when we can all hear her sobbing from inside her room as Dad and Priya try to help her.

"Go send him away, Vo," Auntie Maise says, crossing her arms. "Be done with it."

"What?" I blurt out.

Keis rolls her eyes at me. "You're the Matriarch. It means you're the only one who can send him away from the property."

He won't stop pacing. He's not even trying to get our attention anymore—he already has it. Now it's like he's waiting for us to come out. "He never comes here," I mutter.

But he *was* here in my vision . . .

"And yet," Alex says, her long nails click-clacking rhythmically on the windowsill. Her gaze is sharp and focused. It's hard to tell what she's feeling. What seeing him is doing to her.

I swallow. "Are you okay?"

"Fine. Go see what he wants."

Letting out a long exhale, I listen to my cousin and walk out the front door, pulling it shut behind me.

Uncle Vacu spots me and jumps back, rushing down the porch stairs. "You! What did you do?!"

"What?"

"What did you do?!"

"I have no idea what you're talking about!"

A white woman across the street walking her dog lingers on the sidewalk, staring at the two of us. She's got her dark hair in a ponytail that swings as she moves. Her dog's name is Herbert, though I've never actually learned hers. Her daughter sells us Girl Scout cookies. "You okay?" she calls, looking between me and Uncle Vacu, who is near trembling in place.

"Yup, I'm fine."

"You sure, hon?"

"Yeah, it's okay, he's my uncle."

"All right. I'll say hi on my way back from the park, okay?"

"Okay."

She gives me a nod and continues down the street toward Marie Curtis Park. On one hand, I appreciate her checking up on me. She's not the type of woman who's nosy for the sake of it. But I wish she hadn't seen this. The back of my neck heats. The last thing I want is to be the Black family having domestics on the front lawn. Not even because I care. But because I know there are people on our block who, deep down, expect it, and I don't want to give them the satisfaction.

"Go around the back," I say to Uncle Vacu.

I rush through the front door, and the family surges around me.

"Is he going away?" Mom asks.

"I'm going to the back." I walk quickly through the kitchen to the back door.

"Why are you talking to him?" Uncle Cathius grumbles. "He's high!"

"He's not high," Alex says again, her voice weary and strained. "This isn't what he's like when he's high."

"Whatever he is, he needs to go!"

"I want to talk to him," I counter. "He never comes over here. He must have a reason. If I know why, then I can make sure he doesn't keep coming back over and over. And you all want to talk about how *I'm* the impulsive one, hack me."

"Tone!" Mom shouts.

"Sorry." I jog out the back door. The cold hits me in an icy slap, harsher out in the back because of how close the lake is, and I wrap my arms around myself. I'm wearing a sweater, but it's not nearly enough. This is winter jacket weather. But I'm not going back inside for one.

As expected, as I come around to where Uncle Vacu is waiting, the rest of the family presses up against the windows. I stop in front of him with my arms crossed.

I hear a sliding sound as Auntie Maise unabashedly opens the window so they can hear everything we say.

"We're not giving you money!" she shouts.

Hack me. "Can you not?"

Uncle Vacu scowls at her. "I know you don't have any money. Broke as hell living up in this giant house like you're NuMoney."

Flames shoot from my aunt's fingers.

"What is it?" I say to him, focusing his attention. "Why are you here? It's not money, so what?"

"What are you doing?"

"Excuse me?" My arms drop to my sides. "What am I doing? What are *you* doing? Why are you here?"

"There's something wrong with my gift," he says finally. "I don't know if you're as shit at being the Matriarch as you were at doing your Calling, but something is wrong."

I flinch at his words and hate myself for it. "I'm having an adjustment period. So occasionally you may notice a pull on your magic. If you don't like it, feel free to pledge to a different Matriarch."

"I'm a Thomas. Always."

"Then deal with it."

He shakes his head. "That's not it. I know what it feels like when you pull on my magic, which, yes, I would like very much if you would stop doing. But it's not that. My gift is hacked."

I blink at him. I thought for sure that's what he meant. But now I'm picturing Aaron Bailey shocking me with his gift. "What exactly is wrong?"

"I was on the subway . . . sitting, minding my business. There was a girl there, Black and tired-looking, you know? Like she was having a hard time with it." Uncle Vacu rubs his arms and looks around as if expecting the woman herself to jump out. My family, blissfully, stays quiet as he speaks.

He continues, "A seat opened up next to her, and I took it so I could brush her with my hand. Use my gift to make sure at least her baby would make it into the world safe. Though the way she looked, it probably wasn't going to be easy for either of them. And then . . ." He trails off.

I didn't even know Uncle Vacu still used his gift. Granny always said that gifts require sobriety, and he was never sober enough to use his properly. But maybe they didn't, and she just didn't want him using it high. Or maybe he was sober then, in between fixes, like he was now.

"What happened?" I push.

"Her water broke right then and there." He shakes his head. "Shouldn't have happened."

I freeze. Her water broke. Uncle is right. That shouldn't have happened. That's not how his gift should work. The same way Aaron shouldn't have shocked me, and Auntie Maise shouldn't have been on fire in my vision. "And?"

His shoulders get stiff, and he keeps shaking his head. "What did you do? What's going on?"

"You left her, didn't you?" Alex's voice comes from the window, smooth and even.

Her dad jerks his head toward her. "Alex." Once he's looking at her, he can't seem to stop. "You're so . . ." He snaps his mouth shut, but I can guess what he means.

The last time he saw his daughter, she was eight years old. Now Alex is nineteen. She's a young woman. She's grown up. And her transition made her more confident and herself than she was when she first came to live with us. But even when I visited him last year, Uncle Vacu knew her pronouns. She hadn't told us that until she had her Calling. Somehow, he must have kept tabs on her, but I'm sure however he saw her from afar, it's very different from seeing her in front of him now.

Alex swallows but stands tall. "That girl, you saw what you did, and you left her there."

"What else could I do?" he grinds out.

"You're a doctor."

"Not anymore."

She sounds worse than mad, she sounds disappointed. "You're the same. You haven't changed at all." She turns away from the window and stalks off toward her bedroom.

He watches her go, and despite the way his eyes follow her, he makes no move to stop her.

"Get rid of him!" Mom yells at me, before rushing after Alex along with Keisha.

"I didn't do *anything* to you. This isn't me," I say to Uncle Vacu. I can't let him go, not without knowing more. "When was this?"

He seems to have recovered from the shock of seeing his now-grown daughter. Or he's good at pretending like he has, anyway. "Today! Obviously!"

"Have you noticed anything else strange about your gift before this?"

"Contrary to popular belief, I don't go around touching pregnant women all day. The last time I used it was like a month ago."

"A month ago?"

He kicks at the frosted grass. "Some of the women in my building . . . they . . ."

"They're like you," Auntie Maise says from the window, her voice surprisingly even. "They do drugs."

He grinds his teeth. "Yes. This may shock you, but it's not that easy to stop that sort of habit, even if you're pregnant. I help them without the judgment they would get elsewhere. I also don't call child services on them before they even have a chance to try and get better."

"For money?"

"We have universal health care, Maise, why would they let me charge them? I do it for free!"

She scoffs.

"Can you please stop?" I say to her before turning back to Uncle Vacu. "A month ago, your gift was fine, but now it's messed up?"

"Yes."

"Okay, I'll look into it."

"You can't be serious," Uncle Cathius splutters from the window. "He's not a part of this family! Let him deal with it on his own."

I ignore him. I feel Uncle Vacu's magic the same way I do everyone else's. Like he said, he's a Thomas. That means I'm his Matriarch. "Don't come back here again. Contact me through my feed."

"You blocked me."

"I'll unblock you."

Uncle Vacu stares at me with his dark eyes so like Grandad's. My lip trembles for a moment. I wonder if Granny is with him now. If she's happy. Or if she's my same grumpy Granny.

"You didn't come to the funeral," I mumble.

His shoulders droop. "I didn't think I would be welcome."

Another failure. He shouldn't have felt that way. She was his mom. He should have been able to come and mourn with us. I should have let him know that. I didn't even think of it. "I'm sorry."

"Unblock me and fix this. That's enough." He breaks his stare with me and walks away. I follow him around the front to see him off. More than anything, it'll give me a moment to think before I go back inside.

Uncle Vacu leaves as our neighbor comes back down the street with Herbert the dog, ponytail swinging. She watches him and raises a hand to me. I wave back to her, and she smiles. All is right with the world now as far as she's concerned.

I walk back into the house as Keis is making her way down to the basement. She pauses and regards me for a moment. "Everyone thinks you're sparking it all to shit. Backtracking on everything Granny did by bringing Uncle Vacu back into the family."

"I'm not bringing him back into the house or anything. But he is a Thomas. I need to help him the same way I would help any of you."

"But he'll ask eventually, don't you think? To be in the house. Be a part of the family properly. And what will you say?"

I press my lips into a flat line. "Could you see in his mind which hospital that girl was taken to?"

"No."

Hack me.

"But I do know."

I raise my eyebrows.

"I need you to lift some restrictions on Justin so he can help me with something on the tablet."

"Are you blackmailing me?"

"I'm offering you information in exchange for information. At most, it's disingenuous."

"I'll just ask Uncle Vacu."

"He doesn't know. He was too freaked out to even think about it. But I noticed."

I pause. "Is lifting these restrictions going to be dangerous?"

"No."

I stare into my cousin's eyes. No matter how bitter she is, she wouldn't put the family in jeopardy to make her game.

"Thank you for your resounding faith in me," she drones.

"Fine, tell me."

"He got off around St. Patrick Station. They would have taken her to Mount Sinai."

My jaw drops. "I thought you knew! That's a guess at most."

She crosses her arms. "Fine, here's another tidbit for you. I trolled through the memory. She had a backpack with her name patched onto it: 'Kairee.'"

"You can do that? Search through memories?"

"When people are recalling them at the moment and I'm paying attention, yeah."

I never realized how strong Keis's gift could be until she actually started trying to use it. Sure, having two gifts *feels* impressive, but the use of them is so specific. If I think about it, Keis has the stronger gift. *She* should have been the one Granny wanted to be Matriarch.

But she wasn't.

Granny said she wanted me.

"What sort of grown woman sews her name onto a backpack?" I ask.

"She wasn't. He said *girl,* and he meant it. She looked like she was our age. Probably why he wanted to help her." Keis turns away and heads down the stairs. Nothing to say about my thoughts of Granny and gifts.

This is the most she's talked to me in a month. Suddenly, I'm hungry for it, desperate for more. I want to stop her, to pull her back.

The basement door shuts with a snap, and I'm left standing in the hallway alone.

CHAPTER EIGHT

I press my blood-streaked forehead to the ground and let out a wet exhale. My room is bathed in a mixture of late afternoon sun and candlelight. The entire space smells overwhelmingly of vanilla and orange. Beyond my room, there are shuffling sounds as everyone gets dressed and ready for the evening. Meanwhile, I'm in the same position that I start every morning in. On the floor, having failed to contact the ancestors again.

Except this time, it's a little more crushing.

It's Saturday, the day of the showcase. I've only ever shared my visions with one person at a time, yet somehow I need to project my vision to both my family and the other Matriarchs. I even extended an invite to Rowen, which is as much of an apology as I'm making to her.

Yesterday, I tried drawing on the magic of everyone in the family to practice sending the vision to both Alex and Keisha. Nothing happened. It just pissed everyone off when their magic was pulled and then suddenly pushed right back into them. But mostly I think they were still annoyed at me for the way I handled Uncle Vacu. Shockingly, Alex was the most understanding.

When I went to her room to ask for help with my experiment and talk about the day before, all she said was, "You're always trying to help everyone, Vo. I get it."

But there was a sort of flatness to her expression that made me wonder if my helping one person was just hurting another. It wouldn't be the first time.

Except I can't let this go. Uncle Vacu could be a lead on helping the entire family, the whole community. I have to keep in contact with him.

But now I know that I can't rely on the family's magic to give me the bandwidth I need to show this vision. I need the ancestors' help. According to the almanac, in times of need, they can lend their power to a Matriarch.

And now is definitely a time of need.

There's just the issue of not being able to contact them.

The door creaks open and Keisha steps inside with a bundle of fabric in her arms. She's in a tight black mermaid-style gown that has a little train that stretches out behind her. She's wearing a short body wave wig in a dark brown that has a wet look to it.

"They're coming," she says.

"I know." Every single one of the Matriarchs and Johan responded to the invite to say they would be. Even Rowen, which Mom will be happy about.

Keisha stares at me sitting on the ground, her eyes trailing from my bloody forehead to the candles almost burned down to stumps. "You need to figure out how you're going to do this."

"I know," I say again.

She sets the dress on the bed. White. I'm so hacking tired of wearing white dresses. "Courtesy of Alex, who you'd better thank later, since you only gave her two days' notice."

"I could have worn something I already had."

Keisha recoils. "To your showcase?! Is your shit sparked? Alex already went over this." She crosses her arms. "Get dressed and come downstairs. Also, I got your fancy appetizers warmed up, except the stuff that needs to be fried. You're welcome."

Hack me, I had forgotten about them. I spent a good chunk of yesterday in a frenzy making appetizers and freezing them to be warmed up today for our guests. Little mini beef and veggie patties with flaky yellow pastry, coconut shrimp ready to be fried to perfection with pineapple dipping sauce, curried chicken wings with crisp breading, an assortment of small cakes with Caribbean and Canadian flavors, and, of course, bite-sized pholourie with sweet tamarind sauce.

"Thanks," I say.

She shrugs.

"I really mean it." I take in a deep breath. "You don't have to help this much, you know? Like . . . if it's too stressful, or—"

"I'm fine, and you need the help." She steps out of my room, and before she closes the door, says, "That's what family is for."

I stay on the ground for a moment, staring at where she disappeared.

This isn't how it's supposed to be. I'm the Matriarch. I'm supposed to be supporting everyone else. Not the other way around.

I stand and snuff out the candles, using an already bloodied rag to wipe off my forehead.

I shimmy into the dress and leave the corset back undone. I'll have to shuffle downstairs with it open and have someone help me. It's a light gown made of layer upon layer of gauzy transparent bits and swathes of lace in half-circle patterns. Instead of traditional straps, there are off-shoulder sleeves that fall below my elbows with delicate pieces of lace free-falling off the ends. It's a perfect complement for my shape, clinging to my smaller waist and gliding over my thick Thomas hips.

At the mirror, I grab a tub of our all-in-one curl moisturizer and dump it on my head. A quick bite on my thumb, and I'm using magic to distribute it throughout my hair and define the curls. This is my last jar of product. Even I don't know what I'll do without it.

I make a part in the middle of my hair, use gel to slick down the front half, and use a soft holder to secure the rest in a low ponytail. The final look is a half-up and half-down style. I push a couple of pearl-accented combs in for decoration.

Finally, I apply a bit of makeup, especially to the growing dark smudges under my eyes.

I'm so hacked. Sure, I'll look good for the showcase, and everyone will be fed well, but that won't mean anything if I can't share my gift properly.

I gather up the hem of the dress and light the candles again, ruining my makeup by swiping crimson across my forehead. I need to keep trying. I can't go downstairs like everything is fine. If I can't summon them, then it won't matter.

I clear my mind and beg for Mama Jova. For the ancestor who first Called me. I plead for her help. For her power and strength.

I clench my teeth so hard that they crack.

Come on.

Come on.

Come on!

Magic rises in the air and stays there. Hovering. Power lashing, crying out, screaming without any response.

The door to my room bangs open.

"Hack me, Keisha!" I snap, but when I look up, it's not Keisha standing in the doorway.

Keis frowns. "You're pulling on our magic up here. Be careful."

"Sorry," I mumble.

She's in an emerald gown that falls to her feet with a high slit up the side. Her hair is in a pineapple bun as usual, but this one is more artful, tied with a matching ribbon with little pieces of hair falling down in front of her face. Keis's eyes are lined in black cat-eyes and her eyebrows are perfect, as always.

"I'm supposed to help you tie the back of your dress," she says plainly.

I swallow.

"Keisha is dealing with your food, Mom had a wardrobe malfunction that Alex is fixing, your mom is running around trying to get everything in order, and Priya is trying to organize Eden into her outfit, so I was the only option left."

"Right."

I rise from the circle of candles and carefully douse them before stepping out with my dress. I come to stand in front of Keis and then turn around so she can tie the back.

In the first days of Keis learning to control her gift and using it cruelly, I tried to hide my thoughts from her, though she could always manage to dig out what she wanted anyway.

Now I don't bother.

I'm supposed to be the Matriarch. I keep telling everyone to believe in me, and I can't even hacking do the things I'm supposed to be able to do. I'm about to embarrass our whole family.

Keis tugs tight on the ribbons in the back. "Stand up straight."

I force my body straight and try and suppress the trembling. Tears drop onto the hardwood, and I wipe at them with my toe.

"You need to stop begging and pleading," Keis says.

"What?"

"You keep asking this family to support you. Practically dropping on your knees to get Johan to be your ally. The only time you actually stood your ground was with Rowen."

"And look what happened."

"Yeah. You had a huge buildup of magic. How terrible."

"Magic I pulled from you all. And we lost Rowen as a client."

"And yet she's coming here tonight to see more of the power that you showed her. Not to mention, it was the first time you've seen Mama Jova since the Pass." I try to twist around, and Keis scowls. "I'm not done."

She's right. *Forward*, Mama Jova had said. She'd wanted me to look into the future. Had known it was important, like I've been saying.

"You're a Matriarch. Do you think the rest of them are sitting in circles begging the ancestors to help them?"

"What would you suggest I do?"

Keis stays silent as she finishes tying up the corset. I turn around to look her in the eye. She says, "The ancestors' magic belongs to this family. And you lead it. Don't *ask* them to come. *Command* them. You call, and they must answer. You're supposed to be a leader, so try hacking leading for once."

With that, she turns to leave the room.

"Thanks," I mutter. "For the dress." For more than that.

"Whatever."

After Keis is gone, I catch myself in the mirror with my back still straight from when my cousin commanded me to stand properly. Besides the streaks of blood on my face and the tear tracks running down it, I almost look like someone capable, like someone who can do this. I trace the scar on my chest. A mark of failure.

I'm not that girl anymore.

And I'm tired of suffering to survive.

You call, and they must answer.

When I get downstairs, Mom and Auntie Maise are arguing about where I should stand. They're over in the area behind the entry-way stairs where our dining room sits. The dusk light shines through the back windows, and Uncle Cathius and Dad stand in place with the dining table lifted a little off the ground, staring at Mom and Auntie with faces halfway between confused and irritated. My cousins hover around the archway leading into the kitchen, watching the entire production.

"We should do it here, because then we'll get the nice view out the windows," Auntie Maise says, gesturing to them.

Mom rolls her eyes. "We can't, because then anyone could stroll over here and see."

"And they can't upstairs?"

"We'll shut the balcony doors," Mom snaps back.

"It's a gift in her head! They'll just see us standing around."

"Have you ever actually seen Voya use her gift? How do you know?"

"Have *you* seen her use it?"

I let out a deep breath and already regret being involved. "What's going on?"

Uncle Cathius and Dad drop the table with a clatter and slouch against it.

"Where do you want to do this?" Keisha says, snapping on a piece of gum. "Mom wants to do it in the dining room, and your mom wants to do it upstairs."

I sigh. "What about the entryway?"

"Right where they come in?" Mom balks. "That's so . . . immediate."

"Yeah, but then I can stand on top of the stairs for a little elevation, and we can leave the dining room table where it is so people can grab food over here."

Both Mom and Auntie scowl but nod.

"So we're putting the table back?" Dad asks.

"Yes."

He and Uncle Cathius both groan and move the table back into place.

I stride into the kitchen, where thankfully Keisha has filled the fryers with oil and turned them on so they're already hot when

I get there. I slide the baking sheet of coconut shrimp out of the freezer and dump them into one of the fryer baskets. Then I grab the pholourie dough from the fridge and use an ice cream scoop to dump dollops of those in too.

Alex leans against the island counter. "You're going to get an oil splash on your dress."

"That's what magic is for," I sing back.

Eden rushes through the archway in an auburn sari with gold edging details and does a spin.

My cousins and I *ooh* and *aah* appropriately. Even Keis, who for all her attitude hasn't taken a single bit of it out on my baby sister.

"You look beautiful," I say, abandoning the fryer to give her a hug. "Did your mom get that for you?"

"Yup!"

Priya comes out from the dining room in her own sari. In the style of the rest of her clothes, it's more like a mashup of several different pieces of cloth, but in green, blue, or a mix of the two that comes together gorgeously. "How are you feeling?" she asks me.

"Good," I say, though it's not entirely true. I rush over to the fryer baskets and lift them, letting the shrimp and pholourie sit there with the oil dripping off them. "A little nervous."

Keis said that I needed to command the ancestors and their power. It's one thing to decide to do it and another to actually pull it off.

"The power of a showcase is in the confidence of its star." Priya nudges my shoulder. "Trust the ancestors. You're a Matriarch now; that means they favor you. They'll be there to help."

I swallow and bob my head in a nod. I can't tell her that I don't know if they *will* be there to help. Priya and Dad seem to have this ironclad belief in our ancestors, but they don't know that I'm the one they should be unsure of. And yet even they had their faith shaken, both of them going against their beliefs when it came down to their daughter's life hanging in the balance.

But ever since, despite how things are, they've come back to it. It's nice that they're—or Priya is, at the very least—on my side, but I know it's because of their confidence in the ancestors, not me.

Dad sweeps into the kitchen, likely drawn by the smell of fresh fried pholourie, and grins at us. "Look at this room full of beautiful women."

Priya is the only one who beams, playfully slapping Dad on the arm while Eden grins. The rest of us roll our eyes but enjoy the compliment anyway. Literally no one in this family is known for being modest.

"Thank you for the dress, by the way," I say to Alex, who is done up in a gown with a train she has to keep ahold of so none of us trip over it. It looks like millions of gold flakes sliding over her body, all in one seamless piece with a draped neckline.

"Anything for my favorite cousin."

Keisha holds her hand to her chest. "Wow. We're right here."

Alex just laughs.

By the time we get the appetizers ready and set out the drinks, sorrel, bottles of Caribbean imported beer as well as other liquors, and some Peardrax and mauby that we had sitting in the basement, the doorbell sounds.

I swallow with a painful gulp.

Mom pokes me in the shoulder. "It's time to greet them. They're your guests."

Hack me.

"You look amazing, by the way," she adds, brushing invisible lint off my shoulders. I look at her and she smiles. "You'll be okay. I know I haven't been great these last few months. Losing Mom . . . This is a lot of pressure on you. I don't want you to break under it."

Part of me wants to say "Too late," while another wants to insist that I won't.

Mom's fingers tighten on my shoulder. "I love you. You know that, right?"

"I know." And I do. She's always been there for me. I just never realized how much Granny was a part of that. Without her, it's like we're missing an ingredient in the recipe that makes us mother and daughter. And even though we both know what it is, we can't find the right substitute to get that flavor back. But there's no one-to-one ratio for what Granny was to us. It's never going to taste the same.

I walk toward the door, but Mom keeps ahold of me. "What?"

"Quick tip. Showcases are about drama. So please, for the love of the ancestors, don't open the door like you normally would."

I blink at her. "What? I'm supposed to throw them open with magic or something?"

She kind of cringes but nods at the same time.

"You're not serious."

"I'm *so* serious. When I was younger, Dorothy Carter sent a flock of ravens to open the door at her showcase, and people gushed about it for weeks. Lost their damn minds over it."

Sometimes I seriously hate witch culture.

As I walk to the front, I catch Justin standing on the threshold of the basement door. He throws his hands up before I can speak. "I know, I know. Not to be seen or heard. Just wanted to experience a bit of the glitz and glam. I live a very boring basement life, in case you hadn't noticed."

"I'm sorry that we can't be more entertaining," I say, voice deadpan.

Justin grins and gives me an exaggerated bow before retreating downstairs. I slam the door shut, and for good measure I use my phone to restrict him from coming up the stairs. The last thing

I need is for someone to discover who we have in our basement on their way to the bathroom.

"What a horrible man," Mom grumbles.

I shrug. "Yeah, well, I'm not killing him, so here he stays." I walk into the entryway and up the stairs to the top of the landing. My family gathers around the bottom facing the front doors.

I feel ridiculous.

Alex turns and loudly whispers, "Glitter?"

"No glitter!" Uncle Cathius says, not at all in a whisper. "It'll take ages to clean, even with magic."

"Candy!" Eden cries out, clearly assuming that we're naming things we like.

I'm trying to sort out in my head what I'm going to do when a thought slams against my mind, so rough that I almost stumble from the force of it. It's of Granny, standing at the top of the stairs right where I am, but she's younger. She looks like I knew her when I was little. I remember the moment. She and Grandad were going somewhere fancy for the night, a jazz club or something. And she had dressed up in a shimmering and sleek black dress with silver hoops in her ears. I stared up at her from the entryway and cried out, "Granny, you're beautiful!" And, of course, she had scowled and asked why I wasn't in bed yet. But there was a little smile on her face. Like I said, none of us have ever been modest.

I bite on my thumb, and with her in mind, I open the doors with a gentle wind.

Beyond them stands Ilana Bailey, Torrin Carter, Avery James, Rowen Huang, and, in place of April-Mae Davis, Johan. Not to mention someone that I didn't invite . . . Eli Bailey from the tech conference, standing next to his Matriarch. There's a moment where they do nothing but stare at me as I stare back. Ilana, who looks to be maybe in her late forties, with salt-and-pepper curls that brush against her shoulders, smirks the tiniest bit. The other two Matriarchs are much younger. Torrin, Lauren's aunt, has a short, tapered cut with blonde tips, skin so light it's almost pale, and her signature glittering nose ring. I've never met Avery, though she's Dad's cousin and looks like him a bit too, with the same wide nose and skin tone. She gazes at me with assessing eyes, her lips rouged and locs down to the middle of her back. Rowen Huang is done to the nines as usual, with her short hair pinned up and her pimple carefully covered. I expected her to look irritated with me, but there's a soft curve to her mouth that reads a lot like approval.

Johan is the only one whose face is carefully neutral, to the point where it feels like he twisted it that way.

And Eli . . . he looks as if he's in pain. His lips press flat as he shifts in place, like this is the most uncomfortable situation he's ever been in.

Considering our awkward encounter the other day, maybe it is.

I finally take a look at my family, who are staring at me.

Mom has her hands pressed to her mouth and tears float in her eyes.

Eden tugs on Priya's skirt. "Did you see Granny too?"

"Yes, sweet, I saw."

I don't even know how I did the cast. I just used blood and intention, the way we're the supposed to. The way Mama Jova taught me to. I overlaid the memory of Granny on top of myself. She may not be here for real, but for a moment, it seemed like she was.

Now the guests can remember that I'm not a little girl. I'm the Thomas Matriarch. Granny chose me. I am her legacy.

"Welcome to the showcase," I say, pulling my lips into a smile.

CHAPTER NINE

I stay standing on the steps while Mom leads the Matriarchs into the dining area to grab their snacks and drinks. It's strange, me up there on the landing in my white dress while my family makes small talk and guests eat, like some sort of home wedding. I did try to step down toward them, but Mom gave me a look that I interpreted as "sit your ass down." I guess another part of the whole showcase thing is that I don't mix with everyone else.

The light from the chandelier casts shadows along the wall, and I sink down to the hardwood, attempting to arrange my legs into something that looks elegant. Probably I should stand the whole time, but I would rather conserve my strength. In a few moments, I'll have to use even more magic to share my vision with over ten people at once when I've only ever managed with one person. I'll need all the strength I can get.

Keis's words play in a loop in my head. She said to command the ancestors. I bite my lip. I know she was the one who sent me that memory of Granny. It could have been because she really wants me to loosen Justin's restrictions, but I've already agreed to do that. A bigger part of me clings to the idea that maybe my cousin, my once best friend, doesn't hate me as much anymore.

It's the one bright spot in this entire thing.

Footsteps sound closer and I get up, trying to arrange myself to look more regal and less like a sweaty mess even as the back of my neck is slick with it.

There's no going back now. I have to do this.

The Matriarchs return with drinks and snacks in hand, their eyes pinned to me. Johan raises a glass in my direction, and I push something like a smile onto my face. The forced expression he had before is gone like it was never there. Maybe he just didn't enjoy the display like the others did. Who knows with him?

Eli continues to look like he would like to be anywhere but here. Ilana must have dragged him here for ancestors know what reason.

"Voya will now go ahead and introduce her gift and a bit about her Calling ancestor, and then she'll begin the demonstration," Mom says to the guests as though she's explaining it to them, though I know she's really telling me what to do.

I'm grateful for it. But at the same time, I know she's probably wondering why I didn't start doing that automatically. The ancestors should have told me that much.

I clasp my hands together to hide the shaking. "I was Called by Mama Jova. She was enslaved on a sugar cane plantation in New Orleans and was made to witness the death of a boy she loved. She was awarded the title of Mama for her efforts to save her fellow people at the cost of her own life." I go to continue, but it feels so rote. None of this feels like who Mama is, really, or who she is to *me*. Even if she won't come to me now, she changed my life. She's more than her suffering. "Mama Jova believed in me. She gave me a task that tore me apart . . . that still does." My eyes flicker to Keis for the briefest moment. "But only because she knew that I could stand on my own and seek a future that didn't require that much pain."

I don't mention that Mama Jova gave me an out. That she gave me a chance to get everything I wanted without nearly as much hardship as I'm going through now. If I had taken it, the choice to destroy Keis's future wouldn't have even been in the running. But I didn't trust her or myself enough. In my darker moments, I think of how different things would be if I had touched Luc instead of Juras in that kitchen when she gave me the chance.

It's too late. I can never go back to that moment. All I have is how I move forward.

I unclasp my fingers. "Granny told me that Mama Jova agreed with her decision to make me Matriarch and would do her best to help me. And she did. She gave me the gift of the past and the future. When my actions in the present forever change the path of someone's future, I can see the past that brought them there, and the future that my actions have created."

Rowen's eyebrows raise along with the rest of the Matriarchs. Even Eli's face finally shows an emotion other than discomfort, his eyes widening. All except for Johan, who doesn't look the least bit surprised. I always thought his interest in my gift was because of the secrecy of it, but maybe it was because he *knew* about it. At the Pass, anyone could have hidden nearby and listened in, including him. I just don't know why he would, if not to find some way to hold it over us. He likes to be informed. But why bother playing ignorant?

Either way, the gift of past and future is vague. This is my first time explaining it this clearly.

Now he knows more than ever.

But I need to explain it all. To show how much trust I'm willing to put in this group to help them trust me back.

It's time to show my gift in action.

"I'll need your blood to share the vision with you," I say. "Don't be alarmed by it."

I picture Mama Jova in my mind, her past and our past, intertwined together forever. I've spent months begging for her to come to me. Keis is right, that was never how it should be. But in the same way, commanding her feels wrong too.

You don't command your family.

But you can't beg them either.

Both of those put a pressure on people that squeezes and hurts. How could she or any ancestor help me when I didn't really understand what I wanted help with? I thought I wanted the secret of Granny's products, or how to make everyone acknowledge me as the Matriarch.

But every time I sat in that circle, my intention dissolved to "help."

Just . . . help.

It was weak. Flimsy. Maybe that was the problem all along.

Now as I think of Mama Jova, of my ancestor who believed in me, who gave me these gifts, who told Granny that she would help, my intention clears.

I'm here to make a better future for my family, for this community, and I need her to help me show them exactly what I saw. The danger looming in the future. I need her, not so she can tell me how to fix it, but so that she can give me the power to find a way to fix it myself.

I call.

Smoke billows out around me, and the scent of ash and burning sugar cane fills my nose. Mama lays her hand against my back and whispers, "You called?"

Tears brim in my eyes. And in the next moment, power floods from my ancestor's fingers and fills my body so fast that I gasp aloud.

Plates shatter as we're thrown into the vision. It's all I can do to make sure the magic doesn't touch Eden. This isn't something I want her to see.

The smoke expands, and the house comes into view, burning. We see Auntie Maise screaming and running out of the front door,

Keis smashing her head against the window and falling to her death, Luc sobbing on the lawn, Eden clinging to Dad and Priya's dead bodies. It fills our minds through mine, and the ache in my chest from watching my family suffer travels too. I feel it squeeze the hearts of the Matriarchs.

But it's not enough.

This is only my family.

They need to see more.

I know this is bigger.

So I call.

Again.

And again.

And again.

And again.

New hands press into my back, their names floating beyond my awareness. Thomases. But not just Thomases. Thomases who are also Baileys. Who are Carters. Who are Jameses. Who are Davises. The intertwining of the Black witch families into our own that has happened over generations.

We see Aaron Bailey lighting up the sky electric blue, his shocks making people tremble and fall to the ground where they lay still, his wife and son included. We watch a James drowning in their home as water pours from every orifice. A Carter is attacked by birds, pecked savagely until their ravaged corpse is all that's left. Johan stands over the body of a girl lying prone on the ground with curls that are blonde at the tips.

"Enough!" Johan roars, his voice penetrating through the rush of visions.

I stumble forward and away from the hands of my ancestors, who do not follow me. The vision ends abruptly. I grip the banister to keep myself upright, the sudden loss of bandwidth threatening to drag me into unconsciousness.

The floor is a mess of snacks, smashed dishes and glasses, and ruby red sorrel leaking through the cracks in the hardwood.

Johan is breathing hard, near panting. Blood dripping from his eyes the same way it is for everyone else who I shared the vision with. Or I assume anyway, as Eli seems to have already wiped his eyes and is staring around the room, pupils darting every which way, while Torrin is sucking at a sliced thumb, her makeup already back to being immaculate. Her fingers shake.

Meanwhile, my sister clings to my dad. She couldn't see the vision, but Johan's yelling must have triggered her, because Dad's glaring at the Davises' stand-in leader, who's ignoring him.

"Well," Rowen says, adjusting her dress. "That was something." She pulls a cloth handkerchief from her purse and uses it to delicately dab away the blood on her face.

"Not to be rude," Avery James says, likely very ready to be rude. "But this doesn't seem to concern you?"

"It might if you don't get this under control." Rowen gives her an indulgent smile. "And I was invited by the young Matriarch."

I swallow.

"Good show," she continues. "But given everything"—this with a gesture to the room—"I'll be taking my leave. If you manage to harness that power to make product as impressive as your grandma did, I'm happy to become a loyal client again. Let me know when you've got it figured out." She offers a final wave to me and carefully steps over the broken glass on the floor toward the door. There she pauses and looks at Ilana Bailey, who draws herself up. "Nice to see you, cousin."

"And you," Ilana replies.

With that, Rowen leaves.

Well, at least I didn't ruin our relationship with the Huangs after all. If I ever manage to figure out what Granny could do to make the product properly, it'll be easy to get her back on board. And I'm sure she won't hesitate to share what she's learned here.

If you're going to have your business spread around, Rowen is the best one to do it, because everyone knows she doesn't deal in common gossip, she deals in secrets that are always, *always* true.

"How about I clean this up?" Mom says, and slices her finger with a pen knife. As the blood in it wells, she uses it to gather up broken dishes back into functional plates and bowls, then floats the fallen food into the garbage and the plates into the sink. "Everyone, feel free to replenish your drinks and snacks, and we can gather in the dining room to discuss everything." If anyone notices the tremble in her voice, they don't mention it.

There's no movement in the room for a moment, the Matriarchs seemingly unsure.

I stand up straight and raise my voice. "I have a proposition for how we can work together to make sure the future you witnessed never comes to pass. Enjoy the drinks and food, and I'll talk to you about it." I don't ask, I tell, because in this case, it's the better option.

And for once, people listen.

I give everyone some time to get food and settle in at the dining room table. I sit across from the three Matriarchs, Eli, and Johan, with my family scattered around us. Everyone picks at the offerings.

My entire body feels weak. Like the soft buttercream layers in a cake—seemingly solid but with a melt-in-your-mouth texture. The ghost sensation of the hands on my back radiates between my shoulder blades. I've never felt so spent. The rapid swell and deflation of my bandwidth has left me feeling emptied out. Even my breaths are shallow.

Hack me, no wonder Matriarchs don't borrow ancestor power whenever. And I only used it for a moment.

"I don't believe we've met," Mom says to Eli, which is her way of politely asking who the hell he is.

Ilana pats his hand. "One of my charges. His mom is having a bit of a tough time." She gives Eli a hard look. "*Someone* ran off on her for a bit. Anyway, she drove herself into the ground looking for him, and now she's sick. They're both staying with me now, and I figured, how often is he gonna see a showcase in his lifetime? So I brought him along. You don't mind, do you, dear?" Her question is directed at me.

I shake my head. I don't care, really. I'm too busy shoving mini patties in my mouth as delicately as I can, suddenly starving.

Eli hikes his shoulders up toward his ears. I guess he wasn't expecting to be exposed like that. His brow seems to have a permanent furrow in it like he's still confused about why he's here even though Ilana just explained.

"He's a good boy, honestly," Ilana adds, maybe feeling bad for airing his business. "A bit of teenage rebellion. He's fine now, aren't you?"

"Yes, ma'am."

"So," Johan says, clearly tired of the discussion. "What is this proposition?"

I hold up a finger while I swallow, and he scowls. I finish what's in my mouth and speak. "I think that we should form a council. Granny, April-Mae, and Lee used to have a group of sorts before."

"Yes, and it imploded," Ilana muses, shaking her head.

"It didn't implode, it was abandoned."

She notches an eyebrow up at me.

"One thing didn't work one time. I'm not talking about forming a group because we want stronger gifts or to avoid anomalies, or even to solve this one problem. We need to form something that lasts. A council that can not only work together to protect the community from threats but also help make it better."

Avery flicks her eyes at Dad for a moment before looking back at me. "What happened with Elaine happened because of involvement with Justin Tremblay and NuGene. I loved my cousin, but mixing up with them got us into this. Now we've got the new NuGene CEO in this vision—who *you* had involvement with. Not to mention whoever this person is whose present you've messed up. Because isn't that what you said? Your gift shows the future that *your* actions wrought. The problem here is starting to feel very concentrated in this family."

Eli chokes on his water, his eyes wide, like he's shocked. I mean, I guess it's one thing to see Luc in the vision and another to learn that I have some sort of history with him. Now he probably knows exactly why I was at the conference the other day.

The back of my neck heats up, and I sidestep the mention of the person whose path I changed. "You saw the vision. What happens affects every family."

"But it's happening *because* of yours, is it not? And if it's not because of you, then because of what Elaine, Ava, April-Mae, and Lee started all those years ago. Which you didn't include the Jameses or Carters in, in the first place. Obviously, this needs to be taken care of. But why should we work with you? Why not work within our own families to deal with this?"

Torrin nods in agreement with Avery.

Dad blanches. "You're part of our family too!"

"Last time I checked, you were pledged to a Thomas. Elaine got married and became a Thomas too. Girl was even out here cooking up Trini dishes constantly when we don't have so much as a distant uncle over there. So I'm confused, now we're family?" Avery shoots back.

My eyes go wide. I didn't even think of that. But it's true. Dad's family doesn't have roots in Trinidad and Tobago like ours, and yet those were the recipes Auntie had in the almanac.

I wonder if she made them to help fit in better as a Thomas.

He lets out a shocked scoff. "Are you kidding me? We grew up together!"

"You grew up with my brothers. I was a baby." She rolls her eyes and leans back. "I'm just saying, you didn't want to involve us when you were trying to get stronger gifts and cure anomalies, which we had too by the way, but now that shit's going to hell, you want us in? Nah. You can handle yours, and we can handle ours."

"This isn't a popularity club," I splutter finally. "If we all work together, then we'll have a better means of helping each other and sharing information. Keeping separate is only going to split our efforts."

"It's a pretty picture, Vo, but I think this can be solved with a one-off communal effort versus the long-term commitment that some of our colleagues would rather not promise." Johan turns toward the other Matriarchs, giving me a view of his side profile. "I would propose a ritual—"

Ilana barks out a laugh. "Are you serious? You already tried that. It flopped. Where is your Matriarch? She needs to be called in on this. That woman has a special talent for getting out of difficult situations."

Johan clenches his teeth and tries to morph it into a smile, poorly. "She's away."

"Wait, what do you mean you tried that already?" I ask, looking between the two.

They both seem reluctant to say anything.

"I visited Aaron Bailey and his family a few days ago and he shocked me. Involuntarily," I tell them. "His wife was worried."

Ilana raises her brows. "And how do you know Aaron?"

"Is that really what's important?" I answer, hoping she doesn't pry deeper.

"Yes, well . . . he came to me to say he was having issues. I didn't know what was going on, and I told him to wait for me to learn more. Did he? No! He went straight to the devil to get his fix, and they slaughtered a man for nothing." She sends a glare Johan's way. "You know it's been messy with our family. Not everyone is happy with the way our purity has shaped up, and this has *not* helped."

The Davis leader looks unconcerned.

Eli, meanwhile, has gotten lost in staring at Johan with an intensity that feels like a touch too much.

"So, this can't be fixed with a ritual," I jump in.

Johan snaps, "It *did* work. It just didn't stick. It started happening again. Then he comes into my office saying I screwed him over and I owe him another rite. My ancestors' ass, I do."

"Look, from the vision, clearly Luc knows something about what's happening, whether or not he's responsible for it. I know him, so I can investigate what's happening there."

"And what exactly is your relationship to him? Is he the person whose present you changed?" Torrin cuts in, twirling her nails in my direction.

I splutter, "Well ... We knew each other—" The family shifts at the table around me. It's awkward to explain how I'm connected to Luc. And I really want to avoid mentioning Justin.

"Are you friends?"

"No, we're no—"

"Lovers?"

"No!"

"Okay." She waves her hand in the air. "None of that is helpful, so that investigation is bust."

"Not necessarily," Ilana cuts in. She nudges Eli. "He works at NuGene."

All eyes at the table zero in on Eli. He shrinks under the scrutiny.

Ilana beams, clearly proud. "And can you believe this boy is so modest he tried to hide it? Michelle—don't know if you all know Michelle—she runs that little supermarket at Queen and John Street, so she's always in that area. Anyway, she saw him coming in and out of NuGene twice. Finally, I had to confront the boy. Disappearing into that building every morning and coming back later, I knew he must have gotten a job. He's volunteered with a genetics charity for years, you know?"

"Why would you hide that?" Keis's voice cuts across the table, and I swallow.

Eli shrugs. "I . . . I don't know. It felt weird to celebrate it with Mom being sick."

"See? A good boy." Ilana nods to herself. "Go on, tell them what you do there."

"I work in PR. I'm just an intern."

Without meaning to, my eyes shoot to Keis. She refuses to meet my gaze. She's fixed on the boy in front of us. That was *her* internship. I don't remember seeing him at the exclusive tour, but I also wasn't paying that much attention to other people. Or maybe he didn't need to go. Maybe that volunteer experience he had was enough.

Ilana beams. "He could look into things. It's probably better that it's him than Voya anyway, if this Luc is already familiar with her."

"Assuming we go through with this, which we haven't agreed upon," Johan practically growls. He shoots a glare at Eli like it's his fault that my plan is coming together instead of the Matriarch who volunteered him. "There can be multiple futures. There's no guarantee that this one will come to pass."

"Do you want to take that chance?" I need to take back the reigns on this conversation. "It's already happening with Aaron. My uncle said he made a pregnant girl go into premature labor, and his gift is safe birth."

"Vacu was probably high." He rolls his eyes.

I grind my teeth.

"He may have an addiction issue, but he was telling the truth," Keis says, her voice cold. "I saw it in his mind."

Each of the Matriarchs shift in their seats.

My cousin grins. "I'm not in any of yours now, if that's what you're wondering. It wouldn't be right, as your hosts."

Their shoulders relax the slightest bit. Even if you have nothing to hide, it doesn't mean you want someone in your head.

"That was your oldest girl on the ground in that vision. Aqua, right? I lost my niece not that long ago. You don't gamble with family," Torrin says to Johan, tapping her long nails against her cheek. "I don't like the idea of having to help them with a problem they created, but it *is* a problem. Did it mean nothing to you, seeing her like that?"

"She is my child," Johan says, his voice low and measured. "My first-born child. *Of course* that matters."

"Then you agree," Ilana says. "Something needs to be done. Like Voya said, this isn't going to be fixed with a ritual, and we can't afford to take chances on it. This must be stopped directly."

I sit up straighter in my chair and smile.

"But," she continues, staring at me, "I also agree that this started with your family."

My shoulders slump.

"*But*," she says once more, and I'm tempted to throw my mini patty at her face by this point, "we do need to work together on this. Why try and fix this within individual families when we could combine our resources? I don't know if the council will endure as much as Voya is hoping, but surely we can collaborate at least on this. I would propose that we have the young Thomas Matriarch work with Eli on his NuGene investigation. The CEO obviously knows something from what we saw in the vision."

I blink at Eli at the same time that he blinks at me.

Keisha grips my hand under the table, and when I look at her, she does a suggestive eyebrow dip that makes me wish my chip would short circuit so I could pass out for a bit and exit this situation.

Hack me. This is giving me too many NuGene Match memories. I don't need to get stuck with *another* guy who seems to very much *not* want to spend time with me. My ego is bruised enough.

Ilana continues, unbothered, "We'll have weekly meetings to monitor progress and share any information that we have, and you and Eli can report on what you've found out. We'll rotate meeting locations at each of our homes. I can do the first shift." She stares into my eyes. "And *you* will lead us."

Johan's eyes go wide, and he's not the only one. My entire family looks shocked. "You want *Voya* to be the head of this council?" he asks.

I preen a bit at the fact that he's using the title of our group like I wanted. Though at the same time, I want to shout exactly what he is saying. I wanted to work together on this council, not lead it. I can barely get my own family on board with being led by me, much less a group of powerful Matriarchs and Johan.

Avery eyes him. "Who else? It's her responsibility. I agree with that much. Weekly meetings will help us oversee what's happening so things can't go belly-up again. 'Cause ancestors know, no one in this family likes to be very forthcoming." She glances at Dad, who grinds his teeth. "I would still rather handle this on my own, but I trust Ilana's judgment. If she wants to try a group, then fine."

"She's not even seventeen!" Johan insists. "She's a child."

I don't even have time to retort before Torrin speaks. "She's a Matriarch." She throws a side look at Johan. "That's more than we can say about you."

The room goes silent, and the look in Johan's eyes could burn cities to the ground.

Meanwhile, I stare open-mouthed at the Carter Matriarch. All I've wanted for months has been for someone to acknowledge who I am, what I am. It feels like a giant leap in the right direction.

"Where is your Matriarch, by the way?" Torrin adds. "April-Mae has been traveling for more time than the average vacation seems to warrant. I know she used to have a reputation as a bit of a runaway, but this is ridiculous. How long has it been now? A year at least, maybe two."

The more people speak about April-Mae, the more I realize how little I know about the Davis Matriarch. Johan said she joined the council as a favor to Granny, but growing up, I barely saw them interact with each other. Or maybe I did, but the memories were too wound up in Auntie Elaine, and I lost them. But after the council dissolved, she definitely was even less a part of our lives. I remember her only as a tall and imposing woman who every Davis obeyed without question.

Johan leans back and rolls his eyes. "My mother likes to be away. She's run the family for most of her life, and now she's enjoying a little retirement. I would like to remind all of you that she's got more than twenty years on the youngest of you. It's a young people's game now, and she doesn't have a family that needs her constant monitoring the way some others do with their Matriarchs." He turns his gaze over to me. "What do you think of this idea?"

If I wanted to get out of this, I could try and push the responsibility onto someone else. But the fact of the matter is that I'm the one who had the vision, who brought this council together and wants it to work, and I stand to lose my entire family if this fails.

So instead I say, "I'm thinking that I won't have much time to work at Roti Roti while I'm leading." Part of me hates the idea of losing my one escape, but it's bad enough giving Johan that power over me while I'm Matriarch. It would be even worse to do it when I'm supposed to be leading other Matriarchs.

"You work there?" Avery says, snapping her head back. "Why?"

"Excuse me?" Johan raises his eyebrows at her.

"I mean, the food is nice, but Voya's a Matriarch, not a random teenager with a part-time job."

"Agreed," Ilana adds. "Johan can find another body for his kitchen. Can't you?"

I can hear the slow grinding of Johan's teeth. "Of course. Consider yourself fired."

Torrin lets out a steups. "You trying to make sure the girl doesn't get any cash from the government? Laid off, you mean."

"Yes, that's exactly what I mean."

Ilana rises from the table and smiles around the room, giving Eli a slap on the back. The boy looks like he wants to run away again and never come back this time. And he seems so confused, his brow permanently furrowed. He probably can't believe he was supposed to just witness a showcase and now he's been volunteered to help with a whole operation.

"Then we'll meet again at my place in a few days to work out details. I expect you, Ms. Leader, to have some sort of plan ready by then." Ilana jerks her head at her charge. "Give her your phone number."

I awkwardly hold out my phone, but he doesn't grab his.

"It'll look suspicious if I have your number," he says, looking somewhere past my head. "Send it to Ilana, and then I'll set up a burner app and contact you."

Ilana whistles. "Okay, I see you, Mr. Spy Guy."

He cringes.

"Cool, that works." I send my number to the Bailey Matriatch and then rise to my feet as elegantly as I can. I don't care if this guy doesn't like me. Judging by him running away from home, I'm guessing he doesn't like to get involved in things. And this is more than a little involved.

"Beautiful." Ilana looks around at my family. "Now, who's gonna pack me a doggy bag, because I haven't eaten this well in a while, and I'm not leaving without some more."

Johan storms out of the dining room without another word. Mom rushes into action grabbing containers for the other Matriarchs, who also want leftovers.

I expect Johan to come back. He doesn't.

A smile pulls itself onto my face nevertheless. Let Johan be mad. The Davises have been the most powerful family in this community for a long time, and his power has always come from being the only one that other families can go to when things get tough—for a price he names, of course.

This council will change everything. We not only stand to save our families but to show the community that we can help them, not for profit, but because it's the right thing to do.

I've formed this council to save us.

But at the same time, it could topple the empire Johan and his family have created and make him hate me more than he already does.

And I'm prepared to do it anyway.

CHAPTER TEN

M om shoos me off to my room to recuperate after the level of magic that I used for the showcase while she and the rest of the family clean up. As I make for the stairs, she stops me with a hand on my shoulder. I turn back to her.

"I'm proud of you," she says.

My cheeks pinch, and if my skin were lighter, it would have flushed red. "Why?" I splutter.

"What do you mean, *why*?" she says with her hands on her hips. "You did wonderful in the showcase, and the magic it took to share that vision? That was something very special."

"Granny would have done the same." It clenches at my heart that she didn't get to see this first-hand.

Mom shakes her head. "I've never seen my mom do anything like that. You're never going to be like your granny. You know that, right?"

I cross my arms over my chest and look away.

"And it's not a bad thing. I may not always agree with everything you do, but you *are* the Matriarch of this family. You'll lead it in your own way."

I still don't know what that way is, and now I'll have to lead an entire council on top of the family. It's part of what I wanted but not quite the way I wanted it.

Mom tugs me into a hug and twists one of my curls around her finger before pulling away. "Go get some rest."

I follow her instructions and drag my feet up the stairs to my room. Flopping onto my mattress, I glance at the candles still sat in that circle on the floor. In the end, that wasn't what I even needed. What worked for other Matriarchs apparently wasn't guaranteed to work for me.

Scrambling into a sitting position on my bed, I focus my intention and call for Auntie Elaine.

Unlike the dramatic way that Mama Jova likes to appear, my aunt shimmers into being with a scent that reminds me of disinfectant. I wrinkle my nose.

She sighs. "The smell?"

"Yeah, what is that?"

"It's the hospital." She flops onto the bed next to me and ruffles her short hair. "Remember that place you met me when you became a Matriarch? At Bridgepoint?"

"You said it was your special place."

"Yes, that's where we ancestors come from when you call us, and we bring scents along the way, for whatever reason. And hospitals don't exactly smell nice."

"Mama Jova's smells like rotting sugar cane and ash."

"She must have her special place in the sugar cane fields."

I couldn't imagine living your afterlife in the same place where you died, but maybe she was in a happier memory than that time. It was the only home she had known, after all.

Auntie Elaine eyes me. "I know why you called. You've figured out how to focus your intention to specific requests, but I can't make this one come true."

I deflate, my back hunching. This time when I called, I asked for a way to speak with Granny. There must be, right? She could have advice about how to lead the council. How to do this properly.

I could talk to her about what's been happening. About the show-case. About anything.

I could say how sorry I am.

"Why?" I choke out, voice more petulant than I want it to be.

"Ava is gone somewhere that I can't follow. Our ancestors can exist in all planes of time, but we're separate from both your world and wherever those who pass go. I wouldn't even know where to find your granny."

"So she's gone forever."

Granny never ascribed to any specific religion, and everyone in the family is basically the same, each of us constructing our own sorts of ideas. I never thought much about it. But deep inside, I had expected to see Granny again one day, yet hearing Auntie Elaine like this puts up a wall between us and them. My grandma feels so far away that I can't conceptualize ever seeing her again if I can't connect with her the way I can with Auntie Elaine or Mama Jova.

"Vo . . ." Auntie Elaine's voice trails off, and she reaches for my hand. Somehow, I expect her grip to be ghostly, but it isn't. Her hands are firm and a little rough, even. Moisturized with some-thing scentless.

Suddenly, I'm reminded of a time our hands were linked together. In a park or something like that. My memories of her have started to come back, like Dad said, but they're not as clear as I thought they would be. It's more like feelings of déjà vu than anything.

But just as quickly, I remember Granny's hand going limp in mine.

"I get it," I say, sliding my hands from hers. I'm not going to see or talk to or touch Granny ever again. "You can go."

"Please don't be like this."

"You can go," I repeat.

"Before I do, I need to tell you something about your gift. Mama Jova meant to share this, but you didn't call her."

"What about my gift?"

"There are limits to it."

Limits? I mean, of course gifts have limits to them. Like how Keis can read minds but only things you're thinking about right at that moment. Not your past or future thoughts. I guess I thought of my limits as being that I could only use the power if I changed the path of someone's future forever. But are there more? "Like what?"

"You can only look three times per person at either their past or future."

I scoff. "Three times? Not four? You know, an even mix."

Auntie Elaine gives me "the look," you know, when adults are both annoyed and exhausted by you. "Three is a powerful number."

I think back on how many times I've called on Justin's past and future. Once for Rena, a second time in Rowen's lounge, and now at the showcase. "Wait . . . but that means I can't look into Justin's future or past anymore?"

"Correct."

"Why didn't someone tell me sooner? Why didn't Mama tell me that at the Pass?"

Auntie sighs. "Mama Jova has her reasons."

"Honestly? That's all I get?"

"She has her own ideas for how things should go. If you knew the limits, you may have done things in a different way."

I give myself a moment to really think about it. If I knew I only had three shots at it, would I have used one showing Lauren to Rena? Yes, definitely. But I might not have gone into Justin's future. I may not have done the showcase. I may have sat on those chances a lot longer. But apparently Mama Jova didn't want that. "Is she allowed to do that? Run the show?"

"She's the one who gave you your gift. That means she's responsible for you. And therefore, she dictates how we deal with you as a Matriarch as well."

Of course my being a Matriarch isn't normal either, because Mama Jova insists on making things as difficult as possible. I press my palms against my eyes. I thought I would be able to call on the past and future of Justin whenever I wanted to help us figure out what to do. Now there's no way that I'll be able to.·

"I could do Luc, couldn't I? I changed things for him."

"Yes, but did you change the entire path of his future? Did you knock him away from the one he was on in such a way that he could never return to it?"

I open my mouth to retort then shut it. Luc was always on the path to be the successor of NuGene. Sure, I changed things. He came into his position a lot sooner than expected, and he doesn't have Justin, but if anything, I briefly tripped him up. He's still on the same path he was always going to be on because I chose to take from Keis instead. Her path in life was definitely forever changed by my actions. But Keis's past and future aren't going to help me with whatever is going on with Luc.

"Is that all?" I say.

Auntie squeezes my hand. "That's it."

"I'd like to be alone now, if you don't mind."

She doesn't say anything, but I feel when her presence drifts away, the caustic scent of disinfectant leaving along with her.

I stay there by myself, staring at the ceiling. I got them to form the council like I wanted and even got out of being an intern for Johan, though now I've lost my place to escape when home gets to be too much. And I have to lead this council. To come up with a plan to fix everything before I see them next. I don't even have the benefit of Justin's past and future to help me.

I'm not prepared.

The door creaks open, and I look up. It's only when Keisha peeks her head in and my heart drops that I realize I hoped to see someone else.

Keisha must see it too because her lips press together briefly before she speaks. "Sorry that I'm not who you expected."

Hack me, she's so perceptive. "It's not—"

"No, I get it." She pulls out a plate of food from behind her. "I thought you might still be hungry, so I brought up leftovers." She sets the steaming plate on my night table and backs away.

"I didn't mean—"

"It's whatever. Don't read into it." She gives a little shrug, but there's a heavy motion to it. "I'm not over here trying to replace Keis. I'm just filling in."

"You're not filling in. We're family. We're friends."

She looks me in the eye. "But we're not *best* friends."

I don't have anything to say back to that, so she turns and closes the door behind her. I drag the plate of food toward me and scarf it down, because Keisha was right. I am hungry. Then, full and still feeling like a horrible cousin and friend, I sink onto the bed and curl up under my covers.

I mean to distract myself with feed videos, but in the next moment I'm waking up.

My entire room is dark. I do a quick double blink to bring up the time, and one a.m. flashes back at me.

I swish my tongue around in my dry mouth.

I need a drink. Maybe some leftover sorrel if everyone didn't drink it all.

I'm still in my showcase dress, though now it's wrinkled. I peel it off of my body and bite my thumb with the metal tooth, using magic to steam the dress back into perfect condition before I slide it into a drawer in my closest that rushes to categorize it based on item type and color.

Tapping on my closet again, I get it to spit out some pj's for me, and I pull those on instead. A loose pair of pants and a matching sweatshirt top. It's too cold outside to wear anything less, and Uncle Cathius wields an iron fist over the house thermostat. Granny put him in charge of the app to control it ages ago. Unlike her, he actually set a strong enough password that none of us have been able to figure it out.

As Matriarch, I could get him to give me control, but I don't think I could deal with the fallout of it. So I suffer the cold instead.

I pull a pair of slippers onto my feet so I don't have to walk on the frigid hardwood and go downstairs.

In the kitchen, I pour myself a tiny glass of the last bit of sorrel left and start to make my way back up to the second floor but find myself pausing at the entrance to the basement. The door is cracked open the tiniest bit.

I nudge it all the way open with my foot and walk a small way down.

Keis is in the same position as always at the little desk with Justin beside her as she taps furiously on the screen. For once, I don't think she actually notices I'm there, she's so engrossed in what she's doing.

She's as obsessed with this game as she was with school. With getting a good internship. Justin is as close to NuGene as she's ever going to get now that I've ruined everything for her.

"You may as well come down if you're going to linger in the doorway," Keis mutters, not looking up.

Guess she *was* paying attention.

I swallow and shuffle my way down the steps.

Justin grins at me. "I heard you put on quite the show," he says. "Pity that I didn't get an invite."

I roll my eyes. "Because that's what I need, a known enemy of our community showing up, especially one who is supposed to be dead." Justin loves to eavesdrop, so I expected it. I have no idea how much he heard, but I won't be giving him any hints. I trust Keis not to either.

"They wouldn't even recognize me." There's a cutting edge to his voice. "Who would? I'm hacking cornflower blue."

Fair enough.

He tilts his head. "Lots of chitchat about this vision you showed everyone. I'm very curious about it."

"If you're curious, ask Keis."

"She won't tell me." He says it with a smile so wide that I'm sure he knows that I know how fake it is.

I knew she wouldn't. No matter how chummy they are, she's not going to tell him anything that would make the family vulnerable.

I hadn't even thought about making sure the vision wouldn't extend to Justin in the moment. But like Keis's gift, I guess it doesn't work on NuSaps. Something about the units does not jive with mental gifts. Physical magic is fine though, like what's holding him inside the house. We even tested it. "Sorry you had to miss the fun."

"No, you're not."

I smile back, fake as his. "No, not really. But if you want more books for entertainment, I can get you some."

"I have over a thousand loaded up. I think I'm fine." Justin abruptly becomes bored with me and looks over Keis's shoulder at the tablet. I don't think he likes interacting with any of us beyond her, but it does mix things up for him.

I stand there a moment without saying anything, just watching him and my cousin.

"Keisha is upset with you," Keis says.

"You heard?"

"Upsetting things are loud."

"I thought you could shut everything out now."

Keis looks over at me. "It's like the difference between an open window and a closed one. The sound isn't gone, it's only muffled. And if someone decides to throw rocks at the window because they're sad their brand-new bestie isn't actually, then it tends to be annoying enough to draw notice."

I fix my gaze on my slipper-clad feet. "It wasn't like that."

"Whatever."

Justin stares at us, his NuSap face so still that it sends goose bumps down my arms. It's almost like he's sleeping with his eyes open, though he isn't.

"We had a deal, didn't we?" Keis says, gesturing to him. "I need some restrictions unlocked for Justin."

She holds up her tablet to his NuSap interface app. It works perfectly even with old units, so we could avoid using the retro remote that Justin came with. Keis has access to see what controls are or aren't enabled because that's how the system is set up. But she can't make any changes without both my password and face scan. It's outdated, but we don't have the new tech that can read DNA off your skin. I scroll over the list of three apps she would like him to be able to access.

"What are these?" I ask.

"It's two research paper sites. It's literally things to read so he can stop having to look at it over my shoulder."

"They're offline?"

"His whole system is set to offline resources only, and it's not like I can access anything not offline, so yeah." Her voice is snippy and impatient.

I give permission, and she snatches the tablet back.

I twiddle my fingers and swallow. "I wanted to say thank you. For . . . what you did today. With Granny and backing me up on Uncle Vacu."

"I didn't do it for you. A bad showcase reflects poorly on our entire family. And a good chunk of our business is fueled by personal references. We need to be able to afford the house, because it's not like I can move out. Backing you up on Uncle Vacu is because we need this issue solved so the house doesn't burn down and I don't die banging my head into a window."

Keis looks up and pins me with a glare. "When we were friends, I did things to help you. Now assume everything I do is because I have to. We're not friends anymore. You made your decision. Live with it."

I grit my teeth and step back, knowing that it's probably time for me to go, but my cousin isn't done.

"You know, you spend so much time talking about how important family is to you. How much we all matter, but you always do the things that hurt us. You hurt Keisha. And you chose a boy over me."

"Keis—"

"No," she snaps. "You wanted me to talk to you. I'm talking to you. You don't get to choose how my future is going to turn out. You don't get to decide that I'm the resilient one and he's the one who needs to be protected. Just admit that you screwed it all up! You passed Mama Jova's task, but you left a mountain of hurt in your wake. And who came out on top in the end? Was it your family that you love so much? No. It was him. And now he's trying to kill us all. Good job."

Finally, she turns to the tablet, blocking me out, and I slowly make my way out of the room. Justin's grin stinging against my back.

I go into the kitchen and stand in front of the sink, slurping down my glass of sorrel while sucking back tears and gasping.

Doesn't she think that I know I ruined everything? I tried my best, and this is what we got out of it.

I bite my lip to quiet any sobs.
I guess it's only fair.
I hurt Keisha.
Now I get to hurt too.

CHAPTER ELEVEN

I crack my knuckles as I stare down at the tablet Granny left behind. Her password is the same one that everyone in the family knows, even though it's her personal one: Thomas1. I clutch the tablet as I settle on the bed in her room.

It's Monday, which means a fresh start to the week, and I plan to get things done. Number one, work on figuring out Granny's beauty supply formula, and number two, create a strategy to bring to the council.

I haven't been able to completely push Keis's words from the other night out of my mind. But I can't dwell on it. I'm responsible for this family. I can't get lost in how I've let them down in the past. I need to think of our future.

I unlock the tablet and stare at the disorganized mess that is her apps. There are a bunch of gaming ones, things like puzzles, cooking games, and even coloring apps. I never saw her play these. She must have done them alone in her room where none of us could judge her.

A smile stretches onto my face. It's cute imagining my grumpy granny up in her room coloring pictures of cafés and little animals. The smile doesn't stay for long. It's followed by the crushing memory that she's not here and will never be again.

I push on and swipe through, opening the app where she

would keep notes, hoping to find something useful there. There are endless grocery lists that have a little yellow icon with the initials VT, showing that I was a collaborator on it. We would make them together, her sometimes vetoing things that I put on them, me only doing that if I messaged her first to say we already had a bunch.

Now I make the grocery lists by myself and share with Keisha as a collaborator. She goes and helps me pick them up. I grimace, remembering our last interaction. I need to make things up to her somehow.

Further on in Granny's notes are some appointments and other reminders of things she didn't want to forget. Feed show times and that sort of thing. There's one with Rowen's name on it that I jump at, but it just seems to be dates marking when she needs to drop off product for the Huang Matriarch.

Searching through the rest of her apps is basically the same. No other clues about the formula.

I groan and tap on her photos. There are so many. I scroll way back and find ones of Granny when she was my age, standing in the background of family photos filled with people I don't know—her family before they left when she decided to make the switch to purity.

I flip further and find ones of Granny and Grandad together with a little boy in their arms. Even that young, I can tell that it's Uncle Vacu. Then Mom comes along, and Auntie Maise after.

I swipe through photo after photo after photo of Granny, Grandad, Mom, Auntie, and Uncle Vacu. They look like a happy family even though Granny puts on a sparked face for most of it. A lot of the early ones are those older types you would have to take on a separate camera since they didn't have good phone ones yet. They have a look like they've been scanned from something printed. I spy one with Granny in a bathing suit, holding up Uncle

Vacu by his armpits as someone sprays them with water and they laugh.

He used to be part of this family. He still is. Whatever is going on with his gift, it's going to get him into even more trouble than he could on his own. Granny turned him away before, but that's when he was fine on his own. Or as fine as he could be, considering.

I look down at my phone. He hasn't tried to call me once even though I took off the block. But knowing him, he wouldn't. It was already debasing enough for him to come to the house to tell me what was going on in the first place.

With a swallow, I make a video call to him.

He answers after the first ring.

His eyes are sharp and clear, and he seems to have gotten over his franticness from the other day. The room that he's in is dingy looking. Not his apartment. Somewhere else. It almost looks like an alley.

"Hi ...," I start.

He rolls his eyes. "What did you find out? Do you know what's happening with me?"

"Not yet. We're working on some leads right now." Or we should be as soon as Eli actually messages me so we can find a way to investigate Luc.

"So you know nothing."

I glare at him. "I've assembled a Matriarch council to deal with it. We're meeting tomorrow." Ilana hadn't wasted any time sending out the meeting marker for our next gathering at her house. It's good that she's being so prompt, but it also doesn't give me a lot of time. "I wanted to ask you a bit more."

"Fine. Ask."

For ancestors' sake, he's acting like he's the one doing me the favor instead of the other way around.

I grit my teeth. "Have you been around Aaron Bailey at all?"

Maybe there's something in common, something that happened to them both that could explain this.

"Who?"

"Okay, maybe not. Have you noticed anything similar happening to anyone else?"

Uncle Vacu rolls his eyes at me again. "Enough. Look at this. I found it." He pulls up a video that both of us can see and presses play.

A newscaster pops on screen chatting with a sweaty Black girl on a hospital bed. Her hair is dark and pressed straight, except the sweat has made the pieces around the crown of her head revert to curls, and she looks about my age. In her arms are two babies, but they're not the only ones. She's surrounded by four more bassinets, each with a tiny newborn inside.

"Identical! The first reported case of natural born identical sextuplets in nearly fifty years!" The newscaster, a young-looking white guy with glasses and fluffy brown hair grins at the screen like this is his big break. "This is Kairee Porter, the proud mother. What would you like to say, Kairee?"

Hack me. They rushed in on her before she's barely had a chance to breathe. She keeps looking down at her kids and shaking her head. "It was supposed to be one."

"And now it's a miraculous six!"

Kairee doesn't look like she thinks it's miraculous. She looks like she barely knew how to handle one of these, and now she's got six.

"Ms. Porter went into spontaneous labor on the Yonge-University line a few days ago and was able to be rushed to the hospital for delivery. Let's hear from her doctor."

They cut to a doctor in scrubs, a young woman with dark brown skin who looks like she may have Latinx roots. "I . . . It's something. Her early scans only showed one, but here we are."

The clip cuts out, not because it's over, but because Uncle Vacu has stopped it. He stares at me. "That's the girl from the subway who I touched."

I want to shout, "Oh, really?!" in his face, but I don't. Uncle Vacu's gift is safe birth, and instead of giving it to one baby, it multiplied them. In the vision, Auntie's fire was huge and out of control. Keis was banging her head on the windows—randomly, I thought at first, but what if it was because of voices in her head, her hearing exponentially more thoughts than she's used to?

"It's amplifying the gifts. Making them ten, maybe twenty, maybe more times as powerful as they usually are, to the point where the witch can't control it anymore. That's what's happening to you," I say, working through it aloud. I press my palms against my eyes.

But *why* is this happening? And why does Luc know about it? It would be so easy to blame him for it, but I don't even know what he could do to cause this. Justin only ever tried to create gifts. What's happening now is completely different.

"What are you going to do?" Uncle Vacu snaps.

"I'm working on it."

The door to the room inches open, and I swing my head around. Alex peeks in through the door and freezes when she spots me on the phone. My privacy settings mean she can't see or hear him, but I've failed to stop the look of guilt that I feel arranging itself on my face.

Alex edges into the room a bit. "I wanted to talk really quick. Didn't realize you were on a call."

Even though I wasn't technically doing anything wrong, I feel like I've been caught. "It's okay, we're done here anyway."

"Are we?" Uncle Vacu grumbles.

"Yes, I'll let you know about any updates." I end the call without waiting for him to respond.

Alex's face is carefully arranged. "Who was that?"

"Uncle Vacu." It would be worse to lie.

She nods slowly. "And . . . ?"

"I . . . I wanted to ask him more questions about what's been happening with him. We have the council meeting tomorrow." I open my mouth to ramble on about how I don't have a plan but shut it. I can't do that. I'm supposed to be the confident Matriarch. I can't start off talking about how I don't know what I'm doing.

Alex's eyes slide to the left, and on the screen is the photo of her dad as a kid with Granny. I freeze, not sure what to do. She comes over and sits down beside me and pulls the tablet into her lap, flipping through the photos.

I watch her without saying anything.

"Sometimes it feels like I'm the only one who remembers that he used to be a good dad," she says, not looking up from the tablet. "Slowly, I'm starting to remember Mom, and so there are better memories now. I didn't have that before. I guess that everything good with him came along with her. And after she was gone . . . there wasn't much left."

"You've been remembering Auntie Elaine too?" Dad did say the memories would come back to us in time. Of course I wouldn't be the only one experiencing it.

"There's one where the ice cream truck is outside. Nowadays you just have to ping it on your phone to stop. But when Mom and Dad were little, you actually had to run outside and catch it. So instead of pinging it, they made it into this race to get there." Alex lets out a laugh. "It was something. Dad piggybacked me so we could be teammates, and he and Mom were dodging around each other to see who could get there first. The people in the apartment building must have thought we had an emergency or something." She looks up at me. "We won, me and Dad. And we ate our ice cream in front of the building."

My throat dries out.

She plays with her fingers—the nails are long and painted purple with a pearlescent sheen. "He looked at me like he couldn't believe it was me, the other night."

"It had been a while," I say quietly.

Her lip twitches. "I wasn't myself yet when he knew me. I was Alex, but I wasn't *Alex*." She waves at herself as she says it and cracks a bit of a smile that fades quickly. "I feel like he only realized that the other night. How much time has passed. How different I am in all the best ways. And I got there without him."

I swallow without saying anything because I feel like, in this moment, listening is the right move.

"I love my dad, Vo. I really do. But just because he's not using right now doesn't mean he's well. He needs *real* help. So be careful about how much you expect."

I tuck my feet up. "I'm not getting invested. I just needed to know a little bit more."

"Okay . . ."

"What was it you wanted to talk about?" I don't want to discuss Uncle Vacu anymore. I don't like the way Alex's face looks when we do. Like there's a weight tugging it down.

My cousin must know I'm changing the subject but goes with it. "Keisha."

"Keisha."

"She's been doing her best with this Keis stuff, and—"

"I know, I know. I was hacked."

Alex looks at me down her nose and gets right into big sister mode. "She isn't trying to replace Keis. She's trying to be your friend in her own right. You two were never close *because* you spent all your time with Keis, you know?"

The sisters clash so hard that being around the both of them is often too much to handle. It's why usually Keis and me would hang out, and Keisha and Alex would hang out. But now there's this gap where Keisha and I have actually been able to get closer. She's been helping me, and instead I've been treating her like a subpar replacement. "I'm gonna do something about it."

"Good." Alex pauses and lets out a breath. "I went in her room the other day to grab something and found lots of snack wrappers in hidden places, but she won't eat with us at dinner."

"Yeah . . ."

"I don't know what to do. I tell her all the time that there's nothing wrong with eating when you're hungry. That that's how it should work. Tried to get her to take that hacked feed addition out too so she's not so obsessed. She won't talk about any of it."

"I don't know what to do either. Did you realize she stopped dating too? She said she didn't have time."

"She's doing so much now. Maybe she really doesn't. But I don't know, how she feels about her body could be playing into it too. We need to find a way to help."

"I know . . . Let's both think about it more and try to figure something out." I fluff my curls and stand. "I'll start with the thing I do know how to do."

Alex follows me over to Keisha's room and she stands out of sight in the hallway while I knock on our cousin's bedroom door.

"Come in," Keisha says from the other side. She doesn't sound upset or sad, just kind of neutral.

I walk into her room, where she's lying on her stomach on her bed, feet swaying in the air. She's swiping through her feed, looks like.

"What are you doing?" I ask, trying to sound casual.

She shrugs. "Apparently Keis used to organize Mom's auctions for her pieces, and of course she's not doing that now, but Mom doesn't know how to, so I'm trying to find a tutorial."

There are so many little pockets of space that Keis occupied outside of me that I didn't even notice until she decided she didn't want to be there anymore, and Keisha was forced to slip into the empty slots. "I could help, if you want."

She shrugs again without saying anything.

I sigh. "Look, Keisha, I'm sorry about the other day. I never meant to make you feel like you're second place."

"But I am."

"Keisha—"

"I don't care." Keisha sits up. "Like I said, I'm not trying to be a replacement. But that's what everyone is acting like I am. I want to be appreciated for being me." She flips her phone around in her fingers. "You know last year in the café with that date when you and Keis came by? That was the first time I ever really talked about how being demiromantic was for me. I never thought I could talk with either of you about that stuff. You were always in your own bubble. And I felt bad laying everything on Alex. Otherwise, I don't really have anyone else I would be comfortable sharing things with. It was really nice. I thought maybe we could be like that."

It felt like we were all friends, me, Keis, Alex, and Keisha. But I guess the two of us set ourselves apart and made it hard for anyone else to join without even noticing. "We *can* be like that. You can always talk to me about anything, and I'll listen. Even if, somehow, Keis and I were friends again, you and I wouldn't stop being friends. We would still be *best* friends." It feels so hacked now. The way I put Keis on a best friend pedestal and acted like that was a spot that only she could have. But people have more than one best friend. After all, I used to have Lauren, too.

Now I have Keisha and Alex.

But I always had them. And I would have noticed sooner if I hadn't spent so much time grieving my lost friendship. Not having

Keis hurts, but I can't let that be the reason I hurt the friends that I have left.

"I really mean that," I say to Keisha. "If you ever wanted to talk about anything, I'm here for you. And if *you* needed help, I would help. It doesn't just go one way."

Keisha squints at me for a moment where I sweat under her gaze. Then she smiles and hops off the bed. "Okay."

"Okay?" That easy?

"You can buy me a present to make up for it."

There it is. That's the Keisha I know and love.

Alex slips into the room. "Seems like you two have worked everything out."

"Why am I not surprised that you were eavesdropping?" Keisha says with a scowl that's too playful to actually be annoyed.

A message pops up in my optics, and I blink at it.

It's Eli, finally setting up that burner app he talked about.

Hey. Make sure you only contact me here. It's encrypted just in case. NuGene has a lot of monitoring security in place to help avoid data leaks.

Keisha raises an eyebrow. "Who are you talking to?"

"Uh . . ." I trail off. Hack me, I don't want to tell her who, but I already know that she's probably guessed.

"Ohh!" she cries. "Is it Eli?"

Alex jumps on it. "You two should go hang out to discuss stuff."

I glare at them both.

"What?" Keisha asks, all innocence. "You have to investigate together, for the good of the family and community."

"I'm not dating anyone. I don't even like him. And he certainly doesn't like me."

"Sounds familiar," Keisha sings under her breath, and I glare at her harder.

Alex at least tries to have more tact. "This isn't about dating, really. It's about, you know, getting your mind off other . . . things."

"And how is hanging out with Eli to investigate Luc supposed to help me forget about Luc?"

Both of my cousins get stumped by that one, and I roll my eyes, replying to Eli's message:

Thanks. Please make sure to monitor Luc, but also his sponsor siblings, Jasmine and Juras. Note if they seem to be working on any secret projects or if they're acting suspicious, and also places where they hang out frequently.

Sure.

Between Luc and Eli, I'm seriously starting to wonder if boys are just this annoying about communication in general. It doesn't matter. This is easy enough. I'll do my investigation and he'll do his investigation, and we can both report separately without having to be involved with each other.

And I won't be upset that I'm not the one looking into Luc. That I don't have any reason to try and get in contact with him or to go looking for him.

It's fine.

The last time that I was at Trinity Bellwoods Park, it was for the cooking competition with Granny. It was also where Luc made it very clear that I was to stay out of his life. It's less lively in the winter. No open patios with people eating ice cream at the bakery on the corner, no couples sipping iced coffees while walking their dogs, and no cyclists with pretty baskets and pastel frames. Instead, there's a lot of brown slushy snow pushed up against the sidewalks and the dull hum of the streetcar driving on the main road.

We're in a paper shop across the street from the park. It's more of a fun hobby and craft store than anything, in business for over fifty years. Keisha is carefully browsing the selection of decorative wallpapers with gold foil details. They sell them here in small batches. Apparently, the popular feed models are updating their walls with these, finding outfits that match, and posting the photos online. It's a trend that she refuses to miss out on, so I'm the purchaser today. Mom is not going to be happy that this is what I'm spending family funds on, but I'm willing to deal with that to make Keisha happy.

Alex strolls alongside Keisha, since she decided to come along too and replenish her supply of glitter and ribbons, which this shop has a ton of. I walk up to one of the window displays and stare out at Trinity Bellwoods Park. I can taste the memory of sorrel on my tongue from the day Granny and I cooked together. The day she told me about her first murder rite that I hadn't even know about. Asked me what I wanted to do with my life, and I didn't have an answer for her. We were just there.

How can she be gone if we were *just there*?

"Vo?" Alex says.

I turn around and wipe the tears from my eyes like it's nothing. "Yeah?"

She frowns, her emerald glittering eyebrows digging in. She follows my gaze across to the park. "We all miss her, you know?"

"I know."

"We're gonna go to the bakery after, right?"

"Obviously!" I gaze sidelong at Keisha. "As long as she's okay with it."

"I'll ask." Alex goes back to Keisha, who immediately thrusts at least five wallpaper options at her.

When I next look out the window, I spot someone who I didn't expect to see there. Chestnut-colored hair and light brown skin, sitting perfectly still on a bench. Maya. Luc's NuSap pet project. She looks exactly like she did at that disastrous dinner last summer.

Or . . . not exactly. She's better than before. Maya scrolls through her phone with ease, none of the jerky movements of last summer. Not to mention, when people pass by close to her, she glances up quickly the way a normal person might. She even smiles a little every now and then, like she saw something funny on her phone.

I wave to Alex and Keisha and say, "I'll be right back."

"You'd better be!" Keisha shouts back. "You have to pay!"

I leave the shop and rush across the street toward the NuSap.

I've only just put my foot on the grass when a voice says, "Voya."

I pause in place without turning around. I know that voice. Of course I do. Whenever I'm out and hear it on a feed, my body turns automatically, because I can't help but want to be close to him. Even after everything. "Luc," I say, finally facing him fully.

And it's a pretty pathetic thought, but all I can think is, *At least I look cute in my coat.*

Hack me.

Luc is outfitted in a black peacoat that ties at his waist but seems to have foregone his usual knit hat for a pair of slick earmuffs. His hands are covered in black leather gloves, and his eyes are Justin's signature red.

I'm careful not to stare too much at his body in a way that I know makes him uncomfortable. Meanwhile, the bionics swirl lazily as he watches me.

I have so many questions, and most of them I can't ask.

Are you messing with people's magic?

Do you know who might be?

Do you ever miss me, even a little bit?

"What are you doing here?" I ask instead.

He nods to his NuSap on the bench. "Socializing her. The AI

improves the more they get out and about." He tucks his hands deep into the pockets of his coat as he looks at me, then quickly casts his eyes to the ground, like he wasn't looking.

Whatever he's been doing with her is clearly working. It's like everything he touches turns out perfect. "Congrats on the upcoming launch," I say. "If Maya is an example of what the new units will be like, it'll be a huge improvement."

"Thanks."

The first few times that Luc and I were together were awkward, sure, but this atmosphere is oppressive. Suffocating.

But he's not leaving. It's not like at the conference where he turned away. He stays in place, scuffing the toe of his boot against the salted sidewalk.

I open my mouth to say something but can't figure out what.

Luc looks up and squints suddenly. "What's inside your mouth?"

"Wha...?" I blink at him, then it hits me. "Oh...the tooth. It's a metal canine...It used to be my grandma's."

He says nothing, just stares at me with those bionics—his own keepsake from his "dead" family member.

"I guess we both kept something from them." As soon as it's out of my mouth, it feels like the wrong thing to say, but it's too late.

Luc digs his hands harder into his pockets. "It was always wrong, you know. You and me."

"I..." I can't even think of what to say to that.

"Everything was a manipulation right from the start. It's not surprising that things were so hacked. We should have known that. *I* should have known that." There's an extra bite on the last sentence. "Why did you come over here?"

"I saw Maya and ..." And I came because I thought I would see you.

It's plain on Luc's face that he's already put that together. "Stop looking for me," he says. "You are making everything so much har—" He cuts himself off and shakes his head. "What do you think is going to change? Seriously? By coming to the conference and coming out here? What is going to suddenly be different between us?"

I can't make my voice work. I don't know. I don't even think I expected anything to change. I guess . . . I wanted to see him.

"Nothing," Luc answers for me. "It's over. Let it be over."

Now it's my turn to stare at the ground. The tears are already building, and my throat has dried out. I don't want him to see. Not ever, but especially not now, not in this moment when in the same place for the second time he's very firmly telling me to hacking leave him alone.

I should want to stay away from him. Especially if his involvement in the future is more than just knowing what happened to my family. If he's the reason our future looks like that. If he really hates me enough to find some way to make that happen.

But at the same time . . . in the vision, he was clearly upset about what was happening. He wanted to stop it. That means somewhere inside this Luc is the same Luc who tried to help us in Justin's office. Who secretly unhooked Eden from those machines to protect her.

Inside, there's still the Luc who doesn't hate me.

But standing here, listening to this version of him, I can't even believe my own vision.

He shifts in the corner of my eye. "Your family are over there."

I turn fully to see Alex and Keisha pressed against the shop windows staring at us. When I finally twist back to see Luc, he's already walking down the street away from me.

I suck in a sharp breath and rub furiously at the corners of my eyes.

I pull out my phone and turn off every alert that has to do with Luc or NuGene. I even delete the screenshots.

Luc is still involved with me and my family. Our futures are intertwined. But I don't need to be the one looking for him anymore. That's Eli's job.

It's over. Exactly like he said.

It's *been* over.

It's time I figured that out.

CHAPTER TWELVE

Ilana Bailey, it turns out, lives in the Junction. It's still in the West End but not as far out as we are. There's a definite aura to the neighborhood that speaks of a somewhat less busy but still vibrant downtown. People walk the streets in their puffy jackets, ducking into the endless restaurants and bars lining the main road, or drag folding shopping carts along the slushy sidewalks from the local grocery store. A group of kids my age hangs out in front of a McDonald's, hands full of fries so piping hot that steam wafts in the air.

I pass by them and turn onto a side street that immediately gives way to detached and semi-detached houses smashed up against each other. They have a lot more personality than the ones in our neighborhood. Every single one is different from the other in a way that makes them distinct without one seeming too far off the mark.

Following the numbers down the street, I stop at 423. It's a two-story house covered in red brick with a shiny black fenced-in porch. I also spy a garage peeking out of the backyard. Walking up the steps, I take in the two Muskoka chairs with what look like hand-sewn pillows and a decorative outdoor mat. The door is a vibrant cobalt blue with a neat little doorbell set into the brick. It's nothing like the big homes that we and the Davises live in, but it's extremely nice for Toronto. And there's something about the feel of it that's homey and lived in.

I ring the doorbell, and after some padding around inside, Ilana opens the door with a smile. Her hair is tucked neatly under a black satin head wrap with wisps of salt-and-pepper hair peeking out. "Look who it is. Come on in."

"I brought you some pone," I say, holding out the tin of dessert to her.

Her eyes light up. "You noticed I ate thirds at your showcase, didn't you?"

"No, no, just thought you might like it." I had noticed that she tucked into more than one piece, though I hadn't kept count. It's in my nature to notice what foods people gravitate toward so that I can bring it out when necessary.

As I walk into the main room, I almost fall over in the doorway. The whole area is open, a straight shot from the front door to the back door at the end of the hall, but everything is immaculate. Soft creams, whites, and grays make up the combination living, dining, and kitchen areas. Everything matches, like it's a magazine layout instead of a real home that someone lives in. There's no flat screen for projecting feeds, just a fireplace set into the wall and made up of the same red brick as the outside.

But more than anything, I notice that I'm the only one here. Well, me and Eli, who is sitting down at the dining room table playing with his phone.

Ilana seems to catch on to my shock, because she laughs. "Don't worry, I gave you an earlier time so we could chat a bit before the others get here. They're coming."

I relax. So it isn't that everyone decided they don't want to do the council after all.

She leads me over to the dining room table, where huge platters of vegetables, fruits, cheeses, meats, and crackers are laid out in the same immaculate luxury as the rest of her house. I settle in and try not to eye the food too hard. Meanwhile, Ilana goes over to the kitchen and sets my pone down, carefully cutting it into pieces and arranging it on a plate.

I sit next to Eli, because it seems like it would be weird not to.

"We have a guest," Ilana says. "Phone away."

He sighs but listens to her and puts his phone in his pocket and forces a smile for my benefit.

I look at Ilana. "Did you put this together yourself?" I ask, waving at the charcuterie display.

"Yup," she says with a smile. "It's a bit of a suburban hobby, but it's a hobby, nonetheless. It's something I took up after I became a Matriarch. Calming. You need those sorts of things once you take on this responsibility."

Looking at her now with her carefully wrapped hair and colorful evening dress, I can't picture Ilana Bailey as the sort of woman who would need a calming activity to be a Matriarch. It's stressful for me because I'm the youngest there's been, without real guidance, and my family is in crisis. Though I guess now all our families are.

I eye the food in its plastic wrap. Eli catches me watching, then looks away.

The back of my neck heats.

"If you're hungry, you should eat some," he says under his breath.

I shake my head. "No, I'm fine. I can wait."

He raises an eyebrow at me before saying loudly to Ilana, "Voya can eat some, right?"

"Of course she can!"

I give Eli a nod of thanks, and he stares back, a little furrow in his brow like he's thinking hard about something. I lift the plastic from the corner of each tray and set about making myself a plate.

Ilana glides over and sets the pone on the table along with the rest of the dishes before sitting across from me and Eli. He immediately shifts his gaze to his Matriarch.

"You have a beautiful home," I say, because it's true but also because it's polite. I never realized how much about interacting with people Granny taught me. Never show up to a house empty-handed when you've been invited. Always compliment the host on something. Pay attention to the things people like and offer them if you can. All these little niceties. Now I wonder if Granny learned them because she was the Matriarch.

And if she made sure I knew them because she planned to choose me.

"Thank you," Ilana replies, and seems to mean it. "How are you doing?"

"Fine," I say automatically.

She laughs. "No, really? It's why I wanted you to come earlier. I know we were tough on you at your showcase about forming this council. Even about having a plan for what we'll be doing. But it's important to give new Matriarchs room to prove themselves."

"I . . ." I don't know what to say. I mean, I don't even actually have a plan for what we should be doing. I'm coming to this meeting with some loose info from Uncle Vacu and from my brief conversation with Luc, without much idea about how it's going to come together. But I don't want to say any of that to Ilana.

Her eyes soften, and she plucks a piece of honeydew melon from the tray and takes a bite. "I was in my thirties when my family decided that I would be the new Matriarch. I hadn't expected it. Our Matriarch at the time had straddled both the Huangs and the Baileys. I don't know if you know that, but you knew about Lee being in that council, so I guess you do."

I nod in confirmation.

"Lee was her own kind of special. All of us expected that her daughter would lead us after her and so on and so forth. Except that didn't quite work out. I bet you know about that, too, eh?"

"I do."

"Clever girl. Or nosy girl?" She raises an eyebrow, and I fight not to duck my head.

Lee's daughter was born without magic due to a genetic anomaly that robbed her of even having a Calling. It's the reason Lee, the former Huang-Bailey Matriarch, joined up with Granny and April-Mae Davis to work with Auntie Elaine and Justin to try and find a cure. Except it went bad. And eventually the Bailey-Huangs realized their Matriarch's daughter had no magic, and they split into two families to use the loophole to crown a new Matriarch. Rowen for the Huangs and, apparently, Ilana for the Baileys.

Except Rowen would have only been fourteen back then, so I guess it was someone else before her.

And yes, I had only found that out because I was nosy about Auntie Elaine's past, but I'm not going to let Ilana know that.

Ilana continues, "We used to crown Matriarchs generationally. But that changed. Everyone voted for me. I had no choice. Why would I turn it down, anyway? Everyone wants to be the Matriarch, right?"

"Not everyone . . ."

Beside me, I feel Eli's eyes shift to me, going a little wide like he's surprised.

But Ilana isn't. "No, not everyone. I knew you would understand that." She finishes off her piece of melon. "I had panic attacks every day for two weeks after being crowned."

I nearly choke on my bit of rolled-up salami.

"I had them before, too. But it was the sort of thing I did feed therapy for. Developed techniques to manage it. But as a Matriarch, it was worse. Anytime I had one, everyone in the family suffered. Using their magic would make them feel short of breath, like they were right there in the attack with me." She taps her nails on the counter. They're a brilliant cobalt that I realize matches her door. "I had Huangs who were my cousins, close as any blood bond, and suddenly we were cut off from each other. Separate. And each of us trying to make our families work on their own created this pressure and competition."

She pauses for a moment, and I don't know what to say, so I say nothing. "Rowen was so young then. She had her Calling already at fourteen. A gift that strong, she was the obvious choice for successor. Even without a vote. It's the reason they chose a Matriarch who was much older than you usually would. She was a placeholder for Rowen, who came into power only six years later. I could tell she wanted to keep us together. Did you know that the lounge she built after being crowned was meant to be a place for all of us, Baileys and Huangs?"

"I didn't." I really, really didn't. I had only ever seen Huangs in there. Now it seemed to make sense, that moment at my showcase when Rowen went out of her way to say hello to Ilana.

"Our family wants to go, I can tell, but a lot of the elder Baileys felt it would give the Huangs the upper hand over us. Whatever that means. And Rowen's parents didn't like it much either, standing out in front of the lounge making stank eyes at any Bailey who even wandered close." She shrugs. "I lost half of my family in one blow, and then they wanted to act like we were strangers, even though we were both suffering. It was a lot of pressure. Hence the panic attacks." Ilana reaches out and pats my hand. "So let me tell you, girlie, when I ask how you're doing, I'm really asking."

I give Eli a sidelong look without meaning to.

Ilana waves at him. "He knows how to keep things to himself. Don't you?"

He nods.

"I . . . I don't know what I'm doing," I confess to her in a way I can't to anyone in my family. "I keep trying to prove to everyone that I can do this. I'm doing my best. But . . . nothing ever seems to go right. I was picked for this. I should be able to do this. But it's like no one but me thinks it. My family questions every little thing I do. At the showcase . . . what Torrin said, that I wasn't a child, that I was a Matriarch. That was the first time an adult even acknowledged me."

I feel the weight of Eli's stare. I wish he wasn't here right now, but if Ilana says he's fine, then I'm sure he is. Still, I can't even imagine what shit he's heard about me that made him stare so hard that first time we met. Every time we interact, I feel like he's trying to figure me out, even as he makes it clear that he doesn't want to be involved with me or the council's business.

The corners of the Bailey Matriarch's eyes crinkle as she smiles. "Oh, honey, none of us had any idea what we were doing when we started. Your granny was no exception. Fake it till you make it to the people who you can't break down in front of, but ask for help when you need it from those you can trust. Plastic coating ain't cute. Try to fake it with everyone, and the cracks will start showing when you don't want them to."

I clench my hands into fists.

"They'll come around eventually. But you need to stop worrying so much about proving to other people that you deserve what you have. All you need to do is act in your family's best interest."

The doorbell rings before I have the chance to respond, and Ilana rises with a grin. "Those will be our guests."

She leaves me alone at the table with Eli, who I know is still looking at me.

Johan, Torrin, and Avery file in through the front door, pausing for a moment to take off their boots and pad into the room in their socked feet. It's an awkward sort of shuffle of balancing on one foot while not trying to overcrowd the entryway. I'm glad that Ilana had me come early so I could avoid it.

Johan recovers first, smoothing down the front of his olive turtleneck sweater and adjusting the cuffs of his slim-fitting black pants. He grins at me in a way that feels like old times, with none of the malice that's evolved since I ruined his ritual.

It makes me suspicious.

He takes the seat across from me and beams at the snacks. "Are these the famous Ilana Bailey platters I've heard of?"

Ilana rolls her eyes and sets down some plates for her guests as Torrin and Avery join us. "Help yourself. Flattery not needed."

"But appreciated?"

That gets a little smile out of the Bailey Matriarch.

Now that Johan is here, Eli seems to have a new staring target. But in this case, I can tell that he's trying hard to seem like he isn't looking at Johan. I guess being the subject of the Davis leader's anger even for that short moment at the last meeting has made him wary.

Meanwhile, I sneak a peek at Avery in her wrapped sweater dress with her locs tied back from her face. She went at me so hard in the showcase, it still takes me aback. This is Dad's cousin. We're blood. But she doesn't act like it.

She catches my gaze for a moment and presses her lips into a firm line.

Guess she isn't harboring a secret fondness for me the way Ilana seems to be.

Torrin spears a green olive with a toothpick and pops it into her mouth, swirling it around. Her short curls have a little dusting of white snow on them. She catches me looking at her hair and peeks at my own. "Ah, to be young with long hair," she sighs. Though she's young herself, even if she's not as young as me.

When curly, my hair isn't that long, just resting on my shoulders, but it is stretched out, which I guess she must notice. "You could probably grow it?" I supply. We have a Thomas Tonic for Hair Growth line that's separated by hair type, but I don't feel confident enough to recommend our stuff these days. It's hacked. It shouldn't be like this.

She scoffs. "Ancestors, no. I have a baby face, and I'm trying to look Matriarch-serious, you know? It's gotta be short. The piercings help too." Torrin does have a sort of round face.

It's strange, looking at them all. Besides Johan, Ilana is the oldest. Torrin and Avery seem like they're both in their twenties. Meanwhile, Granny and April-Mae are older. And now me, I'm the youngest by a long shot.

"Thinking, thinking, always thinking." Johan points a finger at me. "There's always something going on inside that head."

My face flushes, and I try not to cringe. "I was thinking that in my head, Matriarchs were a lot older. I guess 'cause of Granny."

"You do realize that my mom and your granny weren't that age when they became Matriarchs, right?"

"Obviously," I mumble, even though the only thing that's obvious was me *not* thinking of that. "But Lee is older too. I figured that, at this point, most Matriarchs would be."

"The ones before them were. That's how it's supposed to be. Everyone here became Matriarchs much younger than their predecessors."

I blink. I hadn't thought of it that way, but it made sense. "How long has everyone been a Matriarch?"

"Eleven years," Ilana says, though I already knew that.

Torrin shrugs. "Four years." I knew that too. Lauren had told me as much. Though she didn't talk about who came before her aunt, and I assumed it was a more distant great aunt or something.

"Seven months," Avery mutters.

My neck nearly snaps looking at her and my mouth drops

155

open. That's barely more time than I've been Matriarch, but we're so different. I would have thought she had been one for years.

Avery scoffs. "Nice to know your father doesn't see fit to tell you anything about your family."

"Probably he was a little preoccupied with his daughter becoming Matriarch and getting two gifts. But who am I to say?" Johan throws out.

That makes Avery hike her shoulders up.

I offer a small smile to Johan. Today would have been one of my Roti Roti shifts, but instead we're here. I even got the alert saying I was laid off yesterday. It's the sort of thing I thought would make him furious, and maybe it has, but somehow we're still tighter as family than even someone like Avery, who is my biological relative.

Ilana fixes up a plate and hands it to Eli. "Here, take this up to your mom."

A darkness passes over his face as he takes the plate and makes his way up the stairs.

Johan watches him and waits until he's upstairs to say, "How is she doing?"

"I don't know. The doctor said it's a whole bunch of things, from the stress. That she needs lots of rest while they work on a treatment plan."

"But he's back now. Shouldn't that stop it?" Torrin asks.

"Unfortunately not, because now she's stressed about it happening again. It was a lot for her to handle. He was gone for *months*. Can you believe that? Poor woman was worried he was dead. And the police wouldn't touch it because he was still posting on his feeds. She's been having a lot of trouble with him the last couple of years."

I'm reminded of Lauren suddenly. She would run off on her Mom all the time. The amount of times Rena Carter came to our doorstep to see where she was . . . and now she's gone for good. I bite my lip. Eli's mom is lucky that he came back. He's lucky to *be* back. But damn, even Lauren was never gone for that long.

"And yet this is who we're trusting to help us with this investigation?" Johan raises a skeptical eyebrow. "How do you know he's not going to run off again?"

Ilana frowns. "He's a smart boy. He works at NuGene, for ancestors' sake. He's just . . . he's been having a hard time . . ." She trails off. "He's fine. He loves that job. He's there day and night. And he wouldn't leave his mom like this. He's always checking up on her. Sometimes I can hear him talking to her, saying he's sorry."

My heart hurts a little for Eli. He's kind of standoffish but clearly feels guilty about how running away affected his mom. Now they're living with Ilana, and he probably feels terrible knowing it's because of him. Maybe that's why he's been the way he has about getting involved in this whole council. Now all of us are in his business. His cousin brought it up too at the tech conference, which probably contributed to the awkwardness.

Maybe it's a lot less about him specifically disliking me and a lot more about just being in a shitty situation.

"How old is he?" Torrin says, tilting her head to the side.

"Seventeen."

"Has he had his Cal—" She cuts herself off as the sound of Eli's footsteps reaches us.

"Why don't we hear what Voya has to say about moving forward with our little issue?" Ilana says, smoothly covering any spots of silence that would make it obvious that we're talking about him.

"Little?" Avery snorts. "If you want to call it that."

Eli takes his seat beside me.

"Um . . . I talked with my uncle more about what happened. I'm pretty sure that whatever this is, it's amplifying gifts to the point where the witch can't control it anymore. And since a few of us have already had contact with Aaron Bailey but don't show any symptoms, it's clearly not something contagious. It's just happening."

"How?" Avery says, tilting her head. More asking widely than pitching the question at me.

"That's what we need to find out."

"We know that boy knows something," Torrin adds. "Luc, right?" She looks at Eli. "What did you find out?"

He stiffens in place. Even though we had a full conversation about him, he's been ignored by the Matriarchs for the most part. Now he has our full attention.

"Um, well . . ." He fumbles over his words and tucks his hair behind his ears.

I jump in. "Eli was looking into if Luc and his sponsor siblings seem like they're working on anything in secret or doing anything suspicious."

He nods at me. "Yeah, so . . . they work on things together all the time that other people don't know about. It's hard to say what's suspicious or what's not."

"There's no new advances that might point to this?" Ilana pushes.

Johan shakes his head. "The boy was only crying on the lawn, but you're acting like he's the mastermind of this. Let's not go so far down this rabbit hole that we miss out on other leads."

This makes Eli look directly at Johan instead of pretending that he's not. In response, the Davis leader scowls, and Eli immediately turns away.

"What other leads?" Avery barks. "This is the only one we've got."

New advances . . . I think back to the tech conference and try to remember if Luc said anything like that but come up blank. He talked about NuSap stuff, and that information is already public.

There was that one guy who talked about that gene hack thing that he insisted NuGene was working on. But he also talked about monkey pee, so who knows how reliable his information is? May as well check with Eli while we're here. "What about gene hacks? Is that a thing?"

Eli fumbles with the glass of water at his side and takes a drink. When he finishes, he says, "Gene hacks are a theory. I mean, NuGene is researching them, but it's not something that'll be made real for a while still."

It makes sense. I knew monkey pee guy probably didn't have any real information.

"Isn't it more likely this is a magic thing rather than a genetic thing?" Eli asks, raising his voice.

"Finally," Johan says, throwing his arms up. "Some sense."

I hike up my shoulders. "I'm not saying one hundred percent that this is something that Luc is doing. But if he is, if this is revenge, then it's going to involve genetics. It seems worth investigating along with seeing if this is a magic thing, like a developed anomaly or something."

"Wait, revenge?" Avery pegs me with a glare. "Revenge for what?"

"There were . . . some issues."

"Hack me, this is some Elaine bullshit all over again. I'm guessing this is why you wanted to avoid saying he's the one whose path or whatever you changed to make this future? Don't think I didn't notice you not confirming that at the showcase."

I shouldn't be surprised that out of everyone, Avery picked up on that, but I'm saved from correcting her wrong assumption by Ilana cutting in.

"It doesn't matter. Voya is leading this council to help take responsibility. But what's happening is going to affect us anyway. I think knowing that the boy has motive is even more reason to dig hard into what he knows." She points at Eli. "You hear me? Learn whatever you can about any new advances or secret projects."

"Yes, ma'am."

"And what will you be doing, Miss Thomas?" Johan flicks his wrist at me.

I wrinkle my nose. He used to call me that in class when I was little. It could be endearing. But now that I'm a Matriarch, it could also be insulting.

"I'll keep investigating the origin of this issue. I've already talked with my uncle. It would be good to get information from Aaron and anyone else in your families who may become affected. That way you can keep me up to date. If I can figure out anything in common that might explain what caused this, that'll be a big help."

"Good plan," Ilana says with a smile. I'm beginning to like her more and more. "Let's go with that, then, and we'll reconvene next week at Avery's place."

Avery gives a brief nod.

Tension rolls off my shoulders, and I try not to show it. "So, then we're done?"

Torrin scowls. "Um, no. That was business. Now is the part where we eat and gossip."

"Girl, yes," Avery says, bumping the other Matriarch with her shoulder.

I blink, sure that they're kidding. But they must not be, because Torrin immediately hits Johan with a question. "Now, I spied with my little eye Topaz walking around with some hot young thing. I haven't seen that boy in ages, since I missed the last BBQ. He's so grown now."

I stiffen in my seat.

"And when was this?" Johan says, keeping his voice level.

She shrugs. "A while ago, actually. Maybe a couple of weeks? I meant to ask you about it at the showcase, but it was a *lot* more involved than expected. So who is the new boo? Or old boo? He was very cute."

Johan scowls. "They broke up. Some ungifted thing, anyway."

Ungifted. I forgot that some people use that term for non-magic people. I'm not sure if Topaz and his boyfriend actually broke up or if Johan has just decided that's how it is. I know a little about how much it hurts to not be able to be with someone you . . . you care about.

"Well, that sucks," Torrin whines.

Avery frowns at Johan. "What's this attitude about *ungifted*? It's good to spread out, you know? We're basically inbreeding at this point."

"Maybe for your family, but ours has some practices that are harder for ungifted to grasp long-term than it is for someone within our community."

Practices like stringing someone up in a basement and plunging knives into their body. My tongue floods with the taste of my own spit, the air hot and humid like it was the night I was down in that room. My toes twitch, remembering the feel of blood squishing between them and pooling in my sandals.

"Some of us in the community don't like that much either," Avery replies. It hits me then that Avery is the only pure witch at the table. I don't care about our family's label as much as I do their actions that led to it, but even if I did, it would be at least a decade of using pure magic before we could shed that label.

Maybe that's why Avery's the least on board with this. It feels petty for something like purity to get in the way when it comes to saving our entire community, but damn if witches don't love petty.

And I *know* that witches love their labels.

If everything goes well with this, maybe I can start introducing the idea of doing away with those for good. I could show everyone what Mama Jova taught me.

"Too serious!" Ilana announces and pushes the conversation to chitchat about her charcuterie boards. And the gossiping goes on like that for an hour. This person has x gift and is using it for this. So-and-so seems like they're going to marry this person, but whose name are they going to take? Blissfully, none of them mention my family's failing business.

There's a moment when I sit back and watch them. We're leaders of five different Black witch families coming together to help each other. That much is obvious. But this, sitting and chatting about anything and everything, it feels like *more*. Like community. Like my dream.

Eventually, they get tired of the chitchat, and everyone gets ready to leave.

Ilana stops me on my way out. "Make sure you two keep in touch," she says, pointing between me and Eli. "This is a collaboration. You two should both be going *together* to investigate things. There are clues Eli may notice from his connection with NuGene that you wouldn't, and things you may notice being a Matriarch that Eli wouldn't."

The two of us stare at each other for a moment, him tucking his hands into his pockets and rocking back on his heels, and me awkwardly holding onto my scarf.

Ilana rolls her eyes at us.

"Yeah, okay, that's fine," I say finally. And it is. It's not like he's actively an asshole the way Luc was. He's a nice enough guy. And Ilana is right. He might notice angles that I could miss. "Does that work for you?"

He crosses his arms over his chest and nods. "Sure."

Well, at least Keisha and Alex will be happy about this turn of events.

CHAPTER THIRTEEN

I spot Eli loitering outside the Cinnabon without any effort. Shifting from foot to foot, he nearly gets knocked over by someone rushing by with a hurried, "Dude, watch out!" Eli stands there in his green puffy coat, hair slicked back into a ponytail, and blinks for a moment before turning and spotting me. I give him a little wave, and he nods back.

Hack me, this is so awkward.

After Ilana's not so subtle pushing that we actually work together in our investigation, I messaged him on the burner app about coming to Dixie Mall. Part of me thought he would say no and I could get out of it without being lectured by Ilana later, but here he is.

It's a weekday afternoon, so it isn't very busy in the outlet mall tucked away over the border of Etobicoke into Mississauga. Shoppers walk around idly, not so much buying things as they are looking around at stuff. Weekday mall trips are usually for browsing or grabbing one specific thing. Our family had piled into the van enough times to come out to do the very same thing. There aren't really any family outings anymore.

But I'm not here to shop.

"You made it," I say, stopping in front of him. "That guy was super rude."

"Yeah, no, I was just surprised by the 'dude' thing. It was fine."

Mortification creeps up on me. I was sure that I checked his profile. "Sorry, have I been using the wrong pronouns for you?"

He shakes his head. "No. I mean, I use he/him. I am a guy. . . . It's really nothing." He lets out a quick exhale and immediately launches into saying, "Look, I'm sorry if I've been weird. There's been a lot going on with me, and this felt like one more thing, but I *am* committed to helping. Obviously, this affects my family too."

And that was definitely not what I was expecting. "So you don't, like, randomly hate me?"

"No! That would be so weird, right? Like, I don't even know you. What reason would I have to hate you?"

Others have managed before, is what I'm tempted to say. But now I feel ridiculous for even bringing it up. It was like I thought. He was awkward because of the situation that Ilana roped him into.

He shuffles on the spot and looks down at his shoes.

"Um . . . okay." I thought this was going to be a repeat of having to work with a boy who wants nothing to do with me, but this is a complete reversal. "I mean, yeah, that's great."

Finally, he looks up. "What exactly are we doing here?"

"I have to see someone in the market."

Eli nods. "Lead the way."

I find myself standing up straighter. I had been so prepared to deal with a weird, sullen, and reluctant Eli that now that I've gotten this new and improved one instead, it's like my entire body is lighter. I have the tiniest bit of hope that this will work out.

I lead him over to the door tucked away in the corner with the witch mark on it. As usual, no one looks over at us, since it naturally causes non-magic people to look away. Pushing open the glass door, I make my way down the steps into the Flea at Dixie.

The market runs in the basement of the mall, shut down to

regular shoppers a long time ago and reinvigorated as a hub for witches to sell their wares.

Only a few months ago, I met Lee for the first time here. I had been thinking about her ever since that council meeting where Ilana talked about how much splitting the families had hurt. To my own shame, I hadn't thought about the ex-Bailey-Huang Matriarch for a while. Or, I had. I thought of her as a unit with Granny, April-Mae, and their council. But I hadn't thought of her as a person. As someone to consult or include. They had already kicked her out of the community, after all. But she's still a witch. And moreover, I want to make sure she knows what's going on, because she doesn't have a Matriarch she's pledged to who can warn her.

That, and I want to see if she knows of any witches going through the same thing as Uncle Vacu and Aaron Bailey.

"Has this place always been down here?" Eli asks.

"You've never been here?"

"... Is that strange?"

"No, I guess if you don't live close by, maybe you wouldn't come. But yeah, it's been here for a while. Though the non-magic people think it closed down ages ago."

"Right ... magic keeps them out, I assume."

I nod, and we make it to the bottom of the steps, where a familiar man calls out to me.

"Hello, brother, sister!" he cries. "Interested in a lighter?" Guess he's still hocking those since I saw him the last time I was here.

"No, thanks." I wave him off and continue weaving through the aisles, trying to find my way back to Lee. To that booth hidden behind dark cloths where I watched a vision of Luc hang Keis by her neck. The image still lays against the back of my eyes, easy to access, though I work hard to push it away.

"You okay?" Eli asks, coming to walk right beside me.

"What?"

"You seem . . . I don't know, like you're uncomfortable."

Am I hanging out with Keisha right now?

"I'm fine," I say, and push forward.

When I find the curtain that I'm sure is for Lee's shop, I stand there for a moment. It's technically into her back room, so I don't know that I should be ducking under. But I also think if I try to find the front of her shop, I may end up lost.

Eli looks at me and then at the curtain. "Is there a reason we're standing here?"

"Give me a minute."

"Exactly who or what is it we're looking for?"

I don't get a chance to answer, because the curtain jerks to the side and Lee steps out. Her head is covered in a vibrant green-and-gold headscarf tied into a knot at the nape of her neck, and her face has that same tightly pulled smoothness to it that makes her age hard to guess.

"Come on, stop standing around," she says, and disappears back behind the curtain.

I look at Eli. "That's who we're here for." I scramble after her, and he stumbles along behind me.

Her shop looks exactly the same as it did when I was there last, though the polished artifacts on the table are different. I guess business is good enough to keep product moving. The air is heavy with the incense coming from two sticks, these ones smelling like something earthy that I can't quite place.

She waves us over to the little table in the middle of the booth, where we both sit while she fusses with the electric kettle in the corner. "I'm making you tea."

Her tone doesn't seem to invite any declarations otherwise, so I nod. Eli wisely stays quiet.

166

She finishes preparing the tea and sets cups in front of us. They're white ones with a mark in gold on each. Some sort of Chinese character. Maybe for the Huangs.

"I haven't seen your face in a while," she says, taking a sip of her tea. Then she looks over at Eli. "And I haven't seen yours in a very long time, though I still know it. Little Elijah Bailey. Mary's boy."

My face heats up on cue, and Eli fidgets in his seat. I say, "Yes, well, a lot has been going on."

"I was sorry to hear about Ava. Sorrier still that I didn't come out to her funeral. I was worried that showing my face might make things uncomfortable, so I opted out."

To hear Granny's name stirs up memories of her fingers slipping, slack, from my hand. My throat goes dry, and I swallow to quench the thirst. "It's okay. Thank you." Accepting people being sorry is a part of grief that I hadn't thought much about. It's painful, because the words do nothing. But I also understand that people say those sorts of things because they want to show they care but don't know what else to say. What *could* you say? So they apologize. And you thank them. And you both move on knowing that words don't change anything.

Lee looks over at Eli. "Now you, I can tell from the way you're looking at me, don't remember me at all."

"I remember." He says it with less confidence than preschoolers use to lie.

"Boy." She waves her hand at him. "You must have been five or six. It's okay."

All of Eli's body relaxes at that, and he lets out a soft sigh. "I don't. Sorry."

"Like I said, it's fine. How's your mom?"

His face darkens, and he gets extremely interested in his teacup. "She's a little sick right now."

"I heard you ran off. For a long time too."

"Hack me," he mumbles, then catches himself and jerks his head up. "Sorry!"

My mouth drops open.

Instead of getting mad, Lee cackles. "That's what it's like in this community, you should know that. Everyone around here is in your business." She pins me with a look. "Speaking of, what is *yours* with *me*?"

I clasp my hands around the teacup and take a small sip that burns my tongue. "There's . . . Some witches are reporting issues with their gifts . . ." Suddenly, I realize what a mistake it was to not invite Lee to my showcase. I didn't even think of it, and now I can't show her the vision anyway. I used up my three chances. "I saw a vision of the future where witches' gifts go wild and we die."

"We?"

"People in my family. And in the others, too. Baileys. Jameses. Carters. Davises. I wanted to warn you since you're not connected to them anymore. And I wasn't sure they would let you know."

"Oh, I know."

I blink at her. "Really?"

She smiles, slow and wide. "Rowen Huang came knocking. Ilana Bailey, too. Not together, mind, but each made their own way over to me." She lets out a little laugh. "And here I thought no one in the community gave a shit about me."

I balk. Ilana didn't even say anything. I look over at Eli, and he raises his hands as if to say, *I didn't know either.*

"We do care about you," I say.

"Yes, yes. Thank you." She sighs. "Rowen was only a girl back then. I've known her and her brother since they were born. Ilana, too, she and I go way back." Lee looks me up and down. "Matriarchs have been getting younger and younger. My ancestor Papa

Xi-Shi said that old Matriarchs mean life and vitality, and young ones mean death and despair."

I look down at my hands. It's true. Having an older Matriarch means they've lived and survived long enough. Young ones mean they're dying off. "I understand our family, and even yours, but the Carters and Jameses, too?"

"More things than you know changed all those years ago when we joined that council. When we let that man into this community. It's some sparked shit, isn't it, how much one white man could change everything? We let him in, and he destroyed us."

Beside me, Eli shifts in his chair again. I wonder if he's heard the whole story from Ilana. There were so many heavy hints about what went down with Justin, Auntie Elaine, and our family at the showcase that she must have had to bring him up to speed.

Lee continues, "The Baileys and Huangs had a loophole to keep their Matriarch alive. But the others didn't. April-Mae and your granny were strong enough. But the others weren't. Families were scared."

"What . . . are you saying?"

"I'm saying that before then, having a strong Matriarch didn't matter as much. How did your granny's family pick their Matriarch before you all came along?"

I wrack my brain and remember what Granny said to me in the park. "The oldest. She said the oldest child became Matriarch. But then she picked me."

Lee gives a sharp nod. "Your granny did go off script there, but traditionally the Thomases did the oldest. Them and every other Black witch family. But the Baileys and Huangs elect their Matriarchs by voting now. That's how Ilana and Rowen got picked. The Carters and Jameses switched it up too. They got scared. Scared of how things could go down. How Justin could expose us. How we could end up back in chains, in experiments.

They remembered their ancestors dying alone in the name of "science" and didn't want to think of what could happen to them. They decided power should choose. Now they both choose the strongest, and if their current Matriarch becomes too weak . . . they replace them."

I swallow. "That would mean their Matriarch would die."

"And die they do."

Beside me, Eli goes so still that I end up glancing at him. His expression is placid. Is this his first time learning about all this too?

I can't make myself believe what Lee is saying. It seems unimaginable. But then again, some of these families will slice into writhing bodies for power. Why not let a Matriarch who doesn't make the cut die to ensure further survival?

Lauren never talked about who the Matriarch was before her aunt. I assumed it was some older relative who died. But now . . . what if it was someone the family didn't think was worthy enough now that Torrin was an option?

And knowing that Lauren would replace Torrin one day, how was my friend living with that? Did she even know? And how did Torrin feel about it all? They always acted like an ordinary aunt and niece. Not two people with that looming over them.

"The Jameses are a pure family," I whisper. I know that doesn't mean much to me anymore, but it does to them.

Lee nods. "That they are. And if their Matriarch volunteers to die, there's nothing impure about it."

This is why these divisions of pure and impure are so hacked. People twist the meanings to suit them. There's nothing about this practice that seems good. Yet isn't that what pure is supposed to be? But it's not, just like how everything impure can't be called evil.

Magic is nothing more than blood and intent. But even as they mold the boundaries around purity, my point of view is somehow too radical.

"I do feel bad for Avery, though, her mom passing like that. Even if it was her choice." Lee shakes her head. "I suppose you already know, though, through your father."

I didn't. I hadn't even known that Avery's mom was the Matriarch before her and definitely hadn't know that she died. Avery said she was crowned seven months ago. That means she lost her mom just before we lost Granny.

We're blood, and I didn't know a thing about it.

No wonder she seems to hate us.

I clench my hands into fists in my lap. "We could have helped each other instead of sacrificing Matriarchs to close ranks."

"I think they had had enough of us 'helping,'" Lee says with a scoff. "Now, I hear you've got a council going."

"Yes, a Matriarch council. We're going to be working together."

"Good, keep me updated. I'll let the Andersons know." She gets up and waves me off.

"Andersons?"

"We changed our name. My daughter said she told you."

"Who else is in your family?" The way she said "Andersons" makes it seems like there's a lot more than her husband and daughter.

She squints at me. "You're sharp, eh? My family. Others, too. Witches that don't want to be part of the big families. Or witches the big ones have forgotten. We gather under the name Anderson. Make our own family."

I balk at her. A whole other family of Black witches that I didn't know about and that I'm sure others don't either. "You're their Matriarch, aren't you?"

Lee shrugs. "It is what it is."

"Join the council."

She lets out a bark of a laugh. "They don't want me there."

"Johan isn't even a Matriarch, and he's there. You lead a Black witch family. You're part of this community. You belong with us."

"They'll never go for it."

I grin at her. "Good thing they made me leader, then, isn't it?"

Lee regards me for a long moment and a smile spreads across her face. "No."

"Why?!"

"Because I trust you to get this done without me. These witches that I lead, they're Andersons because they don't want to be involved with those families. I'm happy to work with you as a liaison, but I'm done being part of the fold."

I want to fight against what Lee is saying. She's the only one of the original council who's available to us, and I'm desperate to be guided.

Her eyes soften. "You'll do fine without me."

It's one more thing that I have to try to do on my own. I never realized how solitary being a Matriarch could be.

"Have you noticed anything in the Andersons? Problems with their gifts?" Eli stares at his former Matriarch, and I could smack myself. I should be the one asking. If he didn't, I might have forgotten, so caught up in wanting Lee on the council.

She shakes her head. "No. But I'm sure I will soon. These things don't tend to stay isolated for long. If it's affecting multiple families now, I imagine it'll affect them all soon enough."

"Was the anomaly like this?" I ask. "We're wondering if maybe this is a magic thing, or—"

"This is *not* like the anomaly." Her voice is firm. "That happened slowly. Over many generations. It's still going, you know? Just because no one's talking about it openly doesn't mean it's not there. But this? It's too fast. The second anomaly case didn't come out until years after the first. It took a while to track it down, but track it down we did because of Tremblay putting together the genetic links."

"Justin."

She nods. "According to him, magic is an adaptation that we developed and then passed down over time. But now that we don't need magic as much as we used to, it's going through the process of natural selection and causing our gifts and magic to die out." She wrinkles her nose. "Don't know that I agree with him about us not needing magic, but it's not like we had an alternate hypothesis. Anyway, that's why we needed him to artificially manipulate the genes and stop it."

"So if it were anything like the anomaly, it would be slow." I swallow. "Maybe there's some other magic thing it could be? A ritual?"

"There's no ritual or cast that could affect a gift. That's the strength of them. Only way to stop one would be to stop magic, and only a Matriarch or the anomaly can rob a witch of that. Outside of genetics, of course. But whatever strides Justin and Elaine made on that front, we never learned."

"That means this isn't coming from us," I say. "It's coming from someone else."

From someone who could make genetic changes that affect magic faster, the way Justin was supposed to do for us.

I look over at Eli, who's staring into his teacup. His grip on it tighter than necessary.

Maybe when he imagined cooperating with us, he wasn't thinking it would involve this much on his part. But now that Lee has confirmed this isn't magic, there's only one option left.

Luc doesn't just know something about what's happening. He's probably the source of it.

CHAPTER FOURTEEN

When I get back from Dixie Mall, I slink into the house through the front door and quietly press it closed behind me. Now that there are bigger things than the beauty business to worry about, the adults aren't so much on my case about it. But now they're constantly harping on me about the gift malfunctions.

And somehow I'm not in a rush to tell them that Luc is probably the source of this, not some natural occurrence like the anomaly. Or maybe that wouldn't upset them. I mean, we couldn't fix the anomaly, but we can do something about Luc.

At the very least, Eli said he would be doing his part to look into things. I don't know him enough to say that I fully trust him, but I have hope that he'll do this best. Like he said, his family is affected too.

But in the back of my mind, I wish there was a way to get *both* of us access to Luc and his siblings. I know he's the one who's supposed to be looking into it, and I'm supposed to be staying away. But Ilana said we should be going places together, didn't she? Maybe he would miss something that I would pick up on.

I walk down the hall toward the kitchen and run right into Keis on her way out of it. I scramble to arrange my thoughts away from Eli.

"Save me the pain of you thinking about him harder by attempting to not think about him," she grinds out. "I don't care that he got the job. Someone was going to get it, and it wasn't going to be me."

"Sorry."

"If you can't change it, don't bother."

I swallow and stay silent. I expect her to walk past me, but she stops and shakes her head. "After everything Luc's done to this family, even knowing he's probably the cause of this, you still love him. You're still making excuses in your head to see him. Do you even realize how pathetic that is?"

"I'm not making excuses to see him," I mumble. "I just think it'll help if I'm around."

"Because you, the girl he hates, are going to get more information out of him than an employee he's completely neutral toward and has no reason to suspect?" She rolls her eyes at me. "Yeah, that makes sense."

I clench my fists at my sides. "He regretted it. In the vision. He regretted what happened. This isn't like him. He did his best to help us with Justin. You weren't there." The moment it's out of my mouth, I know it's the wrong thing to say.

"Whose fault was that?!" Keis's nostrils flare. "You are unbelievable. You know what? Keep your pity thoughts. You sparked my shit to hell, but don't worry, I'll be fine. I'll pick myself up. Just like you thought I would. But don't forget what you did to me." She stalks off down the stairs into the basement, and it's only when I look that I realize Justin is there, hanging out in the doorway. And he doesn't follow Keis down.

"How are you there?" I swear that I changed his area controls to keep him off the stairs for the showcase, and I don't remember changing it back.

He grins at me. "Glitch with the older models. They have

trouble recognizing stairs as an area limit. It shows up like you've done it on the app, but it doesn't work." He shrugs. "But see, I stayed in the basement exactly as you told me like a good robot. That's called trust."

I glare at him. He's clearly happy to have not reported that glitch before this moment, and it wasn't something we tested either. We were concerned with keeping him inside the basement and inside the house. Not about whether he could come up the stairs.

Justin continues, "There's been a lot of talk of Luc and NuGene lately. You know, I could help you with that."

"Because that went so well the last time."

"Yes, well, last time I wasn't hacking trapped in a NuSap body. I'm *very* motivated now."

"No deal."

"You haven't even heard what I want in exchange."

"No deal."

"Good God, girl, I just want to have the slightest of roaming privileges. It's very dark and very boring down there."

"No. Deal."

Keis stomps back up the stairs and throws Justin a look. "Give it up."

He swears under his breath and makes his way down the stairs. I expect Keis to go with him, but she doesn't. We stare at each other for a moment before she nods. "I'm glad I don't have to tell you not to do it."

"I thought you would tell me to do it."

"Why would I tell you to make a deal with the devil?" With that, she turns around and returns to the basement, shutting the door with a snap.

At the same time, the sound of the front door opening floats in, and Mom comes around the corner. She looks at me, then looks at the basement door, and her eyes soften. "She'll come around. She and Maise are a lot alike, you know. Your aunt can hold a grudge like no one else. But we're family. That always wins out in the end."

"How long will Auntie hold the one against me?" I say, it spilling out of my mouth before I can stop it.

The corners of Mom's eyes crinkle, those wrinkles I never noticed before. "Maise . . . She, and me too, I won't pretend . . . Being the Matriarch was a dream we both had. We wanted to be the ones who helped move this family forward after Mom was gone. We're mourning losing her, but we're also mourning losing a dream."

I don't know what to say to that.

"It's easier for me to get over it because you're my daughter. I'm a lot more preoccupied with how you're handling everything. But Maise . . . like I said, it's harder for her and Keis to get over feelings like that. But they both still love you, you know that, right?"

I don't know that. In fact, I feel confident that Keis is on the opposite end of love from me. Not to mention, Auntie has barely spoken to me in the last six months except to snap at me for something.

Mom frowns. "It'll all work out. But you're the leader now. That means you have to do the things that leaders do."

"Yeah." I press a smile to my face so she'll stop looking at me like I'm a kicked puppy. She's trying. I know she is. But . . . it's not the same as if I knew she had complete confidence in me.

Mom heads into the kitchen, and I make my way upstairs to my room. I want to flop onto the sheets and mindlessly scroll through my feed. Get lost in videos of recipes and cooking shows that I missed when I was obsessively watching Luc stuff. At least watching those can help distract me from being tempted to continue to watch Luc stuff.

I can still picture him. Standing there at Trinity Bellwoods looking perfect and telling me in no uncertain terms to leave him alone.

Well, too bad. He's the reason that I can't.

I reach my room with intentions to carry through on my feed-scrolling plans, but when I open the door, Mama Jova is sitting on the bed, waiting for me.

For a moment I just stare at her.

"Aren't you going to sit down?" she asks.

Because I don't know what else to do, I go inside and park my butt on the bed. "I didn't call you."

"You did."

"When?" I think I would have remembered.

"At your showcase, you called, didn't you?"

That was all the way back on Saturday; it's already Wednesday. This woman really does what she wants. "Uh, yeah."

"There you go." She shifts on the bed to get comfortable. In the back of my head I do have some feelings about her grinding her bare behind into my bedsheets but don't dare say anything. "I sensed that you need guidance as a Matriarch."

I needed guidance months ago when I became one, I'm tempted to snap. "I mean, yes, I'm trying to figure this out, but it isn't exactly easy."

"You can start by monitoring the push and pull of your magic."

"What?" I thought she was going to tell me something to help with my future disaster vision. Not this.

"Sometimes you get upset, yes? Angry, like in Rowen Huang's shop, and what happens then?"

The magic. It seemed to bubble under my skin until it was crawling to the surface. "It . . . rose up. The magic."

"That's the pull. Some of that magic is yours, but often you've tugged it away from your family."

Everyone has told me as much.

"And the push?" Mama asks.

"Pushing the magic into a cast?"

"There." She nods, satisfied. "You put your family at risk when you pull from them without warning. You can't be free with your emotions like the rest of them. Keep your anger in check." She crosses her arms and leans back. "The eldest Davis should be helpful. You're friendly with her, aren't you?"

"Aqua?"

"Yes, she's got a very special hold on her emotions. You should make a point to spend time with her and learn what you can."

It's so strange to hear her basically tell me to hang out with Aqua. But the emotions thing . . . I think of Aqua managing to calm down Topaz. She's definitely good at it.

"Can I get an affirmative on this?" Mama Jova says, voice firm.

"Yes, ma'am," I intone, even though it feels ridiculous to call Mama Jova that when we look the same age. I peek over at her and try to picture her as living. Running around with that boy. A bit of happiness in what was likely a sad life. But even she must have had her own hopes and dreams back then. Things she wanted to do. An idea of the person she wanted to become. I only got that small glimpse into her life, completely overshadowed by trauma. I can't help but wonder what she was like outside of that moment. Before that life was gone.

"Save your pity for the living," she says, catching my eye.

My face gets hot. "I—"

"The moment you were born into our family, with our history, and our skin, life became hard. When Mama Bess was Matriarch and they reclaimed this house and brought it here, when they saw that the Promised Land was not what had been promised, she said, 'It was better, but it was not good.' Those words are still relevant today. Our motto is not 'we suffer and we survive' because we like

179

pain, or even because we think it makes us stronger, though some people seem to have forgotten that. It's a premonition based on the way life has always been for us. They've done away with their harsh words, and they don't own us anymore, but they've never stopped the violence. That's what this is. Violence carried forward. And he's down there, in your basement, coiling his whip."

"Justin?" I blurt out. "I'm taking care of him. He's annoying, but he's not a threat. He's even helping Keis study stuff."

Mama Jova grins at me. "And some masters liked to teach their slaves to read."

Her words send a chill across my back.

I'm reminded of Keis calling Justin's offers a deal with the devil.

I get it. I'm not about to let Justin get involved even if all he wants in return is a back rub.

She continues, "You are the one who has to stop this chain of violence and hate. *You*. People can help, but in the end, you're the one that can change his future, and yours in the process."

"Justin?"

Mama rolls her eyes.

"Luc." I gape at her. "You know, don't you? It really *is* him doing this, isn't it?"

She does nothing but disappear in a whisper of smoke and ash.

I cough a bit and collapse onto the bed. Why can't Mama Jova be like Auntie Elaine? Straightforward. Easy to communicate with.

But she's right. I have to do this. Keis can say what she wants about this being an excuse to see Luc, but I can't rely solely on Eli to get things done. I don't know him well enough to let him handle it alone, even with everything that I already have on my plate.

I open the burner app and start a video call. We need to come up with some sort of plan.

Surprisingly, the video opens immediately. It's Eli in a plain white room. It could be his bedroom, but I guess it could also be NuGene if he decided to go to work after our meetup.

"Hey," he says. He's kind of got a vacant look. Like he's there but also not. Distracted. Maybe he *is* at work.

I shake the strangeness off. "Sorry, are you working right now?"

"No."

"Okay . . . Look, I was wondering if there was any way that you could get us both into the same space as Luc. Like, I don't know, is there a way to do that?"

"An event with me and Luc?" His eyes get an even more faraway look, I assume him checking his schedule.

"Yes, ideally."

"Tomorrow, I'm volunteering at Helping Hands with Luc, Jasmine, and Juras."

My eyes go wide. "That's perfect!" Was he even going to tell me about that or just go on his own? Wasn't he the one who said he was committed to this? "Can you sign me up as a volunteer?"

He smiles. "Sure. I'll send you an invite."

That was shockingly easy. Maybe he really did mean what he said. "Okay, perfect, um . . ."

"Is that all?"

"Yeah, I guess. Oh! I'll pretend that I don't know you outside of the volunteer program to make sure they don't get suspicious."

"Okay." He pauses, then repeats, "Is that all?"

Hack me, he is so hot and cold. "Yeah, bye."

"Bye."

He hangs up without saying anything more while I sit with my phone in my hand. That's it.

Tomorrow, I'll be seeing Luc again for the third time in little more than a week after not seeing him for months. Not to mention, this time Juras and Jasmine will be there too.

I have absolutely no plan for what I'm going to do, but at least I'm going to get a chance to do *something*.

I can fix this. I can try and reach the part of Luc that regrets what he's doing. I can do my best to remind him of the boy in Justin's office who didn't want anyone to get hurt.

The one who didn't hate me yet.

CHAPTER FIFTEEN

A banging downstairs has me jumping up from bed. I stumble out of my thick sheets with full pajamas on, bleary-eyed and disoriented. My room is too dark for me to properly see where I'm going. I shake out my arms, partially to help wake me up and partially because I feel like I need to move.

I stuff my feet into slippers and pull open my bedroom door—

Where Auntie Elaine is waiting.

For a moment, I freeze, wondering if the sound that woke me was her knocking, but then the banging comes again. She's in her nurse scrubs with her hands clasped in front of her and her head down.

"What's going on?" I ask her as I stumble into the hallway.

Dad comes out of his room, shooing Priya back inside. Keis's door stays shut, but Keisha shuffles out of hers down the hall while rubbing her eyes, and Mom ambles around the corner.

Auntie Elaine doesn't look up. "He's outside. In the back."

Dad's eyes are sharp on me. As if he can sense me speaking to his sister, though he wouldn't actually be able to see or hear her. "What is it?"

"Downstairs," I say, loud enough for everyone to hear. "In the backyard."

All of us rush down the stairs and get to the bottom as Keis is walking up from the basement, her pineapple bun askew in a way that suggests she fell asleep working again. She meets my gaze and then heads for the backyard without a word, easily pulling the thought from my head.

I shove open the back door, and all hell breaks loose.

Auntie Maise is in the yard shouting at Uncle Vacu while Alex stands a little ways behind her. Their rooms are closest, so I guess it's not surprising that they responded to Uncle Vacu's knocking first.

Auntie Maise at least had the foresight to cast some sort of sound dampener, because by the back door I can barely hear her, but as soon as I get within a couple feet of Alex, her voice is on full blast.

"Pick up your bags and get gone!" Auntie screams at him. "You lost your right to be here a long time ago."

Uncle's shaking his head. "This is my house too!"

"Over Mom's dead body it is."

"For ancestors' sake," Mom mutters behind me and shoots forward. "Maise, get back inside."

Sparks shoot from Auntie's fingers. "Don't tell me what to do. Last time I checked, you weren't the Matriarch."

"No," I say, stepping forward. "I am."

Auntie Maise pauses, and her lips press into a thin line. But she stands her ground, refusing to move. It feels like a standoff, the two of us against each other, months of her resentment hitting me in a single look.

In that moment, I remember a day, only a couple of years ago, of her helping quiz me for some sort of test. The two of us sitting at the dining room table, cracking up over a joke that I can't even remember. It feels like ages ago.

Now she's standing against me. Disrespecting me and my position at every turn. Like all the adults in this hacking family except for maybe Dad and Priya.

Uncle Cathius ambles out from his microshed toward us. "What in the . . . ? What is he doing here?"

"That's what I would like to know," I say, shifting my gaze to Uncle Vacu.

He grinds his teeth together and points at his bags. "Isn't it obvious?"

"Spell it out for me."

"I got kicked out. A woman wanted my help, and I was trying to explain to her that I can't do that anymore, on account of issues with my gift, and she got *very* vocal. The housing said I was 'causing disturbances,' and I'm suspended for a few weeks. I'm not allowed on the property." He shook his head. "Not that they say anything about the white lady down the hall who's screaming at her boyfriend day in and day out."

I press my hands to my eyes and take a deep breath in. Hack me. I pull them away. "And now you want to stay here?"

Uncle Vacu says nothing but he doesn't need to.

Auntie Elaine grips my arm, and I turn to her. She's staring at her husband with tears in her eyes. "He'll only get worse if he has nowhere to go."

I think of the photos in Granny's tablet. Of her hugging her son tight to her chest. Once upon a time, she turned him away. If she loved him that much and couldn't let him stay, why should I?

"*Please*," Uncle Vacu croaks. "I don't have anywhere else to go."

Alex's head snaps up.

All of us focus in on Uncle Vacu. Never, *ever* has my uncle begged.

My cousin turns to me. Despite what she said in Granny's bedroom about not expecting much from her dad, the look in her eyes is pleading. Alex said that it was like no one in the family remembered that he used to be a good dad.

Auntie Elaine's grip on my arm increases.

"What should I do?" I whisper to her.

"You're the Matriarch. Not me. It's your choice."

I almost laugh. My choice. Everything is always my hacking choice.

But I knew what I would do from the moment Alex looked over at me.

"Uncle Cathius, you'll come into the house and stay in Granny's room. Uncle Vacu, you can stay in his shed. Do *not* come into the house under any circumstances. If I find out you've been inside, you won't be welcome here again."

"Voya!" Auntie Maise snarls. "You cannot be serious."

I ignore her. "You will also leave Alex alone. Don't talk to her. Don't send notes to her. Don't try to communicate with her. Don't even *look* at her. If she wants anything different, she'll let you know."

Uncle Vacu's gaze slides to the ground, and he nods.

"Wait a second," Uncle Cathius snaps. "That's my house!"

"No," I snap back. "It's *my* house. *I'm* the Matriarch." I throw my hands up, and I'm so tired suddenly. Tired of running around trying to protect this family, and save the business, and deal with this Luc shit, and *still* having my authority questioned at every turn. "Granny chose me. And maybe she didn't have much of a choice in the moment, but neither did I. I didn't ask for this! But it's what I am, so you *will* listen to me. Or you can consider yourself spitting on her memory."

Uncle Cathius's mouth drops open, and he jerks back as if I physically slapped him.

Meanwhile, Uncle Vacu picks up his luggage and makes his way to the shed without so much as a thank you.

"This is a mistake," Auntie Maise shouts, her hands coating themselves in fire. "You are playing a game you are not equipped for."

"Control your gift," I say, voice cold and sharp. "Before you bring the house down."

For once, Auntie Maise is speechless.

"Voya!" Mom gapes at me.

Every single decision I make is challenged and picked apart. I clawed my way to this impossible point where I could finally make them, and now every time I do, someone finds a way to throw it back in my face.

Alex's eyes make me draw in a sharp breath. In them is not pride at me for helping her dad but something else. Something that makes her lips press tight and turn down into a frown. She shakes her head at me.

I can't stand to look at her.

"Everyone go to bed. I have volunteering in the morning." I turn away and walk back to the back door, where Keis is loitering.

She opens her mouth, and I cut her off.

"Save it! Whatever hateful thing you have to say. Save it. You're not exempt from criticism because you're stuck here. You're barely a part of this family. You don't contribute. You don't help. And Keisha is hacking starving herself off the pressure of having to take over everything that you can't be bothered with." I shake my head at her, content to explode. "Have you ever thought that maybe you deserve this?"

I'm halfway to striding to my room when I hear my name called, so soft, that I could have easily missed it.

I turn back, and Keisha is standing in the hallway next to her sister, whose gaze is downcast.

Keisha says, "Do you ever actually think about us?" Her voice is strained. "You always say everything you do is for the family, but sometimes it feels like what you do is actually for *you*. And we're always collateral." She shakes her head. "Be selfish if you want to be selfish, Vo. I get it. It's been a lot on you. I try to help, Alex tries to help, and it's still too much. But don't pretend like it's about us. Don't pretend like what you did tonight was for *us*."

I run the rest of the way to my room without looking back, slam the door behind me, and throw myself onto the bed.

The weight of Auntie Elaine sitting beside me appears and doesn't go away, even after a few minutes of me trying to sleep.

"What?" I grumble. "You have something to say too?"

"You didn't have to hurt them."

"If you think that, then you clearly don't know this family well enough." I can't stop it. All the pain inside of me keeps escaping. Whether it's me tugging magic or lashing out.

Maybe Keisha and Keis are right. Maybe everything I've done that I thought was for the family was for me. Maybe I don't actually know how to truly put them first.

Maybe this is the sort of Matriarch I was destined to be.

Just when I thought I was finding my footing, I've messed everything up again. I used to avoid decisions for this exact reason. Now I keep making the wrong ones over and over again. But I can't go back to how I was. Before my task, it didn't matter if I avoided choices. Now it does.

Auntie Elaine lets out a soft sigh. "I think we both know the family better than that."

She doesn't wait for a response before disappearing.

I stay awake under the covers for almost an hour before sneaking downstairs and softly knocking on Alex's door. Even if she wanted me to help Uncle Vacu, I'm sure it's affecting her that after being absent in her life for so long, he's now literally outside her window.

That voice in the back of my head asks me if I'm doing this for Alex or for me, and I don't know anymore.

She's not exactly a heavy sleeper, but not a light one either. "Alex," I whisper through the crack in the door. "Alex," I say again, with a louder whisper.

There's some shuffling before the door opens, and my cousin

appears. Not bleary-eyed. She wasn't asleep then. "Go to bed, Vo."

"I . . ." Suddenly, my voice abandons me. I don't know what to say. I can't stop thinking of the way she looked at me. And how Keisha couldn't.

"I know this is hard for you," Alex says with a sigh. It sounds exactly like the one her mom let out before she left. "I know that. But this is hard for other people too. You're not the Matriarch of nothing. You're the leader of our family. You're supposed to protect *all* of us."

"I am! I'm letting Uncle Vacu st—"

"This isn't about you letting my dad stay. I'm grateful for that, of course I am. But you kicking Uncle Cathius out of his shed and bringing him into the house without even asking him if he was okay with it? He probably would have said yes, but you didn't even give him a chance. Now he's mad. You don't think that's going to cause trouble for Keis, Keisha, and Auntie? Or how about that shit you yelled at Keis? She *deserves* this? Or how about you shouting about Keisha's eating when she's right hacking there. I'm proud of her for saying something to you instead of just taking it. We said we were going to bring that up with her delicately. You told her she could talk to you about anything. How comfortable is she going to feel doing that now?"

I shrink under her words, each one burying me deeper.

"I gave you a pass on my mom. You should have told me about her first, not gotten sparked to shit at the family for hiding her and screaming about her in the kitchen. I had to find out about my dead mom with zero warning. I was upset, but I knew you were going through the most back then. But you can't keep making excuses for hurting people in the family. I'm not gonna back you up on that anymore." Alex crosses her arms, and the beginnings of tears shine in her eyes. "It's like how you keep pulling at our magic, you know? You can't just take from us. If you need help, *ask* for it. Don't suffer and lash out when it gets to be too much. I know you love us, Vo. I know this is *so* hard for you because of that. But the way you're acting . . . that's not the sort of love any of us want."

My throat is completely dry. I have nothing to say.

"I'm not going to harp on you being selfish, because honestly, for so long you never gave yourself the time of day. But I get where Keisha was coming from. This is about you, but it's also about us. There's a balance there. You want to be respected as the Matriarch, but I don't even think you understand what being the leader of this family looks like for you. You're leading us like you're the one and only authority, and you're surprised that they're pushing against that?"

"Granny—" My cousin waits for me, but I can't make the words come out. Only . . . isn't that how Granny was? She told us what to do, and we did it. Except it's not like that with me. No one listens unless I force their hand.

"You aren't Granny, and you're never going to be."

I flinch.

"Maybe you should think about why you assume that's a bad thing." Alex steps back into her room and starts to tug the door closed. "Go to sleep."

Before I can say another word, it's shut, and I'm staring at the wood.

It *is* a bad thing, isn't it? Granny was our Matriarch. She was good at it. Everyone looked up to her. Respected her. Followed her. First Mom and now Alex have told me the same thing. But if I can't be like Granny, then what do I have?

I keep thinking that I'm doing what a Matriarch would do, what Granny would do, but nothing works.

I let out a deep, shuddering breath, my face wet with tears, and start the trek back up to my room.

CHAPTER SIXTEEN

T he next day, I go alone to volunteering with Helping Hands. I'm bundled up in my thick coat with a knit hat pulled over my hair. Alex made it for me a couple of years ago when she got into working with yarn. When I left this morning, I snuck out like a coward. Not wanting to face her, Keisha, or anyone else. I drop into a seat on the GO train, the aboveground transit that runs from Historic Long Branch into Union Station downtown, and stare out the window as we speed by.

As we pass Exhibition Station, I think of Caribana last year, the gunshots, and those two people who died: Lucas and Henrietta. The ritual that I ruined could have protected us. I know that the real blame is with the officer who decided to shoot. But if I hadn't done what I had, it wouldn't have happened. I don't think we should have to take a life to protect each other, but I didn't do anything to help in place of it.

It's been fumble after fumble after fumble since I was given my task. And even when I passed it, what did I really get? A miserable cousin who hates me. A boy I saved who wants to destroy my entire community.

Granny. Gone.

And me with these gifts.

If I can't use them to save us, it's just another failure.

I flood out of the station with everyone else and get a naviga-tor going on my phone. The Helping Hands building entrance is buried in the PATH, and I always get lost if I don't have help. The series of underground hallways that run along the subway have been in place for years, and more keep getting added to it.

The PATH is like its own city right underneath Toronto. I pass by cupcake shops opening bright and early for people looking for treats to bring their coworkers, grocery stores with rows of grab-and-go lunches, and every sort of shop in between—bookstores, LCBO liquor stores, even stores selling luggage.

It's packed as it usually is on weekday mornings. Sometimes it's suffocating down here. The bakery smells mixing with the panic-sweat from people rushing to work, and compacted into the smaller hallways, made stronger by the lack of fresh air.

I turn down a corridor with a line of elevators, checking the board at the front for the right floor and room. A dozen other people pile into the elevator with me, mostly dressed in sleek peacoats and trenches, their hair immaculate and their skin clear. The sort of people who I expect get NuGene mods with the same casual nonchalance that other people use to get Fade Ink.

My brain fills in an image of tawny brown skin and a DNA helix design inscribed on it.

Luc.

In a few moments, I'll be seeing him for the first time since Trinity Bellwoods.

Leaving the elevator, I walk into another hallway and fol-low the posted numbers until I get to 8670. It's a door with a semi-transparent screen to block whatever is happening inside, and the Helping Hands image is pasted on the front.

I walk into a modestly sized waiting room that looks like it could fit twenty people. I thought it would look sterile like the rest of this building or the NuGene public offices. Instead, it has the more welcoming atmosphere of the employee areas in NuGene but with significantly less teal.

The chairs are a stylish cream with a slim but comfortable-seeming cushion, and there's a huge screen projecting these photos and videos of people—previous Helping Hands patients probably. I walk up to the receptionist, who greets me with a smile.

They have a tag pinned to their chest that says their name is Leon and they use he/they pronouns. He's Black and maybe a little older than Alex with dark maroon locs that hang to his shoulders and gold-rimmed glasses perched on his nose. "What can I do for you today?" he asks.

"I'm here to volunteer. Eli put me in the calendar. I'm Voya Thomas."

They look on the computer and say, "So you are. Can you tap your ID to the scanner, let me know your pronouns, and I'll get you a badge. You'll have to sign a few forms, then you can go on back. Eli is already here with the others."

I tap my wrist to the desk and tell Leon my pronouns. They give me a badge that has them listed along with my name and the photo pulled off my ID, and I sign the forms.

Leon grins. "Perfect, I'll send Eli a quick message to let him know you'll be on your way. You can head over to room eleven."

I thank them and make my way down to room eleven. Based on the door numbers, I assume that it's at the end of the hallway.

I'm going to see Luc again, but I can't get distracted by that. I need to focus on learning more about whatever he has planned. About how I can change his mind. Or at least make him hesitate enough to let something loose.

With a deep breath, I'm about to reach for the door to room eleven, but instead it bursts open and Eli charges through. I jump back, and he closes the door behind him. His eyes are darting absolutely everywhere.

"Hi . . . ," I say, watching him. "Are you okay?"

"What . . . Why?" He rubs the back of his neck and looks around. "You're here."

"I'm here . . ." He seems to be expecting me to say more so I add, "Remember? Last night? I said it would be good if I could get into a room with you-know-who? And I asked if you knew about anything like that. You said you were volunteering with those three today?" I don't mention that if he was as committed as he said, he should have told me about it earlier, though I want to.

Eli nods frantically, but his eyes are wide the whole time. "Around what time last night did this happen?"

"I don't know, like six, maybe?"

"Okay . . . okay . . ."

"Is everything all right?"

"Yeah, no, I just . . . sometimes I get a little foggy and forget things."

This is a pretty hacking huge thing to forget, but this is also the guy who ran away for literal months. It's not that easy to guess what his thought process is.

"Maybe we should reschedule to a day when I'm more prepared?" he tries.

I raise an eyebrow. "Do you want to explain to the council why we've postponed this? When we're trying to do as much as possible as quickly as possible? In my vision, there was snow on the ground. Weather conditions are already predicting that won't be a thing in March. We can't exactly waste time." Is this boy completely sparked?

His face drops. "Okay, okay, we'll just . . . We're doing this, okay."

"Look, it's cool. I'll act like I only know you from volunteering. If anything, they'll think I snuck in here. I won't blow your cover. Your job is safe. Relax." I'm reassuring him with how I hope things will be. I mean, they have to know that he's a witch if he's a Bailey, but not all witches know each other. It'll be fine.

Probably.

Hopefully.

Even if we did know each other, I think Luc and his siblings would assume that I'm not going around telling everyone that I murdered the former head of NuGene.

"Okay, let's do this. This is happening," Eli mutters to himself as he goes to open the door. He waits a moment before finally pushing it open.

The room is a lot bigger than I thought it would be, with a small lab area off to the side consisting of some glass equipment and computers, and a patient area with a couple chairs, a hospital bed, and a setup of machines that must be genetic modification devices.

Juras and Jasmine are seated in the lab area chatting with each other, while Luc is in a little booth in the corner, focused on a screen. The three of them aren't in those white NuGene lab coats like I would have expected, but dress pants and button-downs like Eli. I'm in jeans, but at least I have on a plain sweater.

"This is one of our new volunteers, Voya. We just met outside. Wanted to get her up to speed a bit." Eli's voice is both too loud and too high.

This boy is worried about *me* giving him away? He has zero spy ability.

"Luc is taking a call right now." Eli gestures to him in the booth. "But here we have Jasmine and Juras, they're from NuGene. And Luc, yeah, you probably know him ... Because he's the CEO!"

I force a hard smile on my face and try to nonverbally tell Eli to stop being so hacking obvious.

"Nice to meet you," I say to Jasmine and Juras, setting the tone. Assuming I'm operating like I don't know Eli, it would make sense for all of us to pretend not to know each other, because explaining how we do know each other would be a lot.

Jasmine pulls a smile that looks so natural, mine slips off my face. It's truly like this is the first time she's ever met me. Like she doesn't know that I "killed" her sponsor dad . . . but she has to. Luc seems so close with them now. He must have told them, right? "Nice to meet you, Voya. Looking forward to working together today."

Juras, on the other hand, physically steps back from us without saying anything. He goes to fiddle with something in the lab, but his hands are shaking and his body is stiff. He was already slim before, but he looks even smaller now.

The booth door opens, and we snap our heads to it as Luc steps out. I meet his eyes at the same time that he meets mine. I expect the cold detachment that he served me at Trinity Bellwoods, but he just looks tired.

"I have to go and greet the patients," Eli says suddenly and turns toward the door.

I jerk my whole body to him and blurt out, "Right now?" There's no way he's going to leave me alone with them, right?

He tilts his head at me, suddenly super calm like he wasn't freaking out a moment ago about me being around them. "Yes. They're at the front desk." Without another word, he opens the door and disappears.

Slowly, I turn back around to Luc, Jasmine, and Juras.

Hack me. Hack me. Hack me.

"Perfect," Jasmine says, the smile gone from her face. "Now you can go. Because I think we all know that you can't stay here."

"Eli—"

"—Yeah, I'm still trying to figure out how you got your claws into him. How you got here at all."

I scowl. "I signed up to volunteer, so I'm volunteering. I literally just met him."

Jasmine is about to say something else when Luc cuts her off. "It's fine. Let her work through her shift."

"You have to be kidding."

He shakes his head. "It'll create more questions to answer if she abruptly leaves. This is a top-rated volunteer program. They're going to follow up if someone comes in and doesn't complete their time. It's fine."

"I still don't understand how she even got in here."

"Drop it, okay?"

Maybe it's the weariness in Luc's final words, but Jasmine doesn't push anymore. She scoffs at me and moves to Juras, gently running a hand across his back. He's still refusing to turn around, but I notice the slight trembling of his shoulders.

Finally, I understand.

He's scared.

Scared.

Of *me.*

In their world, I'm the villain.

And in mine . . . I meet Luc's stare across the room. Bionics swirling. In my world, they should be the villains too. Except, I understand. I threatened their family. I could picture Keisha or Alex doing the same thing. I hurt Juras because I couldn't trust myself and my ancestor. And Luc . . . even after seeing the vision, I can't help but think of the boy who pressed his lips to mine in a park on a warm summer day.

"May as well take your coat off," he says with a sigh, gesturing to the coatrack in the corner of the room.

"Right." I shrug off my giant parka and hang it on the rack.

I did not think this through enough. What am I even supposed to ask them about? Anything is going to seem suspicious. I guess I thought that if I was around them, I would learn something more than Eli would. But now I'm wishing he would come back.

As if on cue, the door opens, and Eli comes in with three people. He guides each of them over to a station where Juras, Jasmine, or Luc is assigned.

Eli looks at me. "You can work with—"

He doesn't get to finish because Luc cuts in. "She can work with me."

Jasmine gives Luc a look so sharp that I flinch a little.

"Okay!" Eli chimes, chipper like it's nothing. He's probably proud of himself for putting us together without even having to try.

"Are you coming?" Luc says, meeting my eyes again. I swallow and nod.

Our patient is Mr. Goban. He's a Black man who seems like he's in his forties, close to Uncle Vacu's age. Nevertheless, he's got deep bags under his eyes like he's lived for a lot longer. He's set up on a bed next to the genetic modification machine. "Hello there," he says to me. "Are you a geneticist too?"

I laugh. "Oh no, that's a little above my pay grade."

"Oh, yeah? And what is that?"

I grin. "Nothing."

"Volunteer?"

"Yup."

"Do you want to be one? A geneticist?"

"Nope."

He laughs. "Then why are you here, if you don't mind my asking?" I can feel the heat of Luc's gaze on the back of my neck while he sets up the computer.

I pause. "My late aunt, she was nurse and spent a good chunk of her life trying to help people who needed genetic intervention but couldn't get it. I think she would have healed the world if she could." It's not like I came here with a practiced answer. I guess if I was good at this whole undercover thing, I would have. It's just what comes out. And sure, maybe it's not why I'm here, but it's still true. I wring my hands together and force a smile for him. "I'm not very good at helping people. I feel like the more I try, the worse I make it. But I figure if I can make a small difference somewhere, that I'm honoring her, in a way."

Mr. Goban nods. "That's very noble."

"A little selfish," I say, thinking of Keis and Keisha's words. I can see it more now. How it matters too much to me what they think *of* me. But I can't stop it. I care if my family and my ancestors think I'm worthy. I always have.

"True altruism doesn't exist."

I give him a small smile, but I don't know if I can let myself off the hook that easy. Maybe he's right. But I'm the leader of my family now. They need to come first. I thought I was putting them first. But I haven't. I've been so caught up in what they think of me that it's somehow taken a back seat to actually helping them. To helping this community. To doing what I promised Mama Jova I would do.

Luc clears his throat. "I'm starting the procedure. You can relax. We'll do about a third of the changes today and give you time to recover. Then you'll come back for two more treatments, okay?"

"Plug away!" he exclaims.

I laugh, and Mr. Goban rewards me with a grin. I wonder if he's a dad. He has that sort of energy. He tilts his head up to look at Luc. "Now, son, are you going to hook me up with a NuSap discount or what?"

This time, Luc laughs. Really laughs. I haven't heard that laugh in a long time. Didn't think I would ever hear it again outside of a feed recording. "I'll see what I can do."

"What will you use it for?" I ask Mr. Goban.

He shrugs. "This and that. Half of us don't even know, I think, but now that we can afford them with those pay plans, we all want 'em," he says with a grin. "I heard some of them can give a pretty nice back massage."

"Can rub your feet, too," Luc adds. "Pick up and put away your groceries. Clean your house top to bottom. Watch a movie with you if you're lonely. Convenience and company are the top things people look for in robotic assistance."

"Oh, all of that!" Mr. Goban says with a low whistle. "You all keep coming up with more and more, don't you?"

Sensing an opening, I say, "Like genetic hacking." Maybe monkey piss guy is full of shit, but I want to see what the leader of the company himself has to say about it.

"Isn't that the thing where you can give people a shot instead of hooking them up to this machine? Some of the volunteers were chatting about it last time I was there."

I blink at Mr. Goban. I didn't expect this to be something noteworthy enough that volunteers would be talking about it. But I guess it's fair to say they must generally chat about new genetics research.

"It's theoretical," Luc says with a thin smile. "Genetic modification as a process was only even invented in the last eleven years. If we could use a shot, we wouldn't be bothering with these bulky machines."

"You wait and see, boy," Mr. Goban says. "I thought the smartphone was the peak of technology, and now we've got chips in our brains."

"Under your skin."

"Pft, it's still sending signals to my brain."

I look over at Luc and say, "I would think that you would know better than anyone how fast technology can advance." Like, do you have something you could advance enough to manipulate magic? To make gifts go wild?

"That's the thing about knowing a lot about technology. You're also very aware of its limits." Luc gives me a long stare before turning away.

The procedure finishes quickly, and I also learn that Mr. Goban lives in Scarborough with his wife and their cat. Cat dad.

Eli jumps up to escort him out. Jasmine and Juras are still working with their patients.

I swallow and say to Luc, "Why did you invite me to work with you?"

"You clearly came here to get something out of me. I figured I would save us both the trouble."

It's so direct that I don't even know how to respond to it.

"Did you have that fake reason for being here prepared, or did you make that up on the spot?" he asks.

"What?"

"What you said about your aunt. That's obviously not why you're here."

I stare at Luc, our eyes level. I could lie, but what would that get me in this situation? The whole point of coming here was to try and reach the Luc in my vision who regretted what happened. How can I do that slinging lies?

"Yes, I came here because I knew you would be here. But as impossible as it may seem to you, multiple things can be true at once. My aunt wanted to help people. And maybe you forgot or didn't know, but she died to protect my family from Justin. So excuse me for also wanting to feel connected to her." I wave my hand around the space. "Isn't that why you're here? Because you want to have some sort of connection to the people who benefit from genetic mods?"

Luc swallows and tries to set his mouth in a frown, but it's not quite working.

"Right from the start, I knew what pursuing a match with you meant. I went into it to fall in love, knowing I would have to kill you . . . Or I thought so, anyway. Obviously that didn't happen. You're alive. And if I had it my way, my grandma wouldn't have died, and Justin wouldn't have died."

"He didn't die," Luc whispers. "You killed him."

"My grandma didn't die either."

He flinches.

Unlike his sponsor siblings, he was there. He knows what Justin did. That he forced Granny's death under threat of hurting Eden.

"I miss her every day," I say, so quiet I don't even know if he hears it. "No one else has to die, you know that, right?"

"No one is dying."

But they will. I don't know if the Luc I'm talking to right now doesn't know that yet. But my vision . . . Things will get worse.

"Time for you to go," Jasmine says across the room. I jump in my seat, and when I look around the room, both of the other patients are gone, and Eli hasn't returned.

Wow, that boy really threw me to the sharks.

I go collect my coat without a fight.

Juras is still sitting at his station, resolutely looking away from me. "I'm sorry," I say to him, because I can't *not* say it, looking at him like this, too scared to even turn around. "For what I did to you. I wish I hadn't, but I did."

Slowly, he turns to look at me. I'm shocked that he doesn't ignore me outright. "I don't accept your apology."

That response, on the other hand, is not shocking at all.

"That's okay." I turn to Jasmine next. "I'm sorry about Justin. I imagine you won't accept that either, but I am." I'm not sorry about what I did. About the man in our basement. But I'm sorry that they can't know he's alive. That they have to grieve like I am. That they think someone they loved is gone forever.

Jasmine doesn't respond at all.

"I hope that we can all move on," I say finally. "Live our own separate lives."

It hurts. The word "separate." Cutting myself off from Luc. But clearly that's what he wants, and if they stick by it and stay out of ours, we can change that future I saw.

I tried. This was only my first real shot at it, but I really tried to make them understand. To hold out that olive branch. If Luc and his siblings are behind this, I've made it as clear as I can that I don't want a war.

I walk to the door and reach out for the knob.

"I'm sorry about your grandma," Luc says. His voice is so soft that I almost miss it.

I pause with my fingers on the doorknob but don't turn around.

"That's the only time I'm ever going to say that."

"Thanks," I reply, then I push the door open and leave.

I manage to get myself out of the Helping Hands office, then stumble into a bathroom and find an empty stall at the back. I sit down, put my hands over my face, and bawl. Choking, deep, and heavy sobs. I cry so hard that a woman taps on the stall door and asks if I'm okay, and I have to tell her in a voice thick with tears that I'm fine.

I don't even know what it is. If it's me being grateful that Luc actually feels bad about Granny. Or if it's the crushing pain of knowing that it doesn't hacking matter if he's sorry because she's still gone.

With a few long, deep breaths, I manage to get enough under control to leave. As I'm coming out of the bathroom, I get a message from Aqua of all people.

Hi, Voya! Hope I'm not bothering you, but I kind of need some help, and Emerald already said no. If you're free this weekend, can you meet me somewhere? I need to do something for Topaz, and I'm nervous to do it alone.

I message her back: *Sure, I'll come help.*

Aqua is the sort of person who is always helping other people, so if she needs it for once, it's probably important. Besides, Mama Jova told me that I could learn from her. No better time than the present.

"Hey."

I jump at the sound of Eli's voice.

"Hack me." I press a hand to my chest. "How long have you been there?"

"Not long. Leon at the front desk said you seemed upset."

I shrug and resist the urge to rub my eyes. "I'm fine." I wave my hand generally in the direction of the Helping Hands office. "That wasn't a complete disaster. Though, honestly, you could have been more help."

He drops his gaze to his feet. "Yeah, I know."

"You need to, like, calm down. Yesterday you were talking such a big game about starting over and working together. You even set this up. Now today you're all cold feet and freaking out. You left me alone with them when we're supposed to be working together. I just, hack me, I have no one else to help with this." By the time I finish, my chest is heaving, and tears are pricking the corners of my eyes again. "I'm sorry, I—"

"Do you really think people are going to die?" Eli asks, cutting me off.

I squint at him, my jaw dropping. Didn't this fool see my vision along with everyone else? Did he forget that too somehow? "I get it, visions don't always come true, and the future is flexible, blah blah blah, but what I saw *will* happen if we can't stop it." I lean against the wall. "If what I said made a difference to Luc and his siblings, then we shouldn't see any more cases of this, right?"

"Right." Eli grips his hands into fists. "And . . . if it doesn't stop?"

"Then I guess we'll have to do something about it, won't we?"

And for the first time since Ilana volunteered him, Eli actually looks serious about this. There's something different today than there was yesterday. "I'm going to do better, I promise. We'll work together." He reaches out his hand to me. "No one dies," he says, voice resolute.

"No one dies."

We shake on it, and there's something official-feeling about it. For this to work, I need Eli, and if he wants to help, he needs me too. We need each other. It feels like everyone has been piling everything on me. I have to lead the council. I have to be the perfect Matriarch. I have to solve this problem.

Everything by myself.

But now I have someone to help. And taking his help doesn't feel like letting anyone down or giving in. It feels like the natural thing to do.

"Can I ask you something personal?" I say suddenly.

Eli tenses.

"You can say no."

"What is it?"

"If Ilana needed help with something and she asked you, what would you think of her?"

He frowns and tilts his head to the side. "That . . . she needed help?"

"You wouldn't wonder why your supposedly powerful Matriarch couldn't do it all by herself? Or think that maybe she must be struggling if she needs you?" I wave my hand at the Helping Hands doors. "I mean, it's not like Luc is always asking other people how to run the company. How would they respect him otherwise?"

"You might be surprised," he says, sticking his hands in his pockets. "Jasmine and Juras are always with him. I doubt he never asks for their advice. Sometimes people respect you more as a leader if you ask for help when you need it. If you're trying to do it all alone and failing, that's worse for everyone. You're just saving face at the expense of the people you're supposed to help."

He's right. Like how Keis, Keisha, and Alex were right. If it's more important for me to seem like I'm a worthy Matriarch to the point where I hurt my family because of how badly I'm failing, who does that help? No one but me. And even I suffer for that.

There was such a relief in knowing Eli would help me. If I had that from my family, maybe things would be easier. I've avoided it because I didn't want to lose respect that I didn't even have. But I keep making things worse. I asked for their help with the showcase, and it's one of the few things that's gone right. Maybe if I asked for a bit more, I could actually do this. Could protect them and the community, because it's obvious that doing it alone isn't working.

"Thanks," I say to Eli with a little smile. "You're surprisingly wise."

"That's borderline insulting."

I balk, and a smile quirks to life on his face. I relax and give the toe of his boot a nudge. "Get used to it, partner. I guess we'll be working together for the next little while."

"Should I also get used to you crying in bathrooms?"

"Yes. I cry all the time. It's my brand."

Eli smiles wider, and I smile back. And for a moment, I get my grasp back on that small feeling of hope that we can do this.

When I get back home, there's activity in the kitchen. I shrug off my coat and make my way over there. Dad and Priya are eating some sort of meal with Eden at the island, while Keisha and Alex chat about something on her phone screen. Uncle Cathius is setting himself up with a cup of tea.

A quick glance into the dining room shows Auntie and Mom chatting over their own steaming mugs.

It's one of those weird weekdays that for our family ends up being more like a weekend. Everyone in the kitchen freezes when I come in.

I drop the dozen donuts I picked up from Tim Hortons onto the countertop. If it were my choice, I would have gone with artisanal cupcakes or something. But I know exactly which Tims donut everyone in my family loves. Even I-refuse-to-eat-non-home-cooked-food Uncle Cathius loves himself an apple fritter.

"Could everyone come in here?" I ask. "You too, Keis. I know you can hear me."

The family gathers in the kitchen, and after a moment, Keis comes up the stairs, dragging her feet along behind her. Thankfully, Justin doesn't come up to spectate.

Mom raises an eyebrow at me, and I smile. "I wanted to say that I'm sorry. About yesterday, especially, but also about so many things these past few months. I know I'm the Matriarch, but I don't want to be a dictator. I don't want to say things that are hurtful because I'm frustrated and upset or because I'm under pressure." I straighten and meet the eyes of my oldest cousin, then Keisha, and finally, Keis. "I'm lucky to have family who help me realize that." Eli, too. But I refuse to mention him and have to deal with suggestive wiggling eyebrows.

Alex gives me a soft smile, and I try not to preen under her approval. It means a lot. Even Keisha shares a little nod. Keis doesn't respond in any way, and that's fine too. This isn't supposed to be about me feeling forgiven. It's about my family feeling that I'm doing right by them.

Luc and his sponsor siblings inadvertently helped too. We're both protecting our family, but they're standing together, whereas

I've been standing apart from mine. There's no version of my life where I think that's okay. Alex was right.

I'm not Granny. Granny is gone.

I can only be who I can be. I haven't figured out how to be a Matriarch as me yet, but I know that I don't want to be the kind who makes my family feel the way they did last night.

"I need help," I say finally.

It takes everything for me not to pull back the words. Saying this, admitting this, it gives them more space to doubt me. To judge my leadership. But I *do* need it. "From everyone. And I need everyone to help everyone else too. I know what Uncle Vacu is like, but I also know I don't have the experience with him that all of you do. Still, I need to give him a chance. And yes, I should have figured out how to do that without alienating everyone else."

Auntie Maise crosses her arms and looks away. "I didn't make it easy for you. I know that." It's as much of an apology as I could ever expect from her. She glances sidelong at Keisha. "You either."

Keisha blinks at her. "What did I do?"

"No! Ancestors help me. I mean that I haven't made things easy for you."

"I'm fine."

"No, you're not."

Keisha frowns but doesn't say anything else.

I dig out a bottle of nail polish from my pocket and slide it over to Keisha, who eyes it for a moment before grabbing it and examining the color. "It's cute, I guess."

That's as good as it gets for compliments from her. But in case she doesn't feel comfortable eating, I still wanted her to have something special.

Alex says, "I'm okay with Dad being out back for now, but it's not a permanent solution."

"I know."

My eyes find Keis across the room, but she doesn't say anything. She goes around us to grab a butter knife out of the drawer,
then comes back, pops open the donut box, and cuts a honey cruller carefully into quarters and starts eating a piece.

"Well, since they're here," Auntie Maise says, and grabs a
chocolate dip for herself. Everyone gets in close to pick at which
donuts they want.

Keisha sneaks out a hand and grabs one of the quarters of the
cruller that Keis cut up.

I meet Keis's eyes.

It's one of the few favorites that she and her sister share.

I know that at any other time she would eat the whole thing.
She cut up that donut so Keisha wouldn't have to battle over eating a whole one, or cut it herself, which she probably wouldn't do,
because we would all be watching.

It was the wrong way for me to say it, but what I said has
clearly made Keis pay a lot more attention to her sister.

"I'll figure out somewhere else for Uncle Vacu to stay." I nod to
Uncle Cathius. "And you'll get your place back."

"Pft," Auntie snorts. "He's in the Matriarch room like he's
always wanted to be. He's happy as hell."

Uncle scowls at her but doesn't deny it. Just chews on his apple
fritter. "I guess he can stay there for a little while."

"You said you wanted our help," Alex cuts in. "I'll find something for Dad."

I splutter. "I can't ask you to—"

"I want to. I know him. I can find something."

"Okay . . ."

Mom brushes a hand across the top of my head as she licks
the glaze from her honey dip donut. She has the worst ways of
eating everything. "Tell us what you need, Vo. We can help too."

"I just . . . I want you to have some confidence in me." I swallow and grip my hands into fists, finally saying aloud what I've been wishing for these last six months. "I know that I'm not Granny. But she chose me, and Mama Jova, too, but you treat me like it's a mistake. It doesn't help me to have every move I make second-guessed and reduced to me being 'a child.'"

There's a balance. I need to focus more on helping the family, *actually* helping, but I also can't be constantly overwhelmed. I beat myself up enough on my own about my choices. It doesn't help me make them to have everyone else join in.

Dad meets my eyes and says, "The ancestors don't make mistakes. If they chose you, if Granny chose you, then you're the right choice."

Mom nods furiously. "None of us should have ever made you feel otherwise. We're sorry."

Slowly, there are nods around the room from the rest of the adults. My shoulders relax, and it's like I had been holding them tense for so long that I forgot they could do that. I know it's not that easy. I can't just ask them to respect me and get it. But at least now they're thinking about it.

And I'm thinking too. About what putting my family first really means.

That small step forward is enough.

CHAPTER SEVENTEEN

I can't remember the last time I baked or cooked something for myself like I used to. The meal before the showcase doesn't count, because it was secretly a bribe, and I was so panicked about the actual showcase that I couldn't even enjoy what I made then. This pastry is ulterior-motive free.

I'm in the kitchen by myself, rolling out a chilled piece of rough puff on the countertop. It's Saturday, which for most families would mean that their house would be full of everyone running around, but that was yesterday for us.

Today is a workday. Mom went off to meet with clients, same with Auntie Maise along with Keisha to help her. Alex has a meeting with a feed shop that wants to carry some of her clothes, and Uncle Cathius is doing ancestors-know-what. He used to follow Granny around and program our drone orders. But now that we basically have none, he's just doing whatever. Dad and Priya are both off at appointments too, and Priya brings Eden to work with her now, too afraid of my sister having a flashback without one of them around to help.

The only other people home are Keis and Justin, and they're not about to keep me company.

It's like being in an empty house.

I work my fingers faster so the dough doesn't have time to get warm. If it doesn't stay chilled right up until going in the oven, I'll lose the layers. Pressing on the metal cutter, I make precise squares and place them on a sheet lined with a slip mat.

In the corner of my eye, I watch the time. Aqua wants me to meet her at the Eaton Center in a bit. She was being cagey about it via messages, which could mean anything, to be honest.

I'll probably only have enough time to bake these and pack one to take along before I need to run to the GO train station.

The doorbell rings, and I jerk away from the kitchen island.

I grab the tray of dough and stick it in the fridge.

As I pass by the basement door, I half expect Keis to come up to see who it is. It's weird to have people visit unannounced. Suddenly, I feel bad for how I dropped in on Aaron Bailey. I don't really have time for anyone.

I pull open the door and blink wide-eyed at Eli standing on the step. He's bundled up in a bomber-style army-green parka and looks his usual uncomfortable self. I can't keep the surprise out of my voice. "Hey . . ."

"Hi . . ." He flounders for a moment, clearly wrestling with what to say. "I thought that I would come by and maybe we could chat about things? Like the NuGene stuff, etcetera."

"Oh, I mean, yeah, okay, but I need to go somewhere in a bit."

"That's fine."

I step away from the door and let him inside. He doesn't make any effort to take off his jacket, and I don't offer.

"I'm just . . . working on something in the kitchen," I say, and start heading over there—making sure to go the long way around through the dining area to avoid the basement door. He follows along without being told, and once I get to the island, I wave him over to a seat and pull my dough back out.

He looks down at the tray. "You still cook a lot?"

Still? Since when does he even mean?

Eli must catch the confusion on my face because he quickly amends, "At the showcase you said you cooked at Johan's restaurant. I didn't know if you liked doing that in general."

"Oh!" I shrug and let out a breath. "Honestly, I haven't done it for fun in a while. I kind of do it to get it done now."

"Like a job."

"Pretty much."

He looks down at the dough as I spread the cream cheese filling over it. "Doesn't that make you sad?"

"Yeah, I guess. Maybe that's why I wanted to do it today? I dunno. I think I always knew that when I got my gift, my life focus would shift, but it shifted a lot more than I ever expected. I just don't have time for it."

"Right." He twiddles his thumbs. "My, um ... dad always liked that quote, you know, the one that's like, 'When I became a man, I put childish things away,' and that it was important to move on. That things you do when you're a kid, even the people around you, it changes when you grow up."

"I don't think I like that very much," I mutter, not meaning to.

Eli chuckles. "It's true, though, don't you think?"

"It is . . . but I would give anything to keep everything I had when I was a kid." Though I hate to admit it, I'm still a kid, I just don't have the same life anymore. I wish that I could have Granny. Grandad, too. That Keis was my best friend again. I wouldn't be the Matriarch. None of us would be in danger. My Calling wouldn't have happened. "Do you ever wish you didn't have a Calling?" I ask him.

Eli's face smooths out for a moment, becomes perfectly blank. "I . . . Why? Do you wish you hadn't?"

"I used to be so afraid of not getting to be a witch. I guess I wonder what it would be like if I had never even had the chance."

"I think if you hadn't," Eli says, looking into my eyes, "you would wish you had. Maybe just as desperately. Magic is power. It's a lot of power. And when you're powerless, it's the only thing you want. Because not having it means being afraid."

I think of Juras in the office, shaking because of how scared he was of me. "I guess. But then I think of everyone who got hurt during the process, and if I could, I would rather not have magic. Just be afraid and spare them the pain."

"You can't mean that."

I raise an eyebrow at him, and he hunches in on himself.

"When is your train coming?" Eli asks, changing the subject. "I'm not holding you up, right?"

"No," I say, shaking off his comment. "They come like every thirty minutes."

"On weekends, too?"

"On . . ." It hits me then. The train doesn't have as much service on weekends. Hack me, I didn't even think of it. "Oh shit, I have to go right now. Uh . . ." I can't leave though. We didn't even talk about NuGene. "Want to come?"

We manage to make the train downtown, and Eli spends the ride catching me up on what happened after I left volunteering. Apparently, it was pretty normal; Luc, Jasmine, and Juras went about their business. He says we should get the Matriarchs to have their people who are showing symptoms create daily logs of how they feel and how their magic is reacting, the same way that NuGene collects qualitative data during their studies. He rambles on about graphs and data points.

I'm hit with a memory of Luc that day we were researching Justin and Elaine, when he talked about genetic modification machines. He and Eli have the same fever and passion. Maybe this is the way NuGene people are built. Though even I don't believe that. Luc is special. He always has been.

"Wait," I blurt out. "Aren't you a PR intern?"

He blinks at me for a moment, then recovers. "Yeah, PR people need to use data too. Besides, volunteering at Helping Hands has kind of gotten me used to that sort of thing."

"True." I hadn't thought of that.

We get off the train at Union Station and then take the subway north to Dundas Station for the Eaton Center. There's not much else Eli has to say after that, but he sticks around anyway. He probably could have sent everything through the burner app. He didn't need to be here, but here he is.

I don't want to admit it, but it is nice. It makes it feel like we really are working on this together instead of doing our parts separately and attempting to meld them later. There's less pressure on me to figure it all out. And now with the family helping, hopefully things change at home, too.

Coming out of the subway is chaos. There's this sudden and constant buzz of people talking and the bustle of them moving past you in what feels like a never-ending stream. The Eaton Center is one of the biggest malls in Toronto, central to downtown, and constantly packed. Coming here on a weekend guarantees being in crowds all day. Me and my cousins are usually lazy and go to Sherway Gardens because it's closer, but Eaton Center has a lot more stuff going on.

We take the steep elevator right outside the subway station up to the unofficial waiting area of the mall. It's convenient because it's a big, empty space that's both close to the subway and easily accessible walking off the street. As expected, there's a huge swath of people milling around, leaning against walls, and taking up charging stations.

"Who are we meeting, by the way?" Eli finally asks.

"Oh, Aquamarine Davis, do you know her?"

One of Eli's eyes kind of twitches. "She's a Davis?"

Poor guy is probably still traumatized from Johan glaring at him during my showcase when Ilana volunteered him. I guess it's not like he would know that Johan wasn't mad at him, that he was mad at not getting his way and having Ilana listen to me. "Yeah, but she's, like, the nicest. You'll see."

I pull out my phone and set a marker for the ping Aqua sent out. It lets my phone lead me to her, so we don't have to spend hours trying to find each other in the space. I follow the yellow footsteps over, and it's only when I'm nearly in front of her that I realize who it is.

"Aqua?!"

Girl is decked out head to toe in black, with her hair tucked under a black knit hat, and black shades on. She even has black gloves.

Eli and I look at each other at the same time with very raised eyebrows. Though he turns away as soon as he realizes what we're doing.

"Hi!" she says, and beckons me into the corner with her. "Sorry I had to be so weird about this . . . um." She looks over at Eli. "Hello."

"This is Eli. Sorry, he was already around, so I brought him."

"Oh, you're the one helping with the council?"

"Yeah," he says.

"That's fine, that's really good, actually. You're a boy. I think it'll seem less suspicious that way."

Eli smiles, and it's surprisingly bright for what seems like a passing comment. "I am that."

I want to back up to how this girl can seriously want to talk about what is and isn't suspicious. "Sorry, what's going on?"

Aqua lets out a long breath. "Okay, so. Topaz and his boyfriend . . ."

"Uh-huh . . ."

"They broke up, but Topaz thinks that Daddy may have said something to him or done something to him. Which I don't think he would, but I don't know anymore. So I said I would go see how he's doing and, like . . . if he looks heartbroken and stuff and maybe, like, probe to see what's going on."

What even is my life? On the train over we were planning how to stop everyone in the community from dying, and now I'm doing this love connection thing? "Topaz didn't want to come for this little operation?"

Aqua shakes her head. "He can't. Daddy cast a monitor on him."

"What?"

"Your parents never used that?"

"Not that I know."

She blinks like I'm the one that's weird. "Oh, well, it's an object, and you link it to a person, and wherever the object is, it can watch them. Usually it's a drone."

"Could you not just avoid the drone?"

"We don't know what it looks like. It could be any drone. That's what makes it so effective. You don't know what it is, so it's really hard to ditch it."

This is so hacked. "Johan does that to you?"

"I mean, only if he feels he needs to." Aqua kind of shrugs. "Is that strange?"

"It's super invasive. Also, doesn't that use a lot of magic?"

"It does, yeah. That's why he usually doesn't use it for long. But I guess he's really devoted to doing it with Topaz . . . Dad's been tired lately." Aqua's voice is low and strained. "He usually wouldn't be this harsh about it. I think he feels like things are getting out of control, and this . . ."

This is something he *can* control.

He thinks so, anyway.

Aqua straightens her back and takes a long, steadying breath, and her face is back to normal. Not that tortured look she just had on.

"How do you do that?" I ask.

"Do what?"

"Just . . . get over it. You looked so stressed a moment ago, and now you're fine."

"Oh, well . . ." She kind of glances at Eli, who looks back at her. "It's related to my gift."

I get it right away. The Davises keep their gifts secret. If Eli weren't here, maybe she would have told *me*, at least, but he is.

He seems to read that his presence is what's holding things back and says, "I can start walking if I know where we're going?"

"The boba place below us."

"I'll meet you there." Eli leaves with his hands tucked into his pockets.

Aqua frowns. "Sorry. I feel bad about sending him away. Is that okay?"

"It's fine, you just met him. You don't want to shout about your gift to a near stranger."

She nods but keeps looking at his back with her eyes narrowed. Then she shakes her head and turns back to me. "I can read people's true emotions. It's like what Keisha does, but for all feelings, not just discomfort."

"What?"

"Like . . . when we work together, sometimes you smile and look happy on the outside, but inside you're sad. You're always a little bit sad now."

I swallow and take a step back, though I don't mean to.

"It can be a lot when you first learn about it." She clasps her hands together. "I guess sensing how people feel all the time, I ended up always helping my siblings try to get a handle on theirs.

My grandma, she wanted us to push everything down. I guess that's what works for her. But I knew how everyone really felt. I learned that the best thing you can do with an emotion is acknowledge it. So . . . I'm still stressed. I'm still worried and sad. But instead of trying to shove it aside, I accept it, I take a deep breath, and then I can move forward with it."

"But . . . you don't look like you still feel that way."

Aqua smiles. "Voya, a lot of people don't look like how they feel inside. That's what makes it so easy to hide."

"Oh."

"I find that it's not hard to feel when I let it happen. It's when I try to pull back the emotions, to tug them deep down inside of me, that things don't go well." She shrugs. "Lucky for me, having this gift from fourteen means I have a lot of practice at it." Aqua jerks her head in the direction of the escalator. "Now let's go before Eli gets there first."

Pulling back the emotions . . . is that what I've been doing? Mama Jova said to monitor the push and pull of my magic. The way I tug at everyone else? Is it because I'm trying to pull the emotion inside instead of letting myself feel it?

I follow after Aqua, still thinking about it, and we find Eli waiting by a huge white pillar. I'm about to head to him when the eldest Davis pulls me in front of her.

"I can't be seen," she whisper shouts.

No one knows who you are in those clothes, I want to say, but don't.

"I can sense that you're annoyed."

Hack me, this is Keisha's gift amplified by a hundred, and yet somehow I think my cousin still wears the crown for employing it in the most frustrating way.

Aqua says, "Let's hide behind the pillar, okay?"

We reach Eli and the pillar but keep behind it instead of coming in front where he is.

He backs over at us. "Um, what is happening?"

"We're hiding," I say. "Get over here."

"Seriously?" Though he does come behind the pillar like we asked.

"Yes!" Aqua whispers. "Okay, that's him at the blender. His name is Mason."

The dude is cute. He's Black with deep ebony skin and dark brown eyes, and he must be at least 6'5". Like a beautiful giant. His hair is buzzed, and he's got a bunch of piercings in his ears. He's methodically blending and pouring drinks with a frown.

"Hmm . . . ," Aqua murmurs. "I can't tell from this far. I need to be closer."

"Can't tell what?" I ask.

"If he's sad."

Eli nods. "Because if he didn't really want to break up with him, he'll be upset, right? He kind of looks like it from here."

But that's not what Aqua means. She means that she needs to get close enough to use her gift to discover his true feelings.

"Okay," Aqua says. "Voya, you go and pretend to order a drink. And then, Eli, you act like you're interested, and ask him dating questions, and I'll hang back and—"

"Or we can just ask him to talk to us."

Both of us blink at Eli.

He's staring at the boy making his drinks. "Chances are, if he didn't want to break up with him, he'll want a chance to say so. He wouldn't say it to Topaz, but he might say it to someone else, knowing it would get to him."

"But then why not say it to Topaz if it's going to get to him anyway?" I ask.

Eli licks his lips. "Because sometimes you're too afraid to know if maybe you're wrong. If maybe this is the right choice, and being together was the wrong one." I stare at him until he meets my eyes, and he shrugs and rubs the back of his neck. "I mean, like . . . maybe Johan said something like, 'Topaz hates you,' and Aqua can confirm if that's a lie, but if he asked Topaz, he risks being embarrassed if it *is* true. You know?"

I get what he means, but it feels like he understood it a lot deeper than he's playing it off. I know he ran away, and now I'm wondering if he did it to be with someone and it didn't work out.

Like Eli predicted, Mason is actually down to talk with us, especially once Aqua takes off her disguise and he realizes who it is. We sit at a table—with boba, because it's not like I was gonna turn down the chance to get one when it's right there.

"So why did you break up with Topaz?" Aqua says, her voice soft and non-judgmental. It feels less like she's a sister come to scope things out for her brother and more like she's a friend.

Mason plays with his fingers. "It . . . felt too hard, I guess. Things were great, but everything was so secret. Like, it's 2050 in Toronto, and we're secret? But Topaz said he was worried about how your dad would take it. That he's, like, super picky about who Topaz dates."

Aqua nods along.

"I guess Topaz could tell I was sparked about it, so then he said he would tell your dad and it would probably be fine. But then it wasn't fine. And now he's always freaking out, and he said your dad is following him around, and it . . . got to be a lot."

So it wasn't Johan, but it was. He hadn't done anything to Mason, but he still had.

"If you love him," Eli says, looking at Mason, "you'll regret letting him go because someone else didn't like it."

Mason scoffs a little. "Easy for you to say."

"It isn't, actually."

All our eyes are on Eli now.

His shoulders hunch up a bit, but he keeps talking. "Some

people are impossible to love—not because of them but because of everything that comes with them. And maybe love isn't supposed to be hard like that. You can let it go if you want. Go for something easier." Eli releases a long breath. "But if you love him, you'll always wish that you tried. Even if it doesn't work in the end. That's what I think anyway. My dad used to say stuff like that, that you'll never regret failing as much as you'll regret not trying."

It hits me then that Eli's dad is probably dead. His mom was the one looking for him. She was the one he came back to. There was not a single mention of a dad. And from the way he talks about him, it doesn't seem like he's the sort of man who would walk out on them.

Aqua lets out a little content sigh and pats Mason's hand. She taps her phone lightly against his sitting on the table. "If you want to talk to him, you can message me."

We get up and leave then, saying bye to Mason, who doesn't look so sad anymore. He looks like he's thinking.

In front of the subway station, Aqua grins at the two of us.

"Thank you," she says to Eli.

He ducks his head. "It's fine."

A message flies into my vision. It takes me a minute to recognize the Matriarch group chat since I just set it up. I left Eli off it so he doesn't get comprised.

It's from Ilana: *Aaron shocked a coworker today. She had to go to the hospital. Her entire arm is numb.*

What? That's not what happened when he shocked me. It stung, sure, but it wasn't strong like that.

My stomach clenches.

It's getting worse.

Torrin sends a message: *Not good. And worse, I have two affected people.*

Then Avery: *I have three.*

Finally, Ilana says what we're all thinking: *We need to go faster on this. Much faster.*

Meanwhile, Eli and Aqua are both looking over at me. I show them the message.

"I have to go," Eli says, his voice low and quiet. "I . . . I have to see what I can find out. I'll message you."

"We're doing this together, you know?" He stops and stares at me, his eyes wide like he truly forgot we're supposed to be a team. "This isn't all on you because you work at the company. I'm here to help."

After a moment, he nods. "Yeah, okay. I'll keep you updated. I promise." Before I can say anything else, he's turning and sprinting into the subway, not to the northbound train that would bring him up to the westbound and Ilana's house. But to the southbound. To ride the loop.

He's going to NuGene.

CHAPTER EIGHTEEN

imico is one of those neighborhoods that makes you smaller when you're in it. It's outside of the downtown Toronto core, and yet it's surrounded by huge, towering buildings. Condo after condo after condo built sky-high and close together. Everything has this shine to it too. Our area is called Historic Long Branch for a reason. Sure, we had a lot developed while we grew up, but a lot stayed the same too. Mimico seems to rebuild itself bigger and better every single year.

The streetcar, where I could easily get a seat when I jumped on, is jam-packed after only a few stops in the area. I have to squeeze my way out to get off before we hit the Humber Loop.

Tuesday afternoon right at lunch rush was probably the worst possible time to schedule this meeting, but nothing else worked until later, and none of us want to put this off. It's already bad enough that we had to wait until now in the first place.

Outside, there are about a dozen big-box stores. You don't have to go more than a couple blocks for anything that you might need in this neighborhood. And half of them are on the bottom floors of the condos. Not to mention the bridges connecting the buildings. It's like its own glass-encased city.

With the quick help of my AI assist, I follow the glowing trail my optics project to a huge park surrounded by no less than twenty towering condo buildings. I'm glad I don't have to figure out which is which myself. Every single one of them is made up of this blue-tinted glass that makes it impossible to distinguish between them.

Avery's turns out to be one of the buildings connected by a glass bridge about fifteen stories up. The golden letters outside declare it to be Lakesedge House, which is a strange branding choice considering that there's still two buildings blocking the view of the lake, but okay.

Inside, I tap my phone to the call box and make my way in, taking the elevator up to the twenty-fifth floor. I don't know how people stand to live this high up. Unbidden, I think of my vision with Keis falling out of her bedroom window. The crunch of her landing on the ground. And that was from one story up.

I shake my head to clear it and knock on door number thirty-two.

The door jerks open, and Avery appears with her locs loose and swaying. She looks me up and down. "Well, come on in."

I shuffle inside the space. It's a big difference from being at Ilana's place. Not because it isn't a house. It's also smaller. Maybe a one-bedroom unit at most. Stepping inside brings me directly into a hallway that immediately gives way to a small kitchen with an island and a door leading into what I assume is the bathroom.

Avery guides me to the living area, which is right across from the kitchen and has a balcony big enough for a couple chairs. Her walls are covered with art pieces. Some are framed paintings, others are drawings stuck on with pieces of black and white tape, and there are also little flat sculpted masks that look African, but that's from someone who doesn't know much about it.

All of the strongest Black witch families in Toronto came over to Canada escaping enslavement in the States, so we're technically of African American descent. But some were those born in the US, and others were those born in and taken directly from Africa. Not to mention that some families like ours blended in with immigrants and ended up more connected to other kinds of ancestry, like us Thomases and Grandad's Caribbean culture. The Davises and Carters are like that too.

As I remember it, Dad's family identifies more strongly with their African heritage, though I'm embarrassed that I don't even know the specific country or countries their ancestors were from. Just that they did their best to stay connected to that culture in secret during their enslavement. Avery probably knows a lot about the masks on her wall.

Overall, it's a nice space, and if it belonged to anyone but a Matriarch, I probably wouldn't be thinking about the size. I'm reminded that even though the Jameses are considered one of the major families, there's a big difference in how they grew up. They don't have an ancestral home. Most witch families outside of our own don't. Only those with gifts strong enough to assert themselves have privileges like we do.

Suddenly, I feel ashamed. This is my family. Half of me is James, and this is the first time I'm even spending time alone with Avery. And I know virtually nothing about the Jameses' history.

I turn to her. "Is everyone running late?"

"No, you're the only one with enough respect to come on time."

"Oh." For a moment, I thought that she, like Ilana, invited me early so that we could have time to chat. But I should have known that she probably wouldn't want to spend extra time with me.

I sit on the squishy couch as Avery moves around in the kitchen. Her balcony has a pretty good view. She's not just looking at another building. It oversees the park below.

Avery sets down a bottle of Peardrax in front of me. "Your dad said you liked these. I happened to have a few from our last Roti Roti takeout night."

"Thank you." I sip the lightly pear-flavored soda. "Do you . . . talk with my dad a lot?"

She collapses into an armchair set a little off to the side. "No. But he's been anxiously messaging me since this council was formed. I guess my 'behavior' at your showcase made him feel ill at ease."

"Are you two . . . cousins?"

Avery rolls her eyes. "Wow, he really doesn't talk about us, does he?"

I shake my head. "It's a pretty Thomas-dominated household."

"My mom, she was the Matriarch before me."

"I'm sorry," I say, because I don't know what else to say. Except it's never helped me when people say that about Granny. But that makes me want to apologize again. I already knew about it since Lee told me, but it's different to be talking to the person who's affected by it.

Avery shrugs. "Your dad came to us when that whole issue with Tremblay happened a while back. Wanted us to find a way to help. Your grandma didn't like that at all, I can tell you that, but he did it anyway. My mom told him that it was a problem for *his* Matriarch." She flicks her hand at a photo behind my head, and I turn to look at it.

It's a group of kids sitting around a table grinning at the camera, some of their faces messy with birthday cake. Without them being pointed out, I spy Auntie Elaine and Dad. He doesn't have locs yet, just a puffy afro, and Auntie's hair is pressed straight and to her shoulders. There are also a couple other boys, one holding a baby.

"The baby is me," Avery says. "I didn't grow up with your dad or aunt, but my brothers did. They tried to push for our mom to do something to help, but she said no. The Thomases didn't want us in their little group, even though Elaine was ours. She didn't fight for us to be in it either. What could we do anyway? We're a pure family. Our gifts dwindled."

Dad tried. He did whatever he could to save his sister. He loved Auntie Elaine in that all-encompassing way you can only love family. But after her death, he cut himself off from everyone. Now that I know what happened to her, and here talking with Avery, it's suddenly so clear that Auntie Elaine was probably the tipping point for Dad leaving. I'd always thought it was something me and Mom did.

Now, with Granny gone, I can easily imagine how strong that desire to run away from everything would be. Even if I still wish we hadn't been included in that "everything."

But he came back to us. I guess he never came back to Avery and the rest of the Jameses.

"Anyway," Avery adds. "Your dad seems paranoid about that bad blood lingering. I won't pretend that you're my favorite family. But we're going to have to work together now."

I nod vigorously. "We will!"

She rolls her eyes at me again.

I spy a painting to the left of her head and squint at it. It's not very big, not like the giant family portrait that the Davises have in their house. But it looks properly old, as if it was done a long time ago.

Avery follows my gaze. "Ah, those are the five original Matriarchs."

"What?"

She squints at me. "Didn't Johan teach you this in school?"

"Yes! I mean, I know what happened. That the strongest Matriarchs of the Black witch families worked together originally to help protect each other and cement their holds in Toronto and stuff. I've never seen a picture of them."

Johan taught us that back in the early days, several Black witch families found ways to flee enslavement and came to Toronto, though half of the Davises stayed in Nova Scotia. They came over on boats from the US as free people and had their names written in the Book of Negros. A faction of them still live there today. Even after all that, things weren't easy. Like Mama Bess said, "It was better, but it was not good."

Weaker families had members stolen away and forced back into enslavement. It was hard enough to prove their freedom in Canada, but if they were taken back to the States, it was basically a death sentence. The five strongest Black witch families made a pact to gather the weaker families under their influence and protection. For that period of time, there wasn't a single Black witch who wasn't pledged to either the Jameses, Thomases, Baileys, Davises, or Carters. When Johan taught it to us, he said "the Baileys," but at some point, they must have joined with the Huangs. I assume now that he skipped over the details to avoid discussing the whole thing that happened with the council, Auntie Elaine, and Justin.

Once enslavement in Canada was officially abolished for everyone, not just some people, there wasn't as much of a need for protection anymore. Families started wanting to establish themselves, and things became competitive.

The smaller families broke off their pledges and returned to their own names. Not to mention, new Black witches started to immigrate over and create more families. But the five that were there in the beginning always remained the strongest.

I walk over to Avery to get a better look at the painting. I recognize Mama Bess from photos in Granny's room. She was a tall and thickly built woman with those famous Thomas hips.

Mama Jova didn't get to come over with her Matriarch. There are a few more of our ancestors in the same position. During the process of enslavement, many of them got separated. If they had pledged to a new Matriarch, they wouldn't be in our almanacs, and our ancestors wouldn't be doing their Calls.

Mama Jova is one of the few who held onto her connection to her Matriarch, even knowing she was far away. Sometimes I forget how strong Mama Jova is. And she was my age.

I turn to Avery and say, "We're going to be like that again. It won't be history. We'll get through this and take a picture to match the portrait."

I don't know if it's something about my voice or what, but she doesn't roll her eyes at me this time. "You really believe that, don't you?"

"Yes."

I don't know how, but back then, our families came together, and we protected everyone. We were a community. We can do that again.

A knock comes at the door, and Avery rises to answer it. But before she does, she says, "I hope you're right."

The mood in the room isn't exactly cheery. It's not like we're silent. There's the usual chatter of who wants drinks or snacks, and did they get caught up in traffic, followed by shit-talking the Gardiner Expressway, and a quick "your nails are looking good" catch-up. But it's like we all know the conversation we're going to have won't to be good.

And as the leader, I feel like I have to break into it. "I think we should probably talk about the cases that have come in from each family."

"Here we go," Avery sighs, leaning back into the couch.

Johan starts, "I don't have any to report, but you know my family isn't very widespread in Toronto. I'm sure Voya has had the same experience."

I nod. The Thomases and the Davises, despite being considered the strongest families, are also the smallest, in Toronto, anyway. And with us, even though Granny had a bunch of siblings, because of her insistence on purity, a lot of them left. The Baileys, Jameses, and Carters, however, all have a bunch of extended family that live in Toronto.

"How about the ones in Nova Scotia?" Ilana asks. "Have they noticed anything?"

"They run their own affairs there. We keep separate unless they have something pressing that they need help with. And they haven't, which I will assume means that this is not something they're experiencing."

"They 'run their own affairs'? April-Mae is still their Matriarch, isn't she?"

Johan levels a stare at Ilana. "I hope you are not making a judgment about how my mother chooses to lead her family?"

"I didn't realize that's how your family operated," Avery says, looking between the two of them. "Not a judgment, just curious."

"My mother was born and raised in Nova Scotia, and her aunt lived in Toronto as the Matriarch. That's where our Trinidad bit first comes in—my great uncle was an immigrant from there. My father as well. My mother visited her aunt often, and so when it came time to choose a successor, her aunt picked her to lead. They had no children, and she was fond of April-Mae. They have a stand-in head in Nova Scotia who communicates with the Matriarch in Toronto. It has always been that way. When my mother was younger, her father was that person. Now it's an uncle."

"It's a man?" Avery asks. "Each time?"

"Not necessarily. It's just how it has worked out."

I never knew any of this. I mean, I knew that some of the Davises lived in Nova Scotia, but I assumed that April-Mae had been born here in Toronto. I remember now what Ilana said in the last meeting, that April-Mae used to run away. Though Johan says she "visited," but he also said that she owed Granny a favor—I still don't know what for.

Johan clears his throat. "If we're done deep-diving into my family history, can we please get back on task?"

"Well, that mess with Aaron happened at work," Ilana says.

Eli sits quietly beside her. I haven't heard anything from him since he ran off to NuGene on the weekend, even though he promised to update me. I tried sending him a message on the burner app, but he didn't respond. Now he won't meet my eyes. Though I notice he keeps looking sidelong at Johan.

I have no idea what Eli's problem is with him. I have history with the Davis leader, but as far as I know, Eli has none. For his part, Johan seems completely disinterested in Eli.

We're going to need to have a talk at some point. I can't have the one team effort that felt like it was working suddenly crumble to pieces.

Johan tilts his head. "What do Aaron's coworkers think happened?"

"They don't know what they think happened, and he was too surprised to make up anything. But you know, he's a big Black guy, so they asked if he wouldn't mind taking a 'brief leave,' and so he's at home now. They're paying him, though."

"Any more people in your family?" I ask.

She nods. "Yes, unfortunately. A girl—she just got her gift, so they figured it was growing pains, but it's more than that. She dream hops."

"For real?" Torrin says with a whistle. "I love that."

"Yes, well, she's hopping when she doesn't want to, sometimes into uncomfortable dreams."

"Uncomfortable?"

"She has a teenage brother with a crush on a kid at school and a very active imagination."

We all cringe.

"And yours?" Ilana asks.

"Two. I won't get into them, but it's the same issue." Torrin spits out her answer quickly but has an air like she's not making a big deal out of it.

Impure families keep their gifts secret. Ilana's family isn't pure, but she seems to handle the Baileys a lot differently. Or maybe she's more willing to be open with us than Torrin is. Another way the pure/impure groupings divide us.

"I have three," Avery adds. "Not particularly serious. But one is uncontrollably growing her nails, which could potentially be dangerous."

Johan leans forward. "I'm sorry, her gift is growing her nails?"

"*At will*, yes," Avery hisses.

The Davis leader looks about two seconds away from laughing in her face.

"Okay, so things are escalating," I cut in. "Eli and I met with Lee Anderson, and she had an interesting note to make."

Johan rolls his eyes. "Ancestors have mercy, is she joining up too?"

"No. She would like to stay out, but she said she would keep us updated on any cases from her end. But the interesting thing she noted is that the anomaly, for example, came on slow. When they were working with Justin in the council, he said it was a natural genetic process. Except this is happening too fast, which probably means this isn't our magic messing up organically. Someone is making it happen."

"And you think it's your boy?" Johan counters, throwing a cool look my way.

I scowl. "He isn't *my* boy."

"Luc Rodriguez," Avery snaps. "Destroying the entire witch community due to this very vague reason as to why he doesn't like you. I think it's high time we learn why that is, don't you? Since you seem so sure that's the reason he's after us. Now it's very important information."

The other Matriarchs and Johan nod along. All of them want to know. Eli looks at me too, but not like he's eagerly awaiting learning what it is, like he feels sorry for me. He's had all of his business exposed left and right since the start of this. I guess now he sees that it's my turn.

I'm a Matriarch like most of the group, but I realize that Eli and I are the most alike. Not just because we're close in age, but we've both messed up. We've both been scrutinized by our families for our mistakes.

And maybe . . . we're both trying to make up for it.

I thought he was getting on board because of the obvious danger. But now I wonder if it's more than that. If this is Eli's chance to prove something too. If we're both trying to show everyone that we're more than our pasts. If we're both terrified of sparking shit up again.

He gives me a little nod. It's such a tiny movement.

But I'm grateful for it.

Now that we're sure Luc probably has something to do with this, I can't get away with not saying why he hates us enough to want to take us down. At this point, hiding it won't help any of us.

Slowly, I let out a long breath. "I killed Justin Tremblay."

"Hack me," Torrin gasps, then covers her mouth like she didn't mean to say that aloud.

Ilana and Avery look at me in shock.

And then Johan . . .

Johan *laughs*.

For a moment, Eli's head snaps to him with so much acid in

his expression that I almost gasp. But as quick as it happened, it's gone, and he's looking at his lap again.

"Is that appropriate?" Ilana barks at Johan.

"I'm sorry," he says, likely not at all sorry. "But you have to know. Voya nearly got *both* of us killed trying to save the life of some random person. Two people died at Caribana for that, by the way. And now I hear she's out here murdering a whole CEO of a multibillion-dollar company? I *have* to laugh."

I cringe in my seat. "I would appreciate if this information didn't leave this circle. For obvious reasons."

Avery stares up at the ceiling, shaking her head. "I knew you all did some sort of impure ritual last year, but you really picked the worst victim for it."

"I didn't do it for magic," I say, grinding my teeth. "Besides, that ritual and this death were two separate things."

She looks over at me. "Wow, so you did *two* murders last year? Even better."

"I only killed Justin because he was trying to hurt my family. Because he wouldn't have stopped. Granny—" I cut myself off and press my hands against my mouth. I can't go there. I can't. Can't go back to holding her hand in mine. To her fingers going slack. To staring at her body.

"Did this happen to occur around the same time you became Matriarch?" Ilana asks, her eyes sharp.

I nod. "He forced the ceremony."

Avery balks. "*What?*"

"He forced the Matriarch ceremony . . . under threat of murdering my little sister. I couldn't stop the ceremony, but once I was crowned . . ."

"You used your wish to kill him," she whispers.

She's wrong, but I don't correct her. I can tell them this much, but they can't ever know that we have Justin. He was enough of a threat before, and now that his sponsor son is behind this new threat, if I let them know he's alive, he won't be for long.

I clench my hands into fists.

Luc is after us. That's how it is now. That's what I have to remember. I was really out here thinking I made a difference at Helping Hands the other day. That because he was sorry Granny died, I had changed his mind. But what if I didn't? What if he would never regret whatever he's doing until it was done?

I can't let it get there.

We need to stop him.

"So the name of the game is revenge," Torrin says finally, twirling a pointed nail. "But now they're coming for all of us."

I nod. "Justin was collecting information on all of the witch families. Not just ours. He . . ." I look up at Torrin. Rena kept things secret for me. It would have created too many questions otherwise. But now I can say it. "He killed Lauren trying to learn about us."

Torrin goes perfectly still, and then her lips twist and her eyebrows narrow. "Him? It was *him*? Does Rena . . ." She trails off and shakes her head. "She knows, doesn't she? She stopped looking for her, and I was furious at her for it."

"I used my gift to show her what happened to Lauren."

The Matriarch's fury slips for a moment and her eyes go wide, her mouth opening to say something.

"I can't do it again. I'm sorry."

Her mouth snaps shut, and her teeth audibly grind together. "And so what's to stop us from bumping off new Mr. CEO?"

My eyes go wide. "You can't—"

She pins me with a hard stare.

No. There's no way. They can't kill him. They *can't*, right?

My eyes meet Eli's without meaning to, and I see my panic reflected in his.

236

"And what do you suggest we do after we kill off the only person with the means to reverse whatever it is that he's set in motion?" Ilana drawls. "Gosh, impure witches are so unimaginative. Kill, kill, kill, doesn't it get boring?"

"You're acting like you aren't one," Torrin snaps.

Ilana grins at her.

"She's right," Johan says, and I almost snap my neck looking at him. "If he's dead, we learn nothing. Besides, he's got two siblings, doesn't he? Maybe it's him, or maybe it's them. Either way, going in guns blazing and picking them off will solve nothing. We need to figure out how to cut off what's happening and then reverse whatever has already occurred."

My chest relaxes, and I slump in my seat. "I can do that. We can do that." I look over at Eli again for confirmation, and he nods.

Everything almost went sideways, and I have Ilana to thank for avoiding that, but Johan, too, of all people.

The meeting ends soon after that with the Matriarchs agreeing to gather data on the movements of their affected people so we can find any commonalities, and me and Eli agreeing to continue the investigation of Luc.

As we're walking out of the condo, Ilana gives my coat a tug. I stop and turn to her, where Eli is standing at her side with his hands in his pockets.

Ilana regards me for a moment before saying, "I noticed that in your story you didn't really talk about your connection to the boy. Only his sponsor father."

I splutter for a moment. "I . . . We were matched, in that genetics thing NuGene did. It was a way for Justin to get information from me. That's all."

"He cried for you in that vision."

I feel Eli's eyes on me, but I can't look at him. "He's not a killer."

"Or maybe he is, but he didn't want to kill *you*."

I swallow.

Ilana reaches out and adjusts my scarf, tucking the ends into my jacket. "You said Mama Jova Called you. I know her. One of my ancestors was there at that plantation. She escaped because of her."

My eyes go wide. I didn't know that. I knew Mama Jova was separated from the rest of the Thomases, but it hadn't occurred to me that she would have been around other witches.

"She wasn't a Mama, my ancestor. Just a woman, separated from her Matriarch like your Mama Jova. Learned to write and noted it down in her memoirs. About that sad girl and boy. How that girl was made to betray him because of an enslaver's whip." When Ilana looks at me, it feels like she's digging past every layer of fabric and covering that I have. "I've wondered ever since your showcase why she might Call on you. Now . . . I'm thinking maybe I get it."

I can't make my mouth form words. I don't know what to say.

Ilana's eyes narrow for a moment. "Mama Jova saved a lot of lives that day. Maybe it's cruel, but she saved more with that boy dead than she did with him alive. Sacrifices for family, those are the only ones worth losing love. Because sometimes, you have to lose love. You have to suffer to survive. Isn't that your family motto?"

My heart beating in my chest feels like the only sound that I can make. I hate that motto. The more I hear it, the more I can't stand it. Ilana pats me on the shoulder and starts to walk past.

She pauses when she notices that Eli isn't following. "You coming?"

He scuffs the toe of his boot on the ground. "Yeah . . ." He looks at me. "In a second."

"Mm-hmm, you'd better be by in five minutes or I'm leaving without you."

Eli nods, and only when she's out of earshot am I able to relax. "That was intense," Eli says. "You okay?"

I bark out a laugh. "Yeah, it was, eh? I'm fine." I rub at my face, her words still in my head despite it. "Kind of opposite from your philosophy."

"What?"

"What you told Mason about, like, fighting for love."

"Are you in love with him?" The words spill out of his mouth so fast that I have to backtrack in my mind to understand what he said.

Once I do, I freeze and meet Eli's eyes. Neither of us says anything for a moment. I know he doesn't mean Mason, obviously.

Finally, I break the silence. "It doesn't matter. Ilana is right. We have to stop him. I used to think I was making the sacrifices needed for my family. But I wasn't doing enough. I know that now."

"Ilana said he cried for you in the vision . . . Were you dead?"

"Why are you talking like you didn't see it? You were there."

He looks away and nods. "Yeah . . ."

"Another spacey moment? Like what happened with the volunteering?"

"Something like that." He shakes his head but doesn't leave.

"Is that all?"

It takes Eli a few moments before he speaks. "Do you regret . . . I mean, it's a lot. What happened with you and Justin and Luc. I get how that could push someone off their life path into something new. That's how we've gotten here, right? That's how your gift works."

Eli must still be operating off the assumption I let everyone believe, that Luc was the one whose present I changed. It doesn't seem worth it to correct him. But what *is* worth addressing is what he started to say before he cut himself off. "You wanted to ask if I regret killing him, didn't you?"

He shifts his eyes away from mine. "Death is such a permanent choice."

"It is." My lips have gone dry. I lick them but it doesn't help. "I wish that no one died, but it's too late now."

"Yeah." He nods without turning to face me. "Two people gone in one moment that changed so much. Justin was going to lead the company, now it's Luc. Your grandma was going to lead your family, now it's you. Now you and Luc are tangled up again. Four people's lives changed forever."

Luc was always going to lead the company. I went over that with Auntie Elaine. I guess I'm the same too, since Granny said she was always going to pick me. But Granny . . . It never even occurred to me. If I could jump into Justin's past and future, why not hers?

"Hack me," I breathe. "You're a genius."

"I know."

"What?"

"What?" Eli parrots back at me, eyes wide. "Um, people say that I'm smart."

I roll my eyes. "Whatever, I have to go! Thank you!"

Without waiting for Eli to finish what he was saying, I run off toward the streetcar. Too distracted to even bring up the fact that we haven't talked about whatever happened when he went to NuGene.

Suddenly, all of that can wait.

Just for a bit.

Because now I have a way to see Granny again *and* save the family business.

CHAPTER NINETEEN

W hen I get home, I rush up the stairs and into my room, not wanting to waste time. Everything else can wait.

Eli was right: Four people's lives were changed that day, but only *two* future paths were completely derailed. Justin's *and* Granny's. It feels so obvious now that I'm kind of mad that I didn't think of it sooner. I should be able to go into her past. I have three chances. I can't mess this up.

The door to my room flies open, and I stare at it in shock.

Keis stands there with her face set. "You really don't learn, do you?"

I blink at my cousin. "What?"

"You're going to jump into Granny's past to figure out how she made the products, right?"

"Um . . . yeah."

"And what are you going to do if she doesn't actually say what she's doing? Do you sit by yourself in a room and dictate out loud what you're thinking?"

Hack me.

Keis rolls her eyes. "Ridiculous. You should be thankful you barged in with your thoughts so loud and distracting. I was about to ignore them when I realized. You would have wasted a chance."

"You're going . . . to help me?"

"I'm going to help *the family*. And me, because Mom said she'll probably have to cut our allowance soon to help cover bills. Losing Rowen was a big hit. Don't think no one's noticed how our meals are suddenly either vegetarian or featuring canned meats."

I flush and resist the urge to press my hands to my cheeks. I've been stretching the groceries further when I shop now. Buying frozen vegetables instead of fresh ones. Doing more tomato or butternut squash sauce pastas. I assumed everyone would just figure I was doing it to save time. But of course Keis knew what I was really doing: finding little places to save money.

"Can you even do that? Read thoughts from my vision?" I ask, sitting on my bed.

Keis nods. "Yeah. I did it during the showcase to see if maybe I could get a clue about what was happening. But Luc's thoughts were too chaotic, and there were too many of our screaming thoughts along with the ones from the Matriarchs watching. This will be different."

My jaw drops. "You didn't say anything."

"Because I didn't get anything useful. It didn't seem relevant to mention."

Before, when we were best friends, Keis would have told me that right away. It would have been something we chatted about long into the night. Now I wonder if she talks with Justin about that sort of thing instead. Is he her new best friend?

Keis snaps at me, "I'm not going to be besties with a grown-ass man who also *murdered* Granny and Lauren. Get the vision going, and let's get this over with."

I stumble to my feet and exhale. I'm more than capable of sharing my vision with one person.

Clasping my hands together in my lap, I focus my intention. It's not hard anymore. Not after all those days I spent trying to call the ancestors. It's second nature now to fall into the right headspace.

I clear my thoughts of anything and everything, focusing on my breathing until even that falls away from conscious thought. Then I bring in my intention.

I think of Granny devising the secret behind our products.

Right before I dive into the past, I reach out with my mind and project to Keis, who lets out a gasp as blood slips from her eyes.

The vision explodes to life in front of us.

It's Granny, but a much younger version. She barely looks like how I've always known her. Instead of a short, graying afro, her hair is thick and long, braided back into two huge plaits that fall to the middle of her back with a bright yellow scarf wrapped around her head. Her face is definitely Granny's—though without any of the wrinkles that I've known her with.

She's at the kitchen island detaching the bowl from a stand mixer that's filled with a thick white cream. For a moment, I think it's whipped cream, until I watch her add a few drops of fragrance to it.

There's screaming down the hall, and Grandad bursts into the room with little Uncle Vacu on his shoulders, both of them hollering as they come in.

She scowls. "Why are you screaming in my house?"

Yeah, that's Granny.

Tears well in my eyes, and they're spilling down my cheeks before I can stop them.

"Sorry, sorry," Grandad says, and sets Uncle Vacu down, who whines to be picked back up. It's only then that I notice Granny's swollen belly where my mom is. "How's it going?" he asks.

"I'm deciding."

"Deciding?"

She leans on the countertop. "I've been consulting with the ancestors. Trying to figure out how we can give our business an extra edge. We aren't using impure magic anymore. My bandwidth has already fallen. Neither of us is going to university or college at this point, and with one more on the way, it's better if we can run our own business and childcare instead of having to work somewhere else and pay someone to watch the kids."

"We'll figure something out."

Granny puffs out her chest. "Already have. Deciding if I should do it."

"What?"

She shakes her head and rubs her belly for a moment. Then mutters, "I'm doing it."

I stare as she puts her thumb in the back of her mouth and bites down. Hard. Blood spills over her hand, and she hastily hovers it over the bowl, letting it drip into the mixture.

Grandad's jaw is basically on the floor. "Why are all you Thomases so intense?"

Granny ignores him and turns the stand mixer back on, where the blood churns together until the mix acquires a slightly pink tinge that I recognize as our Fluffy Face Cream.

The vision fades away and ends.

I meet Keis's eyes, slightly redder now. "Is that . . . hygienic?" I ask.

"Definitely not. Probably also not up to code in any way, but I guess now we know why we never sent our stuff in for Non-GMO certs."

Blood. *That's* the secret. All this time. Now it seems so obvious. Isn't that what magic comes down to? Blood and intent?

Keis says, "It's more than that. I got into her thoughts. She definitely didn't learn that guarding her mind stuff until later on, because it was an open book. But Mama Bess, did you know she did Granny's Calling?"

I shake my head.

"Well, she did. Anyway, she told her that Matriarch blood is special. We couldn't just use any blood. It has to be from a Matriarch."

Of course. I understand now why Granny didn't tell us. It's her blood, so it's not like it's impure magic, but once she sold it, it would mean pure families using product with someone else's blood. Which isn't even real so-called impure magic, but I could see pure witches turning their noses up at it.

Despite her insistence on purity, Granny was already practicing a kind of magic that didn't quite fit within the strict margins the community decided on. This just hits home even harder how useless the whole pure/impure thing is.

If she were here, I could have shared that with her.

I rub my hands across my face to dispel the tears there. But suddenly they come harder and heavier until I'm near sobbing. "It's my fault," I cry. "It's my fault that she's not here."

"No, it's not."

I gasp and look up at Keis. She is the last person I expected to refute that.

"It's not your fault that she died. It's not your fault that I'm stuck here either."

I'm practically gaping at her. This is the exact opposite of what she said the other day.

Keis narrows her eyes. "That doesn't mean I'm not still mad at you about it or that I don't think you shouldn't own up to the parts you're responsible for. I just mean that all of this comes down to that man in the basement. This is *his* fault."

"I thought . . . you and Justin . . ."

"He's playing nice because he has no other options. And of course I'm going to take advantage wherever I can. But his being here is a sentence. A punishment. And one day, when I don't need him anymore, I have no problem leaving him locked down there forever."

Damn.

"Now," Keis says. "Let's get these products sorted out so we can go back to barely breaking even. It's not great, but at least we can eat meat and keep an allowance."

I have this moment when I think about whipping out my phone and telling Eli all about it. Showing him my win. I know that he would get it. After all, aren't we both trying to prove ourselves?

Keis rolls her eyes at me, and I flush, shaking the thought out of my head. "Let's do this."

Granny used to keep the secret of the products from us, but I decide to share it with everyone. There are a lot of skeptical looks around the kitchen island while everyone watches me bite my finger and drip what I hope is an appropriate amount of blood into the mixture, then set the machine going.

But once it's done mixing, everyone's faces go slack.

"It looks just like it," Alex breathes, coming close to the mixing bowl.

Mom meets my eyes. "Try Rowen's mix."

My family runs around getting the ingredients that we know go into the Matriarch's serum and mixing it up. At the end, I drip my blood in until it matches the hue that Granny used to get. Something we haven't managed once since she died.

Testing the mix is even better.

I swallow and turn to them all. "This is what I've been trying to explain. There is no pure and impure. There aren't these stark divisions. Magic is nothing more than blood and intent."

"It's still pure magic," Uncle Cathius protests. "It's Ava's own blood."

"But what about when it goes on someone else's face? Then they're using blood that isn't theirs," Keisha says, crossing her arms. "Granny must have known it wasn't super pure, or she would have told us."

"She wasn't *tortured* for it!"

"But it wouldn't be their blood, and you know that would be enough for them to call it impure," I cut in. "Every time I use my gift to share a vision, I take blood from others. But I'm not about to kill people either. I don't have a higher bandwidth now just because I'm the Matriarch. I have it because I've quit pushing myself into boxes that were created to divide us. If you all tried to do the same, it could happen for you, too. We could become a stronger family without needing to hurt even one person. Stop holding your magic back."

The adults shift around me, Priya in particular. I know that her family has been strictly pure for a long time, but she broke for Eden. She says, "When I think about last year, I remember how quick I was to turn against what I had supposedly devoted my life to. But the same pure witches who thought of themselves as better were the ones who turned their noses up at my sister. And I wonder why I continue to hold those people on a pedestal even as we went to Johan for help." My stepmom nods at me. "I'll try."

"You've already shown that sometimes you know better than us," Auntie Maise adds with a shrug. "If all you want is for us to start thinking a little differently, we can do that, can't we, Cathius?"

I watch Uncle look at his ex-wife and deflate a little. "Fine." He looks down at the bowl of face cream and pats me on the back. "You've turned this around. Why not purity, too?"

Mom's eyes well up, and she gives me a hug.

"Now, let's celebrate!" A soft pop sounds as Auntie Maise, careful to consider Eden and loud sounds, opens a bottle of champagne that I didn't even know she had, and the whole family breaks into laughs. She grabs glasses for absolutely everyone, and we clink them together. Even us kids, besides my little sister, get some.

My aunt pulls me close and says, "Good job, leader," and it takes everything in me not to dissolve into tears.

"Keis helped," I add, and my cousin shrugs and turns away.

I know that she did it for the family, not for me. But it doesn't matter.

Finally, I managed to do something significant as the Matriarch. And the fact that I had help doesn't make it any less of a win. Maybe this isn't how Granny would have done it, but it works for me, for us.

And more, now everyone has started thinking about how they use their powers. We have a chance to bring back the strength of magic that we used to have without torture or murder.

It makes me think of the house, where our powers sit. This entire time, it's been a weakness, a vulnerability. But now I wonder what it will mean if our magic inside its bones grows stronger. If it can turn into something that protects us instead of something we're afraid of.

Dad slides over beside me. I notice his presence immediately.

"You did good," he says. "You always do."

"Thanks."

"No, you really do." He glances over at Mom and then back at me. "Ama and I weren't really a good team the way we wanted to be, but she's always been better than me at telling you what she feels. I always assume that you'll just *know* that I think you're strong and amazing and capable. But I don't say it to you enough, and I sometimes forget how much that can matter."

My brow raises, and he lets out a little chuckle. I thought Dad's strength of belief in me rested on how he felt about the ancestors who chose me. Not for me in my own right, even if I finally realized how much he loved me.

"See? That expression tells me that I don't do that as much as I should."

"Thanks," I say again, but this time I look him in the eyes and try to convey how much it *does* matter to me.

Dad pulls me into his arms for a quick hug, then tends to Eden's dwindling cup of apple juice.

I look around at my family laughing and clinking glasses.

In this moment, for the first time since she passed, it feels like Granny is here, even if she's not.

This was her business.

Her way to take care of us.

It's not going anywhere. And neither is this family.

CHAPTER TWENTY

I yank up the collar of my coat against the wind and suck in a deep breath. People make their way beside me, holding their hoods up against the cold. Meanwhile, I stay where I am, looking at the sign with its familiar witch mark in the corner—a dot surrounded by an almond-shaped circle with one more circle around that—a bag full of products clutched in my hand.

Finally, I step inside the store, and the woman at the register blinks at me, clearly surprised.

I wave to her and say, "I'm going to the back."

Without waiting for an answer, I keep my head high and march to the door near the freezers. I push it open, and a waft of vapor smoke weaves in front of me.

It's easy enough to spot Rowen on her favorite lounger; she raises an elegant eyebrow at me. It's the first time I've seen the Huang Matriarch in foundation. With Granny's serums, she never needed it. The color is a close match, but not enough for me to think she doesn't have any on. It's a little too bright in comparison with her neck.

"Look who it is," she croons, and waves to the seat in front of her. "Come join me."

The Huangs sitting at the bar eye me, clearly curious about what's going down.

I didn't bring Alex or Keisha on purpose. Some things I need help with, but this is something that I need to do on my own.

Sitting down on the couch, I reach my hand into my pocket and dangle the little bottle of elixir in front of Rowen. My grip is firm. "Full payment up front."

Her smile slides away. "What if I want a refund?"

"You won't."

The corner of her mouth quirks a bit. "Look at you. Don't you have bigger motherboards to fry? Why are you still knocking away at this?"

"My granny built a business from the ground up. The same way she built our family. We've been brought down. Product quality dropped. Our very existence is in danger. But that doesn't change the fact that I refuse to let anything she worked for be destroyed."

I thrust my hand out farther.

Rowen looks at it and then looks at me. "This is your last chance. Maybe it seems petty to go this hard for cosmetics, but this is about more than that. It's about mutual respect. You know that, don't you?"

"I do."

"Fail me this time, and don't you dare walk into my lounge again."

"I won't." I don't even blink as I stare into her eyes. The room seems to fall silent around us.

Rowen takes the serum from me and swishes it from side to side.

"Try it," I say.

Both her eyebrows shoot up. "It usually takes a day to work."

"And now it's faster."

She barks out a laugh that fills the space. "My, my, my, you're confident, aren't you? No impure magic, right?"

"We're no longer a family that puts ourselves in boxes. But no one was tortured or murdered for it, if that's what you mean."

"Hmm, I'll be interested to see how long that stance lasts. Categories exist for a reason, you know."

"And sometimes divisions need to be torn down."

That gives Rowen pause. I wonder if she's thinking of the divide between her and the Baileys like I am. Not only are they separate, but the Huangs are strict purists while the Baileys are impure. All these things separating two families that used to be one and the same.

Rowen turns to a boy in a corner and says something to him in Mandarin.

He squishes his face up, but one sharp word from a woman at the bar, and he scrambles to his feet.

Within what seems like seconds, he's back with a soaked face cloth and a mirror. Rowen cringes at the dripping cloth but takes it and wipes the makeup off her face. Underneath, there are barely perceptible wrinkles at the corners of her eyes, but there's also an obvious flush to her complexion and patches with angry red spots. Not to mention the pimple that started it all.

She uses the depressor to squeeze up the fluid.

"Three drops," I say. "One on the forehead, two on the cheeks."

Rowen follows my instructions and rubs the serum into her skin. She fans her face to help it dry before pausing and eyeing me. "That's a very big smile."

I grin wider.

The woman at the bar gasps and starts speaking rapidly in Mandarin to Rowen, who snatches the mirror and turns it to her face.

For a moment, she doesn't say anything, just stares. Then her lips quirk up. "Looks like I underestimated you."

Her entire face is clear. Not only that, it's got a dewy shine to it, and the already tiny wrinkles have completely disappeared.

When I had the family try the products with my blood, not only did they work, but they worked faster and more effectively than anything Granny had ever made. I thought we would have to wait a couple of days for the serum to kick in, but the third trial batch cleared up both the under-eye and corner-eye wrinkles I had been noticing on Mom lately. We just waited one more day to be sure there weren't any ill effects.

Mama Jova told me that when I understood what magic was, that it was only blood and intent, without letting divisions like pure and impure get in the way, that my magic would be stronger. That I could be a great witch.

All I wanted was to be a good Matriarch.

It never occurred to me that I could be stronger than the ones who came before.

But here it is, right in my blood.

I have the potential to do more than just maintain what Granny had. I can make our family, our community, better, exactly like I promised Mama Jova that I would.

Rowen looks at the bag at my feet and raises her brows. "Do you have more for me?" She grins. "Because I'm ready to clean you out."

I leave Rowen's place on a high. My bag completely empty with a very large deposit in our bank account and more on the way. A bunch of people at the bar who watched how the serum worked on their Matriarch put in huge orders for products right away. Though I assured Rowen that her special mix was just for her. Keeping her happy was worth her word of mouth.

I'd put my phone on Do Not Disturb for the meeting but take that off as I'm leaving. I'm about to share the news with the family when I see Keisha's messages.

Shit is so sparked at the house.

Keis is going off.
You have to get back here NOW.
Hack me.

I'm in such a rush to get into the house that I almost miss the drone sitting on the porch. I squint at it. It looks like the standard model that gets used for the mail. Ours are exactly the same except they're cheaper knockoffs. But it's hard to tell unless you already know. That's why we got them. I pick it up and spot the white sticker with our Thomas Brand decal slapped across it with a tiny logo of the drone brand beside it. It *is* the standard mail one. I thought all of ours were off-brand. I guess not.

I turn it over and find a box of our product with a return label taped on. I scowl. Of course. At least this won't happen anymore now.

Usually it would go directly to Uncle Cathius at his micro-shed and I wouldn't even see it, but he's staying in the house now. I guess that's why it's here. He must be out.

The door slams open, and Keisha pokes her head out. "What are you doing? Get in here!"

"Yeah, sorry."

I rush into the house and drop the drone on the floor. The first thing I notice when I get inside is screaming. Not terrified cries. Just explosions of frustration. It must have taken me half an hour to get back home, and this is still going on?

Keis rushes around the corner, her eyes narrowed, and points at me. "You deal with this. You're the Matriarch."

"Deal with what?"

"He stole my shit!" she shrieks.

My shoulders slouch, and I exhale. "Who and what?"

Alex comes around the corner behind Keis with her arms crossed. "Calm down."

Keis glares at her, then looks back at me. "Uncle Vacu stole a very important, very expensive chip upgrade to my tablet that I saved *for months* to buy."

I look at my other cousins for confirmation.

"She didn't actually see him do anything," Keisha says. "But honestly, he's the most likely."

Alex clasps her hands together. "Granny put up barriers to stop him from being able to come into the house, and Voya didn't take them off, as far as I know. It's the same magic keeping Justin in here."

Keis spits, "Granny is dead. Why would what she cast hold?"

I press my lips together. "Her protection of Eden is still holding."

"That's after years of having the house and ancestors recognize her as one of ours. It's not the same as something she cast. Those need active magic, remember? Just like what we're using to keep Justin trapped. A witch needs to be inside the house and have bandwidth."

She's right. I shrug off my coat and press my palms against my eyes. I had thought about using the magic in the house to keep Uncle Vacu out, but it already took the entire family just to do the cast for Justin. It didn't seem worth it. "When did you realize it was missing?"

"Today."

"How long have you had it?"

"Like, barely a week. He must have seen the delivery drone come in."

"How would he have known what was in it?" I jerk my head toward the basement. "Have you considered that maybe *he* took it?" There's a reason that Mama Jova said not to stop paying attention to Justin.

Keis crosses her arms. "I've looked everywhere in the basement. It's not there."

"Searching spell?"

"Did that. Nothing. It's not in the house because Uncle Vacu took it."

I grit my teeth. Justin wouldn't be able to hide anything from a cast like that. And he can't leave the basement, so there's no way he would be able to hide it somewhere else.

Alex tilts her head to the side. "If the shape of the object is different from what you're focusing your intent on, the searching spell won't work, remember?"

"Why would the shape change?" Keis snaps back. "If Justin stole it, he would be using it for something. He wouldn't break it for no reason."

"Maybe you accidentally broke it? Stepped on it or something."

"I wouldn't do that! Your dad took it!"

"Careful how you talk to me," Alex says, her voice low.

Keis steupses and turns to me. "I know it was him. He's gone into the basement and stolen things for money before. We know that he's broke."

I walk over to the entryway stairs and park my butt. "Did Justin see anything at least? He's down there all the time."

"He says he goes into sleep mode if he's bored. Which is usually the case when I'm not there."

"Would he say anything even if he *did* see something?" Keisha asks, playing with her nails.

"Yes, because he would use the information to bargain for something."

That's the murderer-turned-robot we all know and hate.

I let out a sigh. "So what now?"

"Glad you asked," Keis sneers. "I'll dig in his mind until I find the answer I want."

This girl. "Why didn't you just do that from the start?"

Keisha laughs. "Oh, he's long gone. She went into Alex's room to shout at him out the window, he said he didn't do it, threats were made, and he bolted."

I glare at Keis. "Really?"

She at least has the decency to look a little sheepish.

"You couldn't read his mind while you were shouting?"

My cousin hikes her shoulders up to her ears. "It's hard to concentrate on reading minds if I'm mad or angry or scared or whatever. Emotions are distracting."

Is this the shit that Granny had to deal with? "Okay, so I guess I'll try to find him. Convince him to come back, and then you can, from afar—assuming you're calm enough to do so—read his mind. No contact."

Alex tugs her coat from one of the hooks on the wall. "I'll come with you. I have a guess about where he is."

"I'll come too," Keisha says, and then mutters, "I'm not hanging around with the screamer."

"I can read your mind," Keis says. "Muttering under your breath doesn't matter."

"Not while you're all pissy like this you can't. You basically already said so."

"Get hacked!"

With a shake of my head, I pull my jacket back on.

Keis throws her hands up. "I guess I'll just stay here forever then."

"If he stole it, I'll take responsibility and get you another one," I tell her.

"With what money?"

"With *our* money. Rowen loved the product, and we already have orders coming in. Which you would know if you weren't so fired up that you can't even hear thoughts properly. I'll send the orders to you. Please get Mom and Auntie started on them once they get back."

Keis scowls, but there's not as much heat in it. "Fine."

"Oh, can you put away the drone too?" I ask her before we leave.

"What drone?"

I look at the spot on the floor where I put it. "It was just here..."

"It probably flew back to the hub."

It's true that our units are programmed to do that. And with all the shouting, I honestly wouldn't be surprised if it took off and we didn't notice. But still, I look toward the basement. "Check to make sure that Justin didn't somehow get a package."

Keis's eyebrows fly up. "If he did, that's the shittiest escape attempt a genius has ever made."

"Do it anyway."

My cousin rolls her eyes but makes her way to the basement. I'm probably being paranoid, but at least her checking will make me feel better.

When Alex said she had an idea where her dad was, I didn't expect to end up in front of a church in Roncesvalles. We're just a couple of blocks down from one of the best cookie places in the city, where they shove all this stuff inside the dough. Though this place lacks any fresh bakery scents; instead there's a strong and sharp smell of pee, which dims the dessert interest by a fraction.

The church is decorated with illustrations and graffiti. It's the sort of place I would have looked at and thought was cool but never stepped inside.

"He's at church?" I ask Alex, shocked. I didn't really peg Uncle Vacu as the praying type. It seems like the sort of thing he would sneer at.

My cousin fixes her gaze on the doors, the bright sunlight making the sparkles on her face stand out even more. "It's a safe injection site. They give out free Mod-M too. The sort of thing that people will use if they don't have the money to get the real stuff."

I glance sideways at Keisha, who hugs her body with her arms.

"How . . . did you know he comes here?" I ask Alex.

She exhales. "I unblocked him when I was sixteen and called, but then I hung up after one ring. Nothing happened for a few days, then he called me back. But not to talk. Some people had beat him up when he went to buy from them, and he needed help getting over here."

"You *went*?" I blurt out. I thought that Uncle Vacu hadn't seen Alex since she was eight that first night he came to the house. But it had actually only been three years.

"I went," Alex confirms.

I stare at my oldest cousin in complete silence for a moment.

"You didn't tell anyone?" Keisha breathes.

"No," Alex says with a sigh. "I knew it would probably make Granny mad. It wasn't smart. I dunno. Dad never hit me, but he can get in a good shove when he feels cornered." She glances over at me, probably remembering when he pushed me in the hall that day years ago when he'd broken into the house. "I should have told someone. But . . . I feel like no one wants me to ever forgive him. And yeah, he messes up. I wouldn't be surprised if he stole Keis's stuff. But I keep wishing that he'll get better. That's why I went." She glances at me. "I told you how he looked at me at the house. Like he couldn't believe it was me. That was nothing compared to when I saw him that first time when I was sixteen. It wasn't bad. It wasn't like he was judging how I looked. You know me, I always loved my eyeshadow, even when I was a kid. He never said anything sideways about it. I don't think he was shocked to see me as a woman. Didn't blink when I made sure he knew my pronouns and used them. But he just . . . didn't know me. At all."

"And then?" Keisha adds, because it feels like there's more.

Alex shrugs. "He just asked for money after the whole thing.

No congrats for coming out. Didn't care how I had been. What was going on in my life. Didn't even ask if I'd had my Calling yet."

"Alex . . . I'm sorry," I say, coming closer to her.

"At least you're trying," Keisha adds. She gives the building a hard look. "But what's important is that *he* tries."

Alex nods. "Yeah."

She takes a moment and then strides forward into the building. Alex explains to the person at the front desk that she's looking for her dad and that he lives in our house. Apparently, that's the only way they're allowed to tell you if the person is here or not. And sure enough, he is.

We can't go inside the rooms, so we wait near the front desk until Uncle Vacu comes out. His eyes look glazed, but he walks steady. He's dressed nicely in a soft sweater and slacks. But he has no coat.

Alex straightens, and he glances at her, then quickly away. "I would say hello, but someone told me not even to think of you," he mutters, shooting me a glare.

"Unless she reached out first was my stipulation," I correct.

I order a car, and we pile into it. Keisha offers Alex the front seat, but she waves it off. Instead of asking me, she takes it herself. Which is so classic Keisha.

I sit between Alex and Uncle Vacu.

"You have the money for this?" he says.

I scowl. "Yes. I've fixed our product issue."

He harrumphs. "Is Keis going to yell at me again when we get back?" I realize that for whatever bravado he has now, back then she scared him enough for him to bolt. I'm guessing he puts a high value on his privacy, and he doesn't know the limits of her gift. Maybe he thinks she can pull any thought from his head, at any time. Even we didn't realize that Keis wasn't in a position to read his mind until Keisha said it.

"No. I told her not to." I eye him for a moment. "Did you go in the house?"

"No."

"No?"

He glares at me. "I'm not a fool. If I went in, you would kick me out. There's nothing in the house worth enough. My gift is hacked. All I have is you. Why would I jeopardize that?"

"Because drugs make people do things that don't make sense," Alex replies. "Like leaving their child alone to go get food and not coming back for days. Like seeing them for the first time in eight years and not asking them a single thing about their life."

Uncle Vacu tucks his head down. "I didn't steal anything," he mumbles.

"I believe you," Alex says without a hint of doubt. "For the reasons you said. But also because if you had something valuable, you would also have Mod-H. You wouldn't be in a clinic getting a watered-down version."

It's painful how well Alex knows her own father. It hurts that she's aware of these things. She's barely had contact with him but can read him without even trying. Meanwhile, what does he know about her?

I move to look out the window when I catch sight of Uncle's hand, which seems to have some sort of burn on it. The skin at the junction between his thumb and pointer finger is enflamed, and there are blisters on it.

He yanks his hand underneath his sweater.

I meet his eyes for a moment. "Did something happen?"

"No," he grunts, and looks away.

When we get back home, Keis gets to read Uncle Vacu like she wants, but this time with his permission. His thoughts were still circling around the accusation alongside his daughter's words, according to her. But he isn't a thief after all.

Besides him, Justin is the only suspect. The searching spell came up empty, but I can't help but wonder if he had anything to do with it.

But maybe I'm being paranoid. Keis found the drone on the hub exactly as it should be, along with the return package. Justin didn't have anything.

Despite being found not guilty, the next day when I go to check on Uncle Vacu, he's gone.

Alex and I stand alone in the microshed while she reads the words scribbled on a piece of scrap paper. The edges crumple in her fingers before she finally hands it to me without actually looking at me.

It reads: *Goodbye, Alex.*

Nothing else.

My cousin gets on the phone, and I help her, calling hospitals to see if he's there, but his name never shows up. It's hard to know if that's a good or bad thing.

Finally, Alex goes over to the bed in the corner and sinks down on it. "I said too much. I shouldn't have gotten on him about leaving me alone and not asking about me."

I sit down next to her. "You were saying how you felt. You're allowed."

My cousin shakes her head, and her eyes start to water. "I feel bad."

"You can feel that way, but you didn't do anything wrong."

"No . . . not that. I feel bad because in a way, it's almost a relief. Like . . . I can stop hoping. I can stop wondering if things will change. I can stop constantly thinking about what *I* can do to change things. I can stop deluding myself into thinking I can control someone else's decisions. Because he's gone again. Even if I'm still worried."

Haven't I spent so much time trying to do just that? Thinking

I can change Luc's mind. But Alex is right. People make their own choices. You can't decide for them. And you have to make yours too.

I choose to hold my cousin's hand and sit with her on the bed in the microshed for as long as she needs me.

CHAPTER TWENTY-ONE

idafternoon on Sunday, I start the walk over the approximate three blocks it takes to get to where Torrin, Rena, and their family live. The entire time I knew Lauren, her aunt was usually with them in some way. Growing up back when they were pure, the five of them lived in a two-bedroom apartment overtop an ice cream shop. But once they made the swap to impurity, their gifts got stronger, money started being easier to come by, and they bought a house a little ways over from ours.

I stare around the neighborhood, remembering when I would walk down here to visit Lauren. Half the time we would end up meeting in the middle because she got too impatient waiting for me, and we would walk back together.

Now I know that no one is going to meet me at the halfway point.

Missing Lauren feels so different from missing Granny. Even though I learned my friend was dead on the same day that Granny was taken from us, it felt like I had been mourning her much longer. There was a relief too, in finally knowing for sure what had happened to her. And in a lot of ways, I expected it. I hoped otherwise but knew she had been gone too long. I was prepared for it in a way I never was for losing Granny.

But even though it doesn't hurt as much, it's still painful.

Just as I'm about to reach the end of the block, Rena swings around the corner. She's in a form-hugging coat whose puffiness somehow manages to cling in an attractive way. The boots she has on are so high they disappear underneath the jacket and they have a sharp heel. She's got a pair of leather gloves on her fingers and furry earmuffs on her head.

"Thought I would meet you," she says.

I stop in front of her, and we both stand there for a moment, each of us knowing that this is exactly what Lauren would have done if she were here.

I wish that I could jump into that period where I don't want to cry a little when I think of everyone I've lost.

Rena reaches out and brushes a flake of snow off my face. "You should come visit me more, you know?"

"Right, sorry," I say, and follow her as she turns and heads back toward the house.

Rena goes off talking about how her husband and son ran off to Marie Curtis Park to find hills for him to rush down on his toboggan. Apparently, he's "thoroughly" Canadian and enjoys the cold weather a lot more than she does.

"We have Caribbean blood, you know? We crave the warmth. Lauren did too, didn't she?"

She did. I used to laugh at her because she would put on multiple coats just to walk to the GO train station and complain the entire time. "But she never let it stop her from going out."

"No, it definitely didn't." Rena gestures to the house as we get close. "Here we are. Home sweet home. I think you and Avery are the earliest. Though she did that to hang with Torrin. Thick as thieves still. I think poor Avery hopes we'll go pure again one day."

"You don't?"

"And lose all this? No. It's one thing to have never had something at all, and another to lose it."

The Carters' house is one of the newer builds on the street. It looks like it's made entirely of rectangles. Even the roof is flat. It's a mix of brick and stone, accented with huge, beautiful windows.

Rena leads me inside, and I go ahead and hang my coat myself, take off my boots, and order them neatly alongside the others.

When I look up, she's staring at me. "Oh, um . . ." I fumble for words.

"It's okay. It's nice that you remember everything. Sometimes, it's like we lost Lauren ages and ages ago, and yet it's still so fresh, too."

"I know what you mean." The idea that it's only been months almost seems like a disservice.

I look at Rena. "I'm sure you know by now . . . but I told Torrin about Lauren."

"I know." She smiles at me. "It's better this way. I think she takes this council a lot more seriously now, knowing what we're up against."

I want to say that Luc isn't like Justin. That we aren't up against the same sort of thing at all. But what would be the point of it? Why defend Luc when he's more than likely the reason we're going through this?

"Who's here?" Torrin and Avery come out from the back room with stemmed glasses that I assume are filled with wine. The Carter Matriarch smiles at me. "It's our famed teen Matriarch."

I resist the urge to scowl. I mean, I *am* technically a teenaged Matriarch.

"Don't you bully her," Rena snaps at her sister. "She and Lauren were good friends, you know?"

When Lauren originally told me her aunt was the Matriarch,

I pictured, as I always did, someone around Granny's age. I certainly didn't expect it to be Rena's *younger* sister. But their family apparently chooses their Matriarchs based on some sort of magic bandwidth test they do when you're Called. Whoever has the highest level in their generation is named the next Matriarch. It was how Lauren was named. I just didn't know that they sacrificed the older Matriarch early to have a more powerful one leading.

Lauren used to spend all this time with Torrin, learning about what it would mean for her to be the next Matriarch. I'm sure now that she must not have known just how soon she could be called on to succeed her aunt. They hid their rituals from her; why not hide that, too? My friend was too carefree. It seems impossible that she could have held a burden like that and still lived the way she did.

And now she would never become a Matriarch.

I think of what Keis said about Justin. This is *his* fault. No matter how docile he seems, we can't forget that.

I chose to save him, but I don't think I fully realized what it would mean to know we're housing a man who's stolen so many lives. Granny. Lauren. And Auntie Elaine.

Torrin rolls her eyes at her sister. "I'm just teasing. Do you want something to drink, Voya?"

"Whatever you have is fine."

"Well, I don't have Peardrax, but I've got some mauby." Rena and Torrin's grandma came over from Jamaica, and so they're on it with the Caribbean drinks and snacks. But I would rather drink nothing than mauby.

My face must twist because she laughs. "Peanut punch?"

"Yes, please!" I chime.

As she goes to get my drink, I join Avery in the living room area. Rena, meanwhile, stays in the kitchen, perching on the barstools by the island. Nearly everything in the space is white or some shade of off-white. It's hard to believe a seven-year-old like Lauren's brother lives here. But I guess that's the bonus of being witches. You don't have to worry about stains.

Their living area faces a huge set of floor-to-ceiling windows that overlook their fenced-in backyard.

I remember laying out there in the sun with Lauren while she complained that they didn't have enough room for a pool. We ended up getting a ride from her dad to the Sunnyside one, which was painfully overcrowded but also the closest outdoor option.

I hadn't prepared at all for the memories of my friend. To be surrounded by them like this.

"Gone too early," Avery mutters beside me.

I turn to her, swiftly wiping my eyes, which I hadn't realized were leaking.

My cousin's gaze softens. "You've experienced a lot for someone your age, haven't you?"

"I . . ." I don't know what to say, so I trail off.

"They all thought I would hate her," Torrin says, coming up behind us with my peanut punch. "Lauren. It would be natural to, given that if my magic ever dropped to what was considered an unacceptable level, she would succeed me immediately."

I swallow and ask, "Did Lauren know that?"

"No." Torrin stares out of the window, and I wonder if she's picturing a scene with Lauren there too. "When I was named the next Matriarch, I knew everything. My aunt who I was to succeed made no secret of hating me for it. I don't know if it was pure vitriol or if she thought it would be easier for both of us that way. But it wasn't." She looks at me. "I wasn't going to do that to my niece. So we kept her in the dark, and I loved her. And I have never been more grateful for that choice because I got to love her for all the time we had her, and she got to love me too." Her voice gets heavy, and her eyes are shining.

The door cracks open and Torrin swipes a hand at her face. She turns and exclaims, "Look who's here, almost on time." Johan and Ilana make their way in. I look behind them, expecting Eli to pop out, but he isn't there.

"Isn't ten minutes late on time?" Johan asks. His locs are piled on top of his head, and he's got on an auburn cardigan overtop of a white shirt, and dark-wash jeans. Ilana follows behind him in a cream sweater that matches the decor and a pencil skirt.

I suddenly feel self-conscious in my leggings and sweater with its strawberry print. Not to mention the peanut punch in my hand with its juice box container.

Rena serves Johan and Ilana some wine that they bring over to the couches in the living area. After she's finished, she weaves her way up the stairs and disappears, I guess to leave us to our Matriarch business.

"You don't have any snacks?" Ilana asks, aghast.

Torrin shrugs. "Wine is a snack."

The grumble from the elder Matriarch says the opposite.

"Oh!" Torrin says suddenly, pointing at Johan with a pointed nail. "I saw Topaz post a pic of him out with his boo. Very cute. Not broken up after all. Glad to see you came around."

Johan grinds his teeth together. "I didn't come around. That boy doesn't listen."

"You can't get in the way of true love."

He scoffs, and I try and keep my face carefully neutral. I already saw the post. Aqua messaged it to me with all sorts of happy faces. What Eli said must have made an impression, because Mason and Topaz worked it out. I'm happy that at least someone is having a positive love life.

"Your mama used to have an iron grip on you all, I remember that," Ilana says with a chuckle.

Johan rolls his eyes. "Then how did Cathius end up with twins at eighteen? Iron grip, my ass."

"Oh, so she just had it on you, then?"

The glare that he throws her way is so intense that the room falls into silence.

Ilana winks. "I'm just playing. Don't get mad." She turns to me with a grin. "I heard that Rowen Huang has been singing your praises. I put in my orders too."

"I saw that you did," I hop in, eager to dispel the bad atmosphere. "My family are working on them now." None of us were prepared for exactly how far Rowen's word of mouth would spread. We ended up having to open a bigger cut on my hand to get more of my blood out while Mom practically shoved cookies down my throat to keep my energy up.

Auntie Maise grumbled that if Uncle Vacu were more dependable, he could probably extract it through a needle and show them how to store it effectively. Which would be ideal. I could basically sit down and "give blood" like I was at a drive, then save it for the family to use as they wanted. Thankfully, Rowen's serum is the only thing that uses more than a few drops, so I won't spend my entire life suffering from blood loss.

"Your family's beauty stuff?" Torrin asks, and turns to Ilana. "You use it? You don't just cast?"

Ilana waves her off. "You think I want to cut myself up to get cast pretty every day? Nah. Plus, you miss spots with magic anyway. Got folks walking out in the morning already low on bandwidth, pft, not I."

Torrin eyes me. "Hmm, maybe I'll look into it. Do you do samples?"

"We do," I say.

"Send some over to me." I nod and toss a quick message to Keisha and Alex to see if one of them can bring some samples over in a bit.

"So you have no updates besides ones that concern facial products?" Johan drawls.

"Hair products too," Ilana adds.

He gives her a look.

"No," I say, wringing my hands. I was too caught up in figuring out the beauty supply business stuff. "Eli was going to look into some things, I think . . ."

Everyone turns to Ilana.

"He's been having to put in some extra hours at work, so he couldn't come. I'm sure he's also trying to find things. He's always running off to NuGene, and if he's home, he's tapping away on that tablet. Boy is so exhausted sometimes that he's completely out of it."

That sounds like Eli, but we agreed to work together on this. He was serious. If he's putting in extra hours, I have to believe that it's because he's looking into something at NuGene for us.

I say, "I'll contact him after the meeting, see if we can't dig deeper."

"Good," Ilana says. "Because we need to move fast." She holds up her phone and shares a photo of Aaron with an open sore on his shoulder blade. The instant I see it, I think of the blistering burn I saw on Uncle Vacu's hand the other day. "Aaron said this sore showed up the other day, and he's developing a few more. I already showed Eli, and he ran off to work right away to see if he could unearth anything." She catches my gaze. "You look like you have something to say."

I swallow. "My uncle—the one who has been having problems with his gift—I saw something like that on his hand."

"How long has he had it?"

I shake my head. "He wouldn't even acknowledge it."

"Can you ask?"

"No. He . . . left home. He won't answer any of our messages."

Johan shakes his head. "Classic Vacu."

"Vacu Thomas? As in Elaine's husband?" Avery says, narrowing her eyes.

"Yeah," I mutter. "He's ... having some substance-use issues." I can picture Granny in my head saying not to tell people about our business. But what does hiding it do for us? We're supposed to be a community helping each other out.

Ilana crosses her arms. "Have you called hospitals?"

"Yes, and shelters, but he's not at any of them."

"You need to find him," Torrin says. "And Eli needs to start coming through. He's been doing a lot of 'looking into things' without a lot of finding things."

Avery chimes in with an "Mm-hmm!"

Both Ilana and I frown at them. "He's a PR intern," I say. "It's probably not easy for him to get enough access to learn information. But he's trying."

Ilana makes a little harrumph of agreement.

"Then you make sure he tries his very hardest." Torrin tilts her wineglass at me. "Because we're not letting that family get away with eradicating us. And we need to do it fast. Messed-up gifts are bad enough, but if this thing starts eating away at our bodies too ... "

I want to snap and ask her what exactly she's done besides come to these meetings and give little reports or if she's putting her future career on the line to help save us like Eli is, but I bite my tongue.

She's frustrated.

We all are.

I swallow, clenching my fists in my lap to avoid shaking. "I'll do something."

With one final stare, Torrin collapses backward into the couch and takes a long gulp of her wine.

The rest of the meeting is taken up arranging for every Matriarch to do welfare check-ins on their family to see if anyone is showing early symptoms. At the very least, we can monitor those people.

We also check in on the location data from the affected witches. I'll put it together at home to see if I can find a pattern.

Meanwhile, I have to figure out how exactly me and Eli are supposed to speed up these results.

CHAPTER TWENTY-TWO

There's a light tone when the meeting ends, but it feels like we're pretending things are better off than they are. Keisha and Alex come in just as Johan and Avery are leaving. Avery brushes past him with a brief goodbye, clearly still not a fan. She does make a point of saying bye to me, though, so maybe our relationship is getting a bit better.

"Look who it is," Johan says, stopping in front of my cousins on his way to his car. "You don't have time to visit your uncle anymore?" he asks Keisha.

She scowls. "I'm busy."

"*Busy*, eh?" He brushes his fingers across the top of the light pink bob wig she's got on. "You're a Davis, too, you know. But you act like you're all Thomas."

"It's my name."

He presses his lips into a thin line. "So it is." He jerks his head at Alex. "How about you? We have a meeting next month about Caribana outfits. Are you going to come? Or are you *busy* too?"

Last year, when Alex found out that Johan was the one who killed her mom in that ritual Auntie Elaine insisted on, I thought their relationship would be forever changed. But Alex made it clear that it had been her mom's choice. Even so, I do wonder how much it affects how she interacts with him now.

Alex crosses her arms. "I go every year, don't I?"

"So you do." He opens his car door and says, "Why don't you all come have dinner before our meeting next week? Voya knows the time."

My cousins nod, and Johan gets into his car and peels out of the driveway.

After however many months of being short with me, now he suddenly wants to be buddy-buddy with the whole family? It's not like he cut any of us off, but his lingering anger about the botched ceremony was enough to keep me at arm's length. I didn't realize my cousins hadn't been around much either. Regardless, he hadn't made any attempts to draw them back into the fold that I knew of. What's different now?

Alex holds up a bag. "Free samples!"

"Oh!" Torrin says, and waves them inside. Though Avery and Johan left, Ilana is still hanging around in the kitchen playing with her empty wineglass.

Alex dumps the contents of the bag onto the island and points everything out. "These are the facial products, and these are the ones for your body. We have foot scrubs and that sort of thing. And over here are the hair products. We brought them all—they're divided based on hair type, but we know some people have mixed textures, so you can try a few out."

The Carter Matriarch nods along as she's taken through the options.

Ilana nudges me and jerks her head away from the others. I follow her as she leads me back to the couches but doesn't sit down.

"I have a family connection at a rehab center in the Muskokas. If your uncle wants the help, I can get him a spot there." She pulls out her phone and shows me a feed filled with beautiful scenery and people smiling. "Evergreen Rehabilitation

Center" is in block letters across the front along with a blurb that says they specialize in addiction and eating disorders. "They have a sixty-day intensive that's really good. It incorporates a bit of genetic therapy, as well, to assist with adjustment of predispositions so it's a little easier to handle. It's private, so they always have beds open, unlike waiting a small century for the government to cover you."

It looks like an amazing facility, but even if I could get Uncle Vacu to agree to go, we could never afford something like that. Genetic therapy included too? No way.

"I . . ." I falter, not sure what to say to her.

She frowns. "You don't think he'll go? Get everyone in the family to talk to him. Even with this thing affecting our gift, if he doesn't get help, he's more likely to end up dead from the drugs than that."

"Yeah, and thank you for offering, it's just . . ."

"What is it? Something more than getting him to go?"

It's embarrassing to even talk about this. Our house is bigger than any of the Matriarchs with the exception of the Davises. Maybe from the outside we look like we're doing better than we are. It's the sort of white lie that Granny was probably glad for.

But here Ilana is, offering to help me, and I can't accept it even though Uncle Vacu needs it. I think of the eating disorder program. Keisha could use that help too.

"We don't have the money," I say finally. "The cost of a place like that . . . We don't have insurance that would cover private rehab, and there's someone else in my family who could benefit too. The idea of sending one and not the other . . . it would be hard. Even if Uncle Vacu's issues feel more immediate." The best we could do is get the two of them on an OHIP waiting list and hope the government could manage something for them. But even without knowing much about it, I'm sure that list would be anything but fast. Ilana basically said as much. Maybe we could get Uncle Vacu to agree to it initially, but would he still want to go possibly months down the line when the list finally got to him?

Ilana regards me for a moment before she speaks. "If I could help with that, would you accept it?"

I balk. "I can't ask you to pay."

"And I wouldn't," she says with a scowl. "But sometimes you can get discounts, or someone can donate a spot. If I could get something like that for both of your people, and if you could get them to go, would you accept that help?"

Granny would have said no. That we should be helping ourselves. But no matter how much I love and miss her, the truth is that she *didn't* help Uncle Vacu or Keisha. But I can.

"Yes, I would."

She nods. "Give me a little bit." She waves me off. "Your cousins are waiting."

Alex, Keisha, and I leave, though Ilana stays behind with Torrin.

"What was that about?" Keisha asks as we step outside.

I don't want to get any hopes up or even float this by anyone until I know that it's a sure thing. "Matriarch stuff. We need to make sure people in our circles aren't showing symptoms." No sooner are the words out of my mouth than I get a message from Lee.

Something is wrong with a member of my family. Can you come over?

I don't miss a beat before messaging Eli on the burner app: *Can you meet me somewhere?*

He responds right away: *Where and when?*

I meet Eli at the bus stop at the end of the block where Lee lives. They're over in Mississauga in a neighborhood I'm not that familiar with. It's one of the many housing developments in the area. It's shockingly uniform. Rows and rows of tan homes with deep maroon roofs and neat little grass yards. Though of course, they've been frozen all winter.

We haven't had any recent snowfall, so no one is out shoveling. It's mostly empty. People are inside.

I can't forget the snow on the ground in my vision.

We're running out of time.

I was expecting Eli to get off a bus, but instead he hops out of an ordered car right on time. "You didn't have to spend money on a car," I say.

He brushes his curls out of his eyes—they're poking out of his knit hat—and shrugs. "Didn't want to be late." I expect him to look haggard from all that working Ilana said he's been doing, but he's exactly the same as always.

"Sorry I ran off like that after the meeting at Avery's place the other day," I say.

"It's fine." He opens his mouth, then closes it.

"Something you wanted to say?"

". . . You never did answer my question. About if you regretted killing Justin."

I blink at him. That's true. I figured he was just asking because it came up in the meeting, but it seems to really matter to him. I remember what he said at Helping Hands: *No one dies.* Ilana did say that not everyone was happy about the Baileys being impure. I wonder if Eli is one of those people. Someone who doesn't want to see lives taken, even if it's to save others.

And given my white lie about Justin's "death," there's no way for him to know that I feel the same way. As far as he can tell, I'm not above murder. "I meant what I said before. What happened with Justin was because I was backed into a corner. But I'm committed to avoiding deaths of any kind."

He hesitates for a moment before saying, "Even if Luc forces your hand?"

My mouth goes dry.

He continues, "Isn't that what Ilana was saying basically? That if we need to—"

"We're not killing anyone." I cross my arms over my chest, suddenly colder. "We're going to stop this without losing lives. That's why we're working together, isn't it?"

Eli nods, but his eyes are on the ground. "Maybe he deserves it."

"What?"

"If you do things that hurt people, then maybe that's just what you deserve."

I take a moment to really look at Eli. Shoulders hunched. Eyes averted. I'm starting to think that this isn't about Luc and whether he should die. Or even a debate about what sort of murder is justified. This is about what Eli did to his mom when he ran away. "I've hurt a lot of people with my decisions. Even when I thought they were the right ones. But when you take a life away, you take away a chance for them to do better, to be better."

Finally, he looks up at me.

"I don't care what Luc deserves. Or what you think *you* deserve. We all have a chance to do better as long as we keep going." I gesture between us. "Isn't that what we're doing? We're making up for past mistakes, the two of us."

"We are, aren't we?" Eli says softly. "But redemption isn't for everyone."

"Hack me, you're dramatic."

He bursts out laughing, and before I know it, I'm laughing too. Out of everyone I know, Eli is probably the only one who comes close to understanding what I'm going through right now. Neither of us wants to have our shortcomings hurt anyone else. We're both working with a sticky dough ball, trying to make something of the mess and terrified that we'll fail.

And maybe that's the sort of thought that, if I said it aloud, would make Keisha wiggle her eyebrows to high heaven. But it doesn't even feel like that. I still can't think of any boy like that without thinking of Luc. However hard I thought it was going to be to fall in love, falling out of love is a lot more difficult.

I don't even know that Eli and I are friends.

But he does feel like a person I don't want to lose. And right now, he's a person I need.

"Ready?" I ask, jerking my head toward Lee's house.

He smiles. "Yeah."

We follow the house numbers down to sixty-eight, and I knock on Lee's front door. Her place is identical to the rest in terms of the tan brick style with its front bay window and 1.5-car-width parking space. But she's added her own touches to it. There's an old rocking chair in the front, covered with burlap, I assume to protect it from the snow. And a beautiful lush wreath on the door filled with greenery and poinsettias. They look real, too. Probably some sort of magic keeping them alive.

The door opens, and Lee stands there, looking less like her normal, assured self and more nervous, which isn't a great sign. She nods to Eli. "Nice to see you again."

"Likewise," he says.

"Wish it were under better circumstances, but here we are."

A chill creeps over my spine, and I shiver.

"Oh, sorry, it must be cold. Come on in." Lee waves us inside the house. It's homey and lived-in even though it's clearly a new unit like the rest. I spy pictures on the wall of Lee and her husband and daughter, and it smells like the spicy aroma of the incense she's got burning.

She leads Eli and me over to a small table off the kitchen.

Lee doesn't ask if we want any tea, just starts making it like before. The pot must already be hot, because she barely has it on before the kettle clicks off. She brings the cups over to us but doesn't sit down herself.

"I'll go get her," she says.

Eli and I exchange a look as she goes to get whoever it is that she's getting.

Lee comes back with a short Black girl with her hair done in mini twists wearing sweatpants and a towel tucked around the upper half of her body. She spots Eli, and her eyes go wide. "There's a boy here!"

"Child, he doesn't care." Lee rolls her eyes.

The girl looks like she could die on the spot. She *very* clearly cares.

Lee pats her on the shoulder. "This is Ailee. Go on, show them your back."

Ailee throws a hard look at Eli.

He clears his throat. "I can look away."

"For ancestors' sake," Lee groans. "You need to see."

"Why don't I take a picture?" I say to Ailee. "And he can look once you're gone."

She nods her head furiously. She must be my age, but she looks even younger like this. I wouldn't want some random guy to see any part of my naked body either.

Eli politely turns away, and Ailee exposes her back to me, dropping the towel away.

I'm so shocked that I almost forget to take the picture.

There are only three sores, but they're nothing like what Aaron or Uncle Vacu have. They're bigger and deeper. The pink of her flesh underneath stands out stark against her dark skin. One is leaking a clear liquid.

I raise my phone and snap the photo.

"Fine for her to turn around?" Lee asks, her voice low.

I wipe away the tears gathered in the corners of my eye and will my voice not to crack when I say, "Yeah."

"Can I go?" Ailee asks Lee.

"Yes, go on."

She races back up the stairs as quickly as possible.

Eli turns around, and I slide my phone over so he can look at the photo. His entire body goes still. For a moment, his eyes get that vacant look in them. The same one he had on the phone arranging the Helping Hands volunteering. Ilana's mentioned it before too. It's like he's short-circuited. Spaced out.

Lee gives me a grim look. "Ailee is staying with us because of family problems. Her dad is all she has, and he's lost his job recently. He's having a tough time, so we said we would take her. She's been sticking to Hope like a second skin, you know? She's sweet."

"Hope?"

"She's fine."

"What?" I blurt out.

Lee smiles.

"Sorry, I don't mean—I'm not upset about it, I just . . ." But it makes sense. Hope doesn't have any magic. There's no gift to affect, and it seems the same applies to whatever this side effect of these sores is. "I guess this was made for witches and witches only."

"It seems that it was."

"How long ago did this start? Or how long has her gift been affected?"

"I told you I would keep you up to date." Lee swallows. "This started today."

Eli finally finds his voice. "Excuse me?"

"You heard me. This morning, she didn't have any of those sores. Her magic was fine. She went out with Hope to do some shopping, and a couple of hours after, she came back. We noticed the first sore. Now it's like that."

It's too fast. That progression is *way* too fast. It's like it's getting worse. Why is it getting worse?

"I don't understand," I mutter. "In my vision, no one had sores like that. Something has changed." And I can't figure out what or how to make it better.

"None that you could see," Lee adds in. "I assume that everyone was clothed in this vision? Maybe they had them, or maybe they didn't. Can you check again?"

I shake my head. She does have a point, but I'm tapped out on Justin's future. Either way, things aren't exactly improving, we know that much.

I imagine Ailee with more and more sores, dying from the pain at the same time that her gift goes out of control. It's a horrible, gruesome way to go.

How could the Luc I knew want this? Manufacture this?

Maybe . . . the Luc that I knew is gone.

I stand. "Thanks, Lee."

My body is hot, and my breaths are short. I just need to get outside. I need to get air.

Stumbling out of the house, I walk away as fast as I can without running. I don't want Lee to see me like this. Don't want to risk Ailee seeing me like this.

At the corner by the bus stop, I collapse onto the bench there.

After a moment, Eli sits beside me.

When I look at him, he's there but not. His eyes are vacant. Staring. But his mouth . . . He's gasping, choking. It's like he's sobbing, but he's not using his whole face, and there are no tears.

"Are you okay?" I say, because I'm so confused about what I'm looking at.

He jerks away from me with his whole body, and sucks in one

huge, deep breath. When he looks back, he's normal again. Or near normal. "We need to do something. Now."

"I'll message Lee and get the location data from Ailee's phone. Since it happened so fast, it narrows down the possible spots."

"Knowing where it happened doesn't matter. We need to go straight to the source."

"Luc?" I stare at him. "We can't convince them. I tried that."

"We're not convincing them of anything," Eli snaps, his voice shaking. "We're shutting it down. There's going to be an intern party tonight. We're going. I'll distract them, and you find whatever evidence you can. All I need to know is if you can use magic to look like someone you aren't." He turns to me. "Can you?"

I mean, technically I could. But only for as long as I had bandwidth. I have more than anyone in our family now, but it's not limitless. I guess I could do it to get into the party, then drop it as soon as I was hidden somewhere. "Yeah," I say. "I can manage it." I pause, then add, "Is there a reason you didn't mention this party before?"

"It seemed too risky. Like it wouldn't be worth it. But now I think it is."

Fair enough. If we tried something like that and got caught, it would be bad. We needed to move fast but sometimes if you move *too* fast, you can ruin everything. Though I can't shake the feeling that makes me wonder why he keeps so much close to the chest.

I need to calm down. We're both devoted to this. It's just like he said. If it was too risky then why mention it at all?

"One more thing . . ." Eli takes another breath before he says, "Don't tell the council until after we've done this."

My eyebrows go way up into my hairline. "Why not?"

"Do you *really* trust everyone in that group?"

I stare back at him. I trust Ilana without a doubt, and now Eli, too. He has a lot on the line, and he's clearly all in. Torrin would not mess around on this, especially knowing that Justin was responsible for Lauren's death. My cousin, Avery, no matter how she feels about me, is committed to protecting her family. I know that.

But Johan . . .

He didn't want this council to happen, and he certainly hasn't been happy about a number of things that he's made no secret of.

And I know that Eli is not his biggest fan either.

Eli nods. "That's what I thought."

"Fine," I say. "I won't mention it to them. What time is it happening?"

"In a few hours. I'll message you about the location."

I blink and look over at him as another ordered car stops in front of us. He gets up and heads over to it.

"What are you going to be doing between now and then?" I ask. "You can come to our house if you want. We can just go together and split up before we get there."

"I can't." He turns and looks at me over his shoulder. "I need to go steal something from NuGene."

CHAPTER TWENTY-THREE

I'm going to get caught.

Apparently even exclusive NuGene intern parties, like everything in Toronto, have a line. I followed Eli's instructions dictated in a very long message along with a package that came via a drone without a readable serial number. I grip the ID pass belonging to an intern named Jayenne Yowel, who, to be honest, looks a lot like me, so it's not like I had to put that much effort into the cast.

But hack me, I expected to walk in, flash the ID Eli sent, and hide in the nearest empty room. Not wait for ancestors know how long in a line.

Not to mention that now, of all times, Auntie Elaine and Mama Jova have both decided to ignore my calls. I guess this isn't important enough for them to help, or maybe it's too soon after the last time.

Either way, I'm on my own.

"Did you know this was going on?" an intern asks behind me.

Their friend says, "No. It's a flash party. HR probably knew about it for a long time though."

I wonder how Eli knew about the party beforehand if it was supposed to be a flash. Unless he got the alert earlier in the day. Or even at some point during our visit with Lee. He has a tendency to be vacant sometimes, so it's hard to tell when he's being himself and when he's getting a message.

"They're letting us in!" someone shouts.

Thank the ancestors.

Sweat beads on the back of my neck as I walk forward with everyone else and hand the security guard my badge to scan. He does it so fast that I don't even have time to be scared. I boot past him inside.

The office is dressed up like it's a nightclub. There are bright flashing holos everywhere and countless NuSap units offering people food and drinks on platters. We're being herded toward the same area.

I concentrate on holding the cast as I follow along with the crowd into the huge first-floor area, which has now been transformed into a giant dance floor. Music pumps through speakers and people wind around each other, standing in groups with drinks or out on the dance floor.

Immediately, I spot Jasmine and Juras off to one side together, nursing their drinks and looking mildly interested in the party. I know that they don't know it's me, but I can't help walking faster and averting my eyes.

Where is Luc? Did he not come tonight?

A hand tugs on mine, and I almost jerk away before I realize that it's Eli.

I cringe. "Hack me, who did your hair?" I don't mean to say it aloud, but for ancestors' sake, it's in two crude braids that he tugged together into one with a hair tie at the base of his neck.

"Ilana said that too," he says with a scowl. "I did it. It's fine. I was trying to keep it out of my face."

"It is *not* fine." I'm shocked that Ilana let him leave the house like that. She could have fixed him up with some cornrows or something, anything but this. "You should have stuck with the wash and go. Or a plain ponytail. Why didn't you do that? Ancestors help me, did you think the braids were *nicer*?"

"Can we stay focused?"

"And why are you wearing sunglasses indoors?" This boy seriously came to this operation a whole ass mess.

"Can you at least pretend to dance so we don't stick out?"

At some point we trailed onto the dance floor, and we're the only people not moving. I force myself not to glance over at Jasmine and Juras, and start dancing. Which is not something that I'm great at. My cousins insisted they couldn't go to Caribana with me unless I learned to wine properly, so I can do that, but I'm not about to pull out those moves in this crowd, so I do an awkward two-step instead.

"You do realize," I say, "that you can't *pretend* to dance. You either dance or you don't."

Eli throws me a look so exasperated that I can't help but smile at it. He's as awkward as I am and can barely coordinate stepping from side to side.

I eye his dark clothes and sunglasses. "Seriously, why are you dressed like that?"

"Because I work here and I'm trying to blend in. Also, that ID I got for you is fake. I mean, that girl was an intern here, but five years ago. I went through the system to find someone who looked like you. But if anyone realizes, I don't want them to remember that I was hanging around you."

Hack me. I did think it was convenient that there was another intern who looked so much like me just when we needed her. "Then why didn't you do a cast to look like someone else too?" Though I could see why he might not want to. I keep having to wipe sweat off my face, and it's not because the room is hot.

"Take this and hide it in your purse quickly," he says, ignoring my question.

I grab what he hands me and try to be casual as I put it in my purse.

I barely finish hiding it when Eli's eyes go wide and he blurts out, "I need to twirl you really quick, is that okay?"

"Okay . . ."

As soon as the words are out of my mouth, Eli grasps my hand and spins me into a twirl. A laugh bursts out of my mouth. This is truly the worst spy operation. I grin. "I have to twirl you now or it'll look weird."

He blinks at me. "Okay." It takes him a moment after I've twirled him for his eyes to narrow. "That . . . wasn't necessary was it?"

"It was necessary for my enjoyment."

"I needed to do that because I thought someone was watching us because we're, you know, on a mission." He tries to sound serious, but I can see the smile tugging at his lips.

"Right."

This is a mission. This isn't fun.

Not at all.

Very serious mission.

Eli rubs the back of his neck and goes to tuck his hands into his pockets, then pulls them out and attempts to wave them in what I think is a dance move. He clears his throat and says, "That thing I gave you? It'll temporarily turn off the cameras. Red button to disable, green to enable. Go hide in the bathroom if you want to take a better look at it, then sneak out. There's an elevator right beside it. Take that up to the second floor, room twenty-three. Your pass will let you in. Once you take out the cameras there, you can drop the disguise."

Thank the ancestors, I'm starting to feel lightheaded. The twirls were a nice distraction, but it wouldn't be fun anymore if I fainted. "What's in room twenty-three?"

"It's their working lab."

"Not their offices?"

Eli frowns. "They don't have private offices. It's a trend with younger CEOs. You work in common areas with your employees to foster better communication and so they're more comfortable approaching you. The working lab has a smaller number of people with access, so it's likely the more ideal spot."

"Or maybe they have a super secret room."

He rolls his eyes. "Have you never heard of the phrase 'hidden in plain sight'? It's less suspicious than using a so-called super secret room. Especially if this is something they're working on regularly. People would notice them constantly sneaking away."

Okay, that actually makes sense. I can tell he knows I realized it too because a sly grin slips onto his face.

"Yeah, yeah, you're a genius, whatever," I say.

"After you're done, we'll meet here again so it looks like we took a walk around and came back. Then we can leave."

I nod. "And what am I looking for?"

"Evidence. Of anything."

"Very descriptive."

"How would I know what to look for?" He bounces on the balls of his feet and looks around the room. I follow his gaze; Jasmine and Juras are still in their corner, but there's no sign of Luc. "Okay, go."

"See you later." I allow myself one long, deep breath and head for the bathroom. It's a lot easier to notice how much this cast is taking out of me now that I'm not distracted. I'll barely be able to hold it to get to the lab. How am I supposed to get back?

I walk into the bathroom and hide in a stall to take out the device Eli gave me and get familiar with the buttons. I leave with my hand in my purse, and as soon as I walk out, I press the red button and get inside the elevator, hoping that it worked. This way, the cameras will see me walking in and then out, totally normal.

I press the red button again when I step out on the second floor because I'm paranoid, and I keep pressing it as I go along. My pass gets me into room twenty-three, where I drop the disguise after disabling the cameras.

Sinking to the floor, I take a moment to catch my breath.

My shit is so sparked. There's no way I can hold this long enough to go back to the party after. Going beyond your bandwidth is not only hard, it's dangerous. That's how Mama Jova ended up practically hollowed out against a tree.

I push myself up. I can't worry about that right now. I start to go through every single drawer I can find, searching around for something.

I'm on the third desk over when I hear the sound of footsteps nearby.

No. No. No.

I rush around the room and find a cabinet to tuck myself inside, only able to see a little through the crack.

The door opens, and Luc and Jasmine come in.

Luc tucks his hands into the black pants he wears, paired with an equally black button-up. "No one is here."

"I swear it pinged a malfunction with the cameras."

"It's probably because of the lighting downstairs."

She turns and glares at him. "Because of *your* party. The one you can't even be bothered to show your face at."

"I'm sorry that I got flocked in the hallway and had to talk to our other employees. Besides, the party is for Juras. It was a surprise. I thought people liked surprises." Luc's voice is short and clipped as he leans against a desk while Jasmine walks around the office.

They came straight here. If that doesn't confirm that something is in this room, I don't know what would.

"Juras is fine," Jasmine says.

Luc stares at her. "He's not fine. He doesn't sleep. He doesn't eat. When he does work, it's on . . ."

"You're still working on it too. What's wrong with that?"

"I'm working on it because it's broken, and I'm trying to fix it. But last time I checked, he was very much fine with those effects. So yeah, there's something wrong with that. There's nothing else for him to do."

Jasmine stops searching the room. "He's scared."

"He doesn't think *you're* scared? That *I* was scared?"

"Oh, so you're not anymore?"

Luc falters for a moment, his hands twitching at his sides. "That *thing* is making it a lot less scary. That's the point, isn't it?" He steps toward his sponsor sister. "What if it kills them? Are you okay with that?"

They're talking about what they're doing to us. They must be.

Jasmine stares straight back at him before looking away. "It won't."

"But what if it does? Are you fine with that?" Luc's voice keeps getting louder.

She ignores him and goes back to searching the room, ducking under desks, and finally, she looks over where I am.

I barely have time to bite my cheek and focus my intention on getting her to look away from me.

Don't notice. Don't notice. Don't notice.

"Jazz," Luc says. "Are you fine with that?"

"No," she says after a beat, and turns away from me to him. "But I'm not okay with *not* doing it either. This is what we have. We don't have time. We can't let them move against us." She goes over to a computer and types something into it that I can't see from my position.

"What are you doing?" Luc sighs, exasperated.

"Just checking on something I'm curious about . . ." She steps away and smiles at her sponsor brother. "You were right. No one's here."

He rolls his eyes and turns around, and she follows after him. I wait a long while after they're gone to come out of the closet.

My heart is thumping so hard in my chest it's like the only thing I can hear.

It *is* them. They're 100 percent the ones behind this.

And Luc . . . he knows. He knows what's happening. That it's dangerous. That he could kill us, and even as he questions Jasmine, he's not stopping it. He's not doing anything about it.

I let out a sob with no tears behind it.

Was I wrong about him like Auntie Elaine was wrong about Justin?

I shake away the thought and stumble over to the computer Jasmine was on, and amazingly, she didn't log out of it.

Why wouldn't she log out of it?

There are two screens minimized on the bottom, and I bring one up. It's a profile . . . a profile of Elijah Bailey. His smiling face stares back at me. And underneath his name it says *deceased*.

What?

I bring up the other tab, and it's the exact same profile of Eli, except this one says he's alive.

What's going on?

There's no way Jasmine left this open by accident. She did this on purpose. Is it a threat? Did she think Eli was the one hiding here? But why? Does she somehow already suspect him? Did she notice despite his disguise that he was hanging out with an intern she didn't know? She can't possibly know every single intern working here, right?

I try to dig around more in her files, but it won't let me. She gave me access to this and only this.

I start clicking all over the place and an email opens up. I peer at it, expecting Jasmine's, but it's not.

It's Luc's.

This is his computer.

The most recent one is marked *Gene Hack Updates*, and it's been sent to two sets of teams, the Geneticist Team and the PR team.

> We're pleased to announce that the liquid gene hack trials have been successful. This is thanks to everyone's hard work and dedication. Accordingly, we're giving the team some much-needed time off, so feel free to take a few extra days this week, and we'll resume on Monday.
>
> As always, I know I don't need to remind you, but this is a confidential trial. Our patent is still pending and in danger should this information be leaked. Legal consequences would be serious.
>
> We will be continuing to rely on our PR team to monitor any news associated with NuGene about this and maintain the stance that this is purely theoretical. Please continue to monitor.
>
> Thank you and enjoy your time off.
> —Luc Rodriguez
> NuGene CEO

I slump into the desk chair.

Gene hacking. A way to manipulate genes using nanites transported through liquids. A technique that is supposed to be theoretical only. A technique that could easily be used to mess with the genetics of anyone in a way that would be untraceable because it's not supposed to exist.

And Eli knew.

He got the email. He's in PR. He must have.

He sent me up here for evidence when he had it all along.

I asked him, to his face, about genetic hacking, and he did exactly as this email instructed: maintained the stance that it was "purely theoretical." I'd let myself feel ridiculous for even entertaining it.

And those files . . . the two files that were both him, one alive, one dead. Why would Jasmine leave that out? Unless she thought it was him snooping around. Unless she wanted to remind him of what she knows about him.

But I don't get it. He's clearly here and alive. Why would he be worried about being seen as dead?

I thought I knew Eli. I believed in him. I thought we were alike. That we were both trying to do the same thing. To show people that we can do good. That we aren't our past mistakes. We were going to save everyone.

But I don't know him at all.

Only one thing is for sure.

Johan isn't the only person on the council who I can't trust.

I use the last of my strength to get my disguise up and get me out of the building. Hack Eli's plan. I can't right now. There's no way that I could trust anything that comes out of his mouth.

I run around to the park behind NuGene and stand in the center, surrounded by snow, the chilled wind hitting my face. Disguise dissolving. Limbs weak from the magic.

I don't know what to do anymore.

Snow crunches, and I turn my head.

Luc stands there.

Maybe it always was or maybe it just started now, but it's snowing. Small flakes fall onto his face and melt on his brown cheeks. And his eyes are the ones I've always known. No bionics to be seen.

I jerk myself away and start walking.

"Where are you going?" he asks.

I stop and turn around. "I'm leaving. Isn't that what you wanted? For me to leave you alone?" The words are harsh from my mouth.

The future is elastic. Just like Johan said. Maybe it's already changed enough that I wouldn't see Luc there either. Wouldn't see him crying on our front lawn for me and my family. *He knows*. He knows what this gene hack is doing, and he's doing it anyway.

My Calling task was that I fall in love with him.

It was never a requirement that he do the same.

And he must not have. Because no one who loved me could ever do something like this to me and my family.

I turn and make it about two steps before I feel his hand on my arm. I pull away, and he jumps back. "What?" I snap. "It's not enough to be killing my family? You want more from me?"

His eyes go wide and his mouth slack.

I laugh. "Surprised that I knew?"

"You don't understand—"

"Excuse me?!" I shout. "I don't understand? What *don't* I understand? What don't I understand about *this*?" I pull out my phone and show him the picture of Ailee's exposed back.

He flinches.

I stand there with my arm out, letting him look, but he won't. His eyes are cast away from me. "No one was supposed to get hurt," he mumbles.

The laugh that comes out of my mouth is sharp and biting.

He looks at me then, the storm of his eyes churning. "I wouldn't do that to you," he whispers. "I would never try to hurt you like that."

No.

I refuse.

I'm not going to get tricked into thinking he cares about me all of a sudden. Not that long ago, he was firmly telling me to stay away from him. He turned his back on me. Now all of a sudden, he wants to act different? Act like he cares? No. I'm not buying it. "So what? We have our gifts get so powerful that we can't control them and die from that instead? That's the goal?"

He shifts in place. "That wasn't supposed to happen either. It was meant to be natural selection."

My jaw goes slack. "I thought you were the geneticist, but you seem confused about how natural selection works. People don't *make* natural selection."

"That anomaly that's floating around? It's natural. Magic dying is natural. We just . . . wanted to make it faster. Obviously, that's not what we got in the end. None of this was supposed to happen." He stresses his final sentence, voice strained.

"Then fix it!" I scream. "Fix it!"

He cringes and turns away.

And I understand, then, the entirety of his conversation with Jasmine. "You don't know how, do you?"

He can't. It's that simple. Luc is one of the most talented geneticists at NuGene, and he created something he doesn't know how to stop. Because of what I did. Because of what he *thinks* I did.

And in that moment, I consider telling him about Justin. Not because it would solve anything. Just to see it hurt. To see him realize that he'll be murdering all these people to avenge someone who never needed it.

Because I never killed Justin.

But I'm the one who gets the dead grandma. The dead friend. The dead family. I get all of that for having mercy on the villain.

"When do I get to be mad?" I say, voice getting louder. "Huh,

Luc? When do I get to be furious with you? When do I get to be vengeful? When do I get to hate your family for what they did to mine? I knew my grandma my entire life. She was like my second parent, and he killed her. *Your* sponsor dad. How come only *you* get to be upset at *me*? Why? Wasn't I wronged too?"

Luc doesn't turn. He keeps looking somewhere off to the side. There's a shine to his eyes.

No.

He does not get to keep acting like he cares. And he doesn't get to ignore this. To ignore me.

"Fine, don't look. But I hope you're listening." I dig my heels into the ground and stand tall when I spit, "Be afraid. Be very, very afraid of us. Because now it's my turn. We're going to come for you. *I'm* going to come for you." His eyes, those big, blue-gray eyes, go wide as they finally meet mine.

The flush of the cold has turned his cheeks scarlet, and my hands are frozen, but neither of us move to warm ourselves.

"Voya . . . ," he croaks, my name falling broken from his lips.

"*What?* What could you possibly say in this moment to fix this? Go ahead."

He opens his mouth and leaves it like that for a second before closing it.

Because there is nothing.

Nothing he could say to make up for what he's done. What he's *still doing*.

I let him go, and this time when I turn around, he doesn't try to stop me.

And in that field of snow, I leave the part of me that loved him behind.

CHAPTER TWENTY-FOUR

When I get home, hair and face wet from snow, the aroma of pizza wafts through the door. For a moment, I stare in the direction of the kitchen, then turn and glance at the stairs leading to my room.

The last thing I want is for them to see me like this.

The anger that coursed through me when I shouted at Luc died somewhere between getting on the GO train and walking home from the station. Now I feel empty.

I wish that I could walk into that room and have everything be normal.

Maybe I could.

I think of that moment when we celebrated figuring out the secret of the products. And it makes me shuffle my feet forward.

They're all there. Even Keis. The pizza must have just come in.

"You're back," Keisha says from behind me. It takes her one look at my face to frown. Everyone at the table stops moving around. "What happened?"

I don't even realize I'm crying until she pulls me into her arms.

Never have I cried this loud and this publicly. It just comes out. All of it comes out.

The last time they had pizza, before my vision, they asked if I was depressed. And I don't think I was. I was just sad.

But I also wasn't *letting myself* be sad.

It's like Aqua said. I wasn't letting myself feel the feeling. I was packing it down, hiding it away, making it smaller and smaller so that I could make space for everything else that was happening.

But I can't do it anymore.

By the time I calm down enough to dig my head out of Keisha's shoulder, the entire family is gathered around me in a circle. And I'm not the only one with tears in my eyes. Everyone else has them too. Without exception, though Uncle Cathius sucks in a breath and brushes his away fast.

"Why are *you* crying?" I blubber, confused.

Keis huffs and crosses her arms. "Because none of us, even the one of us that can hacking read minds, realized you were hurting this much."

I meet my cousin's eyes and end up sobbing all over again. Because for the first time in months, she doesn't look like she hates me. She looks like she did when she was my best friend.

Except it won't ever be like that again, will it?

That was the other thing I stamped down. My relationship with Keis is fundamentally changed. Even if it gets better, it will never be like what it was, and I don't know how I feel about that.

"Why don't we sit down and eat?" Alex suggests. "Or are we just going to stand here and cry all night?"

I laugh and reach up to Eden, bundled in Priya's arms, and brush tears from her eyes. "It's okay. I'm not fine. But it's okay."

Priya gently passes her off, and I clutch her to my chest. She's still so small even though she's so heavy.

A pressure sets on my head, and I look up at Dad. He's not using his gift on me. He's just there. And it's enough. I'm not guessing at what he feels, because he's already told me. I only need to remember.

I set Eden down, and she grips my hand as I collapse at the table. I pick up a slice of pepperoni and pause with it halfway to my mouth. "We got Heritage this time."

"Of course that's what you notice," Alex says with a laugh.

"I'm just happy it's *good* pizza."

Mom shakes her head. "You didn't say anything about not having it last time."

"I held my tongue."

"That's new."

The whole family bursts into cackles at that, and even though I'm pretending to be annoyed, I smile. I hesitate for a second. Thinking over the words I want to let out. Finally I say, "Before my showcase, none of the ancestors would come to me. Granny said they had stopped talking to her, too, when Auntie Elaine died. That they were disappointed in the sort of Matriarch she was. I guess I figured that's why they didn't want to talk to me either. If all of you thought I wasn't doing a good job, then why should they be any different? And I was ashamed. So I didn't say anything." It's like something has unwound between my shoulder blades now that I've confessed it.

Keis meets my eyes, her lips etched in a frown. "I made it worse. I know." She opens her mouth like she almost wants to say more but doesn't.

"You were upset," I say.

"I know I had a right to be upset. But I've been a brat this whole time." She wrings her hands. "To everyone. I got on you about being selfish, but it's not like I'm any better. I messed up things with Uncle Vacu. Now he's maybe on the streets somewhere, and he doesn't have to be."

"You don't know what really made him leave," Alex cuts in, shaking her head. "None of us can unless he tells us."

I pull myself straight. "But if we find him . . . Ilana Bailey said she has a rehab opportunity for him. It's a facility called Evergreen something. They do all sorts of things. She said she may be able to get discounts for us."

Auntie Maise, Uncle Cathius, and Mom frown simultaneously.

Dad cuts in, "Don't you dare give her grief for 'telling people our business.' What have we gotten for keeping everything to ourselves? For just putting this on Voya? Nothing. If we all shared with and helped each other, Vacu wouldn't be the only one who could get help."

The other adults actually look properly shamed, and I smile at Dad. I know he's thinking of Eden, but I also know that he's thinking of me too.

"Evergreen," Keisha says quietly, poking her pizza slice. "It's in the Muskokas, isn't it?"

I blink at her. I didn't want to bring up the idea of there being space for her too in front of everyone. "You know it?"

She shrugs. "AI searched a few places . . . That one is really nice. Expensive, though . . . I know a girl online who went."

The table is quiet as we look at her. I share a quick look with Alex, who nods at me. "Ilana said she could possibly get discounts for a couple of spots."

Keisha looks up from her slice. "I could go?"

"If you wanted to. I would find a way to make it happen."

She pauses and picks at a nail. "I don't think I need to be an inpatient. But . . . talking to someone, or a program I could do with them from home . . . I would like that."

"If it's about the money—" I start, and Keisha shakes her head.

"It's not. If I talk to someone and they say I should do inpatient care, then I will. But I don't think it's right for me. I've done some research . . . I think something I can do from home would work better."

I nod at her. "Of course." I want to cry all over again and feel myself pushing it down before I remember Aqua's words. I feel it, let the few tears roll out of my eyes and brush them away. And it feels a lot better than holding it in.

"Now," Keisha says, pointing at me. "What happened?"

And so I tell them everything that's gone down in the last couple of meetings. That I had to share that I killed Justin with the council. I tell them about the sores on Ailee's back and the progression of what's been happening, sneaking into the intern party, the gene hack email, and the conversation with Luc.

Auntie Maise leans back and whistles. "Wow, you just declared war with him, eh?"

My face flushes. "It was already war."

Luc is not the boy I thought he was.

I spent so long clinging to that feeling of first love. Of feeling like he was truly a good person who was hurt. Now I can see him like everyone else has. Maybe he was that once, but not anymore.

As hurt as I was by him turning his back on me, I should have been the one turning my back on him.

The Luc that I knew is gone.

Keis says, "So we can't trust Eli and therefore can't completely trust Ilana. We can't convince Luc not to do this. And we can't trust Johan."

I hadn't messaged Eli on the burner app, and strangely enough, he hadn't messaged me either. Hadn't asked about why I had ditched. Maybe he was just that sparked. But I hadn't even thought of Ilana. Does she know about whatever is going on with Eli? She can't. She's been so ridiculously nice to me even when she's been tough. "I don't think Ilana knows about it."

"But she might. Either way, the council is comprised. And you can't tell them it's not secure without comprising it more."

Keisha taps her nails together. "So what? They're putting the hack in something we're drinking? Do we just not drink anything anymore?"

"Good luck with that," Keis says.

Alex chews thoughtfully and swallows before she says, "What about the location data from Ailee?"

The location data! I sit up straight in my seat. "I have to go there!"

"Whoever or whatever was there won't be there now that you've talked with Luc. They probably moved."

I deflate. She's right.

"You need the data."

"And how do I get that?" And yet the second it's out of my mouth, I remember the conversation that I had what feels like so long ago in the Roti Roti kitchen with Aqua.

Aqua, who had wanted to work in data processing.

The next morning, I meet Aqua in a little bakery on Lake Shore. It's the only place I trust to make decent scones that's not too far from either of us. I offered to find somewhere closer, but the eldest Davis daughter figured it would be best to be farther away from her dad.

The space inside the bakery is small, more catered to people doing takeout than dining in. But when I enter, Aqua has managed to claim a spot in the back for us.

She smiles, but it's not as big as hers usually would be.

"Hey," I say, pulling up a chair. "Hard day?"

"Hard few days. Dad is still mad about Topaz and Mason. And I think he's freaked out about what's been happening in general."

"I wouldn't blame him."

Everyone in the family agreed that I needed to say something to the council, and so I ended up sending the photo of Ailee's back to the Matriarchs. Now the meeting at Johan's is an emergency one, happening not that long after this meeting with Aqua.

"Anyway," she pipes up. "You needed my help?"

"Yes! I need the live feed data for a specific location. But I know it's not really public facing. I was hoping you could use your data knowledge to find it?"

Her mouth drops open a bit. "I . . . yeah, I can. Oh, wow. I haven't done this in a bit, but . . . do you have a tablet?"

I thrust one out at her, and she goes to work. It reminds me of watching Luc hack through our tablet to find out about Auntie Elaine. I let myself feel warmth for that version of Luc but remind myself that he doesn't exist anymore.

"Any specific time period of the live data that you want?"

"Yes," I say. "Like two to five p.m. yesterday."

Aqua scoots her chair over beside mine, and we scroll through different locations during that time period that match the data from Ailee's phone. "Do you know what we're looking for?" Aqua asks. "Maybe I can help?"

"I don't, to be honest."

I'm just hoping that I'll know it when I see it. The video keeps going until I spot something familiar. "Stop!"

Aqua freezes the video, and I stare at a girl sitting on a bench. She's got brown skin and hair, and I've seen her before.

"Maya," I whisper.

Luc's personal NuSap unit. His pet project. Sitting exactly as she had been when I saw her at Trinity Bellwoods. Right before Luc called out to me.

And she's seated herself on a bus-stop bench next to Ailee and Hope.

"Play it, please," I ask.

Aqua plays the clip, but nothing seems to be happening. It's not like Maya is injecting them with anything.

How did Ailee get infected?

Suddenly, Maya blows out a breath. Nothing unusual. Just like anyone else could see their breath in the cold.

Except that you can't see Ailee's and Hope's breath. It's not cold enough.

What's coming from Maya isn't breath.

Luc's email said liquid trials had just finished, but Aaron's been having trouble with his gift for at least a few weeks. Which means that they succeeded with the liquid form of the gene hack before they publicized it as completed within the company. But what I'm seeing from Maya isn't any liquid hack. Is it possible that they've moved on from liquid trials by now? If so, the next logical step would be . . .

"It's a gas," I say, jaw dropping.

It's the NuSap units.

They're releasing them from the units. From ones without blue skin so you can't tell them apart from other people.

And on Wednesday, a couple of days from now, the project will launch.

The city will be crowded with NuSaps.

And still, Luc hacking Rodriguez had made sure that I wouldn't go near Maya even as he told me to stay away from him. I grind my teeth.

Why can't he let me hate him? Why does he have to keep complicating this? And if he didn't want me to die, then why couldn't he hacking put a stop to it?! Even if he can't reverse what he's done, he could stop the units from going out. But he won't. Because he doesn't really care.

"Voya?" Aqua asks. "You're panicking. And you're angry."

"I'm thinking," I spit out. But she's right. "I need a way to find as many NuSap units as possible."

Aqua tilts her head to the side. "Do you have one of your own?"

"What?"

"We used to have one. They can tell when other ones are around them. It's one of the functions. The new ones are supposed to be able to do it too."

"No," I lie. "We don't have one."

But we do. We have the first one.

Justin makes no attempt to hide his smugness over me coming down the stairs toward him. It's like he has Keis's gift and knows exactly what I'm going to ask him. He's sitting on the couch but hops up and makes a great show of welcoming me.

"Look who it is! You haven't visited in so long, I was almost missing your presence," he booms.

Keis rolls her eyes. "He's actually been grumpy for a while now for no reason. This is the happiest he's been all week."

The corner of Justin's mouth twitches, but he's otherwise unfazed. "Keis said you wanted to talk to me?"

I wish that I didn't need him. But this location data is the closest we're going to get to protecting everyone.

"You can tell where other NuSap units are, can't you? As one yourself, that's a feature, isn't it?"

"NuSap units can only sense other ones when they're close together, so that's out of the question unless you agree to take me on a walk." I frown, but he continues before I can say anything. "What I *could* do without leaving your makeshift prison is tell you the location data signature you can use to find them."

Keis adds, "And we'll have some way to confirm this, won't we? To be sure they're really units and not random data?"

"You won't without taking them apart if their skin isn't blue, no," he says, voice strained. "But you can trust that I'm being truthful because if I lied, I wouldn't ever get a chance like this again."

"Unless you use this one chance to escape," Keis retorts.

"You know," he says with a sideways glance at her. "I thought we were friends."

"We aren't."

"What do you want for it?" I say, getting straight to the point.

Justin grins. "Internet access."

"No."

"I thought so. Had to try. Limited internet access."

"No."

"You drive a hard bargain. Access to five to ten webpages or a single app of your approval."

"No."

Justin finally lets the glower I assume that he's been holding back leak onto his face. "I think you need this data a little more than you're letting on. And may I remind you that if you all die, there's no magic keeping me in the house. Truly, it's in my best interest that you fail."

"The controls would still keep you in the basement," Keis says. "So it would actually be a lonelier existence."

I add, "You're not getting any internet access. Ask for something else."

"Fine," he hisses out between his teeth. "I would like to leave the basement and wander around the house."

I open my mouth and then close it. It's not terrible. The magic would prevent him from leaving, and it's not like he looks like himself. He looks like a blue old NuSap unit with Justin's hairstyle. Even if someone saw him through the window, now with the launch, enough people will have their own NuSaps. It wouldn't be strange. "You want to be able to leave if we all die, don't you?"

He grins. "You can't blame me for wanting a little insurance."

Just like Keis said, even if the magic holding him in was gone, the controls would keep him inside the basement. But if he could wander around the house, and we fail, he could break a window and find a way to topple himself outside. Wait until someone decided to come by and have them change the programming.

I don't like it, but there has to be some give. "You can wander the halls, but you won't be able to go into any room that isn't a common area. And you can't go anywhere outside of the basement without supervision. I'll give Keis the access to change your area settings, and you can leave only if she's there to watch you." I look over at Keis. "Fine?"

"That's fine."

Justin presses his lips into a thin smile. "That's the best I'm going to get, isn't it?"

"It is."

I wish that I could make this deal, take his data, and then go back on it. But like him not giving us the right data means we would never go to him again, me going back on my word means that if we ever needed him like this in the future, we couldn't make it happen.

I tilt my head to the side. "I don't suppose you would accept this bargain in exchange for you putting together something to counteract whatever your sponsor kids cooked up?"

He grins wide. "To get me to do that, you would need to set me free."

"Not going to happen."

"I didn't think so. At least this way, if you all die horribly, which I hope you do, I can leave. Humans burn a lot faster than NuSaps." He says it with a smile. I'm not even shocked that with his eavesdropping he found out about the possible fire.

But too bad for him, we're not going to die, and Keis is definitely not going anywhere. There will always be a witch inside the house to keep him in with them.

And if things go wrong, that will be the time to go back on our deal. Because if we're gone, the last thing I'm going to do is unleash an immortal Justin Tremblay on the world. He can burn with us, stuck in this basement. At least I'll know that I tried as best I could to spare his life.

"Then we have a deal," I say.

"That we do." He thrusts out his hand, and reluctantly, I shake it.

It feels like making a mistake, but it's the only option I have right now.

CHAPTER TWENTY-FIVE

I walk out of the basement, shoulders heavy with the deal I made with Justin. But at least now we'll have a way to avoid the units. The challenge will be how I spin it at the council meeting without revealing what I know. As I turn the corner to head to the Davises' for the meeting, I pause, hearing a specific sound that I've learned to recognize over the course of my life.

The slow slicing of a honeycrisp apple.

Several times now, the other Matriarchs have asked Johan about his mom, and each time he hasn't had much to say, but I've also learned more about April-Mae than I ever did before. And it's only now that I realize I could have asked my uncle about her this whole time. There's no guarantee that she would be more on board with helping the council than Johan is, but she at least doesn't seem to have a grudge against me. Besides that, I can't help but wonder what her and Granny's relationship was really like.

I take a quick detour into the kitchen and, as expected, there's Uncle Cathius sitting at the kitchen island, peeling his apple. He looks up at me. "Don't you have a council meeting now?"

Of course he would start by scolding me. "I'm going to go in a minute, I just wanted to ask you something."

Uncle's eyes fill with glee, and he sits up straight.

"Not your advice about being a Matriarch."

"What then?" he grumbles.

I pull up a stool next to him. "It's about your mom . . . You don't know where she is either, do you?"

"No. Mother was disappointed about my leaving the family and didn't keep me updated on her comings and goings. I think she thought bringing Maise over into the Davises would be a one-up on Ava, and it didn't go her way."

For as long as I've known them, the Davises have maintained this competition with us even though we've been "family." I swallow. "Johan said that your mom owed Granny but wouldn't say what he meant."

"Ah, that." Uncle Cathius puts down the knife and offers me a piece of apple, which I take. "However harsh and cruel people think my brother is, he's a saint compared to our mother. It was difficult to be raised by her, but if you can imagine, she had an even tougher upbringing. She was born over in Nova Scotia, and our grandfather was the de facto leader there who communicated with the Matriarch here, who was his sister. Our families had been split like that since the beginning. Half of them left Nova Scotia nearly as soon as their ships landed to come to Toronto and establish themselves with the rest of the Black witches."

I knew that much from what Johan had talked about during the meeting at Avery's place.

"But my grandfather has always held a wish that we would all come back to Nova Scotia and be one family. He resented what his sister was contributing to, this splitting of the family. He . . . resented women in general, I think. He had no sons, only four daughters, which most witches would see as a blessing, but he did not. My mother often ran away to Toronto covered in bruises that she said were from falls. According to the chatter going around, anyway—whispers people probably didn't expect the little boy in the room to hear."

My teeth clench, and I fight not to interrupt.

"I think my great aunt figured that by naming her as the next Matriarch, she would save my mother from him. But it made things worse. And you wouldn't know it to see her, but April-Mae was not always the force she is now. People used to see her as whimpering and meek and were bold enough to say so to her face."

"April-Mae?!"

He laughs. "Yes. I know it's hard to imagine."

"And Granny?"

"Yes, your granny. She was hard as nails from the start. I guess she must have seen something in April-Mae. They started to spend time with each other every day. Meanwhile, our aunt took ill, and they decided that my mother would be assuming the mantle earlier than expected. Our family decided the process should be . . . expedited and chose a date for my mother to become Matriarch."

Between the discomfort on Uncle's face and the careful use of his words, I assume that they decided his great aunt would be killed so April-Mae could ascend. Meaning the idea of doing that has been in practice for a lot longer than I knew about it.

"On the eve of her crowning, my grandfather came with her younger siblings, I assume to forcibly bring her back and stop her from taking the title. I don't know the details of what happened or why he brought the kids. Only that when he left, and he *did* leave, it was with a scar across his face, and without his children. They stayed with my mother until they got older and decided to return to Nova Scotia, where they lived outside of their father's home. But after that day, April-Mae became a Matriarch to be feared instead of ridiculed."

"You think that Granny helped her stand up to her dad, and that's why April-Mae owed her?"

Uncle Cathius nods. "That's the impression we all got. I think she resented that, too, even as she was grateful, and so we were always so competitive with the Thomases. I think that once my mother learned to stand strong, she forgot how to be soft. Or maybe she came to hate that part of herself. But I do know that anytime someone in Nova Scotia under my grandfather's care sent word that they wanted to come to Toronto, she would make it happen, no matter what. Right up until the day he died."

"She let him lead all that time?" Given the history, I understand why those parts of the family stay apart like Johan said in the meeting. But I can't wrap my head around the decision to not kick him out. "Why not remove him from his position altogether?"

"For a man for whom control is everything, if you don't give him something to feel powerful, he'll find something instead." Uncle Cathius twirls the knife in his hand. "That's what she told me when I asked that same question."

There's so much untold history of this community that keeps coming out. I used to think that because we had the almanac, because we had our ancestors, we knew everything there was to know. But there were modern secrets too. Things that didn't get recorded. I'm sure the same can be said of the past.

"She's a hard woman, my mother, and I don't agree with what she does. But she came from harder roots. I thought that was why she was tough on Sapphire, because she saw a child as soft as she had been and wanted her to survive."

Sapphire with her big brown eyes and gentle smile. The youngest of Johan's girls, lost more than a year ago now. She couldn't bring herself to participate in her first ritual, which made the magic backfire. The cost was Sapphire's life. She's also the reason Johan saved me when I messed up the one last year. He refused to let another child die in his basement. And this time, his mother wasn't there to stop him.

Uncle Cathius licks his lips and continues, "But Sapphire didn't survive. *Because* of my mother. I think even she acknowledged that as a failure, and that's why she left." He pauses and looks me in the eye. "And maybe that's why she won't come back."

The Davis house is as grand as ever when I walk up to it. It's about an hour before noon instead of the dinnertime we'd originally planned for because the urgency of the situation seemed to demand that we not wait around until evening. Accordingly, neither Alex nor Keisha is with me, and there almost definitely won't be a meal.

I push open the gate and let myself in, steps heavy. I don't even know what to tell them. The whole point of this was to come together, and for that, we need trust. But that can't happen if I'm suspicious of Johan, Eli, and potentially Ilana. But I also can't leave them in the dark and put their families at risk.

I knock on the front door of the house before stepping in. Most people in the city don't leave their doors unlocked, but there is a scanner on the front gates. Besides that, I guess the Davises feel they have a certain sense of security. Maybe that's the sort of thing that comes with power. That assurance.

I wish desperately for something like that.

The instant I walk in, Aqua seems to materialize. She hops up from the steps and makes her way over, like she's been waiting for me.

"Hey, again," I say.

She smiles, but it doesn't last long before dimming. "Thought I would greet you."

"Am I the first here?" I have been every other time.

Aqua shakes her head. "No, everyone was early actually." She laces her fingers together. "It's bad, isn't it?"

I bite my lip.

"They're scared. Daddy, too."

My eyes go wide. Johan? If he's got something up his sleeve, shouldn't he be more confident and calmer? Or maybe I'm wrong and he's got nothing to hide, he's just sparked that I'm the leader, the way it always seemed. Or what he's planning has nothing to do with us. Of course, Eli was the one who hinted that Johan was up to something in the first place when Eli is the untrustworthy one. "Your dad is actually scared?"

"He's been scared for a long time," she whispers. "The only time he's not is when he's in control. I think that's why he gets so intense about power. Maybe he figures that the more he has, the better he can protect us. That way he would never have to be afraid to lose any of us like Sapphire."

Sapphire again. Her death lingers. Like Granny. Like Lauren. Like Auntie Elaine.

I think about saying "I'm sorry," but instead I say what I mean, even though it feels awkward to say aloud. "It matters to me how much it must hurt you to not have her around." I pause and look down the hall. "Is it okay? For you to say stuff about your dad like that to me?"

"If I can't talk about it with family, who can I talk about it with?"

The back of my neck flushes.

Family.

It's true. That's what we are. But things have been so strange between Johan and me that everything is thrown off.

"I envy you," Aqua says so softly that I almost miss it.

"Why?"

"Because no matter how much I know, I can never do anything. If you hadn't agreed to come with me to talk to Mason, I don't think I would have had the strength to go. I love this family, but I can't help them the way you help yours."

"You do, though. You support them all the time. I see it."
Besides, it's not like I'm perfect.

"But it's not enough," Aqua insists. "It never is. I wish that I could have stood up to Daddy and Grandma and told them not to make Sapphire do that ritual. You chose to form this council even though others didn't want it. You made them see your vision and do something about it when you could have folded when no one believed you. I could never do something like that for my family, even if I wanted to."

"It's not your fault that Sapphire died," I say, though I know it won't help. How many times have I been told that Granny wasn't my fault, and yet the guilt is still there.

"I miss her a lot. Daddy even took me to see her in her petri dish before she was born. Just a tiny bundle of cells. She came out squalling and screaming, but after that, she was quiet. She was a girl of few words."

I remember. She was attached to Aqua too. At our annual BBQs, Sapphire would always sit on her oldest sister's lap. "She was."

Aqua gives a sharp nod. "Daddy loved her the most. She missed being the youngest by a few months, so Peridot got that title. But she was his baby girl, you know?"

"Yeah . . ."

My eyes drift over to a portrait of the family hung on the wall. It's gigantic, taking up a huge amount of space in the room. Still, I haven't really looked at it for a while. Now, I stare. That portrait with Johan and his brothers at the front, Kane and Uncle Cathius, with April-Mae standing tall and proud, and all of them surrounded by Johan's kids. In it, Sapphire is twelve. I recognize the dress because Alex made it for her. The portrait was taken only a month before she died.

Now she'll be twelve forever.

April-Mae looks regal as ever in the portrait. Nearly as tall as her sons, with the same rich dark brown skin tone and that dewy sheen that Johan seems to have perfected. She wore a black-and-gold wrap on her head. It's so hard to picture her as Uncle Cathius said she was when she was younger. Nothing about the woman hints at anything other than confidence and power.

"How long has your grandma been gone?" I ask.

Aqua tilts her head to the side and regards the portrait along with me. "A year and a bit. She left not that long after Sapphire died to travel with Uncle Kane. I figured she felt guilty about Sapphire's death. It was better for everyone that she hasn't been around for a while."

"Was it hard, living with her?"

"I think my siblings found it okay. I always felt like . . . she was disappointed in me. Daddy, too. I don't like cooking, but I work at the restaurant anyway. I can't think of any other way to be useful to them."

I shake my head. "You don't need to be useful to them. They're your family."

"Don't I?" She smiles at me. "Don't you want to help your family however you can?"

Listening to her is like being thrown back in time. To the Voya I was before my Calling. I want to cry out that she's wrong. That she can do more with her life and still help. It's like when people ask what you could say to your past self, but I can't come up with anything convincing enough.

"There you are," Johan says, striding down the hall. "We're waiting." He jerks his head at Aqua. "Don't hold her up."

She looks sheepish immediately. "Sorry, Daddy." I can't imagine living with Johan day in and day out. Protective and strict seems like an overbearing combination.

"See you later," I say to Aqua, who waves at me with a tight smile, and I follow the stand-in Davis leader down the hallway. We enter the dining room, where I've only been a handful of times in the past. The ceilings are sky-high, of course, and their dining room table is even longer than ours. Not to mention it's decked out like a staged room for a special edition of a magazine.

There are large lit candelabras, elegant table runners, and so many accoutrements. Snowflake doilies and other winter decorations—holly and bits of wreaths.

The other Matriarchs are already there like Aqua said, and Eli, too, though he doesn't even look up when I come in. I'm glad. I don't know how to face him now.

"I hope you have something for us," Torrin says, looking at me and then down the table at Eli, who's staring at his clasped hands. "Because clearly things have gotten a lot worse."

Eli refuses to raise his head even though he's being addressed. *What's wrong with him?* Is he really that sparked about me not adhering to his plan last night, or does he somehow know that I know he's a liar? That he, to our faces, said that NuGene didn't have access to technology that it does have access to—technology they are now actively using against us. Maybe he doesn't know that part of it, but he still hid information from us. Why?

The table is quiet while I stare at Eli and he stares at his lap.

Avery narrows her eyes and gestures between the two of us. "Am I missing something?"

I shake my head. "Eli was able to get me into the NuGene building. While I was there, I overheard a conversation between Luc and his sponsor sibling Jasmine that made it clear they *are* the ones behind this."

"I'm sorry," Johan interrupts. "You broke into a secure facility without telling any of us, and all you learned was that your boy is definitely behind this? Something we already knew?"

"We didn't know for sure," I grind out.

"Didn't we?"

Ilana presses her palm to her forehead. "And why were the rest of us not let in on this plan?" She looks over at Eli. "This one told me he was going out with friends, so you actively lied about what you were doing."

I don't have any excuse for it. Nothing to say. I can't blurt out that we didn't say anything because we're suspicious of Johan. And Eli isn't going to jump to my rescue.

"Isn't it obvious?" Johan drawls. "Because they didn't want us to say no or stop them. Classic teenagers."

"I also saw an email from Luc to his genetics department," I hiss out. "It confirmed that NuGene is, in fact, doing genetic hacking. They're able to create genetic changes through liquid form and as a gas. I think that's how they're doing it." It's a bit of an edit to avoid saying how I know it's a gas, but it gets the information across.

I need to tell them this much information so they can have some idea of how to protect themselves. But I can't bring myself to tell them about the NuSaps. The information is too specific. And I can't trust everyone in this room anymore. Can't risk Luc and Co getting wind of this and deciding to switch their transmission method to something I don't know about and can't anticipate. Right now, it's not like we can stop the gene hack even if we're aware of it. So that seems safe to share.

The heat on me disappears as everyone turns their heads to Eli. They remember that he said gene hacks were theoretical. I want to let them stare. Let them question him. Let the truth come out. But then I remember the boy who looked so crushed bringing food up to his mom, the one who said those things to Mason, who vowed that we would beat this together. He lied, but I can't picture him doing it to sabotage us. There must be some other reason.

I add, "The email was addressed to the genetics team only and was marked as confidential. I assume that's why Eli didn't know. Since he's in PR."

Finally, he looks up at me, his face not even shocked. Just blank.

Torrin groans. "Hack me. So, it's invisible?"

"I was able to narrow down the location data more, and I think that I've found some hot spots that we can avoid." With Justin's data I know exactly where the NuSap units are, but I'll give them information that shows more general areas, so if someone isn't working in our best interests, it won't seem like we've pinpointed the units.

"Those areas in the location data are huge," Avery says.

"I've narrowed them down."

"Based on what information?"

I grip my hands together. I can't tell them that I know it's the NuSaps. So I say the first thing that comes to mind. "I spoke to Luc."

Everyone at the table collectively groans, and I force myself not to shrink in my seat. "I—"

"Enough," Ilana says with a shake of head. "You don't need to be distracted by a boy right now, and particularly one actively trying to destroy us. You know that we set you as the leader of this group. Just like being the leader of your family, you have to be impartial. You can't let yourself run away with your emotions. You know that, right?"

It stings, especially coming from Ilana. Out of all the Matriarchs, she's the one I admire most. She's done so much to help me already.

"I wanted to see what he might know. I got the impression that the gene hacking was restricted to certain areas."

"Wait," Torrin cuts in. "So you told him that you know it's a gene hack?"

"I—No . . . only that we know he's doing something. I was trying to dig out how involved he might be. What he knew." A lie. I didn't want to see what he knew. I wanted to yell at him. To ask him why he would do this. I couldn't stop myself.

Avery, Torrin, and Ilana shake their heads at me, and this time I do shrink in my seat. "What does it matter that he knows we know something?" I add. "It doesn't change anything."

"It does!" Avery snaps. "Because now he knows that we're going to be looking into this. That we'll be avoiding it. We know this is being spread in outdoor areas, likely via this gas, and maybe we could have stayed inside for a while until we figured things out. But now, if we do that, he'll know exactly what we're avoiding!"

I open my mouth to rebuttal, then snap it closed.

She's right.

Maybe it doesn't make a huge difference, but I still told him more than he needed to know.

I feel Eli's eyes on me, but I can't look at him. Don't want to see what's there. It's not like he's going to back me up, anyway.

Avery shakes her head. "Just like your aunt. You're wasting time trying to make him something more when who he is is staring you right in the face. If he were secretly good, as your vision suggests, would he be doing this to us? Would he have done this at all?"

I slink lower into my chair, thinking of Auntie Elaine. Of how shocked I was that she could believe in someone like Justin. Care for someone like him. Be in love with him.

I remember her face in that video we found, the one where she said that he had become someone she hadn't expected.

Auntie Elaine hadn't thought he was capable of the things he did either.

I wasted so much time thinking Luc was above that, but I know better now. That conversation in the park showed me everything that I needed to know. Even if he did try to save me from Maya at Trinity Bellwoods, that doesn't change what he's doing now to the community.

I'm done being in love with Luc Rodriguez.

Hack me, I basically declared war.

But I feel like if I say any of that now, no one will take me seriously. It'll look like I'm just saying what they want to hear. So I say nothing.

"You're the leader of this group," Torrin says. "You remember that, right? We chose you. If you're going to lead, then *lead*. Don't get caught up in this extracurricular bullshit."

I nod and face the Matriarchs and Johan. "I'm sorry. I'll do better."

No one says anything to Eli. I feel like he's trying to catch my eye, but I don't meet his gaze. Even if he had a legitimate reason, things went sideways like this because he held back information from us.

Besides, why should the Matriarchs get on his case when he's not their leader. He's not a Matriarch. I am.

The words of the others brush over me as they discuss their plans for dealing with everything. No one seems to have any good ideas, even knowing that it's released as a gas. The information that would really help would be about the NuSaps and the launch, but I can't give that to them without potentially exposing everything.

Thankfully, they decide to use the location data that I have, though I can tell they're only doing it because there are no other options.

At the end of the meeting, the room clears out, and I drag my feet along behind the other Matriarchs.

A firm hand lands on my shoulder, and I stop. I look up, and

Johan stares down at me with his smooth face and rapt eyes. "How are you doing?"

It's an innocent question, but it seems like he's asking me something else. I want to snap at him. It's not like he went easy on me either. From the start he didn't want me to be the leader of this group. He wanted it to be him.

He looks away abruptly, and I follow his eyes to where they land on Eli, looking at us. "Can I help you, boy?"

Part of me almost expects Eli to come over. But, of course, he doesn't. Just turns away and leaves with Ilana.

"I'm fine," I say finally, my voice barely above a mumble.

He laughs. "Yeah, okay. I'm sure you're doing anything but fine."

"Then why ask?"

"Watch your tone," he says, his voice low and strict. The same voice I remember coming out in the classroom.

"Sorry."

Johan tilts his head as he studies me. "You're out of your depth, Voya. You've never been a hard girl. Even from school days. I can sense that in you, you know. You remind me of Sapphire. You want so much to believe the best of people and the world." His eyes sharpen. "My daughter died thinking like that. This world will eat people like you up."

I don't have any response, so I keep my lips pressed together.

"Why are you pushing yourself? Trying to be strong like Ava. You're never going to be your granny. You know that, don't you?"

Spit clogs my throat, and I choke it down, but a whimper escapes, and once it's out, I can't stop the rest. Tears flow from my eyes.

It's not like I haven't been told this before. But when someone like Johan says it, what he means is *You'll never be good enough.*

And maybe he's right.

The triumph of using my blood in the products, that time I felt like maybe I *was* good enough, feels so far away. Like I walked to nearly the top of a hill then tripped over my own feet and tumbled down. And I'm still falling.

Johan pulls me into his chest and pets my hair. I find myself sobbing there. Grateful that the other Matriarchs are gone and don't have to see me like this. "Let me protect you," Johan whispers. "You're my family. You, and Keisha, and Keis. My little brother. Sweet Alex. All I want to do is be able to protect my family. You can help me do that."

"What?" I mutter, confused.

"Have your family join themselves to us. You too. It's the only way to stop being a Matriarch without dying. With the two of us combined, I'll be able to keep both groups safe. You can stop pretending that you can lead."

I push away from Johan, and he lets me, but his stare holds me in place. "What are you talking about?"

"It'll be a true binding to create the Davis-Thomas family. You'll keep your ancestors, your name, your house, and all the trappings that come with it. It'll be better, really, because you'll have our help. You don't even need to participate in rituals. By association you won't be pure ever again, though you don't have that going for you anyway. You know that my family has the power to take care of you. Especially in times like this. I'm not like my mother, you know? I can be kind." He smiles, and it raises goose pimples on my skin. "Do you even want to be Matriarch? Maybe one day I'll let you be in the running. But you're not ready for it now."

"I can't do that," I cry. He says Davis-Thomas, but it would never be that equal. It would be our family under the control of his.

"There's no downside to this, Voya. Combining the two strongest

Black witch families, think of what that would be like. Think of the power. The protection. The legacy."

"I can't—"

"Think before you say no to me again, girl," Johan says, his voice authoritative. "Really think. Because in this situation, the way things are now, I don't see it going well for you. You should know that too with your vision. This is a generous offer. This isn't a pledge that would put you in our service and have you lose your family name, but a true melding of ancestry. Join with us before it's too late."

I bite my lips to stop them from trembling.

"I'm trying to help you," Johan says, coming toward me. "I saw Aqua in that vision as well as you did. I'm not going to let anything happen to her. But I only have the means to look after my own. And I'm sorry to say that if you're not with me, you're against me."

"We're supposed to be a community."

"Community?" He laughs. "Is that what you call that group of women? Those ones who shouted you down in that room? They're looking after their own too. It was the same way in your granny's day. And what happened? Lee became disgraced, and you all lost Elaine and your status. The Davises were the only ones who came out on top. What are the Thomases now, huh? Nothing but a shadow of their former selves."

"Voya?" Aqua comes out into the hall and waves at me.

Johan scowls. "We're having a conversation right now."

The Aqua that I know would have bowed her head and left. But that's not what she does now. She stands firm. "Keisha messaged me to say Voya needs to get home. They're having some sort of issue and need their Matriarch."

Johan grits his teeth but backs down.

Grateful, I speed-walk toward Aqua, who links arms with me as we walk toward the front door.

"This offer won't last forever," Johan calls out behind me.

I don't respond.

Breaking out of the house into the cool air is like coming out from a summer's day into a freezer. And yet I gratefully suck in the frigid breeze. Aqua's grip on my arm tightens for a moment.

"What's happening with Keisha?" I ask.

She raises an eyebrow at me.

Oh.

It was a lie.

"Is that okay?" I whisper. "That you did that?"

"No," she says. "I'm sure he'll be mad if he ever finds out. But I'll be fine." She smiles. "It's kind of fun, actually, being disobedient. Between this and Topaz, I might even have my own monitor soon."

I let out a small laugh. "You didn't need to do that for me."

"I did. Like I said, you're our family. Regardless of whether you share our name." She grips my fingers between hers. "Something is going on with him. I don't know what. But since you formed the council, the other Matriarchs have been asking about my grandma."

"April-Mae?"

She nods. "No one but Daddy knows where she is. But no one has been able to get in contact with her or Uncle Kane the entire time they've been gone. All I know is that when people ask about it, he's more scared than ever. I don't really know what's going on, but I think he's afraid for them? Or for us? I don't know. This whole gift malfunction has made a mess of things. He's pulled all of us from working at Roti Roti, I guess so we don't catch it."

My eyes go wide. I didn't know that. "Really?"

"Yeah. After he saw that vision . . . I think he's really scared to lose us. And I think he's scared to lose you all too. But he doesn't know how to go about it right. I'm worried about him . . . and you."

I think about Johan's words. How he wants us to join with the Davises. How would we even do that without April-Mae around in the first place?

Aqua looks into my eyes. "Be careful around him, okay? . . . . I'd like to think he would never hurt you. Any of you. But sometimes he forgets who is and isn't on his side."

And I'm sorry to say that if you're not with me, you're against me.

I swallow. "Thanks."

I leave the Davis property and look back to check on Aqua as she goes inside, only to find that she's still watching me. And behind her, Johan stands like a dark shadow, looming.

CHAPTER TWENTY-SIX

The house is quiet when I get home. Which doesn't make much sense. Everyone is staying inside now that we know there are NuSap units milling around. Justin's information is helping to keep us safe for now, but at some point, there's going to be too many to keep track of.

And that "some point" is in two days: the NuSap launch.

I peek around the corner and spy the basement door closed, then make my way to the kitchen. Empty. Finally, I duck into the dining room, and there's a single person waiting for me there.

Mama Jova smiles. "You called?"

Is she serious right now? "I called for you yesterday when I was almost keeling over from pushing my bandwidth."

"Attitude," she snaps.

I hunch my shoulders. "I'm sorry. Thank you for coming." I sink down into the chair across from her. "Where is everyone?"

"I had them go to their rooms." It's practically unheard of for ancestors to appear outside of the Coming-of-Age and Caribana. I'm sure that gave everyone a shock. Mama Jova laces her fingers together. "And for your information, some things you can handle on your own. I decide whether it's an emergency that requires our assistance." She regards me. "What do you plan to do?"

"I don't know," I say honestly.

"Then come up with something."

"Oh, it's that easy?" I blurt out, and Mama Jova gives me the most severe stink eye that I have ever had to endure. Strike two.

She scoffs. "Your mom was right. You *are* mouthier since becoming a Matriarch."

"I can't even tell the council what's really happening! What if it gets back to Luc and his siblings somehow? Besides, now the others on the council wouldn't even want to do any plan I came up with. If I had any respect from them as a Matriarch, I've lost it."

"Then whose respect *do* you have?"

I struggle to answer.

"Why are you having a hard time with an easy question?"

Because I don't know if I'm right. I curl my hands into fists. After yesterday . . . I could say my family. That they believe in me and respect me. That if I came up with a plan, they would be in on it. But what if I'm wrong? What if I get it spat back at me? If, once again, my best isn't good enough for them?

"The thing about trust is that it goes both ways. Trust in their trust in you," Mama Jova says. "And decide if what you can do to help the family is worth the risk of proposing it. So I'll say again, come up with something."

She's right. I asked them to trust me; I need to trust them too. And even if my plan isn't the best, if it can help, then maybe it's worth it.

"We have to get rid of the NuSaps," I mutter to myself.

The launch will be the largest exposure. If we could stop it, then we could stop the danger. It would buy us the time to figure out how to reverse the gene hack. I don't know how we could reverse it, but that step can come later. Right now, the priority is to stop that launch.

But it's not like I can get into the facility or have any idea how to sabotage it . . .

I need Eli.

But that email . . . Do I really trust him enough to reveal this to him? Besides, the way he's been acting lately seems to suggest something is off. And yet I didn't expose him in that meeting because part of me still believes in him.

I stand abruptly from the table.

Mama Jova smiles at me. "Looks like you have a plan."

"Thank you."

She says nothing, simply dissolves into smoke.

I rush up to my bedroom and close the door, though already I can hear the family poking their heads out to see what I was talking with Mama about.

That can wait.

I make a video call to Eli and wait while it rings. And rings. And rings.

Hack me, pick up!

Just when I think he's going to ignore me, he answers.

"Do you still want to stop this?" I ask.

He blinks at me. "Don't you want to ask about the email? Why I didn't say anything about the gene hacking? Why I lied about it being theoretical?"

"Do you still want to stop this?" I repeat.

"Why did you cover for me? Why didn't you tell them everything? What if I'm a spy for Luc and his sponsor siblings? You could have let the Matriarchs try to get the information out of me!"

"Do you still want to st—"

"Yes!"

I smile, and Eli makes an exasperated face back at me. I don't know what's going on with him, but whatever it is, him helping me get into that party was not part of some master plan on NuGene's behalf. After all, Jasmine tried to expose him for it. But no matter how he came into this, he was trying to help me. And that's what matters right now. We're still in this together.

"Okay, I have a plan," I say. "The hack is in the NuSap units. If we can stop the launch, that'll buy us some time to figure out how to reverse it."

I haven't forgotten what Justin said. If I set him free, he'll figure out a cure. It's not a bargain that I ever want to make . . . but if it's between that and the lives of my family and community, I'll do it.

And I'll destroy the chip holding Justin's consciousness with a blood whip the second his foot touches the ground.

We said no one dies, and I still want that. But I can't give that man mercy a second time if it means leaving him free to destroy this community.

"How do you plan to reverse it?" Eli asks.

I shake my head. "We'll figure that out later. For now, where are the facilities for the NuSap launch, and do you have any idea how we could stop it?"

"There's only one."

"What?"

"There's only one building doing the launch. They're releasing a bunch of units from there in a parade. It's a surprise."

"An army of blue-skinned robots marching is a fun surprise?"

He cracks a grin. "PR told Luc and his siblings that it wasn't the greatest idea, but they insisted on it." His smile slips. "The facility is in Mississauga. The parade goes straight down Lake Shore Boulevard."

That's the main street just north of where we are. "What are the chances of some of those detouring south to visit us?"

"High."

That's why they need this parade. We're probably going to get the same hack that Ailee did. One that works fast. Fast enough to hit us before we know it's coming. Except this time, we do. "And how could we stop the launch?"

Eli takes a moment before he finally says, "A leak. If anything confidential from the project gets out to the public ahead of time, it puts a stall on it. And everything relevant to that happens in this warehouse. PR monitors if anything comes out that isn't supposed to. But everything inside the facility is on local servers for that reason. Someone would have to get inside and use a tablet on that server to leak photos."

Unable to help it, I ask, "You didn't want to share this as an option in the meeting today?"

"How? I knew that something had gone wrong between us, because you abandoned the party. If I pitched any sort of plan, you could have shot it down. I was still trying to figure out how to get the council to realize it was in the NuSap units, something I noticed you left out. This entire plan wouldn't make sense to anyone unless they knew that."

"I left it out because I couldn't trust you anymore after that email and didn't want to endanger anyone by saying what I knew when you were there. And I wasn't off the mark, because you purposely kept information from us!"

Eli's gaze drops to the floor. "Look, I'll tell you everything once this is done. I promise. And . . . it's okay if you don't forgive me. But let's get this done first, okay?"

I narrow my eyes at him for a couple of seconds before saying, "Fine." At the start of this call, I already decided that if he still wanted to stop this, we would work together. So we will. "I can do it. I'll sneak in and leak the photos."

"No," he says, looking up. "*I'll* do it."

"If anyone catches you, you'll lose your internship. No way."

A laugh bursts out from his mouth, but it's dry and humorless.

"I think there are more important things on the line right now. You asked me if I wanted to stop this. I do."

"What about cameras? Can you use that device from before?"

He cringes. "No. And any outside tech would be detected right away too."

"I'm sorry, but we've done, like, *two* covert operations so far and you're not good at it. Even considering magic, do you have the bandwidth to stay concealed from cameras that entire time?"

Eli's eyes go wide for a moment, and then he scowls.

"Do you?" I ask, already knowing the answer.

"No."

"See?! I can get help from the ancestors."

He shakes his head. "*No.* It doesn't matter if someone sees me. We just need to get the leak done."

"And what about Jasmine and Juras?" I push. "How about when they get an alert or whatever about you being in the facility? Don't you think they'll freak out if they realize you're actively sabotaging them? They might do something even more extreme. Whoever does this *cannot* get caught. And I can do that a lot better than you can."

Eli runs a hand through his hair and gnaws on his lip. I'm sure he's trying to think of a reason to go himself, but there is none.

"I'm the best person for this job," I say. "You have to admit that."

"This is serious, Voya. You'll be alone inside a facility you know nothing about."

"No, she won't." We both jump, and I spin around to see Keis standing in the doorway. "Tell me everything about the layout. I can project it into her head, and she can shout out to me from her mind if she needs us. And Voya's right. She has a better chance of getting in and out unseen than you will, unless you can call on your ancestral magic too?"

Eli sighs. "No. I can't."

"There you go."

I raise my brow at Keis. I know she can project things into my head since she did it with Granny's memory. And of course, she can read my mind but . . . "I'll be in *Mississauga*," I say.

"I know," she says rolling her eyes. "Trust me. I spent nearly two years exclusively in your head. You're the only person I can hear from that far."

I stop and stare at my cousin as she stares back at me. I remind myself that she's doing this for the family, like she said before.

"I'm not," Keis cuts in. "I mean, I am. But I'm doing it for you, too." She shrugs. "I meant what I said. I don't think I can ever forgive you for that choice. I can't let go that easily. But that doesn't mean I don't still care about you."

I swallow, unable to say anything in the moment. Before, I understood that even if me and Keis made up, it wouldn't be the same. It's fair for her to never forgive the decision I made. I used to think that I had to tell myself it was the right one, otherwise how could I live with the consequences of it? But if I'm honest, I don't know if it was. It was what felt best at the time. And pretending that it was the right answer has not once spared me the pain of the fallout. All I can do is know that I made it, and it's done, and it can never be changed.

Me and Keis have a different relationship now. I didn't know how to feel about that before, but I think it's okay. And maybe that all-consuming friendship we used to have wasn't right for us anyway. That friendship was the reason there wasn't room for Keisha. Or Alex.

We're building something new between us, and I'm glad for it.

"So we're settled," I say, voice chipper.

Eli frowns. "Maybe we could try another plan . . ."

"Do you have one?"

He says nothing.

"All right, then. It'll be fine. You share what you know with Keis, I'll use ancestral magic to do what needs to be done, and we'll stop the launch. Jasmine and Juras won't realize it was us, so they should stick to protocol, and we can use the extra time to plan next steps."

Finally, Eli nods. "Okay." He doesn't seem happy about it, but this is the best chance we've got.

"I just need to check in with the rest of the family, and then we're good to go."

"Too slow," Keis drawls. "I already dictated the entire plan to them before I came upstairs." She pushes my bedroom door all the way open where the whole family is standing with their coats on.

"What?" My mouth is hanging open.

Keisha grins at me. "In case something goes wrong, we'll be nearby to jump to the rescue. Priya and Eden are going to stay so homebody over there has cell phone access."

The twins nod at each other.

I think it's the first time I've ever seen those two work together without being forced.

"You're good with this?" I ask, looking around at the family.

Uncle Cathius scoffs. "It's our Matriarch's plan, isn't it? Let's put a stop to this."

"Mom?"

She lets out a long breath and closes her eyes. "I wish that I could make you stay home. Make you not do this. Because you're my little girl, and if you went there and you caught this thing . . ." She shakes her head. "But you're not just my daughter anymore. You're the Matriarch. And if you say this is what we have to do, then it's what we have to do."

I smile at her. I know this can't be easy. Getting into the

NuGene party was one thing, but this is another. The NuSap units that have the gene hack are waiting there.

"The units at the facility should be inactive," Eli says on the phone. I change my settings so the whole family can hear and see him. "NuGene legally can't make people share their data. They have no way to know who is and isn't a witch. If the units there were already active, people would be showing effects to their magic, and it would be too obvious where it was coming from." Then he mutters under his breath, "That's the only good thing about this plan." I don't think Mom catches that bit though.

She presses her hand to her chest and grins at Eli. "Thank you."

He stutters over his words and manages something akin to English, though still indecipherable. He takes a breath, looks at me, and says, "Please, *please* be careful."

I slap a smile on my face. "I'll be fine. Don't worry."

Eli tries to smile back without much success.

After Eli had had a chance to run through the plan, the family starts to walk down the stairs, but I hold Keisha back for a moment.

"Thank you," I say.

She laughs a little. "For interacting with Keis? It's not that bad. Sure, she's grumpy, but she's family."

"For being my friend. My *best* friend, even when I was too wrapped up in my own shit to appreciate you properly."

Keisha's mouth goes slack for a moment before she smiles and links arms with me. "I would never hold back the gift of me from you."

I roll my eyes at her and we follow the rest of the family down the stairs to the front door. I half expect Justin to poke his head out of the basement so he can make a series of cryptic and annoying comments before we leave. But nothing happens.

Keis, Priya, and Eden stand back and away from the doors, ready to be on standby in case anything goes wrong.

"There's one more thing," I say before we leave. "This can't get to the council, and this can't leak to any of the Davises. We can't risk it getting back to Johan." I let out a breath before saying, "He wants us to join with the Davises as one family under their Matriarch."

That gets a reaction. My entire family starts talking at once. Uncle Cathius is the loudest, and he isn't even saying anything coherent. He just keeps saying "Excuse me?!" over and over.

"Quiet!" I hiss, trying to avoid startling Eden with a shout. Which maybe for some people of authority would get the room silent, but of course it's my family, so instead they launch into grumbles about me telling them what to do. Once they've calmed down, I can talk again. "He says that he wants to protect us. But also . . . he thinks I should give up being a Matriarch. If we join families, it creates the same loophole as when the Huang and Bailey families split up. It'll technically be considered a new one. Davis-Thomas. That's what he strongly suggested we do."

Auntie Maise's palms spark. "We can be Davis-Thomas over my hacking dead body."

Everyone else nods along in agreement.

"I don't think Johan has anything to do with the Luc stuff." If he's this afraid for his family, how could he? Besides, how would he have gotten in with NuGene in the first place? "And Eli is helping us, so I don't think he's a leak either, even though he lied about the gene hack. But if we take this to the council, I'm sure Johan will try and stop it to make me more desperate. We'll have to go this alone."

Everyone around the room nods.

I open the door and take one last look back at Keis, Priya, and Eden standing there.

Keisha grips my arm. "She'll have your back here," she says. "And we'll have it there."

"I know," I say.

We leave. And I hope that when we come back, it'll be to a brighter future.

CHAPTER TWENTY-SEVEN

The NuSap warehouse is in an area of Mississauga that's a maze of industrial buildings and offices. Lots of companies love to have their fancy downtown spaces with sleek modern fixtures and elaborate amenities, but at some point, they have to get realistic about the space they need. That's where Mississauga comes in.

Brands and corporations will buy out huge buildings and run most of their major shipping and packaging operations from there. Meanwhile, their marketing teams and customer-facing ends stay in downtown Toronto.

The area where NuGene has their facility is packed with identical redbrick buildings, separated only by huge holo signs that declare the dozen or so businesses that reside inside that block. It's driving me out of my mind trying to navigate the thing.

Because of what Eli said about detection of outside electronics, I left my phone at home. It's not like the people working there don't have phones, but theirs would be registered with the company, and mine is very much not. I have my chip off too, which is super weird. It's like going from high definition to standard. Sounds seem duller, and my vision feels like it's the worst it's ever been. Even though I know it's probably fine. Your chip can't actually improve your vision, but I'm used to seeing things like the time and weather floating around constantly, and using optic filters to trick my mind into seeing more vivid colors, or playing background noise so I don't get bored.

Now, instead, I have some ancient watch of Granny's that we dug up to help me check the time. It's not even digital. Mom had to painfully teach me how to read the thing.

The entire family, minus Keis, Priya, and Eden, are parked in the minibus twenty minutes' walking distance from the facility where they dropped me off. But they're far enough that they're able to have their phones on them in case something goes wrong and Keis has to relay the message to them.

I'm sure she's crawling out of her skin being stuck at home. It feels too much like last year.

Sweat slides down my brow, and my fingers shake.

"Calm down," Auntie Elaine says.

Her hand is pressed against my back, feeding magic into my body. If I tried to do this on my own like at the NuGene party, my bandwidth would already be near spent before I even made it inside. Mama Jova must have agreed because Auntie Elaine showed up when I called this time. But still, at my showcase after having their magic pumped into me, I was so weak, so we have to be fast. Their power can eat into my body as surely as extending past my own bandwidth.

I make sure to keep my intention focused on having no one notice me. For the first fifteen minutes of my walk, we used that system to be sure that people's eyes would slide away whenever they happened to look over at me.

According to Eli, NuGene only has monitors on the actual facility itself. So there's no point in trying to be completely undetected by them until we reach it. Pushing attention off me is enough, and I only have to do it occasionally, because there aren't many people around.

We pass by the holo sign that lists NuGene Industries in its dozen or so buildings, and I let out a long breath. I spent some time deciding on the intention I want to use. There are risks to all of them. I could use the intention to be invisible, but it would be easy to get disoriented by seeing my visible hands and lose focus. I also thought about disabling the cameras, but that would be noticed right away.

The best combo is the simplest.

Keeping the intention to not be noticed and extending it to cameras and equipment.

I close my eyes, hold that intention in my mind, and bite my thumb with the tooth in the back of my mouth, letting the blood fall onto my tongue. The last thing I need is DNA splattered somewhere. Auntie presses her hand harder into my back, and I can feel my bandwidth expand.

While holding my intention, I try to remember Eli's instructions on how to get into the building. There's a sort of back warehouse entrance, and there's supposed to be a delivery around this time. Apparently, they're notorious for leaving the door propped open to make it easier to go back and forth even though they're not supposed to.

I see the metal door hanging open with a piece of wood propped underneath it, and the odd person walking in and out. I make my way over and slip in.

It's disorienting for a minute, and I press my back into a corner away from the camera on the ceiling to collect myself in case my intention breaks.

The warehouse is gigantic. Eli told me it was a wide-open space, but somehow I still wasn't prepared for just how much. There are huge conveyor belts and drone arms slapping cornflower-blue NuSap limbs together and sending them through assembly lines, and it's all happening at a speed that's dizzying. It reminds me of those feed videos that show behind the scenes of food facilities where these machines do the cooking and packaging.

The ceiling of the building is higher than I realized most ceilings could go, or maybe it just feels that way because it's so huge. There are not only cameras on the walls but drones with cameras floating around the space.

Near the middle, there's a giant white block attached to the ceiling with glass windows around it that I know is the oversee station. That's where most of the people during the afternoon shift will be—watching the space in case anything unusual happens, or according to Eli, more likely scrolling through their phones and relying on the computer and video system to alert them if anything goes wrong.

Which works better for me, because there are barely any people on the floor right now.

Eli said that to the right there would be a little alcove by the washrooms where I could probably pause if I need it. I dart out, and Auntie Elaine hisses in my ear, "Your other right!"

"Right," I mutter, and then remember that I shouldn't be talking because that'll make it a lot easier to notice me. I duck into the bathroom alcove and take a deep breath.

I need to stop freaking out.

I am a Matriarch of a founding family.

Granny chose me.

Mama Jova chose me.

Auntie Elaine squeezes my shoulder. "You can do it. Just calm down and remember the plan. We need the communal tablet."

I nod, remembering this time not to speak. Eli said there was a room he didn't expect anyone to be in where I could grab a tablet, take the photos, and leak them.

After that, I can leave.

I dart out from the alcove and force my steps to slow. The intent is to have people and cameras not notice me, but the sound of running footsteps in a seemingly empty hallway won't be good. It's one thing to trick a machine that's programmed to monitor regular functions and another to trick a person.

So I walk lightly down the hall instead. I think about tiptoeing, but it would make the whole thing feel too ridiculous.

The perimeter around the warehouse space seems to be the only one that has halls and rooms. The first one I pass is the break room. People stand around with their coffees, and I focus my intention extra hard as I pass them.

I get to a point with two ways to turn and try in vain to figure out which way I should be going.

"To the right." Keis's voice slams into my mind like a freight train.

I stumble, and my intention drops, but I manage to snap it back into place.

"Sorry," she says, not as forceful this time. "Not used to doing this."

It's fine, I think, and focus again on where I need to go. I follow Keis's instructions and go right. Of course, my cousin has done a much better job with her memorization than I have.

"Soon there's going to be a door on the left. Go in there—it's up the stairs," she says.

It's a lot easier now to focus my intention since I'm not also trying to remember how to get around. I wonder if Keis realized that and that's why she's helping out now. Auntie Elaine probably could do it, but if she's silent, I assume it's because of some Mama Jova reason stopping her.

I try not to think about it too much and keep following what Keis is saying.

"This room, here," she says.

I nearly skid to a halt in front of a room with a metal door and a little sign next to it that says TESTING OFFICE.

This is the part that's less great. If someone is inside the room, I'll have to work that much harder for them not to notice me. It's one thing to use the intention when I'm sneaking by someone in the hallway and another if we're going to be sharing a space while I do things.

I swallow and open the door quickly before rushing in.

There's no one inside.

The whole thing is a lot bigger than I would have thought for a small office space. It's pretty much the size of our kitchen and dining room put together, with tables decked out with tablets or full-on computers and little stations filled with spare NuSap parts. To my left is what looks like a giant mirror, which seems strange in the room, but I ignore it. In front of me is a glass observation window that looks out onto the floor, making it easy to take the photos that I need.

I grab a tablet from the table and boot it up. It asks for a username and password, and I use the communal credentials. It's not that hard to figure out since they're posted in huge print letters on the wall, I guess so that anyone who comes in can use them.

Now all I have to do is take the pictures. I lift up the tablet, but it's set on the selfie cam. As I reach to turn it around, I notice a part of the mirror swinging open like a door.

Someone rushes out too fast for me to see, and the next thing I know, pain is screaming through my body. Panic and fear seize me, and my brain goes blank. It's like being back in the Davises' basement again, the searing pain of the magic whipping my chest, but worse because it spreads across my limbs this time. Every part of me shaking with the force of electricity ripping through it. I must bite my tongue with the metal tooth because blood drips out between my lips. My magic rises underneath my skin, but another jolt of pain has it shutting down.

"More," a voice growls. "It's got to be more. That's what he said."

Something prods me again, and the pain explodes. I'm desperate now. Panicking. I reach for magic with everything that I have inside of me and feel it being tugged roughly into my body. Someone is screaming in my ears, but I can't concentrate. I'm lost to the pain.

"More!" the voice shouts.

"Any more and she'll die," someone else snaps. They poke me with the toe of their shoe, but I can barely feel it. "Look, that last time she didn't even use any magic, according to the monitor. She's out."

The pain isn't coming anymore, but I can barely get my bearings together before the door to the room slams open. I can't see it; I'm facing away from the entrance to the room, sprawled on my stomach, twitching. But I hear it.

"Look who it is," someone sneers. No, not someone. Him. Juras. "Get him!"

There's a sound of scuffling, and the electric buzz of something else.

Then a thump, and someone is lying beside me.

Slowly, I turn my head and come face to face with Eli's eyes. Wide open and blank.

Dead.

Dead.

I let out a whimper that sounds inhuman.

He came here to save me. To help me. And now he's dead.

It was too fast.

This isn't real.

This can't be real.

Jasmine sinks down until I can see her by tilting up my head. She says, "Don't be too heartbroken. He was already dead."

346

What does that even mean?

My side explodes with pain as someone kicks it, and I'm flipped onto my back by the force of it. I end up looking into Juras's furious face. His dark skin is ashy, and his eyes have a sunken quality to them.

"Give me the baton," he says to Jasmine.

I look over at the girl who, instead of giving him the sleek black metal stick in her hand, grips it tighter. "We're not killing her."

"Why not? She's going to die anyway."

Jasmine presses her lips into a thin line. "Luc would be upset."

"Luc can get hacked," Juras snarls. He tries to make a grab for it, but Jasmine smoothly pulls it out of the way. "Jazz!"

"I have a better idea," she says. "Let's lock her in the room with the units. We'll set them on a timer. She can wait and suffer, knowing she's going to die while her family are in peril." She looks at me. "Which they will be if they come for you."

Juras glares down at me, naked hatred in his eyes. "Okay . . . yeah, okay."

"Good. Then let's get her up."

Both of them haul me to my feet and drag me into the mirror room that they came out of. Where they were waiting.

They knew.

They knew that I would be there. But how? Eli came in to save me, so it couldn't have been him.

I'm dropped on the floor roughly, and the light flickers on. NuSap units fill the space. They're already dressed in civilian clothes. Dresses, and shorts, and sweaters. No regard for the weather at all. Just clothes over blue skin.

Juras grins down at me. "These are special units. Accelerated. The symptoms will come on a lot faster." He shrugs. "Not until they turn on, of course. But that's coming. We've decided to do a bit of an early release with these ones. They'll go on in about an hour. Though I think now we'll make that twenty minutes instead." He looks at Jasmine to see if she'll protest, but she doesn't say a word.

"Is this really equal to what I did to you?" I choke out, staring at Juras. "Me and my whole family dead? A whole community. Is that really revenge?"

His lips turn into a snarl. "You were going to come for us. You and your little council. This time, I'm not going to wait around unknowing for you to attack me and my family. We're prepared. We're getting you before you can get us."

"We only formed the council because of what *you* did."

"Don't lie. We know all about you gathering other witches to take us down. You're furious that Justin didn't give your aunt a piece of the NuGene pie. You're coming for us. Justin was just the start."

"What are you talking about?" I croak. It makes no sense, this stuff he's saying. I can't tell if he's making excuses for what he's doing or if he really believes this. I don't even know how he knows about the council at all. Did Eli leak that to them before he decided to help?

I try to drag up magic, but it's impossible. I'm too shaky and weak.

Auntie Elaine is gone too.

I look over at Jasmine, who only narrows her eyes at me. "You were coming for us. You were always going to. That's why we had to come up with this plan. That's why we had to protect ourselves and everyone from you and your kind."

"We weren't," I wheeze. "We only wanted to grieve and move on. I told you that."

Juras scoffs. "We should kill her now."

"Fine," Jasmine snaps, and tosses the baton to him. His eyes go wide as he holds it. "Do it, then."

"Luc . . ."

"Luc can get hacked. Isn't that what you said? Go on. Kill her." Jasmine steps close enough to get up in her sponsor brother's face.

I squirm frantically, trying to move, trying to get my magic to work. Anything.

Juras holds the baton and grips it hard between his hands. Then he looks at me. Then at Jasmine. Then back at the baton. Then repeats it. Over and over.

It takes three cycles for me to realize that he's not going to do it.

He was a big man when he was ordering his sister to kill me, but that's gone now that he's the one holding the weapon.

Jasmine sighs. "See? You can't. That's why you designed this, isn't it? Why you messed with Luc's original formulas. Added a little cellular degeneration in the mix, which did create some other unexpected side effects, but it ultimately does what you want it to. Because you knew you couldn't do it yourself. Not face-to-face like this."

"You knew?" Juras says, lips going slack.

"I know you." She points into the room beyond the mirror. "I have to put the monitor on her. Can you go grab Eli and drag him in? We don't want anyone finding him."

Juras nods, sticking the baton under his arm and leaving the room. Meanwhile, Jasmine comes over and squats beside me to slap a monitor on my wrist.

"Our families have lived here for over a hundred years. Why would we wait until now to do something?" I say. "Entire families— *children* are going to die."

For a moment, I think she'll ignore me. In the other room, Juras grunts as he tries to move Eli. But then, "I've never seen Juras as scared as he is when he looks at you. Talks about you. Hears about you." She clenches her hands into fists. I think she might punch me, but she doesn't. "He's my brother. I'm going to make the world better for him." She shrugs and whispers, "Besides, I don't know how to stop it . . . but if he really loves you, he'll save you."

"What?"

"Juras put in an upgrade on this monitor. If it detects that you're using magic, you'll get a lovely shock, like the one before. It doesn't come off without our say-so either."

Jasmine stands and leaves the room, helping Juras drag Eli next to me where they drop him. I look away. I can't watch his lifeless body. There's a cracking sound, and I cry out. His skull. I didn't think they dropped him that hard, but they must have.

"Let's go," Jasmine says, and leads Juras out of the room. She flicks off the lights before they leave, and the lock of the door clicks behind them.

I'm alone in the dark.

No, not alone. Eli is here too.

The door swinging shut behind them is final.

Trapped.

I reach out for Eli, to see if maybe, just maybe, he's alive. My eyes squeezed shut. I touch his head, expecting blood from the crack, but instead, it's . . . rough. I open my eyes and squint, dragging myself closer, pushing him to the side, and freeze.

That can't be right.

I reach for his head, press my fingers to his exposed wound, and *pull*. Something snaps loose, and when I bring it close to my face it's obvious, even in the dark, that it's wires.

Eli isn't dead.

He isn't dead because he's not real.

Eli is a NuSap.

But . . . people knew him. Not just Ilana, but Lee, too. His cousin from the market. There is a real Elijah Bailey. I think immediately of the two profiles that Jasmine pulled up. One where he was alive, and one where he was dead.

He ran away.

Like Lauren.

Except Lauren *didn't* run away.

She was taken by Justin.

Killed by Justin.

Justin, who was investigating kids from witch families.

Eli was gone for months, they said. Now I'm guessing that it was exactly six months ago when he first went missing. That Justin got in one more experiment before he "died." Or maybe Eli was before Lauren? I have no idea.

But someone realized and put in this NuSap to take the real Eli's place. Programmed it for that. But then . . . why would a NuSap they programmed turn on them? Was it coded *too* well? Did it develop human feelings or something? That's some feed show bullshit.

I can't think about this right now.

My family. Jasmine said if they tried to come for me, they would get hurt. Probably they have more of the NuSaps like the ones in this room.

I scream in my mind and hope Keis hears it.

Don't come for me. Too dangerous. Trap.

Then after a moment.

I'm sorry. For everything.

CHAPTER TWENTY-EIGHT

I lie in a snowflake position on the floor, waiting to be hacked. I should be trying to find a way out of the room. But after dragging myself off the ground to confirm that the door was, in fact, locked, the whole thing seemed fruitless. Jasmine and Juras have their bases covered between this room and the monitor. There's no way out of here except that door.

I decide to call Jasmine's bluff and attempt to summon up the tiny bit of magic I have left and am rewarded with a shock so strong that all I can do is lie in place and twitch for the next few minutes. And even once I'm able to move, there isn't any point in doing it.

Keis hasn't pushed any thoughts into my head. I hope that she heard me so that the family doesn't try to come.

My reign as Matriarch is going to end so soon after it started. Tears fill my eyes. I let everyone down. From the start, they knew that I wouldn't be good at this. I finally made them believe in me, and now I've failed.

Granny was wrong.

Mama Jova was wrong.

Anyone who ever believed that I could be a good Matriarch was wrong.

I knew that I wasn't cut out for this, but I kept trying to trick myself into thinking that maybe I was. That somehow I could be as good as Granny. Better even.

I laugh out loud, and it's a dry, wispy thing.

Imagine that. Me thinking that I could do a better job somehow. That I could change things.

Now the family will wish that we took Johan up on his offer. That we joined the Davises and were part of their family. Though the Davises aren't immune to this either.

I look at the watch on my wrist. I still can't properly tell the time. I'm either ten, fifteen, or five minutes away from certain death.

I wish Keis would talk to me.

I wish that everything were different.

That Granny hadn't been forced to die and leave us. That I hadn't needed to be the Matriarch. I wish that Auntie Elaine hadn't died. That none of the bad things that ever befell my family happened. It's so exhausting. Nothing ever seems to get better for us. Is this what life is? Struggling over and over again for the smallest wins, only to end up with bigger disappointments?

We suffer and we survive.

I thought I could change that. But maybe we were always meant to suffer and survive.

Except this time, the last bit is less certain.

I wish that I could see the future that my mistakes have wrought. But even if I could access my gift, maybe I wouldn't want to. Not to mention, I've never changed my own life significantly. I've always been useless and a disappointment.

A gentle sound like a tablet starting up fills the room, and the air turns misty.

It's time.

I bite my lip as tears stream down my face. I can't even be bothered trying not to breathe in. What would be the point? I can't hold my breath forever.

This is supposed to be an accelerated version. Ailee's was already so fast. How long will I have with mine? A few hours until I die? Or even less? Minutes? Seconds?

I hope that the next Matriarch will do a better job than I could.

I'm supposed to choose, but I can't.

For the first time in months, I'm gripped again by indecision. I don't trust myself anymore. I can't pick someone new. Not me. I'll have to believe that Mama Jova will do it for me.

It's shameful, not making a choice and leaving it to the ancestors to choose for you. But my legacy is already dredged in shame, so what's the harm in a little more?

Whoever she is, I'm sure she'll be a much better Matriarch than I was.

The door to the room bursts open, and the lights flash on. They're so blinding that I have to put a hand over my eyes, since my chip is turned off and can't help them adjust. When I put my arm back down, Luc is in the doorway, leaning against the frame, panting.

I don't even know that I've seen him sweat before, but he is *so* sweaty. It drips off his forehead and into his face in huge splashes, some falling into his blue-gray eyes.

. . . but if he really loves you, he'll save you.

"What are you doing?!" he shouts. "Get up and come out!"

I scramble to my feet and rush out the door with him. He slams it shut. Immediately, he collapses onto the floor, his breathing labored.

I can't think of anything else to do but blink and watch him.

Finally, he hops to his feet and grabs hold of my shoulders. "Are you okay?"

"I . . . don't know." And I don't. I'm confused. And I'm not actually sure if the minute I spent in there with the machines was enough to hack my genes. But mostly I have no idea why he's here. "What are you doing?"

His jaw drops. "What am *I* doing? What about you?! I knew this was a hacked idea. I tried to be positive and get on board when I should have pushed harder to come up with a different plan. But you *had* to, didn't you?!"

"But why are you here?" I say, because I can't reconcile me almost dying and Luc holding onto me.

"I came here because I didn't want to hacking lose you! You're impossible!" He shakes his head at me, furious and covered in sweat.

I think of what Jasmine said, and the words slip out before I can stop them. "Because you love me?"

"Obviously!" he cries.

"But you hated me . . ." *And I hated you too.* Or at least, I was furious with him. But now I don't know.

Luc shakes his head and lets out a laugh. "You know, I really tried to do that. I really did, but you make it so hacking hard." It's then that I realize that some of the sweat isn't sweat at all.

It's tears.

A choke comes out of the back of my throat, and my eyes well up again, and suddenly I'm clinging to him, and we're both crying, which is ridiculous, but we are.

I'm crying because I'm alive.

Because I've been saved.

Because he's here.

"Wait . . ." I pull back abruptly. "You said that you should have pushed harder to come up with a different plan . . . But you didn't . . . Eli . . ." And then it hits me.

Eli, who was supposed to be a PR intern but knew a lot about genetics.

Eli, who was so hot and cold. One moment not wanting

anything to do with the council, and the next moment dedicated to finding a solution.

Eli, who stared at me from across the room at the conference. Moments after I had seen Luc for the first time in months.

Eli, who declared we would be breaking into a NuGene party that spontaneously sprung into being.

That Jasmine said *Luc* had planned.

Eli, who was supposed to be dead but instead was running around as a NuSap.

"It was you," I say. "It was always *you*."

Luc swallows and tucks his hands into his pockets, but he doesn't look away. Eli did that too. Ancestors help me, now I feel like my shit is so sparked for not realizing. But who would have guessed that?

"Not . . . always. Sometimes I had things to do," he says. "Then I left the unit on autopilot. Which it isn't great at. The units need time for the AI to build up to that level of natural human-like behavior, and I couldn't wait for that. I didn't think I would have to. During off hours, I was hiding him at NuGene for that reason, but then Ilana realized, and I got caught in that trap and had to pretend Eli was an intern there. Not that I would ever actually let the autopilot work and expose him to NuGene employees who would know what he was right away. Especially now that they're constantly around units. He sits in a room during 'shifts.'"

The spacey-ness. Those weird times where Eli seemed so vacant and far away. It's because he was just a robot, operating like usual. No wonder he was totally cool with scheduling me into the Helping Hands volunteering. NuSaps are programmed to serve. Then Luc saw me that day and that's why "Eli" was panicked about me being there. Because I wasn't supposed to be.

"You were him, this whole time?!" I shout, repeating myself

because I can't get over it. "Is your shit *sparked*?!" We had spent so much time together. And he had been in all our council meetings. Knew everything we talked about. I had trusted him, leaned on him, felt understood by him.

And all the while, he was the same boy who was the reason we're in this position in the first place.

But then . . . he had been helping.

Anger rushes up, but I don't know what to do with it. I had just reconciled with the idea of letting go of the Luc I knew. And yet I had immediately thrown myself into his arms like a lovesick little girl. Now I was doubling back because he had helped as Eli? He had also kept secrets. He hadn't told the truth. The NuSap danger was still very real. "This is your fault!"

Luc cringes. "Look, I know. I'm sorry. I can explain everything, but we need to leave now before Jasmine and Juras come back. Let's go." He races out of the room without waiting for me, and despite everything, I follow him. I can't cast to keep us concealed, but he hasn't said anything about us being noticed, so I guess it doesn't matter.

The big concern over getting caught was his sponsor siblings finding out what we were doing, and that's already happened.

Luc takes us down the stairs into an underground parking garage. A microcar zooms toward us, and he instructs me to get into it. We both tumble into the back, and the car starts driving away.

He takes a deep breath and reaches out. "Give me your wrist."

I don't. "This whole hacking time! How did this even start? Why have a NuSap of Eli at all?"

"They'll track us if you don't give me your monitor!"

Begrudgingly, I give him my hand. He uses some sort of small tool to get the monitor off my wrist and tosses it out the window.

"Littering," I mutter.

"Really?!"

"Explain," I snap.

Luc sinks against the back of the seat and stares at the ceiling. "Don't you want to know if you got hacked and are possibly dying?"

"Explain!"

"Fine," he says, and finally looks at me. "Elijah Bailey . . . He was killed by Justin. Must have been. But we didn't realize until we found someone trespassing on NuGene property who discovered the body. Someone was looking for Eli, which I guess Justin hadn't counted on. Or maybe he wasn't able to hide it better before he died."

"Looking for him . . . because they thought Eli had run away."

Luc nods.

I was right. He hadn't really run away the same way Lauren hadn't run away. "What about Lauren's body?"

"I'm sorry. We don't know where it is. We looked around after that for more, but nothing. Justin must have had time to . . ."

To dispose of her. Justin had murdered them both. Someone had been looking for Eli and found him. Someone strong enough to get into NuGene. Ilana was Eli's Matriarch . . .

Does that mean that she's the traitor? That she's been working with Luc and his siblings this whole time? Tears well up in my eyes, and I let them flow. I'm so hacking tired of crying. It hurts. This entire time, Ilana has been the only person on the council who I felt really cared about me and believed in me, even when she was chewing me out.

Luc looks at my tears and lets out a sigh. "I'm sorry. I know you're close. Or were close, anyway, before things went bad."

Were close? I turn to him fully. "Wait, who are you talking about?"

"Who are *you* talking about?"

"Ilana Bailey."

Luc balks. "No! Ilana is . . . Ilana doesn't know anything. She's been, honestly, so nice to me. To Eli, anyway. She's been taking care of his mom and everything." He shakes his head roughly. "I'm so sorry about Eli's mom. He did that before I could stop him. He was worried she would notice that Eli wasn't Eli."

He.

Were close.

"Johan," I whisper.

Luc nods.

It all makes sense. Of course it does. Eli was so hyper-aware of him in every single meeting, and Johan seemed annoyed with him in turn. Though he mostly ignored him. Clearly, Johan is a lot better at playing the game than Luc is.

I swallow thickly. "When he found Eli's body, you all were there. And you decided to work together, and . . ." I look into Luc's eyes. "He told you I was going to come after you. For revenge." That was what Jasmine and Juras were talking about.

"Yes."

Johan started this.

"When did this happen?" I say.

"September."

From the moment my gift was announced and I became Matriarch, I started defying him. I helped the people who he wouldn't without a price attached. I became the leader of the family in a way he never could. He never liked any of it.

Now I see his offer for us to join his family for what it really is. Not an offer. A threat.

Join us or die.

Luc continues, "So when the council was formed, it just seemed like another step in your plan. Meanwhile, I pretended to be Eli, even doing things he did while he was alive, like volunteering, so that I would have access to the community and could observe the effects of the gene hack. Everyone agreed, because we needed the data. But it wasn't working right. It was supposed to get rid of your magic. Accelerated natural selection, like I said before. But it was messing with your gifts instead. Jasmine and Juras didn't want to stop it. Then Ilana brought me to your showcase and volunteered me to help, and I couldn't say no without it being suspicious. So I tried not to be helpful."

I shake my head at him. "You still did this. You started this. Even if it was just to take our magic, what gave you the right to decide that? Did you ever think of how I was feeling? My grandma was dead. Our family was completely uprooted. You had lost Justin, but you also had everything you wanted. We were both hurting, but you were the one who decided to hurt us more." And I was the one who made it possible. I chose to let him keep his future and stole Keis's instead. It's clearer than ever that I completely hacked that decision.

Luc bites his lip and stares down at his lap. "I know . . . I didn't think of how you felt. And I was afraid too. Afraid of losing the bit of family that I had left. Of being vulnerable." He raises his head, and his eyes meet mine. "At volunteering, that's when I realized how wrong I was. When you apologized, when you said no one had to die, you were so sincere. And when I saw you as Eli, you were so hurt, so . . . broken. I knew that Johan had lied. But I still couldn't let go. I kept thinking that I could fix the hack and everything would be fine. Magic gone without any lives lost. But then we were spending so much time together. You were trying so hard. And after seeing Ailee's back, knowing that you could die from this, that they all could? That was the day I decided to try to stop the whole thing."

I think about the NuGene party. That was him, as Eli, twirling me on the dance floor, laughing with me. He was in that room, trying to convince Jasmine to think of the lives at stake. He was in that park with me, trying to explain.

"I wouldn't do that to you. I would never try to hurt you like that."

But he *had* hurt me. He started this, and he didn't know how to fix it.

Though part of me acknowledges that I had done the same. I made choices that I thought were right that weren't. I messed up in ways that would last a lifetime. Keis's life is ruined because of me. Granny is dead because I didn't touch Luc when Mama wanted me to.

I connected with Eli because I felt that we had both screwed up, and the two of us were bonded by a desperate desire to make up for it.

Luc says, "Maybe it doesn't mean anything, but I'm sorry. I'm sorry for realizing how wrong I was too late. But I'm trying to fix it now. Like I said, you don't owe me your forgiveness, but I'm going to help you anyway."

That part of me, the part that I thought I left in the snow, rises up again, but I squash it down. Just like me and Keis, what me and Luc had is ruined. It's never going to be the same, and I don't even know if it can be a single percent of what it was. But I do need his help, and I'm not going to turn it away.

"Johan's family is in as much trouble as ours," I say, shaking my head. "How can he be okay with this?"

Luc turns away for a moment. I can't tell if it's because of the question I asked or if he's realized that I'm not going to say that I forgive him. "Yeah, they are. That's why he was in favor of having me continue to pretend to be Eli even though some of his cover was blown." Luc turns back to me. "His family wasn't supposed to be affected. I didn't see your vision, since I was in a NuSap body, but from how the others talked, people he loves ended up in danger anyway. He knows I'm the only one working on a cure. But for now, he has a monitor thing on his kids and sends that data to us, and we make sure the NuSaps don't go near him."

In the end, he put his family in danger because he couldn't stand that I was a threat to his power. Aqua was right. He's scared, and his fear is driving him to make risky choices. I can't understand how he could put so much trust in Luc, Jasmine, and Juras. He can barely trust his own flesh and blood.

Luc reaches out for my wrist. "Can I check you now and make sure that you weren't affected by the NuSap? Please?"

"No point," I say, and lift up the edge of my shirt where a sore is forming. I could feel it burning while we talked. "I'm hacked."

Literally.

CHAPTER TWENTY-NINE

The car stops in front of the house, and I turn to Luc, who keeps glancing at my shirt where the sore is hidden and looking away. He's bitten his lip so much there are little indents in the flesh. I can't help but put together the interactions that I had with Eli knowing now that it was Luc. He has hacked this situation to death. He participated in this revenge, but he's also been frantically trying to stop it.

"How is it that you're the CEO of this company but can't stop your siblings?" I ask. "You're a genius."

Luc lets out a laugh. "They're geniuses too, you know. Trust me. They were brought over as candidates like me. They're not lackeys. If I'm honest, I think Justin picked me just because he liked me best. But those two, they're smart." Luc shakes his head. "Justin has a catch-all gene hack that's supposed to reverse everything. You can think of it as an antidote, but it's basically bringing your genes back to factory settings by destroying all the nanites and whatever programming they implemented on your body. He was the one who figured it out. Gene hacking. We found his notes on it and managed to push from the liquid state to the gas."

My eyes bug out. "We can—"

"We can't," Luc bites out. "Because by the time I'd smartened up to what was happening and went to grab the vials of catch-all that Justin had made, they were gone. Jasmine and Juras *knew* that I would go back on this. And they prepared before I'd even thought of it."

"Does Johan know about the catch-all?"

"No, Jazz and Juras said we shouldn't tell him because then he would make demands to have it, and we might need it. But I'm guessing they just never planned to keep their word to him."

Hack me. Luc is right, I had been thinking of his siblings as lesser-than this whole time. It was hard not to. They always seemed to be in the background. Constantly second best. Now they had shown they weren't to be underestimated. "They realized you were betraying them with Eli too, didn't they? That's how they knew I would be in the facility today."

Luc nods. "I was monitoring your progress to make sure everything went all right. I had Eli hidden nearby in case you needed help. They must have latched onto the feed somehow and realized what was happening." He crosses his arms over his chest. "They had so many contingencies based on me backing out that I didn't even hacking think of because I made the mistake of assuming we trusted each other."

"It's because they know you," I say. "Family always does."

"*They* did. I didn't. Otherwise, I could have predicted everything getting sparked to shit."

"So how do we stop them?" I ask, changing the subject.

"They must have put those vials somewhere."

I jump out of the car. "Someone in my family can do a searching spell. We'll find them."

Luc stumbles out after me, and I walk into the house. The second I come through the doors, Keis is rushing down the hall, and the entire family after her. Luc kind of shrinks behind me, but they're not even paying attention to him.

Everyone rushes at me, and I'm lost in a sea of limbs. There are hugs, petting of my hair, and I get a wet kiss from who I'm sure is Eden being held up by someone.

Then everyone is talking at once, and I can't understand any of them, and can't even see half of them with some of the hugs still in progress.

Finally, the words "SHUT UP!" scream through my head, and I wince along with the rest of my family sans Eden, who blinks at us as Priya sets her down on the ground.

Keis.

My cousin looks terrible. Her pineapple bun has come completely undone, and her face is caked with tears. "Why don't we give her some space?"

Everyone steps back except Mom, who stays a couple of extra seconds to give me one last squeeze.

"I'm not dead," I say, trying to lighten the mood.

Auntie Maise rolls her eyes. "Obviously not, or we would have a new Matriarch."

Keis jerks her head at Luc. "That asshole messaged your phone from a burner app to say he was coming for you and a bunch of other cheesy shit."

Luc's entire face flushes. I didn't even realize he could physically get so red, but he does now. "You have her phone?!" Then he continues, "Besides, I messaged Priya, too! You didn't have to look at Voya's phone."

Keis grins. "I wondered if you had messaged her, too, so I checked it."

"How did you get into my phone?" I balk.

"Emergency manual passcode. It's very easy to guess."

Luc looks like he wants to die. Now I really want to know what he put in those messages.

"Anyway, that's why everyone came back here. I was listening to your thoughts but lost everything when you tugged."

"Tugged . . ." When I was being shocked. *Oh no.* I pulled on so much magic. I must have yanked on theirs. "I'm sorry."

Keis gives Luc a hard look. "Why don't you hang out here for a bit." It sounds like a question, but it isn't. My cousin leads the way toward the basement, and I follow her down with the rest of the family.

When I get to the bottom, I'm looking at Justin's form, slumped over on the ground.

"We found him like that," Keis says, her fists shaking at her sides.

I look back at her. "I don't understand."

"He's gone," Dad snaps. He's practically vibrating with rage. "We should have killed him when we had the chance."

Auntie Maise sighs. "When you pulled on our magic . . . no one inside the house had bandwidth anymore."

No.

No. No. No. No.

Holding Justin in required active magic. The witches inside of the house needed to have bandwidth to make our home keep him in. It's not like the passive magic in the bones of the house that power Eden's life.

When Jasmine shocked me, I hadn't even thought about it, I just pulled. Tugged in my panic, and effectively expended the bandwidth of everyone in the family, including Keis and Priya, the only witches inside the house.

I can't believe that at one point I thought anything to do with our magic working through this house might be a positive instead of a negative.

"But . . . he's here," I say. If he were going to escape, shouldn't he be outside? Not down here exactly where he was supposed to be.

Keis holds out a device. It takes me a moment to realize that it's a phone. "I found this on him."

"Whose is it? Yours doesn't even have internet access. Did he steal someone else's?"

She shakes her head. "It's none of ours. I have no idea how he got it." Her eyes well up with frustrated tears as she gnashes her teeth. "I'm sorry. I was supposed to be watching him."

How in ancestors' name did he get that? No one in the family would have given it to him. Was it at the showcase? That's the only time other people have been in the house. But that was so long ago. We avoided Justin having internet access out of fear that he would use it to escape. Why wait until now? Unless . . . the magic of the house was still holding him in. Forcing him to wait until this moment.

"Someone gave this to him," I say aloud finally. "Someone outside our family."

"Johan?" Dad asks. "I mean, he's the only person we would suspect. Or Eli? What's going on with him?"

Luc is Eli. And he came to save me. If he knew Justin was alive, he would have already tried to get the solution from him. Everything Luc has done shows that he thinks his mentor is dead. "It wasn't Eli," I say.

Johan . . . maybe, but why? Besides, he shouldn't have even known that Justin was here, and he was already working with Luc and them. What would be the point in also helping Justin?

But that was before my vision. Before he realized that Aqua's life was in danger when he had been told that it wouldn't be. He must have figured that he couldn't trust Luc and his siblings to protect his family.

That night, I thought that Justin's settings kept him away from the basement door . . . but later Justin revealed that those settings didn't count staircases. He could have come up and made a deal with Johan during the time when I assumed the Davis leader had left. He was angry and stalking toward the front door; I didn't think I needed to follow his path out. But he could have easily made a quick turn toward the basement if he was being nosy and discovered Justin. Or Justin could have even tried to get Johan's attention after eavesdropping and realizing Johan was against the council. In a situation as desperate as being held captive in a basement, why not shoot your shot?

But Johan wouldn't have already had the phone then. There must have been some other time he delivered it. And Justin would have needed access to the drone too. I wrack my brain, but the only moment I can think of is that drone I found on the porch the day that Keis's chip went missing last week. We checked Justin, and he didn't have anything on him. Or . . . it seemed like he didn't. But that drone . . . From the monitors he puts on his kids, Johan would have access to lots of them, and he actually owns the on-brand stuff and would be smart enough to package it like a return. But he might not have realized that ours are actually knock-offs. I knew it was strange but brushed it off.

We were so busy arguing about that missing chip and if Uncle Vacu stole it that the drone could have easily gotten over to Justin.

It didn't make sense for Justin to steal the chip and break it if he wanted to use it. But it did make sense if he was manipulating us. Creating a distraction. We were doing searching spells for chips, not phones, and if the chip wasn't in its original form, we wouldn't have been able to find it anyway.

The only reason Justin wasn't gone as soon as he got the phone must have been the magic in the house. Even though he was trying to escape with data, it still held him inside.

Does that mean that Johan already has the cure? Did Justin give it to him? Or did Jasmine and Juras get to it first?

Either way, Justin is gone.

Now I have nothing to bargain with for us to get the cure straight from the source. And a murderer is loose in the world again.

I let out a little sob. Mama Jova told me to watch the push and pull of my magic. She told me to be careful about Justin. And like every other time that I've sparked something to shit, I didn't listen. I was so focused on the loosening of restrictions on that hacking tablet and thinking he had stolen that piece of tech Keis was missing, and it didn't even matter. He was patient. He was ready to wait for this chance. He's a genius, after all.

Hack me. Hack me. Hack me.

"Justin is the least of our problems right now," Keis whispers, looking at me.

Keisha looks between us, and like always, hits on it before everyone else. Tears spring to her eyes. "No . . . no . . . you weren't, right? Vo?!"

I swallow. "I was gene-hacked. It's faster acting than Ailee's . . . I probably don't have a lot of time."

The whole family goes quiet.

Until finally a wail bursts from Mom's lips, and Auntie Maise bundles her into her arms. I press my hands against my mouth to stop myself from doing the same. I know I'm trying not to stifle my feelings, but if I cry, Mom will completely break. This is what she was worried about this entire time. She was terrified that something would happen to me, and now it has.

There's a loud knock at the door that shocks everyone.

We rush back upstairs, and Luc throws up his hands as if to say, *It's not me!*

Before I even get a chance to tell him to leave, the door opens on its own, and a rush of people come in: Ilana, Torrin, Avery, and Johan—the Matriarchs with furious faces, and Johan with a cool neutral expression. Behind him, Eli slinks in.

Wait, *Eli?*

He's got a hat pulled over his head, probably to hide his "wound," but that's him.

There's no way this is Luc.

And when Eli pulls a sly grin, I know it isn't.

Jasmine or Juras. One of them is piloting him.

"So, it's true," Ilana spits, shaking her head. "You're here with him."

I immediately swivel my head to Luc, who stands in place, just as frozen as I am.

"What's going on?" Mom says, jumping into action. "You're just going to barge into our house?"

Avery holds up her phone, and on it is a video of me and Luc tearfully embracing in the NuGene warehouse. Despite myself, the entire back of my neck heats up. Thankfully, there's no sound. But it also isn't showing the whole story. It's not a video of him saving me, only that embrace.

Avery points to Eli. "He managed to get a recording and send this to us. Traitors! All of you!"

I'm starting to experience firsthand just how smart Luc's sponsor siblings are.

"Luc came to help me," I grind out. "He's trying to help all of us."

The James Matriarch lets out a cruel laugh. "Oh, and we're supposed to believe that?"

"It's true," Auntie Maise snarls, her fingertips sparking.

I jerk my head at her, shocked. But my whole family aren't trying to distance themselves from Luc. They're standing *with* us.

I brought him here. I believe in him, and they believe in me. That's why.

It's a show of their trust in me.

"Like we'll believe you now," Torrin snaps. "Going behind our backs to the NuGene party was one thing, and now going behind our backs to a NuGene facility? All these 'conversations' you had with this boy that conveniently leaked information?"

"I've been gene-hacked!" I shout. "If I were betraying you, why would I do that to myself?!"

"Because you have an antidote," Johan says smoothly. "Just for you and yours to use at any time."

My jaw drops. The real traitor is trying to pin everything on me, and none of them would even realize it until I was dead. Maybe until the NuSaps had killed us all.

Even as I look at Johan, I can't imagine how he's so fine with this. So willing to let us be wiped out in his obsession with thinking that his family is in constant danger.

"Why would we even do that?" I say. "Why create a council to stop it if I had the antidote the whole time? If I wanted this to happen?"

"To track our moves, obviously." Torrin crosses her arms. "Show them the other photos, Avery."

Avery scrolls through and shows the photo of me and Luc at the park with Maya that day. "You didn't tell us about this little meetup either."

"What are you talking about? I—" I didn't tell them. Because I couldn't trust them, so I didn't talk about seeing Maya or knowing it was the NuSaps.

"Mm-hmm," Torrin says smugly.

Uncle Cathius puffs out his chest and glares at his brother. "We're your family. Why would we do that to you?"

"*Are* you?" Johan says, his voice smooth like honey. "I remember that Miss Voya over here messed up my ritual. Everyone acted like it was so hacked that I thought it was on purpose. How about now? Two people died at Caribana last year. Maybe that's what you wanted."

"Why would I want that?" I scream, tears gathering in my eyes. "I know that was my fault. I know I messed up. Do you know how much guilt I carry every hacking day?! I have been trying to do everything I can to protect this community. To make up for my mistakes." No one is even hearing what I'm saying. They're just shaking their heads. He's fooling them. He's winning. "Ilana!" I cry.

She turns away from me. "Your family is removed from this council. We cannot trust you. And we *will* find a way to get that antidote from you. If you have any humanity left, you'll share it with us."

"We don't have it!"

She shakes her head and pins me with a look. "Your grandmother would be so disappointed in you." With that, they turn and head out the door.

My legs are so weak that they drop out from underneath me and I crumble to the ground.

We're ruined.

Nothing left.

Shut out of the witch community that I dreamed of building up.

Ilana is right.

Granny *would* be disappointed in me.

"The searching spell," Luc jumps in. "We can do that and find the antidote."

Keisha pegs him with a look and points a sharp nail his way. "Just so you don't get your wires twisted, buddy, you're here and you're being tolerated because Voya is vouching for you and because we need you, but don't get too comfortable ordering us around."

Luc shifts in place and nods. "Right, um, yes. I am sorry for everything. Also, sorry, I wasn't trying to order you around, I just—"

"You're very uncomfortable right now."

I rub my palms against my eyes. "Searching spell! What does the antidote look like?"

"It's just a regular vial with clear liquid," Luc says.

My stomach drops.

He looks at me and then around at my sighing family. "What?"

"Searching spells won't work on something that vague when we don't even know where it is," Alex says, running her hands over her scalp. "We'll ping a million places that we could never search."

"If Justin were alive . . . would he know where it is?" I say, my voice low.

Luc lets out a surprised laugh. "Well, he isn't, is he?"

"He is."

He does nothing but stare at me. "What?"

"I never killed Justin. I transferred his consciousness into a NuSap unit that we kept in our basement. And he's just escaped."

I watch as the truth rushes over Luc. As his face twists and he tries to fight against the reality that his revenge was always unfounded.

"He's alive?" he croaks.

"He's alive. And we need to find him."

CHAPTER THIRTY

T he searching spell on Justin immediately fails.

I flop onto the entranceway stairs and fold in half, tugging my knees up to my chest and pressing my face into them.

Wherever he is, he doesn't look like he did anymore. It's useless.

"I'm starting to think the searching spell might be the most useless cast," Keisha says, very matter of fact.

It's like her voice is far away. Everything is tumbling in on itself.

We're kicked out of the council, and everyone thinks *we're* the traitors, not Johan.

I've been gene-hacked and can feel as more sores painfully sprout on my body. I will likely die in a few hours.

Not to mention that in two days, an army of NuSaps will be doing their absolute best to hack every witch in the city.

And the one person we could get the antidote from is missing. Even if we could find Justin, why would he give it to us?

Luc paces the floor in front of me. I watch his shoes cross my field of vision, then leave it, then cross back again. He stops. "I'm going to look for Justin. He must have gone to NuGene. The launch isn't for another couple of days, so—"

"No, it isn't," Alex interrupts.

My neck snaps up so hard that something cracks. "What?"

"It's happening now." She holds out her phone, where it says, *Breaking news! NuSap program launched early!* It was posted literally seconds ago.

Thank the ancestors it didn't happen when the Matriarchs were here. Things would have been too desperate. I don't know what they would have done to try to get that antidote from us. The one we don't have.

And the army is coming now. Not later.

"Hack me," Luc snaps. "Is this my company or not?!" He shakes his head. "I have to go. I have to do something about Jasmine and Juras and find Justin. I'll message you, okay?" He squats down in front of me and hesitates for a moment before grabbing my hands. He makes a face like he's both delighted and mortified to be doing it. Despite how conflicted I feel about him now, I don't pull away. "Everything is going to be okay, okay?"

"How long do I have?"

His lips press into a line for a moment before he speaks. "It's going to be okay."

"How long?"

" . . . Three hours, maybe. Optimistically."

"I didn't picture you for being the optimistic type."

"Either I'm optimistic or I'm accepting that you'll die before we can save you, and I can't do the latter." He stands up and faces my family.

Mom steps toward him. "You really think you can find him?"

"I need to."

"If she dies, you die. You know that, right?"

"Mom!" I shout, eyes wide.

"I'm not playing," she says, voice low and dangerous in a way that I've never heard it.

But Luc doesn't back down. "I won't let her die. This is my mess. I'm going to fix it." He gives me one last long look. Part of me is still furious at him for starting this, for pretending to be Eli this whole time, for not immediately being able to fix it. But another part of me acknowledges that he's doing his best to help us right now.

Luc turns and rushes out of the house.

And it's just me and the family.

"I failed," I say, looking around at them. "I'm so sorry . . . I thought . . . I thought that I could be a good Matriarch. I tried so hard. But I—"

"Excuse me?" Keisha snaps. "Are you dead already? I don't think so, because I can still hear that trash coming out of your mouth."

Keis steps up beside her sister and nods. "A couple missteps don't ruin everything that you've done since becoming Matriarch."

"And you have done a lot," Alex adds.

Auntie Maise crosses her arms and hums, "Mm-hmm!"

"This isn't over," Mom says, though her voice shakes. "We're not going out like this."

"We're here to help, whatever it takes," Dad jumps in as Uncle Cathius was about to talk. The latter throws the former a glare and grumbles something under his breath.

"What's that, Cathius?" Auntie says, voice high and singsong.

He huffs. "I was going to say that's all well and good, but we need a plan."

They look at me, but I have nothing to say. No ideas.

All I can do is picture one failure after another after another.

I have nothing left to give.

Everyone is downstairs. Their voices float up to me without meaning. Just mumbles. Meanwhile, I'm outside of Granny's room, bundled up in the sheets from her bed, staring out at the glass doors of the second-floor balcony.

I never really paid attention to the view out here. I don't know if any of us did. When we go out on the balcony, it's usually to BBQ and eat and chat. We just pay attention to each other.

All you have to look at is other houses and the neighborhood. It's not like the view of the lake in the dining room. It's everyone's mismatched homes and people jogging or walking their dogs. Even in winter. A family heads toward Marie Curtis Park bundled up in their snowsuits.

Like it's any other day.

Like an army of blue-skinned NuSaps won't be coming down the street at any moment.

I figure if anything, at least I can watch for them.

What will they do when they get here and our doors are closed? It's not like a break-in will go unnoticed. Or do they have a plan for that, too? Break the windows in the back where people are less likely to see and breathe the gas inside. Or will they hang around, waiting until we're forced to leave the house?

Luc was right. His siblings are geniuses, like him. Why would Justin have picked them otherwise? I'm sure they've thought of it all.

Meanwhile, I can't think of a single thing.

And I've stripped our family of bandwidth. The ancestors could push magic into me, but there would only be so long that my body could keep up with it. I would end up like Mama Jova against that tree, emaciated from pushing my bandwidth too far. And that's assuming the weakness from the cell degeneration wouldn't kill me first.

Luc has sent several updates to my phone. Seems to be sending them every ten minutes on the dot. He hasn't found Justin yet. But he has confirmed that he can't do anything to stop the launch.

I expected the Matriarchs to already be storming back to our house, but they're not. Even if they did, what would happen? An all-out magic brawl that we end up dying in anyway? No. It's in their best interest to form a plan.

But one way or another, they'll be coming for us. There's no way they'll let this stay as is.

This is life or death.

They don't even realize how dire it is yet.

None of them have been exposed to the newest upgrade. They think the worst version is what Ailee is suffering. And she is. I got my phone back and saw the updated photos that Lee sent. I had to put it down. Couldn't look. Her entire back is ravaged. Lee keeps trying to heal it over with magic, but it's not doing much. The skin is better, but the sores are still there underneath.

She's going to die. I need to think of something, but I can't make my brain do it. Anything I even have an inkling about comes along with a crushing sense of despair. Because it'll just fail, like everything else.

Footsteps sound up the stairs, and Keis appears. "Hey."

"Hey."

She clenches her teeth into something like a smile before it drops off her face. "I realized that I've wasted months being angry at you. Upset with you and the family. That I could have spent that time understanding your choices."

"They're all bad," I mumble. "Nothing to understand. I've always made bad decisions. Over and over again. You were right to be mad. You're still right to be mad." Keis opens her mouth, but I shake my head. "Just let me say this: I thought I was making the best choice that I could at the time. I really did. But now I think back on it and wonder if maybe it was selfish after all. Maybe I was so terrified of you leaving that it leaked into what I thought was right. Keisha said that sometimes I act like I'm doing something for the family, but really it's for me. And maybe that's what it was. I thought that I had to act like every choice I made was the right one, because it would be like shitting on everything that happened if I didn't. That it wouldn't be fair to you, or Granny, or those people who died at Caribana. Even though every time I think of where I went wrong, that's all I see. Mistakes. Bad choices."

"But they weren't bad when you made them," Keis says. "Like you said, you thought they were the best choices at the time. And yeah, maybe you screwed over my life so royally because a part of you didn't want me to leave. I know I've said that to you. But . . . I also believe that you really thought I would create a new future for myself."

"How can I ever make up for that? I can't." Tears slip down my face.

"No, you can't."

I look over at Keis, expecting her face to be cold and set, but instead, she has a faint smile on it.

"You can't make up for things that are already done, Vo. Not unless you can reverse them. You can't bring Granny back. You can't bring those people from Caribana back. And you can't free me from this house. Stop trying to make up for everything and just keep trying your best."

"But my best isn't good enough."

"Isn't it? Didn't you figure out the secret of the products to save our business? Didn't you bring this family together when we were breaking apart in the aftermath of Granny's death? Even if you mess up again, you can keep trying. That's what we're all doing, you know? That's all this family wants from you."

I let out a sob and have to gasp to catch my breath. Is that really all? It feels too easy. That burden of guilt, all I want is to find a way to cast it off. But maybe I can't. Maybe all I can do is what Keis said. Keep moving forward and trying my best, even knowing that I've messed up in the past.

Keis nudges my shoulder. "Can I tell you a secret?"

"What?"

"You were right about me."

I blink at her.

"You still didn't have any right to decide how my life would turn out. But I know that, either way, you had to make that choice for someone, even if I wish it hadn't been for me. It's not like you wanted to be in that position. And over these months, however much losing that internship hurt, I've realized that I *can* shift. I moved right into learning to program and getting on that game with Justin. My dreams have been changing since. And finally, I understood what you meant." She shrugs. "Being at NuGene was never really my dream. What made me happy was knowing that I could get in. That I could be more than just a witch. And frankly, I can do that from wherever I want. Even this house. I think I wanted the freedom to leave so desperately because this place felt like the embodiment of not being able to do anything else. I love Granny, but that's what it was like. But that's not the kind of leader you are. And I wish you could see that."

I still don't know how to respond, but my throat is clogged up. I'm afraid that if I try to say anything, I'll choke.

"And if I'm honest . . . I was always ahead of you. And then suddenly you were in front, and I was watching you instead of the other way around. It felt like you tugged me back to your level. That was part of hating you, how you shifted the status quo. I had never been the one left behind, but now I always am."

I swallow and flex my fingers. I knew that's how our friendship was, but we never talked about it. Keis was the smart one. The talented one. The one going places and doing things. But suddenly, that changed. She's trapped inside and I'm not.

"I'm sorry," I say. "I pushed you so hard at NuGene. I wanted you to realize how special you are. But . . . I think maybe I liked it that way too. Being in your shadow. Because then when I inevitably messed up, people wouldn't pay attention." I laugh a little. "But everyone's paying attention now."

The corner of Keis's mouth quirks up. "Isn't that your MO now? Performing under pressure."

"Ha ha," I say dryly.

"Did you tell her about the good stuff yet?" Keisha pipes up from over at the staircase.

"Do I get to?" Keis grumbles. "Or have you come to jump in?"

Alex comes up behind her and shakes her head at Keisha. "They were having a heart-to-heart."

"I thought they were done!"

"It's not done until you've cried and hugged."

Despite myself, I laugh, and Alex and Keisha smile at me.

"Come on," Keisha says. "Some people are here to see you."

I point outside. "I'm watching for—"

"Girl, come!"

Letting Granny's blankets fall away from me, I get to my feet along with Keis and follow my cousins down the stairs. Keisha links her arm with mine and frowns when I wince. She tugs up the cuff of my sleeve, where a sore has sprouted on my wrist.

We look at each other for a moment without saying anything.

"Some people are here for you. Let's go." She carefully guides me down the staircase and into the dining room, where three people are sitting along with the rest of the family.

My jaw drops.

Lee. Rena. And Uncle Vacu.

My eyes bulge at the last one. "Uncle Vacu?" I squeak.

He regards me with a cool stare. "So you went and got yourself hacked?" Clearly he's been updated on the recent events.

"I wasn't trying to," I mutter.

He smiles a little, and I try to recall if I've ever seen him smile without some sort of malice. "I know."

My arms go limp at my side. "We were looking for you."

"I know that, too. I didn't have any access to internet or anything." He shifts in his seat. "I was in detox," Uncle Vacu says finally.

"Detox?" I blurt out. "Like 'getting sober' detox?"

"Yes. I just got out when messages about what had happened here came through." He crosses and uncrosses his arms. "It was only because you gave me a chance that I was able to stay here. Seeing Alex after so long . . . so grown up without me . . . It was a lot to take in all at once. The last time I saw her, I wasn't even in the headspace to really *see* her. And now here I was again, and she was even more of a young woman than before."

He looks over at Alex, and my cousin draws herself up. I can't tell if she's steeling herself because she doesn't know what he's going to say, or if it's because she's trying not to expect anything.

"In the past," he continues, "I understood that I was letting people down. I wasn't fine with it, but it was done. I was kicked out. I didn't have my child anymore. It was over. My family was gone. I guess I thought that you were all living your own lives without me. But in that cab . . . you remembered everything." And from the way he's meeting his daughter's eyes, I know he's talking to her now. "I could tell it still hurt you. Even if I wasn't around, I was hurting you. Every time I got worse, I was dragging you down with me. Because you still cared anyway, even if I wasn't around. I wouldn't have realized any of that if you hadn't given me a chance, Voya." He shifts his eyes to me. "You could have turned me out, but you didn't. I want you to understand how much that meant to me."

I don't want to do anything to disrupt the flow of him speaking, so I just nod. It's like I'm afraid that if I say something, he'll disappear, and this moment will be gone.

"I knew about your vision. I overheard Cathius and Maise talking about it when I was in the yard. And I realized that I could die. So I did the detox. That way, at least when I came back again, Alex could see that I was a little bit better. Maybe it wouldn't hurt her as much." That's when he turns back his daughter.

Alex wipes at her eyes and says, "I'm really proud of you."

Uncle Vacu immediately stands straighter, and his eyes are glassy, but he holds it all back.

"Dad . . . Voya has a rehab spot available. They may be able to get you in. Would you go, if you could?"

I'm not about to bring up the fact that Ilana isn't currently our biggest fan, but if we sort everything out with her and the council, it could still happen. I jump in. "I'll find a place for you after. One that you and the family agree works. You'll have something to come back to."

For a moment, he looks to me, to his crying daughter, and back to me. He opens and closes his mouth, then presses it into a line.

It feels like no one in the room is even breathing.

Finally, he nods. "I'm open to it, but I need to think about it. And I need to know there's a guaranteed place for me."

It's like we all exhale at once. It's not a yes, but it's not a no either. There's potential. And it's not an easy decision to make right on the spot. Not to mention, I understand him not wanting to get his hopes up and prepare in case it doesn't pan out. But I hope that he now knows that this family is here for him.

Already, Alex is standing right beside him. And I know that matters, to both of them.

"I think there are some other people here to see you," Uncle Vacu says, waving to Lee and Rena.

Lee steps forward. "I don't believe for a second that you betrayed the council and all of that trash Ilana decided to "warn" me about via messages. I had to come see you right away, and now that I've got the whole story from your family, I know your side is the one to be on. From the start, Johan has been gunning for April-Mae's position even though he can never have it. Maintaining power over the other families has been his way for too long now. I'm here because I want to help you stop him."

It feels like the tears flowing down my face will never stop. But for once, they're not ones filled with sadness or regret or frustration and anger.

Rena clasps her hands together. "I feel the same way as Lee, no matter what Torrin thinks. She doesn't know you like I do. And she doesn't know Johan like I do either. Maybe it's because I've lost a child, but I remember the desperation that he had after Sapphire died. He changed. He is obsessed with collecting power and protecting his family's interests. The fact that you've become so powerful so quickly is a threat to him. A girl with two gifts from the only Black witch family that has ever rivaled his? I would say that's enough for him to organize this whole thing. I'll keep working on trying to convince Torrin, but none of them will move without solid proof."

They look at me expectantly, waiting.

Waiting for . . .

It takes me a minute to realize they're waiting for me to give them a plan. To say what to do next. To lead.

They're waiting for me because I'm the Matriarch.

Keisha squeezes my arm gently, not too hard so as to bother my sores but enough to make me look at her. "I know how hard you've worked to be the best Matriarch that you can, and how you didn't think that anyone else could see that. But this is proof that they have," she says, waving at our guests. "You know we're behind you. But it's more than just us."

"That's what you do, Vo," Keis adds, nodding at her sister. They smile at each other, and I wonder if they've ever been this in sync in their lives. "You always try to look out for us. You always remember that we're your family. Even the people not connected to you by blood. You keep this community together. And you can save it."

Looking around at Keisha and Keis, the rest of my family, at Rena and Lee . . . it changes something. Even though I'm standing here with painful sores breaking out, with maybe only a couple of hours left before I die, this changes *everything*.

In me, there's the tiniest spark of hope.

From behind my family, Mama Jova and Auntie Elaine appear.

They believe in me too.

I've worked so hard for this. It was a struggle to get my family on board, but seeing Rena and Lee, too, knowing that I could have this impact beyond my family means so much. It shows that the *community* could see me as worthy of the title of Matriarch. That I could create real positive change, even if I can't make up for the choices I regret. I can move forward, and try my best to make better ones.

I wipe my eyes and clear my throat, a plan finally starting to form. And this time, I don't shut it down. "I need to meet up with Luc and find Justin. He hasn't had any luck yet, but somehow I think we can figure it out. And everyone else, I need you to find out where April-Mae is. Everything that Johan is doing, I'm guessing she doesn't know about it. Or maybe she does. But I talked to Aqua, and they haven't heard from her either. If we can get in contact with her, she can take over his place, and maybe that will help us out."

"About that," Keis says to me. "I think I know how to find Justin."

"What?" I gawk at her.

She shifts in place and holds up her tablet. On screen are little characters—one looks like her, and one looks like me. It hits me

385

then that I've never actually seen her game before. "It's a genetics game, but it's based in real life and on real places. You get these genome puzzles, and when you solve them, you can change the genetic structure of items to complete tasks."

"Is that me?"

She rolls her eyes. "Focus! Do you know about genetic signatures?"

"No."

Mom groans. "Did you learn nothing in school?"

I scowl. I wasn't very invested in science at school. "I feel like you could have read that out of my mind instead of exposing me."

"I couldn't because you weren't thinking about it," Keis huffs. "Genetic signatures are how the government tracks us. It's in the chip on your wrist. It's like a short code for your full genetic data. And unless you opt out with the government, they can use your location data at any time. Most people leave it on because it makes it annoying to use apps and stuff to have it off. Anyway, Justin told me all about how he has his blocked because he didn't want to be tracked."

I nod along with her, trying to stay focused. "Okay . . ."

"But when you die or are declared dead, the government reverses those permissions."

"Wait, how can that work if he's a NuSap now? Or *data*, I guess, or whatever. He's not human anymore. Shouldn't he not have one?"

"He doesn't have one himself, but he needs to use it to get access to certain locations. It would ping every time he does it, which means it would significantly narrow down the number of places he could be."

"So if we know Justin's signature, we can find him?!"

"Yes."

"And you know it?"

"No."

I deflate. Girl seriously took me for a ride.

"The reason this came up in the first place was because of that chip, the one that I thought Uncle Vacu stole. Justin said he had one in his old apartment but that I would need his signature to get in. He put it into the game as the hardest boss in a puzzle because he didn't think I would figure it out. It was obvious that he did it because he was pissed about me not trying to get him roaming privileges. So I didn't bother and saved up to buy it instead. But it's still in the game."

For ancestor's sake, he really didn't lose an ounce of his arrogance becoming a robot. "So what now?"

"Now, you give me some time. I can't do his puzzle. He was right about that. But we made that game together. Somewhere in that coding, he had to have put in the signature so the program would have an answer. I'll start digging. In the meantime, you go meet with Luc."

Looking at my cousin, I know that she can do this. "Thank you."

"Just go."

"No, really, *thank you*."

She smiles at me. Like old times, except not. Different, but maybe, someday, even better.

I let Luc know the plan, and he messages me back right away:

I'm coming to get you.

CHAPTER THIRTY-ONE

I hop into the same car that Luc had before. He looks disheveled. His hair is a complete mess, and he's covered in drying sweat. Still, he looks me up and down, maybe surprised that I'm still alive or worried that I'm on the brink of being gone.

Somehow, I don't feel any different yet beyond the pain of the sores. But maybe it's the nature of my gift. Unlike most of them, mine does require blood, and I haven't shed any yet. Though some of the sores are looking like they're ready to start bleeding.

"Come over here, I'll help," Luc says.

I slide over in my seat to him, and he pulls my wrist close, wiping some sort of cream onto them. I sigh as he does it. The cooling sensation helps with a lot of the pain. He layers it on thickly and wraps a bandage around the whole thing. "Could we get some of this to Lee for Ailee?"

"Already sent it over with a drone. Anywhere else that hurts?"

I stare at him for a long moment, and he shifts under my gaze. "Sorry, the staring, I know you don't like that."

"I've actually gotten better with it," he says with a shrug. "Comes with the whole being-a-public-figure thing. Though, and don't take this the wrong way, sometimes it was a nice break to be Eli."

"Like in not having to deal with people scrutinizing you as the head of a company?"

"That, yeah, but honestly just how easy it was. People always assumed I was a guy without question. And sure, more diligent people would check Eli's feed to make sure. But their knee jerk reaction was 'this is a boy.' And *I* knew without a doubt that they thought I was. I didn't have that voice in the back of my mind wondering if I was really passing."

"I never even thought of that," I admit. My mind went straight to the pressure of everyone looking at him as a leader, I guess because that was what I thought someone would want to escape.

"Well, it had its time, but I won't be using that NuSap anymore obviously. I'm hoping that at the end of this, we can lay them both to rest. With a significant apology to everyone affected, Ilana . . . and his mom." Luc holds up the bandages and bottle of cream. "Anywhere else?"

I lift the bottom of my shirt to show where one is on my stomach and try not to fidget as he slathers on the cream. It's more intimate than I expected. He's never actually seen this much of my naked skin.

I look at him, and he's so obviously uncomfortable. I smile a little. At least I'm not the only one who's flustered by it. "Did you find Jasmine or Juras?"

"No. They're both coordinating the launch somehow, though. The NuSaps are out in the streets already." He crosses his arms. "But I think they're looking for Justin too. He must have contacted them or something. Every data spot that I was in trying to find him, someone else had already been there."

"Wouldn't they know where to go? He wouldn't tell them?"

"No, because that would risk you finding him if he knows that I've fallen out with the two of them. I guess after everything that happened last time, he didn't trust me not to flop on him. And I guess he was right."

"What about their genetic signatures?"

"Blocked. All of ours are."

I knew it couldn't be that easy, but Keis has been working on this nonstop since she thought of it.

Luc finishes applying the cream to my sores and putting bandages over them, even though some are forming as he helps. He bites his lip, and his eyes get this faraway look.

"Is someone messaging you?"

He blinks and shakes his head. "I'm just looking at the time. It's fine. It's going to be fine."

I try to smile for his sake. "I'm sure it will be."

It's weird, but I don't have the space to be afraid for my life. Maybe because I cried in the NuGene warehouse where I was sure that I would die. Or maybe because I'm so distracted by everyone else being in danger.

Or maybe, somehow, I believe Luc.

I get a call from Alex, and immediately answer it. On screen, Keis pops up, and I adjust my privacy settings so Luc can see her too.

"I got it!" she says with a grin. "I'm sending the location to Luc's phone. He *just* used his signature to access this place, so he'll hopefully still be there. But you need to go fast. I think when I did the search it pinged Justin, because it disappeared right away. He must have hacked in and erased data proof of his presence. That means he probably knows we're coming, but you can try and catch him before he leaves. Even if you miss him, at least you'll be in the same area."

Luc fumbles with his phone, and the car takes off at a speed that I didn't even know self-drive units could go.

"You're a genius!" I shout at Keis.

She smiles. "Go shut down the robot."

I'm about to hang up when I spot Uncle Vacu in the background fiddling with some sort of medical-looking equipment. "What is that?" I ask, distracted.

Alex comes into the frame. "I guess Dad had some old equipment stashed here. He's taking samples from his body. He wants to see if he can find way to slow down the progression. He's not very optimistic, but I think he just wants to do something."

Luc presses his hand against his face. "How did I not think of that?"

"Because you've been panicked about me dying?" I try.

His shoulders hike up, and he scowls. "I've been trying to reverse the process. What I have in my lab isn't a cure, but it should slow things down. If you can go there and get it, we can give it to Voya."

"We'll go," Uncle Vacu says immediately.

Luc nods. "I'll send another car for you."

The call ends, and Luc and I share a relieved look.

I turn away almost as soon as it happens, a flush working up the back of my neck.

Focus, Voya. Focus!

We pull up to a tower of condos and rush into the building. Luc pushes his phone against the screen, which gets us inside, but once we get into the elevator, it won't bring us up to his floor.

"Hack me," Luc grunts. "He took me off the access list. My genetic signature won't work. Can Keis send me his?" I message my cousin for it, but when he tries, it doesn't work either. "I guess it did ping him. He's removed access for his, too, now. He probably won't reinstate it until he leaves."

"Stairs?" I try.

Luc shakes his head. "You need to scan for access to the stairwell, too."

"What do we do? We can't let him leave."

"He won't." Luc starts to punch in things on his phone rapidly, pulling up windows and settings that I've never seen. "He seriously thinks the worst of us. Like Keis can't figure out his puzzle, and I can't get through his security because *he* had to use his genetic signature instead of hacking it. Justin has a special skill for picking out talented people, but he always assumes that he's the smartest person in the room."

The elevator turns green and flares to life. Luc grins at me. "Usually he is. But not always."

He's right. Justin underestimated my cousin, and he did the same to the boy he chose to lead his company after him. And to Auntie Elaine, too. I swallow and face the doors as we ride the elevator upward.

I imagine that Alex and Uncle Vacu are almost at Luc's lab now. Assuming things don't go over well here, at least what they grab will be enough to lend me some time to come up with another plan.

The doors to the elevator open, and just like Justin's old condo in Regent Park, we step directly into the space.

There, on some couches arranged near the balcony, sit Jasmine, Juras, and a very different version of Justin than the one I've gotten used to seeing.

Not running. Not going anywhere. Just waiting for us.

He didn't underestimate Keis and Luc at all. He was playing with them. Giving his protégés little puzzles to solve like our lives are just mini games to him.

My fingers slowly clench into fists.

He looks exactly like himself. The way he used to be. No more cornflower-blue skin or stormy eyes. No clunky machinery. He's sleek and polished but in a way that looks entirely too human.

"You like my upgrade?" he says, rising from the couch. "It's not too bad, if I say so myself. Though in some ways I have you to thank, Voya." Justin turns his gaze to Luc. "Can't say I'm surprised to see you over there on her side. You really revealed your true colors in my office that day. Though I hear from your siblings that you mourned me terribly. But apparently not enough to shun my killer."

"Last time I checked, you're alive and well," Luc says, though his voice is shaky. I expect that he never thought he would see his mentor again in the flesh like this. But here he is.

Resurrected.

Justin grins at me. "But you were right. I did get my wish in the end."

He's truly immortal.

And I'm the one who made him that way.

Jasmine and Juras have serious expressions on their faces. Juras, at least, I would have expected to be smugger about the whole thing. Here I am, dying, coming here for the antidote, only to realize that Justin has been able to transfer over his data to a new, sleeker unit than what he had before. He should be delighted.

But his eyes look dull and worn out like the rest of his body. He doesn't look happy. He looks resigned.

"How did you end up with a new body?" I ask Justin. It's a perfect replica. I can't imagine he built that in the last couple hours.

"I have Luc to thank for that. I'm flattered, honestly, that you would build this in my honor."

I turn to Luc.

He at least seems sheepish about it. "I built it because your family didn't have anything for your funeral. They were upset. I said I would construct a model for them using the new NuSap tech so that they could say goodbye properly. So that we all could."

My chest tightens. I never thought much about Justin's remaining family and how this would be for them. Luc and his sponsor siblings seemed to be the only ones around him, but it makes sense that he would have a complete family that would miss him.

And Luc made this model for them.

It's exact and precise.

If I didn't know that Justin had been in a different body before, I would have thought that his living one never died at all.

It hits me then the sort of power that this gives him.

His grin gets wider. "Have you finally put it all together?"

Even though they declared Justin dead, they never found a body. I made sure of that.

But here he is.

No one would ever know that this Justin is a NuSap unit. Luc didn't give him the signature cornflower-blue skin. It's his exact shade. How could anyone guess this was an android when the new models are so perfectly lifelike and this one has Justin's brain and all his memories? After all, that Eli model fooled us, regular witches and Matriarchs alike. I bet Justin could even trick most scanners into missing his machinery insides. He would need to be cut open for anyone to find out.

He could walk right back into his company and take it over like nothing ever happened. Back in power. Except now it would be forever. He never has to hand over the company. Why would he? He could transfer his mind into a new body and claim that was his successor. Even make copies of NuSaps that looked like him but older so that he would age appropriately.

I swallow so hard that it hurts going down.

"You even transferred your consciousness without an issue," I add. I don't really care. I'm just wasting time by talking. How are we supposed come out of this for the better?

"We both know that you don't care about that. But here's the important part. I have backups so I can survive any unprecedented events."

I assume he means like me killing him for real this time.

He raises his hands toward me. "You've given me the gift that

394

I've been searching for all these years. So soft-hearted. Now things aren't going your way, are they?"

I want to cry. To curl into a ball and bury myself in a hole. My skin burns as new sores collect along my body. Soon enough I may be dead, but Justin, meanwhile, will keep living.

"Now I'll be taking back over my company, Luc. And I think, given everything that's happened, that it's time for you to go home."

Luc's hands shake at his sides, and it travels until his whole body is near trembling. "The antidote, your catch-all gene hack reversal? Give it to us. You have everything now. Let us at least have that."

Justin laughs. "Why would I do that?"

"You said that Voya gave you everything that you wanted. Pay her back with her life."

"No," he breathes. "I don't think I will. See, witches make things difficult. And I suspect that if Voya lives, she'll make things hard for me, and I don't really like the idea of that. I think it's better if she gets wiped out along with the rest of them. That's what you wanted, isn't it?"

"That's not what I wanted!" Luc shouts. "That's *never* what I wanted!"

Justin shrugs and flicks a hand toward Jasmine and Juras. "Well, it's what most of you did. Now everyone wins. Except for Voya, of course. Sorry about that."

Hack me, of course Justin isn't going to hand over the antidote. That would be excruciatingly easy and not in his best interest in any case. And I knew that, but it felt like maybe something would come together when we got here.

I look over at his sponsor kids and their serious, melancholy faces. I can't get over how limp and dour they look. Shouldn't they be happy? Justin is alive.

Justin is alive.

And that means they're no longer in the positions they were before.

Luc is the successor, but he kept them on and gave them powerful roles in the company. Both of them are on the board of directors now when they were only interns under Justin's lead. They were able to make names for themselves, showing up alongside reports of Luc when before they were just Justin Tremblay's sponsor kids, and beyond that, in the shadow of Luc, who was always seen as the most talented.

Now they'll be in the background again.

Except this time, it's different.

"You won't need successors anymore," I say to Justin, reiterating aloud what I already worked out.

His lips quirk up a bit but he says nothing.

I jerk my head at Juras and Jasmine. "What will happen to them, then? You'll send them home, like Luc?"

He narrows his eyes at me, realizing what I'm doing. "They'll stay here. I'm happy to have them continue at NuGene."

"As board members?"

"Of course," he says, but it rings like a lie.

If he didn't have them on the board before, why would he do it now?

I look at Jasmine and Juras. "And you're fine with that?"

"You're not going to turn us against each other," Justin says, his voice ironclad. "But good try."

I fight to make my brain work faster. My bandwidth is shot. It's building, bit by bit, but it's not enough to do anything helpful. But I have to do *something*. My entire family—our entire *community*— is at stake. I'm an hour away from death myself. I need to move. The problem is what can I even do right now? Destroying Justin's body won't make a difference.

Maybe—

A loud buzz rings out through the room, and for a moment, I look around, trying to figure out what's happening . . . until I see Justin slump over on the couch, his body jerking and twitching.

Jasmine stands with a baton in her hand. The same one that she used on me.

Both of her sponsor brothers gape at her.

Juras recovers first, his lips forming a grim line.

Luc is a different story. "What . . . what did you just do?!" he gasps. "The antidote!"

"He doesn't have it," Jasmine says.

I snap back, "Because you already took it?"

She narrows her eyes at me. "No. We moved it. But clearly someone was able to find it. We thought it was Luc."

Jasmine and Juras don't have it, and Justin doesn't have it.

"Who else could find it?" I ask.

"Anyone, maybe. But it was in a place that no one but us three and Justin should have been able to access."

"Yeah," I say. "I lot of people without magic think that."

Jasmine gives me a glare for that but doesn't protest.

My mind immediately goes to Johan. Outside of Jasmine, Juras, Luc, and Justin, he's the only one who would have even known the catch-all existed before today. And the antidote is the only reason that makes sense for why he would have been working with Justin. The question is how Johan found it.

"Did Justin know where it was?"

Jasmine frowns. "I mean, he could have figured it out . . . but he would need to have monitored or searched NuGene camera footage to see us moving it. We didn't try to delete any footage or disable any cameras. For one, it's suspicious. Something you clearly didn't think about during your infiltration of our party." She scowls, and I choose not to respond to that. "And for another, you can always find a way to recover data. But even with an AI search, that would take days. I assume that's why Luc and you are chasing us around instead of doing that."

"How could you check the footage? Like, could you do it remotely?"

Luc says, "Yeah. With any device, really, as long as you have access to our system."

"... Like a phone?"

Jasmine and Luc both nod, and I swallow. Justin had that phone for nearly a week before he escaped. He couldn't transfer his consciousness because of the magic, but he did have internet. If he made a deal that required him knowing where that antidote was, he would have enough drive to do it.

Johan.

The only way he could have known where it was was with Justin's help. All Johan would need to get what he and Justin wanted was to make sure our spell holding the former NuGene CEO failed.

I lock eyes with Jasmine. "When you were shocking me, you said that you had to do it until I was out of magic. Who told you that?"

"Don't say anything," Juras snaps, suddenly deciding to participate in the conversation.

Jasmine ignores him. "Johan. He said that pain made it hard to control magic. That you didn't have a proper hold on yours and that enough pain would make you pull magic from everyone in your family. That way, we would know that at least you Thomases couldn't defend yourselves against the NuSaps."

Because he knew. He had realized that I didn't have control of the push and pull of my magic.

And if none of us had magic, Justin could escape, finally fulfilling his and Johan's contract to each other.

Everything must have happened today. Juras and Jasmine attacking me. Justin sharing the location with Johan and escaping. And Johan taking the antidote before the siblings realized what was happening.

Except, that entire plan would rely on Justin keeping his word. There's no way that he would have given Johan any of that information unless he was guaranteed an escape. Johan would have known that too.

Witches use blood vows exactly for that purpose. You can't break it without bleeding to death as punishment. Only, he couldn't do that with Justin as a NuSap.

Someone would have had to give in. Would have been forced to trust in the other before getting what they wanted. Johan had his family's lives on the line, and Justin was bargaining with his freedom.

Justin, who spent months begging for the privilege of leaving our basement.

Justin, who was constantly angry, frustrated, and lashing out about his circumstances.

Justin, who must have tried for six months to escape without success before the Davis leader came along.

Justin, who would have to live forever as a prisoner.

What wouldn't the NuGene CEO have been willing to give up when he was already so close to freedom? When he could practically taste it? If he knew that it could be snatched away in an instant by one person?

This plan needed our family bandwidth to tank. Needed Johan to set that in motion.

I think back to the way that Johan walked in with the council when they told us we would be kicked out. When the accusations came through.

The antidote is missing.

And that did not look like a man who had been played by an android.

Johan looked like he had *won*.

He has it. I know he does.

I tear myself out of my thoughts and stare down at Justin's body. "So, what now? Didn't you do all of this for him?"

Juras scoffs. "Maybe that's why Luc was doing it. But that wasn't why *I* was. I would rather he stay dead."

His sponsor sister, however, doesn't seem to share his feelings. She looks down at Justin's body with her lips pressed into a firm line and shining eyes. "We need to protect each other. Justin . . . I could tell from his voice that he was going to cut us out as soon as he could." She looks over at Luc. "I know you're not our biggest fan right now. But we're thinking about you too. He can't send you home." Juras grumbles something unintelligible, and Jasmine shoots him a sharp look. "We're family."

Luc laughs, sharp and bitter. "*Now* you want to talk about family? When you gene-hacked Voya? She's going to die!"

"Lovers come and lovers go, but family is forever," Juras says. "You'll get over it eventually. But having Justin around, it wasn't going to be good for us." He nods at me. "She had that much right."

Jasmine shakes her head at Luc. "You should have been faster."

"You shouldn't have done it!"

Juras lets out a strangled cry of frustration. "She's already dying! Justin has backups. He's going to come back, and he's going to be mad."

"We're three geniuses, aren't we?" Jasmine says. "I'm sure we'll figure out how to stop him."

"Why would I help you now?" Luc gapes at both of them. "Do you even realize what you're doing? You're going to kill an entire community."

Juras looks at the ground for a moment and grips his hands into fists. "The antidote is gone, Luc. It's too late."

"Don't bullshit me!" Luc roars. "You *want* her to die. You've wanted her to die from the start."

"Is that so wrong?!" Juras screams back. "She could kill us at any time! Whenever she wants! Any of them! And get away with it too! Justin is the richest man in the country, and she wiped him off the face of the Earth without even a hint of suspicion. Now everyone just thinks he's dead!" He's practically baring his teeth, and spit flies from his mouth as he speaks. "You know what I thought after she touched me? After she did whatever she did to me? I was dying, and I thought, 'What a waste.' What had I done besides walk in your shadow? Be second-best my whole life? I won't feel like that again. I won't." His breathing is labored when he finishes.

And finally . . .

He breaks.

Juras dissolves into tears and sinks to the ground beside Justin's body. "He's going to send us away. Go back home? Like this? I could never. They'll look at me like a failure. I was picked for this. I'm supposed to be a genius. More than half of my life spent here, for what?"

Kneeling down next to him, Jasmine pulls her brother into her arms.

It's agony to watch. Tears slip down my face before I can stop them. "I'm sorry," I say. "I'm so sorry."

Jasmine looks at me. "I didn't know it before, but I do now. You're not a killer. Justin is alive, and that's because you never murdered him at all, isn't it?"

I nod.

"Your council . . . they were never coming after us. Johan made it up, didn't he?"

I nod again.

"Geniuses without any street smarts," she says with a laugh. "It should have taken me barely any interaction with you to realize that. I thought maybe you weren't killing us because you needed the catch-all. But then I figured you could at least hold one of us captive for it. But you never did. I kept trying to find the angle . . . but there in that room, when I shocked you and you were so worried for Eli . . . Eli was already dead. Didn't even know who you were mourning, but you did. Then I understood why you might be someone Luc loves."

Luc splutters beside me, and I turn to him. "Help them with Justin."

"What?! But—"

"Justin coming back is a problem for all of us. Besides . . . I know where the antidote is."

Johan has it. But he's a powerful witch. However he's hidden it, there's probably no way we can get to it.

Not without joining his family.

I grit my teeth.

Hack me, this is so wrong.

Was he really that threatened? Did me becoming Matriarch really change his whole life enough to do this?

Changed his whole life . . .

Maybe I did?

Johan and the Davises have always been at the top of the food chain, even when Granny was here. But things have been changing since my Calling. Even if I did it by accident, I ruined his ritual. Not to mention, I came into power as a Matriarch younger than anyone in mine or his family, and have two gifts, something unheard of for a Thomas or Davis. The reason that he's done all of this, that he's started acting like we're his enemy instead of his allies, is a direct result of me coming into power.

I changed the path of Johan's life forever, which means I also have the power to see what lies beyond it. Maybe enough to know what he did with the antidote.

"I have to go now," I blurt out. "I know how to get it."

"Wait!" Luc shouts. "I can come too."

"No, no, you stay with them, like I said. Deal with Justin."

I have to go back home. I don't have much time. Besides, now that I'm hacked, it'll be hard to tell what will happen when I try to use my gift. It might work strangely, or it might not work at all. And if my time runs out during, I want to know that I at least got to see my family one more time.

Luc grinds his teeth and looks at his sponsor siblings. "I don't have time for this." He turns to me. "And you're dying!"

"And Uncle Vacu and Alex are getting what you have to slow things down. I should be okay, and if I get to do what I plan to, we'll have the catch-all soon enough."

He shakes his head. "I'm not going to leave you."

"You're not. You're helping me. Because if I make it through and Justin comes for us, there won't even be a point in being saved. I'll be okay." I reach out and squeeze Luc's hand. "We're a team, aren't we?"

Even though I made that pact with who I thought was Eli, it still holds. We said that we would stop this together. And no matter how upset the other things Luc did have made me, that hasn't changed.

He looks down at our laced fingers for a moment and finally lets out a long sigh. "Let me know the moment you have the antidote. I'll have to come and get enough of a sample to replicate it. Promise me."

"I will."

"Promise me one more thing."

"What?"

"If you know you're going to die, call me. I already had some-one die on me once before I got to say goodbye. I don't need to deal with it another time."

I look into Luc's eyes and nod. "I promise."

Though I don't know if it's one I can keep.

CHAPTER THIRTY-TWO

L uc orders me a car back to my house, where I'm jittering in the back seat. Sores are spreading over my body, and Luc sends me an equal parts helpful and terrifying estimate of how much time I have left. He also has a second one based on if Uncle Vacu gets the serum to me in time. Both have alarms set to go off when the time gets close. For right now, I'm using the time that assumes the worst, just to be safe.

Thirty-five minutes.

That's it.

I can't conceptualize it because it feels so unreal.

How could my life end in a little over half an hour?

The car stops, and I rush out into the house. The family comes running to the entryway when they hear me, Keis and Keisha leading the pack. Uncle Vacu and Alex aren't with them. They must still be getting the stuff from Luc's lab.

When Mom sees me, she slaps her hands over her mouth. "Ancestors help us."

There's a sore developing on the side of my lip, slowly spreading across my face like a rampage. I have the urge to bite it but don't—it would probably hurt like hell.

"Please don't do this, Voya," Keis says, ahead of everyone as always after reading my thoughts.

"What's she mean? What's happening?" Mom cries.

"I think that Johan has the antidote, and I realized a way that I might be able to find it. I'm going to use my gift."

Keisha's eyes go wide. "Isn't it going to be messed up because of the hack? Besides, using your gift this low on bandwidth . . ."

"I know," I say, but we're down to the wire.

"This might kill you before the hack does."

Keisha, always so absolutely hacking intuitive. She figured out everything her sister knows without even needing a mind reading gift.

Mom keeps shaking her head with her hands over her mouth.

"Find a way to bring Johan here," Keis argues. "I'll pull it from his mind."

I sigh. "How would I even get him here? It would take too much time." I give Keis a significant look. She's the only one here who knows how limited my time is. "Besides, you've never been able to get into his head. He's too strong."

"That was before. I bet I could do it now," she mumbles, and her eyes fill with tears. Because she knows that even if she could, we don't have the time.

I look over at Mom. "I need to do this."

She doesn't say anything, just sort of cringes and looks down at her feet. She stops shaking her head at least. "I wish you weren't the Matriarch."

Her words hit right at my heart and make me feel like I'm going to gasp at the pain of it.

"Or maybe I just wish you were a bad one," she continues, looking at me finally. "One who didn't care about doing what needed to be done. Who just looked out for yourself so that your mom would never have to worry."

The pain in my heart subsides. "Mom . . ."

"Do what you need to do."

Auntie Maise lets out a little humph. "Be careful. We'll keep an eye on you while you do it to make sure that everything is okay."

"You'll be okay," Dad says, his voice shaking.

I meet his eyes and look away, because I can feel mine welling up. But I don't say anything.

I wish desperately that Alex were here. That I could see her one last time. Uncle Vacu, too.

"I'm going to use my gift now," I say.

Mom's choked sob rings in my ear.

I gather my intention, homing in on Johan's past. I need to know where he hid the catch-all, and we can work out how to get it after.

I try to make my gift work, but it's difficult. It's like it's stuck. Like a piping bag filled with cream and fruit, and one of the fruit chunks is stopping the whole thing. If I press down too hard, it'll explode out of the bag and ruin everything. I have to be gentle with it, slowly pressing on it until finally . . .

There.

Except something's not quite right. I shift off balance, and my inner ear goes wild. It's like I'm on a roller coaster, and I can hear voices in the background shouting.

"Focus," someone snaps in my ear, and presses the full force of their palm on my back.

The slap of it sends me careening forward, and suddenly I'm rushing face first toward a tiled floor. I hold my hands out and barely manage to not smash my face into it, landing in a kneeling position.

When I look up, I'm in the kitchen, but not.

It's kind of like our family's kitchen, but it's missing things. Some of my kitchen gadgets aren't here, and the communal tablet that usually sits there is gone. Not to mention, the island looks kind of old. The top is some sort of wooden surface instead of the sleek faux marble top that we keep on it. And yet somehow, it looks familiar.

I push myself to my feet and pause.

Something's different.

I touch the corner of my lip, and it's smooth. The sores on my face are gone. What's happening here?

"You need to keep that boy on a shorter leash. You have Vacu running around too wild," a voice complains, and it sounds . . . like April-Mae?

"You're too hard on yours," another voice replies, and I know it instantly. The sound makes me stumble back.

"You're too soft on yours!"

No.

That can't be right.

There's no way.

I take another step back into the counter, and a mug falls to the ground and shatters.

I stare at it, confused. I touched it, and it shattered? I couldn't touch things before. Last time, my whole body went through a wall of the house, and I couldn't grab at Eden, either.

It must be the hack. How it amplifies the gifts.

But does that mean I'm actually in the past? No hacking way. But this feels way too far back, and that voice . . .

A chair squeaks and someone starts to walk around the corner.

Hack me.

I scramble around, not sure where to go or what to do, when finally she comes into the kitchen.

Granny.

Her little afro is a bit less gray than I remember it, and she's got a few less wrinkles, but otherwise she's the same Granny that I've always known.

"Granny," I choke out, my throat clogging. "I messed up."

This is wrong. I was supposed to go into Johan's past but somehow, I'm much further back in time than I was supposed to be. And I'm not even in *his* past. This is Granny's. I screwed up my intention somehow.

My grandma gives me a hard stare as she walks over.

"Ava," someone calls from the dining room. No, not someone. That's Lee. "What is it?"

"A mug fell off the shelf," she says. "Just give me a minute to clean it."

"Avoiding the subject," April-Mae grumbles from the other room.

I swallow hard as I face Granny.

She comes closer and closer to me, and I find that I can't move at all. I'm stuck. Rooted to the spot. I don't know what to do.

Granny cups my face within her hands and peers straight into my eyes. They're watering. Overflowing with tears, and I have to bite my lip to keep from sobbing.

"You . . . ," she says. "You're Voya, aren't you?"

My entire mind goes blank. If this is the past, will what I say screw up the future? Or is my future one where I've already done this?

She cracks a half smile. "I'll take that as a yes."

"How . . . ?"

"You do look like yourself. But it's those eyes. Always thinking, thinking, thinking. That's the way you are." She puts her hands on her hips. "Now, what's this about messing up?"

"I was supposed to be going to Johan's past."

"Johan?"

Hack me, I shouldn't have said that.

Granny pokes me in the forehead. "Too much thinking."

"Ow," I mumble.

"If you're here, I'm sure it's for a reason. And so you're in the past, though not the one you wanted, but that's not bad. And if it's a problem with Johan, get his mama to set him straight. That's her speciality, you know." Granny frowns. "Though she could stand to pull back sometimes."

I blink at Granny. It's true. April-Mae is who the family was supposed to be looking for, but no one can find her. If I went into Johan's past with her, I could figure out where she is. Maybe she could stop him and get the antidote. But maybe that would take too long. Maybe it's better to try to get where I wanted to go in the first place. But what if I mess it up again?

"Thinking, thinking," Granny mutters.

I wipe the tears from my eyes and throw myself at Granny, tucking my head under hers and stealing this one last hug.

She pats the top of my head. "You're the Matriarch now, aren't you?"

I jerk my head up. "I . . ."

"That's good."

"What?"

She grins at me. "I always knew that I would pick you."

That's what Granny said back then too, in the circle when we were holding hands. I've been clinging to her belief in me, to that feeling that I must be good at this because she chose me. But deep down, I never understood it. *Why* would she pick me?

But like she said, she knew it would be me a long time ago.

This is why she was so calm in Justin's office. She *knew* that this was coming. Because that's how time works, isn't it? Even though this is happening now, it has also already happened. She would have remembered me at this age and known that it was her time. That's how she could let go like that.

"Did you pick me because I'm like you?" I guess.

She shakes her head. "I chose you because you're something

this family has never seen. And that makes you a better leader than I was." She grunts. "Now, enough, you're making me sweaty. Don't you have somewhere to be?"

Yeah, that's Granny.

I disentangle myself from her arms. I have to go into Johan's past, but how far back? Maybe it's nothing, but there must be a reason that I'm here with Granny. A reason that she's telling me about April-Mae. Even if neither of us knows it. "I won't mess up this time."

"You didn't mess up," Mama Jova says, appearing in the corner of the kitchen. Granny must see her too, because her eyes sharpen. "I brought you here."

"Why?" I ask.

"Because you needed it."

I swallow hard. Maybe I did. Being here one last time with Granny, knowing that she truly wanted me to be Matriarch, that she thought I could be better, it matters. It matters a lot. I look over at her. "Bye, Granny."

She gives me a sharp nod and heads back toward the dining room.

As I focus my intention, I hear the last words she says to me.

"I'm proud of you."

CHAPTER THIRTY-THREE

When I went into Granny's past, I was thrown on the kitchen floor. Now it's a completely different sensation. I seem to curl out of nothing and find myself pressed against a concrete wall on a set of steps.

Mama Jova grips my shoulder. "Focus on concealing yourself. Focus very hard."

I form my intention into not being seen, or heard, or noticed.

I'm using more magic, magic that I know I barely have, but I can't feel it in my body. It's like whatever the hack is doing to my gift, it's too separate. Part of me worries that I'm killing myself faster, but I trust Mama. If she said to use magic, I'm gonna use magic. I've been burned enough times by not listening.

Once I have my intention running on a loop in my mind, I can split my attention and start to look at some of my surroundings. The concrete stairs lead down into a basement rec room. It's got huge U-shaped couches, a massive TV, and an empty space in the middle where I distinctly remember a man hanging from his arms, bleeding out, punctured by knife wounds.

It's the Davises' basement.

When I used my gift, I tried to focus on figuring out what happened to April-Mae. Some sort of clue so we could get into contact with her. But I don't understand how this place is supposed to relate to that.

"Can we get this little meeting over and done with?" April-Mae steps into view of where I am on the stairs. She's the same imposing woman that I remember, slim and dressed immaculately. She looks upper class where Granny kept a homier look.

Johan walks out from the shadows. "I'll make it fast." In two swift steps, he has a gun pressed to his mom's temple.

I jerk in place seeing it. I've never seen one not in the hand of a cop before. It's hacking Canada, for ancestors' sake. People don't just have handguns. People barely have *any* guns.

Looking at the smooth metal, knowing what's inside, makes me shiver. The shots at Caribana. The popping sounds. The screams. The people running. Lucas and Henrietta, dead. Shot and trampled.

How could he hold one of those and not immediately think of that? I know it's the past, and it hasn't happened. But . . . it also has. Years of people like us staring down the end of that barrel.

But the only surprise that April-Mae allows is one slow blink.

"Now, you'll be nice and cooperative unless you want to see your brains splattered. And there's no blood for you to work with right now either. That's the positive about guns instead of knives." He grins at her. "And here you felt so superior taking out your metal tooth and getting a whole new set of shiny veneers."

Hack me. What the hell is happening?

"You encouraged it," April-Mae snaps.

He smiles. "I know."

"I can still pull on your magic, boy."

"You could, but you won't. Because that would definitely make me kill you."

She moves to bite her lip, and Johan presses the gun in harder. "Don't."

"What is this about? Tell me," she says finally. "Is this about Sapphire? I'm sorry about her. I am. You *know* that."

"Don't you say her name," he snarls before composing himself. "I want you to name Aqua as the next Matriarch. Say it out loud with intention so the ancestors know."

My body is shaking. *That's* what this is about? Johan wanting Aqua to be Matriarch one day? Ilana said the Davises used to pick the oldest child, but that was the past. Aqua wouldn't be guaranteed the spot anymore.

"Why? The girl has no talent. Her gift is too sentimental. Keis, however, did you see the gift she has? The ability to read minds like that? *That's* power." A sly smile slips onto her face. "She could give your gift a unique challenge. She may start to notice all the ways you make sure to get what you want. Ancestors only know how they managed to get that in their family now that they've gone pure."

I've never known what Johan's gift is, but from what April-Mae is saying, it's something that Keis could compete with, but clearly my cousin has no idea either. She would have mentioned it.

"She's a Thomas," Johan grunts.

April-Mae lets out a steups. "Keis is a Thomas now, but there's no way she would turn down the chance to be a Matriarch. I've already told the ancestors. I'm just working on getting her to claim the Davis name for the future. She's so attached to her cousin, but I get the feeling she doesn't want to stick around forever."

"*Aqua* is the eldest."

The Davis Matriarch rolls her eyes as if there isn't a gun pointed between them. "The eldest is so old-fashioned. Can't you see the changes in the other families? It's about *power* now. Age is a useless marker."

"There's no point in wanting Keis. Ava will name her as the next Matriarch anyway," Johan snaps. "Name Aqua instead."

"You don't know Ava like I know Ava."

"Excuse me?"

"She's not interested in giving the title to that child. Trust me, that title already belongs to Voya. She's had her favorite picked out since Voya was a little girl."

Johan presses the gun in harder. "I don't. I don't trust you. Especially not after you let my daughter die."

"I knew this was about Sapphire."

"Name Aqua!" Johan roars in her face. "Name her, or I'll put a bullet through your brain!"

"If I name her, you'll do it anyway."

Johan smiles. "Thought you would say that, so I'll give you a vow etched in blood not to kill you after you make your promise."

April-Mae's face changes, and she looks behind Johan, where a body steps out from the shadows. I recognize her instantly.

Aqua.

She's trembling, and her eyes are wide and bloodshot. "Daddy, please don't do this."

"I told you to stay back there," Johan says, his voice surprisingly soft. Nothing like the way he addresses his mother. "You sit there until this is done."

"I know you're scared. But it's okay. You can be scared. I can help."

"Sit."

He doesn't raise his voice, but Aqua falls to her butt on the floor nevertheless.

This is so completely hacked. I can't do anything but watch. Maybe Mama Jova knew it was fine for me to interact with Granny but clearly, she doesn't have the same feelings about this moment. She keeps her hand firm on my shoulder, and I force my intention to remain steady. My forehead is starting to bead with sweat, and my stomach cramps painfully.

"Besides," Johan says. "Grandma will be fine so long as she does what I'm telling her to do."

Maybe because she truly doesn't have any more options or maybe because she really thinks this is the best way to do things, April-Mae complies, and she and Johan go through the process of enacting a blood vow. I've never seen one done before. It seems to just involve mixing their blood together while Johan states the intention he promised. Johan only pricks his mom the tiniest bit, enough blood for what he wants but not enough for her to cast anything.

Not unless she moves faster than he does, but she doesn't.

April-Mae is a Matriarch, but she's also an older woman. And I guess she doesn't really expect him to kill her. He's her son, after all. He wouldn't.

He wouldn't.

"Ancestors of my blood, hear me: I name Aquamarine Davis as my successor. In the event of my passing, she is to claim the title of Matriarch." April-Mae finishes talking and rolls her eyes at her son as if to say, *Happy now?*

He puts the gun down and steps away from her.

She smiles.

A bullet hits her between the eyes before she can speak.

Aqua doesn't even scream. She just lets out a whimper that breaks my heart more than any screech could. Her grandma drops to the ground.

Out of the shadows walks a man that I didn't even notice before. Like me, he must have been concealing himself.

Kane. Their youngest brother.

Of course. Johan promised not to kill her, but her other son made no such oath.

They worked together to do this.

Kane's face is more serious than either of his brothers', and he's taller, too. He squats down in front of his mother's dead body. "Too bad. But it'll be better this way. We'll have a lot more control, just like you planned. I'll get on the next plane to Nova Scotia and let our dear uncle know that I'll be taking over."

One more shot rings through the room.

I'm not prepared for it, and my intention slips completely for a moment. Not that it matters. Johan is entirely consumed by the two corpses in front of him. His mother and brother, both dead.

Aqua is crying quietly in the corner. "You could have just made him forget," she sobs.

Johan jerks his head toward her. "You knew?"

"I guessed."

"I couldn't. There was too much planning. Too many individual moments. You can't create that many holes. This is the only solution."

Aqua shakes her head and says nothing more.

Made him forget? Like the ritual Johan did with Auntie Elaine to make us all forget her? There were lots of holes in our memories for that, and he did it anyway. But I guess this is a much more dangerous situation.

Johan rolls his neck as if the murder has created a tension there and says to Aqua, "You know what to ask for, don't you? You get one wish."

Her Matriarch wish.

Aqua nods and closes her eyes. There's obvious magic in the air as she sits there. But when she opens them again, they're filled with more tears. "They said no."

"*What?!*" Johan snarls.

"They said no, Daddy. They can't bring Sapphire back."

I have to clutch at my chest, because the pain is so much that it's physical.

Johan stares at his daughter. It's just the two of them, matching eyes, watching one another. Finally, he comes forward and lays his hand on her head. "Forget this. Forget what you saw here. Your grandma and Kane have decided to go on vacation. Remember? Remember me telling you that? You didn't see them leave, and that's too bad, isn't it?"

"That's too bad," Aqua mumbles, mouth slack.

"You woke up late. Then you went downstairs, and you noticed they were gone. Remember? That's when I told you they went on vacation. Do you remember that?"

"I remember . . . I slept in . . . I came downstairs and noticed they were gone, and I asked you where they went. You said they went on vacation. I didn't see them leave . . . I didn't get to say goodbye. That's too bad."

"It is too bad." He pauses. "You think you know what my gift is, but you don't. You realized that you were wrong, remember?"

"I remember . . . I was wrong about your gift."

"Good. Now sleep."

Instantly her eyes roll into the back of her head, and she drops to the ground with a sound eerily like her grandma's body. The rise and fall of her chest shows that she's still alive. However unbelievable it is for Johan to kill his mom and brother, I know that he would never do that to any of his children.

And then he falls to his knees and weeps.

Long, heavy, gasping sobs.

His thumb that bled when he made the vow with his mom is dry. It wasn't a cast. There was no ritual because he didn't kill with pure intent.

And yet he made Aqua forget and even put in a false memory, including one to make sure she forgets figuring out her father's gift.

Her father's gift of memory modification.

My fists clench, and I struggle to hold onto my intention as tears gather in my eyes.

Modifying memories is his *gift,* and he let Auntie Elaine die to change Justin's. He *knew* that he could make Justin forget without the ritual, but he refused to share his power. He let her die a martyr when he could have helped.

I suck in a sob, because I can't let him hear me.

Maybe it's like he told Aqua, too many holes left in the memory, but it's not like the ritual was perfect anyway. It hadn't held either. Except it left my aunt dead.

Mama Jova grips my shoulder harder.

Focus.

Johan finally rises from the floor, gathers Aqua into his arms, and turns in my direction. My breathing gets labored. Mama Jova digs her fingernails into my shoulder, and my intention becomes everything, repeating it over and over and over.

Johan walks up with Aqua, and for a moment he's so close to me that I can barely breathe.

He stops right next to where I am and looks around. His brow furrows, and tears leak out of my eyes.

Stay hidden.

Stay hidden.

Stay hidden.

Finally, he turns away and heads out of the basement.

I wait for several minutes to pass before I let out a huge exhale and drop on the concrete stairs to my knees.

This is where April-Mae and Kane have been this whole time. Not traveling around the world. Dead. And probably long buried where no one will find them. Aqua is the Matriarch without knowing it. She said that Johan seemed worried about Kane and April-Mae. Scared for them. He wasn't. But he *was* scared of someone finding out about them.

Someone like Aqua, with the control of emotions that she has, she wouldn't have ever pulled on her family's magic the way that I do. Wouldn't have had the ups and downs that would have showed in their casting. Not to mention that given how in tune she is with her family's feelings, she probably wouldn't have noticed the new connections between them. No wonder none of the Davises realized their Matriarch had changed.

"You're running out of time," Mama Jova says.

I stare down at my phone with Luc's countdown. I still had thirty minutes left when I started to do this. And now it's down to fifteen minutes, except the seconds are moving a lot faster than they should be. It's like they're double the speed.

This plan failed. I came here to find out what happened to April-Mae, thinking that we would know where to grab her in the present. But she's nowhere we can grab. And Aqua . . . I don't know that she could stand up to her dad, not like this. There's no way she could hope to force him to give us the antidote.

"The future," Mama Jova says.

I blink at her and open my mouth to protest, then shut it. I trust that she has her reasons. "Okay."

"This is your last chance," she adds. "I'm telling you when to go, but it's up to you once you get there to secure the antidote."

I blink at her. "What do you mean? I've only gone into Johan's past once so far. I still have two more times to go."

She gives me a stern look. "That first one *was* his past."

"What? I thought it was Granny's!"

"No, it's his. That's the moment that Ava solidifies her choice to pick you as Matriarch. That's also when April-Mae notices that choice, so later when Keis gets her gift, she knows that Keis is up for grabs. Her noticing Ava's pick is the reason that she changed her mind away from naming Aqua in the first place. I couldn't completely change your gift's intention from Johan to Ava. I could only shift you further in the past so you could see your granny."

"You couldn't have told me where to go then?!"

"No. I'm not here to spoon-feed you." She pokes me. "You're wasting time!"

"Sorry!" I say, and snap my eyes closed. I need to go to the future.

No. I need to go to a point in the future when I have the most opportunity to find the cure. That's what's important. I only have one chance at this.

My intention needs to be perfect.

I close my eyes and let my gift rise.

In the smoothest transition of this entire thing, I stand on my feet in the entryway at the Davises'. I'm about to walk forward and look for Johan, but then I see that he's already there.

It takes me a moment to recognize him, because he looks so different.

His back is to me, but his locs are a complete mess. Dozens of the strands are falling out of formation, and instead of their deep black hue, they're gray and look dry. I then realize what he's doing.

He's sitting in front of the portrait of his family. There's something at his feet, but I can't see it properly. He's in the way.

I look down at my phone, where time is ticking away.

Ten minutes left. It's jumped so much already.

Hack me.

Ten minutes to save my family.

Looking at his back, knowing exactly how much Johan has hurt my family, could still hurt them, all I want to do is scream at him. To rage and ask why. But I don't have time for that.

"Johan," I say, my voice loud enough to echo in the space.

He doesn't turn right away. He sort of slowly pivots until he's facing me.

His face lacks the dewy glow that I've grown up with, but more than that, his eyes are empty. The fire and power that I'm so used to seeing in them has disappeared. Hollow. Completely gone.

He stands up and faces me, fiddling with a little box in his hands, and it's only then that I notice the thing on the ground is a girl. She's older, but recognizable all the same.

Aqua.

But she's limp, and her entire body including her face is covered in angry red sores leaking yellow pus.

It's my vision but worse. *Much* worse.

I gasp and press my hands to my mouth.

Johan throws me a grim smile. "The future is an ugly place, isn't it?"

"You're not surprised to see me?" I choke out.

"The ghost of Voya Thomas come to punish me at last? No." He stumbles forward. "The ancestors say that when you've truly wronged another witch, they come back for you. I've been waiting for you for a long time."

I've heard of that too. Witches said that to betray your kin— even if they weren't blood family—meant that they would come back for your soul one day. Johan was the one who taught us in school that it was a lie. The fact that he seems to think I've come for him must mean that in this future, we died.

I shake my head. "But you have the antidote. Your family should have been okay."

"Should have been," he says. "I saw Aqua in your little vision and made what I needed to make happen to ensure that all of my children would be safe. But I kept it just for us. Pretended like we were just more cautious than the others. But it had been in too many people by then. The nanites in the gene hack started to jump from one body to another. Didn't need the NuSaps anymore. Turns out, a catch-all is not the same as a vaccine. It can reverse the process, but that doesn't mean that you can't get it going again. And so it kept spreading, and other families kept dying. And they were too weak at that point to even come after me. You would have been the only one who might have managed.

"Your boy kept trying to fix it, but he couldn't. And before I knew it, our antidote supply had run way down. I thought about bringing it to him to try to make a proper cure . . ." Johan grinds his teeth. "But I was too proud, I guess. Too proud to expose to him what I had done. And I guess in some ways, I thought that he would turn me down. Let my family die as revenge for you."

"Luc isn't like that," I say.

"Isn't he? Isn't that how this started?"

"You know how this started," I spit. "This started with *you*."

"No," he snarls. "It started with *you*. With *you* coming out of nowhere and becoming a threat to everything I had built. I knew it would be a matter of time before you figured out everything, and then I would be ruined."

"About April-Mae?" With my gift, if I ever chose to look into why no one could find her, I would realize what he had done. "And about how you modify memories? How much have you done with your gift besides letting my aunt die for nothing?"

"So, you know everything, then?" A grim smile spreads on his face. "Of course you do. I would do anything to protect my family. *Anything*. If I had to shift memories, then I did. That gift had to be kept secret. I couldn't expose it, even for Elaine. And I had to keep that antidote. But now it's gone."

My stomach drops, thoughts of my aunt whisked away. "Gone?"

Johan holds up the small wooden box in his hands and opens it. "Except for this one." In it lies a vial. He jerks his head at Aqua. "I tried to make her take it, but she refused. She never forgave me for what I did to you." Tears gather in his eyes, and he brushes them away. "She wanted to be like you. She never felt like she was good enough for this family. I guess she could tell you felt the same about yours. But you kept going. Kept trying to be better. I think she wished she were like that too. My mother stamped out that girl's fire before she even had a spark." His voice pitches lower, and he whispers, "I did too."

He takes the vial out of the box and grips it in his fist.

I could bite the inside of my cheek and use magic to take it from him. But if he got too spooked, he might drop it.

My phone starts to vibrate.

Luc told me it would do that when I had five minutes left.

But in these visions, a minute is less than a minute.

"That sounds dangerous," Johan says, glancing down at my pocket, where my phone sits.

"I need that antidote."

"I know."

"I need it, Johan. Not just for my family. For yours. For everyone. To stop all of this."

He smiles. "And I need it to live."

My hands shake at my sides, and tears gather in my eyes. This is my last chance to save everyone. This is the only chance I'll get. "*Please*, Johan, give it to me."

"Why? My family is gone; why should yours keep going? Did you know that when they were younger, my mother and your granny were the best of friends? April-Mae, if you can imagine it, was the weak one. Meek. Picked on."

"Abused," I croak.

Johan nods. "That, too. But Ava helped her. Raised her up. Held her hand until my mother realized she could be powerful too. And what did she do with that power? She brought up a family to crush yours. To be on top. And she never let that position go, no matter what it took. I learned everything I knew from Mommy Dearest about how to get what you want. Anything to keep this family going. I would call that tyranny, but I guess some ancestors see it as sacrifice. They never showed any displeasure over it." He laughs, and the glee lights up his gaunt face. "But joke's on her, because she didn't become an honored ancestor, did she? Otherwise, I'm sure she would have used Caribana to expose me."

I try to picture Johan on that first Caribana day after she was gone. Wining down the street in his mas costume, not knowing if his mom would show up and tell everyone what he'd done. But she hadn't. He got away with it. In this future, he got away with everything for a long time.

Johan continues, the mirth draining from his face. "We all still pretended we were family, but that wasn't true, was it? Because Cathius got to leave and be with Ava, that hacking Matriarch's pet. But I stayed with Mother. I protected my family the only way I knew how, and I lost my little girl for it. And now I've suffered to save the rest of my family, and they still died. But when *you* suffer, when a *Thomas* suffers, they survive, don't they? But not this time. Now we can all be equal."

I never thought about what life would be like for Johan living under his mom's rule. Kane, too. What the pressure must have been like for them to make that decision. Because Uncle Cathius isn't like them. He's been a Thomas since he was eighteen. We see each other as family, but Granny couldn't protect them. Maybe she *wouldn't* unless they held our name.

He's right. Us being family was a lie. Us being a community was a lie. But it doesn't have to stay that way.

"None of us have to suffer to survive. Not anymore. You wanted me to join you. You wanted us to be one family that protects each other, right? We can be that. That's why I formed that council. To protect us all. I can still do that. Just give me the antidote."

The alarm on my phone reaches its loudest volume.

The final alarm.

In less than a minute, I'll be gone.

Johan stares at me for a moment as the vibrating of the phone becomes urgent. Fiercer. So violent that my leg shakes with it. "I remember Ava saying something similar when she formed that council. We were going to work together. Things would change. We wouldn't have to be scared anymore, but that's not what happened, is it?"

That's been the theme of my life since I was crowned. Living up to my granny's legacy. Leading this family in her image. It pained me to hear that I wasn't like her. But in her own words, she picked me exactly for that reason. Because she knew that, for however much good she had done, she had messed up, too. We all did. I would never not make mistakes. But when I took on the mantle of Matriarch, I promised that I would be more. That I would lead us into something brand-new. That I wouldn't repeat the mistakes that were already made.

I look Johan in the eyes and say, "I will never be like Granny."

The corner of his mouth quirks up before it falls again. He holds his hand out, palm up, and opens his fingers. "Take it."

I don't hesitate; I move forward and snatch the vial from him as sirens burst out of my phone in the background.

"Save them . . . and save me from me. Be better than what came before you," he says.

"I will."

And in an instant, I let go of my gift and force myself back into the present as my phone sends out one final tone.

The end of my life.

But my fingers clutch the vial that can save them.

And finally.

Finally.

I know that I was the best Matriarch for my family that I could be.

CHAPTER THIRTY-FOUR

The feeling of hardwood on my back is strange and unnerving. I guess that I never quite knew what to expect of an afterlife. Not that I would feel things. But maybe it's not that. Maybe saving everyone was enough to be named one of the chosen ancestors, and this is the place where they go. Or maybe this is my special place, like Mama Jova's sugarcane fields or Auntie Elaine's hospital?

"Voya!" Keis's voice is sharp and loud.

My eyes flash open.

Above me is our familiar ceiling, and my fingers are still wrapped around the vial.

"I'm alive . . . ," I say. "I'm alive?!"

"Not for long unless you have a lead on the antidote," Uncle Vacu grumbles. I turn my head, and he's sitting on the floor next to me. "You have him to thank for why you're still here." He jerks his thumb over to Luc, who's standing by the banister leaning against it in a way that suggests he needs it for support.

Luc shakes his head. "You and Alex went and grabbed it. It's thanks to you, too."

His imperfect serum.

"Glad to see you're still with us," Luc says. I can tell he's trying to sound nonchalant, but his voice has a breathiness to it, like he was holding it and only just let go.

"Me too," I say with a laugh.

Uncle Vacu pokes me with his foot. "What's in your hand?"

"The antidote."

He jumps to his feet. "You have it?!" He turns to Luc. "What are you waiting for? You can look at her more when she's not on the edge of death. Don't you have to get this copied?"

Luc flushes but comes over to me. "I'll have to get it back to the lab." I rise to my feet and hand it to him. He looks at it in his palm. "That easy?"

"What?"

"I'm the bad guy, aren't I? You're just giving it to me? I started this."

I fold his fingers over the vial and grip his hand over top of it. "And I trust you to finish it."

Luc stares into my eyes, and I look back at his. It feels like everything is narrowing down to this moment. And maybe it's because I almost died or because things are finally looking up, but I can't bring myself to be furious that this started because of him or even that he was pretending to be someone else this whole time. Honestly, when I think of it, Eli was so very Luc-like that it's kind of hacked that I didn't notice.

Keisha clears her throat. "So, like, are you going to kiss or go figure out how to copy this antidote? You can do both if you want, but we don't have a lot of time."

Luc and I jump away from each other like we've been shocked.

He splutters but hands the antidote back to me. "Here, take a dose now. It doesn't take much, one sip will do it. I don't need it all."

I take a tentative sip. I kind of expect my sores to immediately recede, but the pain of them remains. I pull back my shirt sleeve and stare at the sore with a frown.

"What?" Luc says.

I raise my wrist. "Shouldn't this disappear?"

He does his lip-biting smile that I haven't seen in so long. I guess it wasn't replaced by that new one after all. "It's science, not magic." He digs a device out of his pocket, and I recognize it as a genetics tester. I hold out my hand, and he pricks it and reads the data on the machine. His smile gets wider. "It's working. The nanites are disengaging, and it's realigning your genes the way they should be. It'll take a little bit to be done, and you'll need to go to the hospital to address the cell damage that's already happened, but it won't get worse."

Mom squeals and tugs me into a hug that has me doing a squeal of my own. "Oops, sorry," she says.

"It's fine," I choke out with a wince. There are a lot more sores on my body than there were when I first used my gift, and my chest aches.

Luc's smile drops off. "You really need to go to the hospital."

"I will. But there's something we have to do first. You go to your lab and get those copies going. Ailee needs one as soon as possible."

He nods and, though he looks reluctant to do so, leaves the house.

I relax a little, but it's not over yet. I give my family the short version of everything that I saw while in Johan's past and future, especially about Johan's gift and Aqua being the real Matriarch. I don't mention Auntie Elaine to try to be sensitive, but I can see the understanding dawn in Alex's and Uncle Vacu's eyes.

"He could have helped her, but he chose not to," Alex says, eyes narrowing. "I'm going to have a talk with him about that after this."

"I would be interested in that conversation," Uncle Vacu adds, sharing a look with his daughter.

Alex nods at me. "What now?"

"We need to find the other Matriarchs, get them together somehow, and explain everything. We'll expose what Johan's done and get them to believe we have an antidote to share with them."

Mom pulls out her phone. "I'll send a message to Rena. She'll know where they are."

"Okay, we get them together, and then what?" Keisha asks, chewing on her nails, which she never does.

"I have a way to show them the truth," I announce. It'll depend on Aqua, but I have to try. "They need to believe us. We can still make this community work. But we can't have lies like this in the middle of it."

"Rena says they're meeting right now at the Davises'. We won't even have to gather them up," Mom says.

Thank the ancestors for small mercies.

"Then let's go," Uncle Cathius says, puffing out his chest. "Johan will own up to what he did."

I know that Uncle Cathius has never liked the way his mom raised their family, but I'm sure he didn't wish that she and his brother were dead. And from the set of his jaw, I gather that he's definitely ready for Johan to answer for his crime.

We move toward the door, and I notice Uncle Vacu lingering behind. Alex has stopped to look at him too.

"Aren't you coming?" I ask him.

He chuckles, but it's stilted and uncomfortable. "Me? I think this is where I fade away. I did what I came to do. I helped. But . . . I stopped being a part of this family a long time ago." He meets my eyes. "I'm sorry for those things I said to you about Elaine last year. She and Alex were my life, and I lost both of them. Maybe Elaine wasn't my fault, but I didn't make things better for her. And Alex was definitely on me. I'm getting better at admitting that and accepting responsibility for it."

Alex gives him a little smile.

I swallow hard, not sure what to say to him about it. "I appreciate it," is what I land on finally. Because I do. The Uncle Vacu that I know would have never apologized about anything. "Now, come on."

He blinks at me. "What?"

"Is your name Thomas?"

"Obviously."

"Then you're a part of this family." I jerk my head toward the adults, who are standing in the doorway. "Let's go."

Auntie Maise huffs. "Didn't you hear the girl? Let's go, Vacu."

"Get moving," Mom adds, waving him over.

Uncle Vacu stares at me and then at his sisters. Finally, he looks over at Alex. She grins at him, tears slipping down her face.

"Welcome back, Dad," she says.

My uncle ducks his head and swipes at his face. When he next looks up, he nods. "Okay. Let's go."

We head out of the house, with only one member left behind. I turn back to Keis standing in the doorway.

Keisha's hand lands on my shoulder, but she's looking at her sister. "I'll make sure she comes back."

"I know you will," Keis says.

The whole family is with me when we make our way to Johan's house. Rena and Lee have come along with us too. We stand in front of the gate to the Davises' home like a makeshift army. All of us except for Keis. I half expected Priya to want to stay behind with Eden, but she holds her daughter close and her head high. This is about standing as a family unit, and she's part of it.

Breathing hurts. My chest hurts. Walking hurts. But I'm here. We're here.

I take a deep breath before pushing open the gate.

Hilariously, Johan hasn't blocked us from entering. I guess maybe he didn't think we would have the gall to go for it.

Mom squeezes my shoulder.

I lead the way into the house.

Aqua is waiting in the entryway tapping her foot and looking up and down the hall. I messaged her to meet us. She jumps up as soon as she sees us. "Voya, what is this about? Daddy will be so mad that you're here."

"Can you please let me explain when we get to the meeting?"

"Okay . . ." She gives me a skeptical look even as she agrees.

We walk down the hall and straight into the room where the Matriarchs are sitting.

The entire space goes silent the minute we step inside. I notice that Eli is there too, standing in the back of the room, gaze vacant. On autopilot.

Johan narrows his eyes at us. "What is this? An ambush?"

"Weren't you acting like you were moments from death?" Avery drawls, her eyes drawn and suspicious. "And yet, here you are."

I straighten my spine and force myself not to be intimidated. "I got the cure."

"Convenient," Torrin mutters.

"Grow up, Torrin!" Rena snaps, coming to the front of our group. "How ridiculous are you being right now? She did everything she could to help Lauren. That's your niece. *He*"—she points over at Johan—"avoided helping because we couldn't find a way to pay what he wanted. And *that's* who you're siding with? Really? Lauren would be ashamed."

Torrin's face twists, and she shifts in her seat.

"What do you mean a cure?" Ilana says finally. She's the only one of them who doesn't look like she hates me.

"I used my gift to go into Johan's past and future." I nod to him.

"He had the antidote all along . . ." I take a deep breath. "The truth is that back when . . . when Granny died, I didn't technically kill Justin Tremblay. I didn't want to kill anyone. So I used my Matriarch wish to put him in a NuSap body, and we kept him hidden in the basement. Johan found a way to meet with him, and they worked together to help him form an escape plan. In exchange, he gave Johan the catch-all to reverse the effects of the hack." I jerk my head toward Eli standing against the wall. "Not to mention, Eli is a NuSap unit. Justin also murdered the real Eli. When Johan went looking for him, he found the real Eli's body at NuGene and ended up forming this plan together with Luc and his sponsor siblings—a plan that he abandoned after seeing my vision and realizing that maybe the deal with Justin would be the better route. Luc was periodically manually controlling this NuSap Eli so that he could monitor the effects of the hack, not realizing that Justin was alive. But once he understood the damage that the plan was doing, he switched to our side. Though I only learned that he was posing as Eli today."

The Matriarchs are a chorus of silence and dropped jaws.

Ilana points to the Eli NuSap. "You're saying he's a robot?!"

"Take off his hat."

The Bailey Matriarch raises both eyebrows, but she goes over to Eli and reaches slowly for the hat. He does nothing to prevent her from taking it off and exposing the smashed skull with its wires. She gasps and stumbles back.

Avery shakes her head. "Okay, so he's a robot. Controlled by your boyfriend."

I flush. "He's not my boyfrie—"

"Whatever! None of that means that anything else that you said is true, because if only Johan has the antidote, how did you get it?"

I try to calm down, my body still overheated from Avery's

assumption about me and Luc. "The gene hack—which I *was* hacked, if the sores on my face aren't convincing enough—it messed with my gift the way it does everyone else. Amplified it. Instead of just viewing the future and past, I was thrown into it and had the ability to touch and interact with the people there." I stare straight into Johan's eyes. "His future self gave me the last vial he had."

Johan lets out a loud long laugh. It's his first reaction to anything that I've said. "Now, that's a story. If I'm the villain here, why would I help you?"

"Because in the future, your entire family is dead. The gene hack starts to spread between people, and you run out of antidote. You gave it to me and told me to save you from yourself."

Johan's lip curls, and he stands from his chair. "Get out of my house. I won't tolerate these lies. You're cured, you say? Clearly you had the antidote all along. The simplest answer is usually the right one. This tale that you've spun is a fiction you created to save yourself. Even trying to wrap me up in your boy spying on us, which you apparently knew about. Now you realize that you're trapped and have decided to share your antidote with us."

I shake my head at him, refusing to back down. "I also went into your past. I know what you did to April-Mae and Kane."

I'll give it to him, he's a good actor. His face doesn't change in the slightest. He looks as calmly curious as the rest of the Matriarchs at the table. "Enough. I'll only say it one more time." He glares at me, and his voice goes dangerously low. "Get out of my house."

"I want to hear what she has to say," Ilana cuts in. Johan schools his face into a neutral expression, but the skin around his eyes is pinched tight. "That boy ... Luc ... he was pretending to be Eli, but he was always looking after that boy's mother. To be honest, I suspected that her illness had less to do with her than to do with magic." Her eyes float over to Johan. "There's a way impure magic feels. I deal in it, so I know. I wondered why someone would ever do that to her. Was worried enough to keep her and Eli in my house so I could watch over them. But if that someone was trying to hide something, like the fact that her son was not her son . . . well, that would be motive."

"Ilana!" Avery chokes out. "You can't be falling for this."

"*Hours*. That boy sat by her bedside for *hours* talking to her. And I know he had faraway moments. I guess that was when the robot wasn't being controlled. But when he sat with that woman, he was very much present." She looks over at me. "A boy like that I could believe would recognize when he made a mistake and try and turn it around. So yes, Avery. I would like to hear what Voya has to say."

I lick my lips, letting a cautious hope rise. Ilana is open to listening. And more, I didn't know Luc was doing that. He knew that Johan was the reason Eli's mom was sick. That it was because of their plan. And he must have hated it.

Torrin throws an apologetic look at Avery. "I want to hear it too. I mean, everything she's saying sounds so sparked. But still, I'll give her the right to say it. If only for Lauren."

Rena beams at her younger sister.

Avery, meanwhile, looks horrified by her friend. "Are you serious?" She shakes her head. "This is ridiculous, and it's *his* house. I don't understand why we're entertaining this."

"Do you hate us that much?" Dad says, walking forward. "Do you really want to bring your grudge against me and Elaine so far that you won't listen to anything my daughter has to say because of it? Really?"

Avery grinds her teeth. "Did I ask for your input?"

"We grew up together! Voya is your cousin. We're your family."

"Then *where were you*?!" she shouts. "We're family, you keep saying that. But where were you? None of you ever lifted a finger to help us. When Mom was struggling. When my brothers were struggling. Each of us working so hard to make ends meet because we wanted to be pure. Elaine with her gift just leaving. You didn't even try to get us on that council. We had to suffer and scrimp for everything we got. You *left* us. But now you want to say that we're family?! Get hacked!"

Dad doesn't look away from her. "*We* did that, but Voya never did. She created this council and made sure everyone was on it, didn't she? She's listened to your opinions and contacted you. You're punishing her for what we've done when she has *never* done the same."

Avery's mouth hangs open, and she looks at me as if finally seeing me properly.

"Are you still against listening to her?" Ilana says to Avery.

The young Matriarch hangs her head and says nothing more.

Ilana smiles at me. "Then I guess we're listening. Aren't we?"

"Does my vote not count?" Johan mutters.

"You're not a Matriarch," Ilana says, her voice polite but hard-edged. "And I have spent this entire time trying to find your mother without any luck. If Voya says she has information, I want to hear it." She nods to me.

I nod back. "Johan murdered April-Mae and his brother."

Avery and Torrin let out audible gasps. Ilana narrows her eyes. "That's a very serious allegation."

"That it is," Johan says, his voice as sharp as a cutlass's blade. "Very serious. There would be consequences, don't you think? For saying something that serious."

I know it for what it is. It's a threat. *Say the truth, and I'll make your life a living hell.*

But if things go the way I think they will, he won't be able to.

"He made her name Aqua as her successor and then erased Aqua's memories. It's his gift."

Johan tilts his head to the side and looks behind me to his eldest daughter. "And what do you think of that?"

All heads turn to Aqua, who is standing at the back of my family looking more shocked than anyone else. I walk over to her.

"This is the thing I needed to tell you," I say to her. "You're the Matriarch of this family. That means *you're* the leader. Not him."

It's one thing to say the words to her and another for her to believe them. She shakes her head. As the oldest child, she's been with Johan the longest. He's had the most time to impress his control over her. But I've gotten to know Aqua. She's shown that she can challenge him and stand on her own. She broke his rules to help Topaz and to help me.

But now she says nothing.

Johan guffaws. "This is truly ridiculous."

"Let's see then," Ilana says. "As a Matriarch, she should be able to call on her ancestors and have them legitimize her." She nods to Aqua. "Call them, girl. Your daddy should have taught you the words in that school of his. They'll show themselves to you and us and tell us if you're the true Matriarch of this family. If they don't . . . then we'll have to throw out Voya's claim."

Aqua keeps shaking her head. It's like she can't stop. She's denying it with every fiber of her being.

This is the part that could go poorly.

Getting the council to believe us depends on Aqua accepting this role and going against her dad.

"Aqua . . . ," I say.

She turns her head the slightest bit to look at me.

"I know that it's scary to be the Matriarch. I wasn't ready to lead. And it's not exactly easy. You might find yourself struggling to prove that you're good enough for the title and that you can do right by your family. I can't force you to do this. Because you thinking I'm right, that's one thing, while accepting being the leader of your family is something else. And . . . I understand if you would rather let things stay the way they are now." I give her a little smile. "I'm sure you love your dad, but you more than anyone can see when he's gone too far. And it'll be hard to stand up to him. But you've already done it twice now. For Topaz. For me. You said you admired me, but we're a lot more alike than you realize. Like me, you would do anything for the good of your family, even if it was hard."

Aqua's eyes start to shine.

"I don't think Johan is evil, and I don't think you do either. But he's so scared of losing any more of you that he's making things dangerous for everyone. You've realized it too, haven't you? Just like you've realized what he's done."

Johan's eyes narrow at that.

"I messaged you a description of a box. Johan had it in the future. And you recognized it, didn't you? How else could I know about that box? I saw it in that vision." Maybe I could have done a desperate searching spell for it to expose the Davis leader, but chances are that Johan's found a way to cover his bases for that. But Aqua knows her family inside and out. If he owns it, she's probably seen it.

Aqua swallows, and tears pour down her face.

"That's what the antidote was in. The one that Johan gave me in the future. If you know it belongs to him, then you know what he's done." I let out a long breath. "I won't be mad if you decide not to do this. We'll still always be family."

The entire room goes quiet in that moment.

Aqua breaks eye contact with me and looks down at her feet.

She can't do it.

And it's okay.

I look around at my family and shake my head. Their faces fall, and Auntie Maise looks like she's about to physically shake her niece, but I hold up a hand.

I walk over to Aqua and touch her shoulder. "We'll leave. No matter what, I'll make sure to get this antidote to everyone. Even if I can't be part of this council. And even if they don't believe me. I would never let any of you get hurt." I give her shoulder a squeeze and move to walk out of the house.

My dream of a united Black witch community shatters. I hope that at the very least the ones left will stick together. That they'll make something, even if the Thomases can't be a part of it.

I'm halfway out of the dining room when Aqua starts to speak. "I call on the ancestors, the blood of my blood. Hear my call and bear witness. If I am the true Matriarch of this Davis family, say aye."

Johan leaps from his seat, but it's too late. The room explodes with bright white light, and as it dims, ancestor after ancestor after ancestor appears in the room, their ghostly figures clear and their faces set. And finally, the last of them appears right next to Aqua.

I recognize her instantly.

Ilana stumbles back.

April-Mae.

The Davis Matriarch was a complicated woman, and I can't say what made her an honored ancestor. Whether it was the people she saved from her father, or if it was the way she protected her family, however ruthless it was. It doesn't matter what I think of her, or what Johan does, or anyone else. Something made the people who came before her decide she was worthy to guide future generations. And now, here she stands.

She smirks at her son and says, "Aye."

Around us, the circle of Davis ancestors repeats alongside her, each of them confirming that Aquamarine Davis is the true Matriarch of the family.

Aqua looks at Johan, tears spilling down her face. "I'm sorry, Daddy. But I can't let you hurt people anymore." She raises her hand to him, reaching out with her fingers, and *tugs.*

I've never seen a Matriarch take magic away from a family member, but I watch it now. The power curls into Aqua's fist, and she holds it with a shaking hand, pressing and pressing until it becomes a jewel.

Bright blue.

Sapphire.

Johan collapses to the floor. "You can't be an honored ancestor," he groans, staring up at his mom from where he lies. "You weren't at Caribana. You could have appeared there and told everyone the truth. Why would you wait until now?"

April-Mae looks down at her son with a curled lip. "I knew that it wouldn't be enough. You're too powerful. The only one who could ever punish you would be your Matriarch. And Aqua wasn't ready to stand on her own." She turns to her eldest granddaughter. She doesn't smile. Just appraises her with a cool gaze. "I underestimated you. I thought you soft and sentimental, but maybe that's what this family needs."

Aqua swallows so hard that I can see her throat bob.

With that, April-Mae and the other ancestors fade away.

"The antidote?" Ilana asks, looking to the newly revealed Davis Matriarch.

Aqua makes a cut on her finger and raises her hand in the air. A box comes soaring into it—the same box from my vision. She turns it around to the Matriarchs and reveals the bottom. On it, it says, "To my wonderful son Johan on the day of successfully passing his Calling, from your loving mother." She flips it back and opens it. Inside are at least a dozen vials filled with clear liquid.

"I wondered why he had me hide it," she says, running her fingers over the wood. "Or rather, I did know. Inside was a birthday gift for Emerald, but it didn't feel right. He was too panicked about it. Too scared. And of course, I forgot where I put it almost immediately after. Now I know why."

All the Matriarch's eyes turn to Johan, still kneeling on the floor.

"I think his Matriarch has already given him a suitable punishment," Ilana says, then she turns to me. "Now, leader, what's next?"

I meet Aqua's eyes and smile.

As if on cue, my phone goes off with a call from Luc. I make the projection public so the others can see his face and he can see them.

"Oh, wow, it's everyone," Luc says, eyes wide. "Um . . ."

"Everyone knows everything," I say to him. "We were just figuring out what to do next."

"Nice to formally meet you." Ilana crosses her arms. "But apparently I've known you this whole time."

Luc rubs the back of his head. "Yeah . . ."

"We'll discuss it later. You must have called for a reason?"

"Yes!" He nods vigorously. "The antidote, I can make copies of it. But it has an incubation period. All gene hacks do. The nanites need time to learn the sequence. It'll take something like twelve hours for it to be available."

"That's great!" I beam. An antidote for everyone who needs it in less than a day.

But Luc doesn't smile back. "It's not, actually. The NuSap units . . . they're still coming."

"Tell Jasmine and Juras to call them off! Aren't you all working together to stop Justin? They seriously still want to do this?"

"It's not us!" Jasmine snaps, coming into the screen next to Luc. "If you must know, we're *helping*."

"I'm not!" Juras shouts in the background.

His sponsor sister rolls her eyes. "It's not us. It's someone else in the system. We can direct where they're going for a time, but we can't stop them from moving and emitting the gene hack."

Someone else . . . Justin. It must be. This is probably a distraction to keep his sponsor kids from stopping him getting back into a body. I never even imagined that he could move through the world fully digitally, but of course he figured it out.

"Why does it matter?" Avery cuts in. "We'll have the antidote in twelve hours. Lee's charge is still managing, and she's had it for more than a day."

I shake my head. "No. The ones in the parade today, they're faster. They'll kill you in three to four hours. We could be dead before it was ready. Even if we used the antidotes that Johan has, it wouldn't be enough for everyone."

"Then redirect them into a lake!"

Jasmine grinds her teeth. "For one, they're waterproof. And for two, that is so incredibly bad for the environment. What is wrong with you?"

"What's wrong with *me*?!" Avery shrieks. "Is the baby murderer seriously asking me that?"

"I didn't murder anyone."

"Yet!"

"Stop!" I shout, glad that Priya already took Eden out into the hallway. "Can't we redirect to somewhere far away without any witches?" I ask.

Luc shakes his head. "No, that's what Jasmine meant by 'for a time.' They're already on Lake Shore. We can redirect them for something like fifteen minutes, being generous, before Justin notices. Once he does, he'll probably find a way to lock us out. He's still trying to guard himself from us finding him, working too fast, which is probably the only reason he didn't have enough protection to stop us from taking over redirection controls in the first place. We can probably also block the units from releasing the hack for longer, maybe half an hour. It's a much more complicated function for Justin to take over. So even if you can't get away from them quickly, you'll have a bit before they're dangerous."

That's not a lot of time at all. "Bring them to Marie Curtis Park."

Mom puts her hands on her hips. "And what are you going to do? You let any more ancestors push magic into you in your state, and you'll really die this time."

"I know," I say. "I can use some of my own magic. But I do need blood and people to donate it." I look around the room. "And some people willing to use magic to stop anyone from coming into the park and to keep the units stuck there until more people can come help."

"I'll go," Ilana says, striding forward. "And I'll get as much of my family to come as I can."

"Me too," Aqua jumps in immediately. Johan doesn't even make a sound of protest from where he sits on the floor.

Torrin clears her throat. "Me too, obviously."

Finally, the room is quiet, and we all look at Avery, who lets out a long breath. "We're family, aren't we?"

I beam at her. "Then let's do this."

CHAPTER THIRTY-FIVE

For the first time in a very long time, I am surrounded by the Black witch community. We're gathered on the snow-dusted grass in Marie Curtis Park by the waterfront, the late afternoon sun dipping low in the sky. Waiting. The lake water, freezing by now, laps gently at the rocks we stand on. The city of Toronto at our backs, CN Tower standing tall in the distance, and an army of blue-skinned androids stuck in a bubble of protective magic. Bumping against the sides, trying to follow Justin's commands to escape.

The Matriarchs flank me on either side.

My already sore chest burns as my heart beats faster.

It's unbelievable, how many units there are. It must be every single one from that factory.

There's a group of witches flanking the east, west, and south sides of the area. Jameses. Baileys. Davises. Carters. And Thomases. Eyes closed, focusing on keeping people from noticing what's happening in the park and others focused on keeping the NuSaps in. There aren't nearly as many of us as there are robots, but the people who could come and live in the area got here fast.

It's only when people start looking at the series of cars pulling up along the street that my attention diverts. The door of a sleek electric sports car opens, and shimmering black fabric pools out as Rowen Huang exits.

My mouth drops open.

More of the car doors are flung aside as people—as *Huangs*—spill out and make their way toward us.

Rowen smiles at me. "A cousin of mine suggested that you might need help. And thankfully I have a charge with a gift for speedy travel."

I pause a moment to really take in the Matriarch. "Thank you." It's all I can manage to say.

She twirls a dismissive hand at me, and her family join the circle. I watch her clasp hands with Ilana Bailey, fingers gripping tightly.

A message comes through from Luc: *Justin is close to taking over the gene-hack releasing controls.*

It's time.

I look around and see my dream—more than it, because I could have never imagined reaching even the Huangs, a huge family that extends way beyond my own. This is our start. One day, I hope we'll get to a point where we can be a thriving community. And we aren't the only group of witches in Toronto. I imagine a time when, outside of our council, we communicate with families like the Huangs and Jayasuriyas, too, and help each other when we need it. But I know that moment isn't now. We're like the beginnings of a sourdough starter, just getting our first bubbles, showing promise. We're figuring out the bit where we live without the pain and hurt, and there's still more to do to fix that. Discussions that need to happen about the true nature of magic that Mama Jova taught me and how to maintain power without torture or murder.

But now those steps feel possible.

Avery, on my right, looks over at me. "I'm sorry."

I blink at her. "You're sorry?"

She nods. "For what I said to you that day. About you being like Elaine. Your boy came through. You were right about him being different. And you came through the most."

"But I do think that I'm like Auntie Elaine," I reply.

Now it's Avery's turn to blink at me.

"I wanted to change things, and now look, we're here together to help each other. That's all she wanted. Us working together as a community. And that's what I want too. Like she did, I made a lot of mistakes, except that this time around, I have the help she didn't."

Avery's eyes get glassy. "Yeah, I guess you do." She clears her throat and faces forward. "Are we doing this?"

"We are." I squeeze her hand and shout, "Now would be a good time for blood!"

Around me, everyone notches cuts into their fingers.

Very little of my bandwidth has built back up, but I don't need a lot of my own magic. I don't need power from the ancestors either. I just have to direct everyone else's power through and out of my body without damaging it more than it already has been.

When I raise my hands, the scent of freshly burned sugarcane explodes in the air, and the blood rises with the motion of my fingers. It forms into a sort of giant cloud, and I drag it around the circle, blocking in the NuSap units and keeping them away from the witches. More and more blood pulls into the cloud.

If mine were the only blood contributed or if I had to pull on my own magic, I would be dead by now.

But it's not just me. It's all of us.

With a flex of my fingers, the blood stiffens, and spikes of crimson rip through the heads of every single NuSap, hitting the exact point in their manufactured skulls where Luc told me the chip letting them function is lodged. One by one, they fall.

Finally, I let go and collapse as well. Chest heaving, burning, my entire body shaking.

The only human on the ground in a park filled with cornflower-blue corpses.

I wake in a room enclosed in glass. It's one box in a case of more and more glass boxes. And I recognize it. The place where my family was kept last year. Where Lauren and Eli died. I jerk up, try to stand, and almost fall over.

"You are so sparked," a voice says with a laugh. "You're fine. Lie down."

I blink and look over to where Keisha is sitting, flicking through a tablet. Her hair is in a completely different style than it was when I last saw her, done in multicolored pink pastel strands down to her shoulders with star pins tugging her bangs back.

"What happened?" I gasp.

She waves around the room. "Luc said this was the best place to put you. Ailee was here too for a bit, but she's already gone home. He said you needed a hospital, but explaining the whole cellular degeneration thing would have been a lot. So here you are." Keisha smiles at me with soft eyes. "I'm glad you're okay."

"I, for one, had hoped that she would die."

I twist toward the other side of the room, and there, in the next glass case over, is Justin—and not Justin in his fancy NuSap body, but Justin in the NuSap body I gave him. The first one he ever made. His room is filled with paper books, a desk, a big lounging chair and couch, and even a small table and chairs as if he'll be expecting visitors. Though maybe he will be.

He scowls at me. "Go ahead. Be smug."

"I'm not smug, I'm confused," I say. "But clearly your kids were able to get you out of that computer."

"Yup," Keisha chimes happily and waves at Justin. "Hey, former-CEO-turned-murderer-who-used-to-live-in-our-basement!"

He rolls his eyes.

I laugh and turn back to my cousin, who comes over and bundles me in her arms. "I'm glad you didn't die," she whispers.

"Me too." I take a moment to really look at my cousin. "I'm happy you're here."

"Obviously your best friend should be around when you wake up. One of them, at least."

"Exactly." A grin spreads across my face. "Everyone else is okay?"

"Yeah, most of them are at the house. They're having many meetings about how to fortify it now." She flips her hair over her shoulder. "I think between the magic being in it *and* Eden *and* Justin escaping, they've realized it needs a failsafe."

The house, of course. For a moment there, I figured that maybe it could be made into a strength. I think of being in the park and the way I manipulated the magic through me. What if we could do that with the house—manipulate the magic to fortify it? "I think I have an idea for that, actually," I say.

The door slides open, and when I look, Luc is walking inside. He glances over at Justin, who is sulking in an armchair. "Sorry to put you next to him, but it's easier to monitor both of you at the same time if you're in the same place." I notice the way Luc looks at his mentor, his gaze neutral, but in a way that seems like it's fixed in place. Like he's trying hard. "Someone made it easier to find them when they got greedy and decided to mess with the NuSap protocols to kill you. Turns out, his mind can only be in one place at a time. Putting him in a body is actually to our benefit. Though we're still working on finding those backups."

Justin grits his teeth and turns away.

"I figured it would be better to keep him here instead of your house," Luc says. "I mean, your house is nice, it's just, this is more secure, I think. I'm the only one with access to this area. Jasmine and Juras know, but they're no longer employees. I programmed everything so he is very firmly stuck here." He shrugs. "Only magic could get him out, and I don't think any of you will be doing that."

"Definitely not," I reply. "Jasmine and Juras . . . They're gone?"

"I strongly suggested that they resign, but I'll continue to sponsor them until they find a new company. I can't trust them to be here. Especially Juras."

"Is that going to be okay?"

"They don't seem to be plotting any sort of revenge, if that's what you mean. I think they're tired, honestly. Not just of the job. They've been second-in-command for so long. Maybe they're kind of looking forward to leaving those positions. Even if they're mostly furious at me."

"They're your family." I look down in my lap. For these last months, they've always been by his side.

Luc nods with a grimace. "They are, but I think that's why they'll come around eventually. Besides, I have another family too. Maybe me and my parents will never have the same sort of bond, but I'm open to it. This whole sponsorship thing, for all the good it's done, it's also done its share of harm."

"That sounds like a great new start," I say, because it does.

I find myself looking over at him. This boy with ocean wave hair and stormy eyes who I fell in love with, who I declared war with, and who I'm sitting here with now, not knowing what's next.

Keisha suddenly jumps up. "Well, I think I'm going to go let everyone know Vo is awake." My cousin barely lets me get a word in before she's running out of the room.

"Urg," Justin groans. "If this is going to involve teen romance, please cut me off."

Luc stabs a control on the wall with maybe a little more force than necessary, and the glass surrounding Justin's room goes dark. It's quiet, too. I can't tell if that's because he turned soundproofing on or because he's just decided to be silent.

"I can't believe Justin killed Eli, too," I mutter to myself. "I didn't actually know him . . . but still."

Luc comes and sits on the edge of my bed. "I looked him up, before, because I needed to pretend to be him, obviously. But I learned more from Ilana, too. You've been out for a day, you know."

"A *day*?!"

"Yeah. Well, you passed out. But then you had to be put out to help everything heal. I was going to bring in a doctor, but your uncle took care of you. I just made sure he had the equipment."

"Uncle Vacu?"

"Yup."

It makes sense. I mean, he *is* a doctor. "You were saying about Eli?"

Luc plays with his fingers in his lap. "I was going to look at Justin's notes, but he just told me. Eli didn't have any magic. He was already seventeen, and I think he was worried he would never have any. Ilana told me they talked about it, but she couldn't do anything. It caused a lot of friction in his family. That's why they figured he had run away. But actually he had been trying to do his own genetics trials to solve the issues based on what he knew from working with Helping Hands."

My eyes go wide. It's not unlike what the council and Justin were trying to do, except that Eli was on his own. He probably didn't even know about Auntie Elaine with the way the community refused to talk about her.

Luc continues, "He was trying to set a meeting up with people at NuGene for months to talk about what he called Shifting Gene Theory. Finally, he booked the free appointment from that ad

450

Justin had sent out to witches, except this was after Lauren died, and Justin was already on to bigger and better things. But an employee recognized his name and told Justin about Eli's theory and his meeting requests. Justin still declined, but secretly he set up the meeting with Eli, put him in one of the glass rooms. It was the same day that everything happened . . ."

"No one knew Eli was in the room," I whisper.

Luc shakes his head. "Justin had just died. I know it wasn't actually 'real,' but it was to me. I was a wreck. The company was too. There were police interviews. We were all under scrutiny. And I knew what happened but couldn't prove it, which made me feel more devastated. No one else was even aware that this basement and these glass rooms existed. By the time I recovered enough to tell Jasmine and Juras what had really happened and come down here to investigate . . . it was too late."

Eli was in that room, alone, waiting. Waiting for this man who he thought would change his life. He couldn't have known that Justin was already clued in about magic—Eli must have guessed that his actions would expose us. But he was so desperate to be a witch. To have magic . . .

We were there at the same time that day. I could have saved him if only I knew he was there. But of course, Justin never mentioned him.

A slow, terrible, painful death.

"Does his mom know? How is she?"

"She's . . . physically better. Once Aqua got Johan to tell Ilana what he had done, she undid it. But . . ."

"But now she knows her son is dead."

"Yeah. Though, Ilana spared her the details of how. She said that Justin killed him during an experiment to give him magic."

I fiddle with my fingers and look over at Luc. His eyes are downcast. "And did you talk to her?"

"I did," he says with a sigh. "I thought she would be mad. I wished she would be. But instead she said that she knew something was wrong the moment I came back. That she was happy and wanted to be, but she still felt like her son was dead. And the more we talked, the more she realized that I wasn't the person she lost; she just didn't know why he was different. And with what Johan had done to her, she was so in and out of sleep, she figured it was her mind playing tricks on her. But she's glad to have the body. Ilana is arranging the funeral now."

At least there's that for Eli and his mother. I hope that with the support of her family, she makes it through.

"I am sorry," Luc says. "I know I keep saying that, but I am. So many people were hurt. I would understand if none of them ever forgave me."

"Part of me doesn't want to forgive you," I reply.

"You don't have to—"

I scowl at him. "Can I finish?"

He ducks his head. "Yeah."

"We don't have a great history with deception." I technically started it last year. I looped him into my life to save my family. And then he pulled me back into his life to do what he thought was saving *his* family. Even if it was based on Johan's lie. "But we both tried to do the right thing in the end, didn't we? Maybe that makes us bad for each other, but I figure that we can decide that for ourselves. So . . . I'm conditionally forgiving you."

The corner of Luc's lip twitches, like he's fighting a grin. "What conditions?"

"No more trying to eradicate magic."

"Fair. Counterpoint, no attempts on my life."

"Also fair. No secrets and deceptions."

"Agreed, with an additional condition of surprises being allowed."

I raise an eyebrow at him. "You plan one NuGene party and now you're suddenly into surprises?"

"It was a very good party. A lot of interns said so."

"I didn't like the end of it."

"Neither did I. A girl threatened me."

I'm laughing before I can stop it. "I was so mad."

"You were rightfully angry. I really am, you know, sorry about your grandma. Even if Justin truly was gone, it's not an excuse. It felt like my entire world was snatched from under me, and I acted like I was the only one dealing with that when I wasn't. You understood that it was a loss for both of us and left it at that. I should have too."

"Thank you." I'm still thinking of Granny. While I was out, I'm sure that I must have dreamed about her. I wish she could see that things worked out in the end.

But I believe that somewhere, somehow, she can.

Luc says, "Though you'll be thankful to know that Jasmine and Juras won't be making attempts on your life either, even if they've moved on from NuGene and aren't currently my biggest fans. Jasmine curtly said she was disinterested in being involved with you in any way, and Juras agreed to talk to someone about what happened. Apparently, Avery has a psychotherapist cousin—she was at the park. She's not a witch but knows about magic, so he can talk about whatever openly. Your dad and stepmom were talking with her too."

"For Eden, likely." A smile spreads on my face knowing that my baby sister will finally get the help she needs. The truth is out there now in our community. We have people that we can trust. "Maybe I'll go too." I don't think that I was depressed, but I don't really know. Grief is a lot. I have nothing to lose by talking to someone. And with the business doing better, the expense shouldn't hit us too hard.

Luc and I sit there in silence for a moment.

Finally, he clears his throat and says, "I once told someone that if they really loved a person, then they would fight for that love." He reaches into his pocket and pulls out a little leaf.

I blink at it. That first time we looked for an excuse to kiss, there wasn't actually one. We just pretended.

But I know what it means.

He hands it to me. "You don't . . . it's . . ." He stumbles for a moment, then says, "I know that I messed things up. Even if you conditionally forgive me, this isn't necessarily for now. But . . . I'm not going to stop fighting for you." He's sitting too straight, and his eyes are darting around like he would give anything to not look at me.

I take the leaf from him and turn it in my hands, smiling at the little veins, brushing my fingers over the stem. There's a stiffness to it, like it was dried. Preserved. "Where is this from?"

"The park in the Beaches where we ate that one time . . ."

"It's winter now. There are no leaves." I look up at him. "Meaning that you got this in summer and kept it?"

"Yeah," he breathes.

"When exactly did you collect this?"

"That same day, when you weren't looking."

Even without knowing what our future would be, he decided right then that he didn't want to forget our unofficial date. He would have had to press the leaf into a book and keep it safe for months, stuck in time between the pages like that moment we shared.

I think of the container underneath my bed.

Neither of us had done a very good job at being each other's enemy, apparently.

Reaching up, I put the leaf on my head and smile. Luc smiles back, that lip-biting one. The real one, I know now. I always had the real one. Slowly, he leans forward, and I lean forward too, until our lips press together.

It's not at all like our first kiss. Or our second. It won't ever be. We've changed too much since then.

There are tears, salty as they slide down our faces. There's a grief between us.

And none of that makes it any less special.

CHAPTER THIRTY-SIX

Six months later . . .

This family is so loud. Cackling and screams ring out from the dining room as Eden and Caleb chase each other around the legs of our giant table, which is now even more giant. Aqua decided to make an elaborate and unnecessary gifting of another antique, non-modded wood table. Apparently so we could all have dinner together. Something that I am expected to cook.

I slap the bake dough onto the table and kick up a whole dusting of flour.

Only when the white powder falls back down and Luc glares at me with a face full of it do I realize that maybe I was a bit dramatic about it.

"I'm never going to help you again," he grumbles.

Aqua stifles a laugh from beside me, much more calmly rolling out her own batch of bake dough.

"This is why I chose not to participate," Keisha adds in from her spot on her stool. She's scrolling through her phone, back on her dating apps now that she and Keis are splitting their time helping Auntie Maise. And these days, it seems to be going a lot better too. Fewer disappointments and more exciting potentials, as she describes.

Luc scowls. "You said you didn't want to help because your nails would get messy."

"It's both."

I scowl at all of them and look around the room. "Where's Keis? She said she would help."

"I can go get her," Luc volunteers, eagerly wiping his hands off on a dish towel. "She's probably tinkering with her unit."

I narrow my eyes at him. "Are you going to come back?"

"Of course!"

"He won't," Keisha adds helpfully.

My eyes become the world's tiniest slits.

"I will!" Luc insists.

"Fine."

He rushes off to the basement, where Keis is likely hiding out. My cousin continued to build her love of game development, and with Luc as an occasional tutor, has been learning more about genetics than ever. They're both such nerds about it. They've been talking about developing an offshoot of NuGene dedicated to educational games designed to teach kids how to manipulate and code genes.

It's incredibly strange to see them together like that. My two first loves. But there it is.

They're even able to communicate when Luc isn't inside the house. It took Mama Jova rolling her eyes at me and saying, "You know that magic has loopholes, don't you?" before it finally clicked.

The burner app.

When Keis uses it, she isn't technically communicating as herself with the outside world, and apparently that was enough. Now she can send messages, take calls, and do anything she could before with the internet, so long as she's using an anonymous app.

She can even do more than that. Knowing what Luc could do with Eli gave my cousin the genius idea of getting her own identical NuSap unit. It looks creepily just like her, but the difference is that it *can* leave the house. Luc's been helping develop a full body immersive system for her to control it so she can get a complete virtual experience. What he used for Eli automatically cast his expressions and movements from the neck up, and he had to manually control everything else. But in both cases, he couldn't *feel* the environment it was in. This system that the two of them develop could very well do that.

It's not the same as being unstuck, but it's as close as we can get. Most importantly, it makes Keis happy. There's an extra spark in her eyes now.

Aqua nudges me. "Sorry."

"It's fine." I know that of all people in the world, she would genuinely feel apologetic. "It's probably better this way. I was just going to mope around and feel sorry for myself."

Keisha grins. "We know."

"But you said Luc was going to come over?" Aqua asks.

"Moping is his favorite thing."

She laughs and Keisha joins in, and I find myself laughing along with them. Aqua is so much more open and free now. She's fully taken control as the Matriarch of the family and Johan is effectively on probation. She hasn't given his magic back, and as a council, we've agreed to keep it that way until we feel it's safe for him to have any—a day that may or may not come to pass.

The council has continued running, though now on a monthly basis instead. We even finally convinced Lee to join. And sure, a lot of it is definitely gossiping, but they've also been helping coach me and Aqua on running our families. And in our last meeting, Ilana announced that she's been in talks with Rowen, and while the two families may never rejoin, they're breaking down the bonds that stood between them in the aftermath, with Lee along to help. Rowen also remains our best referral customer.

And one day, I'm hoping to float by her that idea of creating interconnected councils. Priya already said she'll help with the Jayasuriyas. That way we can look after the families under our council on a smaller scale but begin to build a larger-scale community in the city for all witches to help each other.

While my relationships with the other Matriarchs is getting better, mine and Johan's will never be the same. Though we've managed to salvage something between our families, led by Aqua.

At the end of our last meeting, I got the courage to ask her how things were between the two of them.

She smiled. "He's the same old Daddy, in a way. Still insists on no back talk, grumbles about me not working in the restaurant—that's his primary focus now—though he also gives me unsolicited advice on being a good Matriarch. He even invited Mason to dinner!" She sighed, but it wasn't in exasperation; it was more like a positive release. "Sometimes I think he's relieved, honestly. He's spent his entire life trying to protect us, and I don't think that will change. But I also think he trusts me to do the job. Grandma, too. I never thought they would. I don't think any of us could have ever predicted that. No matter what either of them have done . . . it means a lot that they believe in me."

Aqua's ancestor who did her Calling has been helping her along, but so is April-Mae. I guess it's like how both Auntie Elaine and Mama Jova help me. "You should be proud, you know that, right?"

She flushed but nodded.

"And . . . the rituals . . ."

I had finally given the Matriarchs my big speech on what Mama Jova taught me about magic. I've gotten them as far as agreeing to stop using the terms pure and impure, but the rest is a work in progress.

"I remember what you told us about letting go of this idea of pure and impure. That if we just understood magic as blood and intent, we could be stronger." Aqua met my eyes. "I'd like to try that theory out."

I beamed at her. Though neither Ilana nor Torrin seemed like they were going to get on board anytime soon, it gave me a special comfort knowing that maybe one day, no one would be tied up in that basement again.

Though I still wish for a time when none of us hurt others to get ahead. And more still, when pure and impure become labels that no one remembers, all of us just witches. Still, the anomaly lurks in the back of everyone's minds, along with the fear of weakening magic. Justin was sure our magic was going away because we didn't need it anymore. Natural selection. Except he doesn't know us because he *isn't* us. There are families with wealth grown from money they made off the backs of our ancestors. Lucas and Henrietta died during what was supposed to be a celebration of our heritage. We haven't stopped needing magic's protection or its benefits.

What we have done is added labels to it and put ourselves in boxes. And maybe that has nothing to do with why the anomaly started. But it's a hypothesis that I like a lot more than Justin's. I hope that once we stop limiting magic by the divisions of pure and impure, it will become a power that grows in strength instead of dwindles.

Our families can be an example of that.

Keis and Luc come back into the kitchen as me, Aqua, and a reluctant Keisha are slapping the bake dough onto sheets and getting them ready to go into the oven. Keis stares at the dough, then back up at me, and smiles but says nothing.

This time, *I'm* the one who knows what *she's* thinking.

It's the first time I've made bake since Granny died.

"Did you move your last box yet?" Keis asks.

I shake my head. "I'm going to do it before we call Uncle Vacu."

Though I wish he could be here today, my uncle is in the Muskokas for his treatment. Ilana got us our discount, but Alex was the one who footed the bill.

Luc made sure to "discover" the truth behind Justin covering up Auntie Elaine's contributions and brought it immediately to the board of directors. He explained at a length that they could avoid a PR disaster because her family was willing to work together.

The fact that he happened to be dating a girl from the family wasn't their favorite thing, but the proof was in the pudding. There were dozens of documents, photos, and videos in Justin's private files that showed how much she was involved.

NuGene had accordingly offered payouts or percentages of the company as needed. For the first time in our lives, my family hired financial advisors and got things in order. Auntie Elaine would be recognized, and her family, Uncle Vacu and Alex, would have a financial stake in what she helped create.

It's something that I know not everyone gets. There are ancestors whose contributions to science were stolen and never compensated for. But thankfully, Auntie Elaine won't be another one.

The money was more than enough to cover treatment for both Uncle Vacu and Keisha. He went to the Muskokas, and she started her outpatient program.

Selfishly, I'm glad she's stayed with us, but she was right. The specialists she met with agreed that she didn't need to be in a facility and would probably do better if she could develop better eating habits and strategies at home.

As a first step, she took out the program in her chip that calculated calories. Alex and I cried at the appointment, and Keisha rolled her eyes at us, though they were glassy too.

We've had family sessions, too, to figure out how we can support her and get rid of some of our bad habits, like staring at her while she eats or commenting on it.

And one day, when he's ready, Uncle Vacu will come home, and our whole family will be together.

We're supposed to call him so that he can join in on the now very crowded festivities that I didn't even want. Though however much I griped about it, I'm glad.

"Are we calling Dad?" Alex asks, poking her head into the kitchen. Her face is absolutely covered in glitter.

I balk at her.

Keisha snorts. "Wow."

She sighs. "I know, I know. Caleb and Eden required a canvas, and I made the mistake of volunteering."

A huge roar of laughter kicks up from the dining room, and we poke our heads in. The adults are perched on the tables with very many glasses of wine. Mom, Auntie Maise, Torrin, and Avery are already two bottles deep and cackling at ancestors know what. Dad and Rena's husband are chasing after the kids, while Rena, Ilana, and Priya have their own chat session at the second table. Uncle Cathius is engrossed in telling poor Avery's dad some long and boring story, if the man's blinking eyes are any indication.

I feel new people approaching the house before I hear the sound of the door opening. I followed through on my theory of using the magic already existing inside the house to strengthen it, and so far, it's been working. Ironically, the fact that Granny and the adults tied our magic to the house is the only reason that I can do it. There's a thread there, from me as the Matriarch to the magic inside it, like the connection between me and the family. It just took some help from Mama Jova and Auntie Elaine to figure out how to teach the house to set its own intention—the intent to protect itself and the magic made up of the blood of our ancestors.

And by protecting itself, it also protects us. I had Auntie Maise try to set a small, controlled fire, and nothing would catch. We even took hammers to the outside of it. No splinters or breaks.

As a side effect, I'm hyperaware of the connection between myself and the house. And it's different from how I feel the connection with the family. Maybe because now, the house is aware of me too. There's something alive about it. Our ancestors' blood and intent in its bones, living on.

Maybe one day we'll still need to tug our magic away from it. I'm working on creating a family with the potential to do it in the future. But for now, this works.

I'm already turning to walk to the door when Aqua shouts, "They're here!"

I follow her to the entryway, where Mason and Topaz come inside, a sullen Johan following behind them along with Emerald, Garnet, and Peridot. Johan holds up a bottle of wine but glances meaningfully toward the dining room. "I brought this, but I'm starting to think that they don't need any more."

"Let them have their fun," Topaz says, and I reach over to hug him, Mason, and the rest of the Davis kids after Aqua has had her turn.

"Thanks for coming," I say.

Emerald rolls her eyes. "Get sparked. I heard you didn't even want to have this party."

"Well, it's already happening!"

I meet Johan's eyes for a moment, and he nods at me. "Happy Calling anniversary."

"Thank you."

It's stiff and awkward, but as he passes me by, he nudges me a little. "You got me with that gift, girl, you and your Mama." Before he leaves, he whispers, "And I'm glad."

I jerk around, but Johan has already joined the fray. He can never enter a room like he did before. Not with everything he's done. April-Mae and Kane were people who mattered. Who were murdered in cold blood. He let Auntie Elaine die instead of helping her. And he would have let us all die to keep only his family safe. That's not something people forget.

None of us are squeaky clean. But there's a betrayal to what Johan did that digs deep *because* he was such a huge part of our community.

He has to learn the lesson that I did. You can't make up for what's past, but you can do better in the future. And I hope he does. That's why he's still here. Aqua is doing her part to help too. She leads her dad over to a spot along the wall and presses a glass of wine into his hands that he accepts with a tiny smile.

Besides, the way others in the room turn away from him when they used to all turn toward him is its own additional punishment. I know that he notices too—the sting of Alex especially. She made good on her word, she and Uncle Vacu, and they had that talk with Johan. I don't know what was said, but I do know that my cousin announced that she would be starting her own mas band for Caribana next year.

"Ready for that box?" Luc asks, tucking my hand into his as he and Keis come over.

My whole body heats up a bit. When Mom first saw us holding hands, we were treated to an extremely uncomfortable conversation about how she would like my door to stay open at all times. Then she showed us both that horrible sex talk feed video. It was a nightmare.

"Yeah," I say. I look around for Keisha and Alex, who join us when they see me waving at them. "Are you coming?"

Alex shakes her head. "I'll leave you to it. I'm going to get Dad's connection set up."

I turn to Keisha, who smiles at me, Luc, and her sister. "I think you'll be good with them. Just for this." She reaches out and grips my free hand before letting go and following Alex.

"Just us, then," I say, and tug Luc forward, Keis following along behind us.

We walk up the stairs to my bedroom. It's completely empty now. My bed is stripped. My posters gone. My closet emptied. All that's left is one box. And then it'll be ready for Uncle Vacu to move in after rehab.

I pick up the box, and we walk from my bedroom to Granny's room.

Luc steps back instead of going into the room. "Actually, why don't I leave you two to it?"

I swallow, understanding, and nod.

I peek at Keis, who has politely found something interesting on the plain, blank wall to look at.

Luc leans forward, and we share a quick kiss before he goes back downstairs. Thankfully, ours no longer involve tears.

Me and Keis go into the room, and I set down the last box on the bed. Inside are the rest of my boxes. The ones I moved one by one, the same way that I moved Granny's boxes out of the room and into the basement.

In the end, I went to the same psychotherapist as Eden and Juras, and it was her suggestion. Everything one bit at a time. That's how I started, and now I'm here.

It wasn't easy. Not for any of us. Juras still refuses to speak to Luc, though Jasmine has reached out since. Eden still has nightmares, but you can make loud noises around her now.

And me. Those first few boxes, I cried. *Bawled*. I would move one and then couldn't move another for a week.

I miss Granny every day.

But I'm finally moving in.

From the box I put down, I pull out the two photos I got

printed and framed. The first is the one me and my cousins took that day at Caribana. Smiling, not knowing how different our futures would look. The good and the bad. The second is of me, Aqua, Ilana, Torrin, Avery, and Lee. An exact match to the portrait that was in Avery's living room, just updated.

Keis smiles at me. "Guess what I found?"

"What?"

She pulls out her phone. "It was on Granny's tablet in the basement." I hadn't looked through that since way back when. I meant to, but I figured it could come after the boxes. Another step.

Keis sits down on the bed and pats the spot beside her.

I sit and squish close to my cousin.

I gasp when she brings it up.

"I think your mom must have taken it when we weren't looking," she says, voice soft.

It's the three of us. Me, Keis, and Granny, covered in flour, kneading bake dough. I don't know what was said, but we're all laughing.

Tears spring to my eyes.

I don't think I will ever stop missing Granny. But it hurts less now. And maybe one day, I'll only be able to smile when I think of her without the edge of hurt.

Keis grips my hand, and I squeeze back.

"She would be proud of you," she says.

"I know," I say back, because Granny told me so herself.

Alex bursts into the room, her face still a whole mess of glitter. "Okay, come now! Dad's on the phone."

Keis and I follow my cousin out of the room and down the stairs, where I'm assaulted by screams of "Happy Calling anniversary" and a massive amount of streamers and confetti. Everyone has gathered in the kitchen around a cake so huge, even all of us might not be able to finish it.

I spot Luc, who has unfortunately been drawn into Uncle Cathius's story. Meanwhile, Auntie Maise holds up a tablet with Uncle Vacu, who has his own noisemakers. I never thought I would see the day my uncle would use one of those, but there he is.

Priya lifts Eden into her arms while Dad shows my little sister how to use her noisemaker. He catches me looking at him and I smile. He grins back. Just like Auntie Elaine wanted, the anger he clung to for so long over her death fades more every day. In the spaces between, me and him talk about all the wonderful parts of her life now that I've finally gotten all those memories back. I even make less spicy Dad-friendly versions of her favorite recipes. And I'm letting go too. I'm finally releasing the part of myself that was obsessed with the time he spent away. Now we can celebrate the time we have together.

I wipe at my eyes and grin.

"Aren't you glad Aqua insisted?" Keis says, linking my right arm with hers.

Keisha comes over and takes the left. "You are, aren't you?"

I scowl. "Yes, fine. You all did this too early! The bake isn't even ready."

Everyone breaks out into laughs, and I find myself joining them.

Behind them, Mama Jova stands, naked as always, her head held high and proud. She grins at me, and I smile back.

I look around at the people who came to celebrate me. To celebrate the moment when my life changed forever—including the boy who was a part of it.

With magic, *real* magic, there are no Latin phrases or wand waving. There's only blood and intent.

The blood that runs through me, ran through Granny, through our ancestors. Through Auntie Elaine, bleeding out to save us.

Through Mama Jova, bound to a tree, dying as her kin escaped to safety.

So much of our blood has been laced through with suffering. So much so that it's become our motto: *We suffer and we survive.*

Now this is *my* family.

And I want the blood that I pass on to know the joy more than the pain.

To think of blood and intent, and see their own hands reaching out, making something new. Something better than whatever came before.

The one thing I know for sure is that we won't be alone anymore. We're a community. We're more than just one family.

We're a coven.

And we survive.

ACKNOWLEDGMENTS

Thank you to the reader first and foremost for picking up this book. If there's anything that I learned as a debut author, it's to appreciate the time that readers take with my work, regardless of how they feel about it at the end. Though, of course, I hope that you enjoyed following Voya's story. When I started this series, I was in this intense state of hope: I hoped that I got an agent, I hoped that the book would sell, I hoped that people would like it. And when I finished this series, I was filled with the feeling of knowing all those things I had hoped for were possible. A feeling not unlike the one that Voya has at the end of her journey. Even though I'm the author, it feels like we did this together, and that's a feeling I don't think I'll ever forget.

A huge thank-you to my wonderful agent, Kristy Hunter, who did such an amazing job championing this series and helping me through the ups and downs of publishing. And thank you to my fantastic editor, Sarah McCabe, who always ends up suggesting things that blow my mind and make my books even better than I could imagine.

I would also love to extend a thank-you to the Simon & Schuster and Margaret K. McElderry Books team, who did such amazing work on this book and series, both in many stages of production and in getting it to readers. And also to the Simon & Schuster Canada team, who have been wonderful champions of the series and a delight to work with. Thank you to Thea Harvey, the absolutely amazing illustrator behind Voya's beautiful renditions on both the *Blood Like Magic* and *Blood Like Fate* covers, and to the fantastic designer, Rebecca Syracuse. I am forever hearing from people how absolutely amazing these covers are, and I'm so appreciative of the work that went into them.

As an author, I always try my best to authentically and respectfully represent characters outside of my lived experience, and I so appreciate the people who helped me with that. A huge thank-you to my sensitivity readers, Gabe Cole Novoa and Sarah Stout.

I am also so infinitely thankful to the wonderful friends who read early versions of *Blood Like Fate* and whose feedback was paramount in this book's journey. Thank you to Cassie Spires, Jess Creaden, and Kess Costales.

Finally, I want to thank my wonderful partner, our little beagle (aka my favorite coworker), and the family and friends who have supported this series since book one. I could have never imagined the huge amount of hype and excitement from all of you, and I appreciate it so much. And a special thank-you to my family, who inspired me to write a group of characters as loving as the people who I was fortunate to grow up with.

ABOUT THE AUTHOR

Liselle Sambury is a Trinidadian Canadian author who grew up in Toronto, Ontario, and her brand of writing can be described as "messy Black girls in fantasy situations." In her free time, she shares helpful tips for upcoming writers and details of her publishing journey through a YouTube channel dedicated to demystifying the sometimes complicated business of being an author.